"SASHA!"

Pressure tightened on my arm, and my scream intensified. "Sasha! Stop. You're okay. You're safe. Stop."

You're safe.

Two words the Groom would never speak.

Jackknifing up and to the side, my flailing hand hit air and I tumbled to the left, right off the bed. I didn't hit the floor.

Cole was fast, wrapping an arm around my waist and hauling me back onto the bed, *against* him. Chest to chest. Skin against . . . *skin? What?* The nightmare faded like wisps of smoke as I slowly became aware of everything. Cole was holding me to him, his breath warm against my cheek, and he'd taken his shirt off at some point, and now my heart was racing for a whole different reason.

"You with me?" he asked.

I was *so* with him . . .

By Jennifer L. Armentrout

TILL DEATH
FOREVER WITH YOU
FALL WITH ME

By J. Lynn

STAY WITH ME
BE WITH ME
WAIT FOR YOU

The Covenant Series

DAIMON
HALF-BLOOD
PURE
DEITY
ELIXIR
APOLLYON

The Lux Series

SHADOWS
OBSIDIAN
ONYX
OPAL
ORIGIN
OPPOSITION

Gamble Brothers Series

TEMPTING THE BEST MAN
TEMPTING THE PLAYER
TEMPTING THE BODYGUARD

JENNIFER L. ARMENTROUT

TILL
DEATH

WILLIAM MORROW
An Imprint of HarperCollins*Publishers*

TILL DEATH. Copyright © 2017 by Jennifer L. Armentrout. All rights reserved. Printed in the United States of America. No part of this book may be used or reproduced in any manner whatsoever without written permission except in the case of brief quotations embodied in critical articles and reviews. For information, address HarperCollins Publishers, 195 Broadway, New York, NY 10007.

First William Morrow premium printing: March 2017

ISBN 978-0-06-236278-0

William Morrow® and HarperCollins® are registered trademarks of HarperCollins Publishers.

17 18 19 20 21   QGM   10 9 8 7 6 5 4 3 2 1

For You. The reader.

ACKNOWLEDGMENTS

Thank you to my agent, Kevan Lyon, for always supporting me, no matter what random book idea I throw in her direction. This book would've never happened if it weren't for my editor, Tessa Woodward, Elle Keck, Nicole Fischer, and the amazing publicity and marketing team at HarperCollins, including Caro Perry and KP Simmons. Thank you Stacey Morgan, Vilma Gonzalez, Jen Fisher, Andrea Joan, Tiffany King, Sarah J. Maas, Laura Kaye, and many others who helped support this book either through me bouncing ideas off of or them reading really terrible early drafts.

None of this would be possible without you, the reader. Thank you for your continuous support, and I hope you enjoyed *Till Death*.

THERE WERE RULES.

Rules that shouldn't be broken, but it had happened this time and damn it, it would happen again. Didn't matter that everything had been under control up until this point. Didn't matter that the rules had been followed and *needed* to be followed.

Everything was different now.

She was coming back.

And *she* would ruin everything again.

The huddled, pathetic shadow in the corner whimpered. The woman was awake. Finally. It wasn't nearly as fun when they were passed out through all the good parts. Planning required patience, and patience was truly a virtue, one mastered over years and years of waiting.

Bloodied, dirtied rope circled the ankles and wrists. When she slowly lifted her chin and her lashes fluttered open, her startled cry came from deep within a well of endless terror. It was in her wide glazed-over eyes. She knew. Oh yeah, she knew she wasn't walking out of here. She knew that the sunlight she'd seen when she'd gotten into her car the morning she'd left for work was the last sunlight she'd see. She knew that was the last time she'd breathe fresh air.

Dim artificial light was her home now. The musky, earthy scent would be with her right down to the very last breath she took, and that scent would clog her pores and cling to her hair.

This would be her final place.

The woman tipped her head back against the damp brick wall. The terror in her gaze gave way to pleading. Always did. So fucking predictable. So pointless. There was no hope here. There was no chance of a miracle. Once they came here, there was no knight riding to the rescue.

Footsteps sounded upstairs. A second later, faint laughter echoed, drawing the woman's wide gaze to the ceiling. She tried to yell, to scream, but the sounds were muffled. Those pathetic sounds stopped when dull light glimmered off the sharp blade.

She shook her head wildly, flinging limp blond strands across her pale face. Tears filled her brown eyes.

"It's not your fault."

Her chest heaved with erratic breaths.

"If she wasn't coming back, this may never have happened to you. It's her fault." There was a pause as the woman's gaze flew to the end of the knife. "She fucked me and I will fuck her back in the most unpleasant manner."

This time it was going to end like it always should. *She* was going to die, but first, *she* would pay. Pay for everything.

CHAPTER 1

MY HEART STARTED racing as my gaze trekked to the rearview mirror. My brown eyes seemed too big and wide at the moment. I looked freaked out, and I was.

Taking a deep breath, I grabbed my purse and opened the door of my Honda, stepping out. Cold air immediately coasted under the thin sweater I wore as I closed the door behind me. I inhaled deeply, surrounded by the scent of freshly cut grass.

I took a step toward the inn I'd grown up in and hadn't seen in years. It was the way I remembered. Wind stirred the vacant rockers. The bushy ferns that hung from late spring to early fall were gone. The clapboard was painted a fresh white. Shutters a deep forest green and . . .

And my throat dried. Tiny bumps raced across my skin, lifting the wisps of blond hair at the nape of my neck. An awful, surreal feeling slammed into my gut. My breath caught in my throat once more.

The feeling was like a slick, too-heavy caress down the center of my back. The nape of my neck burned like it had when *he* would sit behind me—

Pivoting around, I scanned the front yard. Tall hedges lined the property. It was a decent distance from Queen Street, the main road cutting straight through the town, but I could hear the cars passing by. No one was out here. I turned full circle. No one was on the porch or in the yard. Maybe someone was at one of the windows or the inn, but I was alone out here despite the way my pulse pounded or what instinct screamed at me.

I focused on the green hedges again. They were so thick someone could be hidden behind them, watching and waiting for—

"Stop it." I closed my free hand into a fist. "You're being paranoid and stupid. Just stop it. No one is watching you."

But my heart didn't slow down and a fine tremor coursed through my tensing muscles. I reacted physically and without thought.

I panicked.

Icy claws of terror sunk deep into my chest and I ran—ran from the side of my car and into the inn. Everything was a blind blur as I hit the stairs and kept running, all the way to the upper level.

There, in the quiet and narrow hallway outside the apartments above the inn, out of breath and feeling sick, I dropped my purse on the floor and bent over, clasping my knees as I dragged in deep, uneven breaths.

I hadn't stopped to notice if the inn had changed in the years I'd been absent, hadn't stopped to find my mother. I'd run like there were demons snapping at my heels.

And that was how this felt.

This was a mistake.

"No," I whispered to the ceiling. I leaned against the wall and smoothed my hands down my face. "This isn't a mistake."

Lowering my arms to the wall, I forced my eyes open as I dragged in a deep breath. Of course I would have a . . . strong reaction to returning home, to coming back here after everything had happened.

When I left, I'd sworn I'd never come back.

Never say never.

Those three words had been cycling over and over from the moment I'd made the decision to return home. I almost couldn't believe I was actually sitting here, that I'd done what I'd said I'd never do.

As a child, I'd been convinced the inn had been haunted. How could it not be? The Georgian-style mansion and the adjacent carriage house were older than dirt, used as a part of the Underground Railroad and rumored to have been occupied by injured and dying soldiers after the bloody Battle of Antietam.

Floorboards creaked throughout the night. Cold spots lingered in rooms. The old dimly lit servants' staircase had creeped me out like nothing else. Shadows always seemed to slink along the wallpapered walls. If ghosts were real, then this inn, the Scarlet Wench, should be full of them. And as a twenty-nine-year-old fully grown woman, I was still convinced it was haunted.

Haunted by a different kind of ghost now.

What roamed those narrow halls on the upper

levels, tiptoed across polished floors, and hid in the darkened stairwells was the old Sasha Keeton from ten years ago, before . . . before the Groom came to the town where nothing ever happened, and destroyed everything.

I'd sworn that I would never come back to this town, but like Grandma Libby used to say all the time, *never say never.*

Sighing, I pushed away from the wall and looked down the hall.

Maybe I wouldn't have flipped out so strongly if I hadn't heard the news on the radio just as I was leaving the interstate—news of a woman missing from Frederick. I caught the tail end of her name—Banks. She was a nurse at Memorial Hospital. Her husband had last seen her the morning she'd left for work.

My breath caught as a cold shiver skated over my skin. Frederick was not far from Berkeley County. Usually a forty-five-minute drive on days when the traffic wasn't bad. The tips of my fingers felt icy as I opened and closed them.

One missing person was horrible and sad, incredibly tragic no matter the circumstances. Multiple missing people was terrifying, major news, and a pattern—

Cursing under my breath, I cut those thoughts off. The missing woman had nothing to do with me. Obviously. God knows I fully understood how traumatic a missing person could be, and I really hoped that the woman was found safe, but it had *nothing* to do with me.

Or with what happened ten years ago.

The brisk early-January winds rolled across the

roof, startling me. My heart thundered against my ribcage. I was as skittish as a mouse in a room full of starved cats. This was—

My cellphone rang, jarring me out of my thoughts. Bending over, I reached inside the oversized hobo bag and dug around until my fingers curled around the slim surface. I pulled it out, lips twitching when I saw the caller.

"Sasha," Mom said the moment I hit answer. Her laugh made my smile spread. "Where in the world are you? I saw your car out front, but you're no-where to be found."

I winced a little. "I'm upstairs. I got out of the car and started to walk in, but I . . ." I didn't want to say the words, admit how unnerved I was.

"Do you need me to come upstairs?" she asked immediately, and I squeezed my eyes shut.

"No. I'm fine now."

There was a pause. "Sasha, honey, I . . ." Mom faded off, and I could only wonder what she was about to say. "I'm glad you're finally home."

Home.

Most twenty-nine-year-olds would feel like a failure if they returned home, but for me, it was the opposite. Coming home was an accomplishment, a feat not easily completed. Opening my eyes, I swallowed another sigh. "I'm coming down."

"I was guessing you would." She laughed again, but it sounded shaky. "I'm in the kitchen."

"Okay." I clenched the phone tighter. "I'll be there in a few."

"All right, honey." Mom hung up, and I slowly placed my phone back in the bag.

For a moment, I stood stock-still, rooted to the floor, and then I nodded curtly. It was time.

It was finally time.

I WAS FLOORED.

The inside looked nothing like I remembered. I stepped through the foyer, blown away by the change that had taken place in the last ten years.

Purse dangling from my fingertips, I slowly made it through the main floor. The vases full of artificial orchids were new and the dated chairs by guest check-in were gone. The two great rooms had been opened up to create one large space. Soothing gray paint replaced the flowery wallpaper. The old traditional chairs with the velvet upholstery had been changed to teal-and-white thick-cushioned wing-back chairs strategically placed around the end tables for easy conversation. The brick fireplace had been stripped back and painted white.

Another surprise waited when I entered the dining area of the inn. Gone was the cold, formal table that forced every guest to eat together if they dined at the inn. I'd always hated that, because hello, awkward. Five large round tables covered in white linen were staged throughout the large room. The fireplace in here was painted to match the one in the sitting room. Flames rippled behind the glass. A station to serve drinks had been moved into the room and sat catty-corner to the fireplace.

The Scarlet Wench had finally come into the twenty-first century.

Had Mom mentioned this at some point? We'd talked on the phone a lot and Mom had visited in

Atlanta multiple times in the last ten years. She had to have brought this up. She probably had, but I tended to zone out anything related to this town, and I must've zoned out way too much.

This was significant; seeing this was important, because now I knew I'd checked out way too deeply.

A knot formed in the back of my throat and stupid tears burned the back of my eyes. "Oh God," I murmured, wiping the back of my hands under my eyes as I blinked rapidly. "Okay. Pull it together."

Counting to ten, I cleared my throat and then nodded. I was ready to see my mama. I could do this without breaking down and crying like an angry, hungry baby.

Once I was sure I wasn't going to have an epic meltdown, I got my feet moving. The scent of roasted meat led me to the back of the house. A pocket door with STAFF ONLY posted was closed. Reaching for it, I was suddenly thrust back into the past, and within seconds I saw myself running through this very door and into the arms of my waiting father after the first day of kindergarten, the watercolor painting I'd done flapping from my outstretched hand. I remembered shuffling through this door the first time my heart had been crushed, my face streaked with dirt and tears because Kenny Roberts had pushed me into the mud at the play-ground. I could see myself at fifteen, knowing my dad would never be waiting for me again.

And I saw myself bringing the boy I'd met in Econ 101 through this very door to meet Mom, and my heart did an unsteady flop, pulling me right out of the stream of memories.

"God," I groaned, shutting that train wreck of a thought process down before those pale blue wolf eyes formed in my mind. Because once that happened, I'd be thinking of him for the next twelve thousand years, and I really didn't need that right now. "I'm such a mess."

I shook my head as I slid the door open. The knot returned with a vengeance the moment I spotted her behind the stainless-steel counter, standing where Dad used to until he passed away from the widow-maker—a massive, undetected morning heart attack.

Forgetting about the dread I'd felt the whole long-as-hell drive up here and what I'd heard on the radio, I felt like I was five again.

"Mom," I croaked, dropping the bag on the floor.

Anne Keeton stepped out from behind the counter, and I stumbled in the rush to get to her. It had been a year since I'd seen her. Last Christmas, she had traveled to Atlanta, because she'd known I wasn't ready to come home then. Only a year had passed, but Mom had changed just as much as the inn had.

Her shoulder-length hair was more silver than blond. Deeper lines had forged into the skin around her brown eyes, and fine lines had formed around thinner lips. Mom had always been curvy—after all, that was where I got my hips and breasts, and belly, and, okay, thighs from—but she was at least twenty pounds lighter.

Concern blossomed in the pit of my stomach as she wrapped her arms around me. Had I not noticed this last year? Had I been gone too long? Ten years was a long time to miss things when you only saw someone sporadically.

"Honey," Mom said, her voice thick. "Baby, I'm so happy to see you. So happy that you're here."

"Me too," I whispered back, and I meant it.

Coming home had been the last thing I wanted to do, but as I hugged her tight and inhaled the vanilla scent of her perfume, I knew it had been the right thing, because that concern grew and spread throughout me.

Mom was only fifty-five, but age didn't matter when it came to mortality. Nothing did when it came to death. I knew that better than anyone. Dad had died young, and ten years ago, at nineteen, I had . . . I had almost taken my last breath after *everything* else had been taken from me.

CHAPTER

2

THE IRON BISTRO table in front of the large window overlooking the veranda and garden had been in the kitchen as long as I could remember. Smoothing my hand over the surface, I found the tiny, familiar indentations carved around the edges. It was at this very table where I colored as a child and did homework in the evenings as a teenager.

The door to the old kitchen, which now served as a break room/storage room, was on the opposite end, also marked with an employees-only sign. That door, like everything else in the updated kitchen, had been painted a fresh white.

Mom brought two cups of coffee over and sat across from me. The room now smelled like a coffee store, and I wasn't thinking about the way I'd freaked out before.

"Thank you," I said, wrapping my hand around the warm cup. A grin tipped up the corners of my lips. Little green Christmas trees decorated the cup. Even though it was two weeks past Christmas and all the decorations were down, the Christmas-themed coffee cups would remain out and in use all year. Glancing around the kitchen, I frowned and asked, "Where is James?" James Jordan had been the chef for at least fifteen years. "I smell something cooking."

"What you smell is two roasts." She took a sip of her coffee. "And there's been some changes. Guests have to notify us by one if they will be having dinner here and then we cook the dinner based on that request. It cuts down on the work and we're not wasting as much food." She paused. "James comes in just three times a week now. Tuesday, Thursday, and Saturday." She lowered her cup to the table. "We're still pretty steady with business, but with the newer hotels springing up around here every year, I have to be careful with what we're spending money on. Do you remember me telling you about Angela Reidy?"

When I nodded, she continued, "She's our main housekeeping staff in the mornings and afternoons Wednesday through Sunday, and Daphne is still here, but she's getting up there in age, so I've moved her to part-time. That gives her more time with her grandbabies. Angela is amazing, but a little flighty and sometimes forgetful. She is always locking herself out of the townhouse she rents, so much so that she keeps a spare key in the back room."

I let all of that sink in as I took a drink of the sugary coffee, just the way I loved it. Basically what Mom was saying was that she was doing most of this all by herself. That explained the deeper lines around her eyes, the new ones around her mouth, and the silvery tones to her blond hair. Running an inn or any business with a skeleton crew would take its toll on anyone, and I knew that the last ten years hadn't been easy on her for a whole different set of reasons.

The same reasons they'd been hard for me.

Sometimes, not often, I was able to forget what had driven me away from my home. Those moments were few and far between, but when they happened, it was . . . the warmest sense of peace I'd ever felt. It was like the way it was *before*. Like I could pretend I was an ordinary woman with a career I sort of loved and a past that was common, boring even. It wasn't that I hadn't come to terms with everything that had happened . . . to my family and me. I had six years of intensive therapy to thank for that, but I still welcomed those moments when I forgot, and I was grateful for them.

"You've been doing all of this by yourself, Mom." I placed my cup on the table and crossed my leg over my knee. "That's a lot."

"It's . . . manageable." Mom smiled, but it didn't reach her whiskey-colored eyes. Eyes identical to mine. "But you're home now. I won't be doing this by myself."

I nodded as my gaze dropped to the cup. "I should've come home—"

"Don't say it." Mom reached across the small table and folded her hand over mine. "You had a very good job—"

"My job was to basically babysit my boss to make sure he didn't cheat on his third wife." I paused, grinning. "Obviously, I wasn't very good at it since number three is on her way out."

She shook her head as she lifted her cup. "Honey, you were an executive assistant for a man who ran a multibillion-dollar consulting business. You had more responsibilities than making sure he kept it in his pants."

I giggled.

The only thing that rivaled my former boss' drive when it came to business was his drive to screw as many women as humanly possible. But what she said was true. Late nights at the office; dinner meetings; and a constant, ever-changing schedule with nonstop flights coast to coast and around the globe had been my life for five years. It had its pros and cons, and leaving my job hadn't been a decision I'd made lightly. But my job had allowed me to save up some money that would make this transition into a much . . . slower life a little easier.

"You had a life in Atlanta," she continued, and I raised a brow. My time had basically been Mr. Berg's time. "And your life back here wasn't easy to return to."

I tensed. She wasn't going to go there, was she? She squeezed my hand.

She was *so* going to go there.

"This town and all the memories weren't easy for you to come back to, and I know that, honey. I *know* that." She smiled again, but it was brittle. "So I understand how big of a deal this was for you. What you had to overcome just to make the decision to do this, and you're doing it for me. Don't belittle what you're doing right now."

Oh God, I was going to start crying again.

Yes, I was doing this for her, but I was . . . I was also doing it for myself.

I slipped my hand free and nearly gulped down the coffee before I burst into tears and face-planted onto the iron table like I'd done way too many times in the past.

She sat back. "So," she said, clearing her throat. "Several boxes of your stuff arrived on Wednesday, and James put them upstairs for you. I imagine you still have some stuff in the car?"

"Yeah," I murmured as she rose and carried her cup to the industrial sink. "I can get those boxes up there. It's only clothes, and I could use the exercise after being in the car for a million hours."

"You might change your mind after you remember how many steps you have to climb." She washed out the cup. "We only have three guests right now, two of them checking out on Sunday, and then others—a newlywed couple—are checking out on Tuesday."

I finished off the coffee. "What about upcoming reservations?"

Wiping her hands off on a dishtowel, Mom rattled off what was expected for the next week, and I loved that she could remember that.

"Is there anything I can help you with right now?" I asked when she was finished.

She shook her head. "Two out of the three reservations are dining here. The roasts still have some time on them. The potatoes are already boiled and cut, ready to go. If you want to help serve dinner, we still have about two hours."

"Sounds good." I started to rise. Movement out of the corner of my eyes snagged my attention.

Turning toward the window, I caught a blur of shadows to the right of the veranda. Branches from the dwarf apple tree rustled. My eyes narrowed as I leaned closer to the window. Something moved behind the trellis that was normally covered with vines, a shadow deeper than the rest and keeping close to the hedges. I waited for someone to step out, but when that didn't happen, my gaze tracked over the garden. Not seeing anything, I returned my attention to the veranda. The chaise lounge and other seats out on the veranda were empty, but I'd sworn I'd seen someone outside.

"What are you looking at, honey?"

Having no idea, I blinked and shook my head as I twisted toward her. "I think one of the guests is outside."

"Strange." She moved behind the hanging pots and walked toward the oven. "None of the guests are actually here. I believe they're all out."

I turned back to the window as Mom picked up an oven mitt.

"Of course, one of them could've snuck past me," she said, and the creak of the oven door opening filled the kitchen. "That has been known to happen."

Nothing moved outside.

There probably hadn't even been anyone outside. Just nerves. And paranoia. Like before, when I ran into the house and all the way upstairs. Being back home had me on edge and I liked to think no one would blame me for that.

Worrying my lower lip, I thought back to the

newscast I'd heard on the radio. My stomach twisted as I clasped my hands together. "I heard something on the radio, about a missing woman in Frederick."

Mom stopped halfway to the wall oven. Our eyes met, and when she said nothing, knots formed and wiggled in my belly like a hundred tiny snakes. "Why didn't you say anything?" I asked.

Focused on the oven, she slipped the mitt on. "I didn't want you to worry, and I know you'd try not to, but I didn't want to upset you." She gave a little shake of her head. "And I didn't want you to change your mind about coming home."

I inhaled softly. Did she think I was that fragile? That a missing woman in a nearby state would change my mind? Right after everything had happened I would've been that frail. I would've broken all over again, but I wasn't her anymore.

"What is happening with that woman is terrible, but you know what they say. Most cases of disappearances are caused by someone the person knows," she said. "Probably the husband."

Except when it happened to me it wasn't from someone I knew. It was a stranger, someone I never saw coming until it was too late.

HOURS LATER, AFTER I helped serve dinner to the cute elderly couple staying on the third floor and the family of three who were from Kentucky and visiting relatives, I stood in the middle of my new apartment.

God, it felt so weird being back here.

Same but different.

Dinner service had gone fine, but it was odd

doing something that felt like second nature even though I hadn't done it in years. In a bizarre way, it was a lot like being an executive assistant. Just like with Mr. Berg, I had to anticipate things that would be needed. These were just different *things*. Like when the diners needed their drinks refilled or a plate removed.

Cleanup still sucked, just like I remembered.

But I didn't think as I cleared off the tables and rinsed the dishes before placing them in the dishwasher while Mom completed the turndown service. My mind was blissfully empty up until the moment I headed upstairs.

The attic had been converted into two and a half apartments. Dad had passed away before the third had been completed, and it remained untouched behind closed doors, separating the two apartments. I wasn't sure if the third would ever be finished, and if it was, what its purpose would be. Wasn't like I was going to need the space anytime soon.

Or ever.

Absently, my right hand floated to my left, and I rubbed my ring finger. Even after leaving this town and spending six years with a therapist, I didn't think that I would ever be able to wear a wedding dress or allow anyone to put a ring on my hand.

My therapist said that could change, but I seriously doubted it. I couldn't even bring myself to go to my former boss' third wedding. The whole thing turned my stomach.

Realizing what I was doing, I dropped my left hand and focused on my apartment.

It wasn't quite like I recalled and I suspected

Mom had had the area renovated. Or maybe just with all of my grandmother's stuff gone, the space seemed larger and fresher. The apartment smelled like pumpkin spice, not musty or old, and it was cute in a comfy, cozy sort of way.

The living area shared space with an open galley-style kitchen that only had a fridge, microwave, and sink. All I needed were barstools for the island. My couch, a thick-cushioned beauty, had been shipped up from Atlanta, along with the necessities. My light gray throw blankets, the soft and warm ones made for cuddling in, were already draped along the back of the couch.

The bedroom was big enough. Small closet, but the bathroom in the narrow hallway between the living room and bedroom featured a soaking tub and shower combo with claw feet that made up for its lack of size.

I spent the rest of the night setting up my apartment, which pretty much meant hooking up the TV and unloading all the clothing—clothing I now wished I'd donated, because my biceps ached from all the folding I was doing.

It was well past midnight by the time I wandered into the bathroom to wash my face. Gaze trained on the white basin of the sink as I rubbed in the cleanser, I bent over and splashed warm water onto my cheeks. Blindly grabbing for a towel I thought I saw earlier, I gave mental jazz hands when my fingers brushed the fuzzy cloth. Drying my face off, I straightened and opened my eyes as I lowered the towel.

And came face-to-face with my reflection.

I jerked back a step, bumping into the bathroom door. "Damn," I muttered, rolling my eyes. I started to grab for the toothbrush, but I exhaled roughly and did something I hadn't done in a very long time.

I looked at myself.

Really looked at myself.

Because it had been *ages* since I had, and I'd become so good at not looking at myself that I was a freaking pro at putting makeup on without a mirror. Even eyeliner. *Upper* eyeliner.

My brown eyes weren't dark like Dad's. They were warmer and lighter, like Mom's. My blond hair was pulled up in a messy topknot, and had been all day, but when it was down, it fell to the middle of my back. My face would've fit the classic heart-shape mold if it weren't for the square jaw.

Clenching the rim of the basin, I leaned in close to the mirror.

Around about my freshman year of college, I'd finally grown into my nose and mouth. Or at least that was how it felt to me, because before then, my nose had been huge and my lips plumper than the rest of my face, and contrary to how it sounded, that had not been an attractive combo. Those lips had come from my grandmother. The jaw from Dad. The body and eyes from Mom.

It was my freshman year when I'd realized that I'd moved from passably average to blonde-girl-next-door pretty. Right now I thought I looked like the kind of woman who'd be bringing baked apple pies to the neighbors and currently be working on percolating my third child.

My lips curled up at the corners, and the smile

was weak and sad, and a little empty. There were faint shadows under my eyes and a wary glint that never seemed to fade, no matter how many years passed or what I'd come to terms with.

If I could go back in time, I would've told the nineteen-year-old Sasha to live it the hell up. To go to the frat parties I'd been invited to. To stay out late and wake up even later. To have more confidence in myself. To know what I had when I'd looked in the mirror.

To take the huge step in the relationship with the boy I'd met in Econ 101.

Out of everything I regretted not experiencing before . . . before the Groom found me, it was probably that, because he had taken my firsts and twisted them into something revolting and cruel.

Pressing my lips together, I glanced down. Pink toes poked out from the frayed edges of my jeans. I placed my hands on full hips and then slid them up to where my waist tapered in just slightly. What did I look like naked?

I honestly had no idea.

Even with the men I'd been intimate with in recent years, I really didn't check myself out. Actually, come to think of it, I never got fully nude with anyone.

There were reasons for that.

Two of them, to be exact.

Uncomfortable with where my thoughts were traipsing around and about to belly flop into, I stopped feeling myself up. Quickly finishing up in the bathroom, I flipped off the light and walked out.

Before crawling into the unfamiliar bed, I padded

out into the living room and into the kitchen, the tile cool under my bare feet. Seeing the apartment key Mom must've left on the kitchen counter, I made a mental note to add it to my ring of keys. Beside the kitchen island was a door. Each apartment had separate outdoor access in the form of wooden staircases that led up to a narrow balcony.

Stopping at the front of the door, I double-checked that the deadbolt was locked. My stomach wiggled with nervousness. Feeling neurotic as hell, I turned the handle just to make sure. Locked. Definitely locked. Breathing easier, I made my way to bed, tugged the warm comforter up to my chin, and . . . stared at the shadowy ceiling. Exhausted from the drive, my all-over-the-place emotions, and the endless folding of clothing, I still couldn't close my eyes.

Sleep did not come easy. It hadn't since . . . well, since I was nineteen. Since sleep had become a time when I couldn't see what was coming at me and I couldn't protect myself. For six days, sleep had been something I'd fought with every cell in my body before ultimately caving in to it and instantaneously regretting it.

I did eventually drift off, and when I did, *it* happened, like *it* always did.

His forehead presses against mine, and I know he isn't ready to let me go—he never is, and I like that about him. Love it actually. "You need to get back inside," I tell him as I slip my hands off his chest. "You still have a lot of studying to do."

"Yeah," he murmurs, but doesn't leave. His lips brush over my cheek and find my mouth with unerring accu-

racy. He kisses me softly and he lingers, dragging it out until I'm so close to asking him to forget about his study group. But then he pulls away and picks up my forgotten backpack. He slips it over my shoulder, scooping my hair out from under the strap. "Call me later?"

Later would be late, but I agree.

"Be careful," he says.

I smile, because he's the one who has the dangerous job when he's not in class. "You too." I wiggle my fingers and turn away, because if I don't, he won't, and we'd be standing outside the university library half the night kissing.

I make it halfway across the lawn when he calls out, "Call me, babe. I'll be waiting."

Smiling, I wave at him and hurry across the lawn, taking the path behind the science building that leads to the parking lot. It is late, the sun already gone, and thick clouds block the stars. The parking lot is barely lit, because three out of five of the tall lamps are out, and the school hasn't gotten around to replacing them. There are only a few cars in the lot, and as I walk down the short set of concrete steps I spot mine, parked where I left it.

My steps slow as I cross the cracked pavement. A dark work van is parked next to the driver's side of my Volkswagen. It wasn't there before, and a sliver of unease shuttles through me.

I bite down on my lip as I draw closer, eyes squinting into the dark interior of the van. I don't see anyone in the front. A horrible thought emerges. What if someone is hidden in the back? I immediately push that aside, because even though with everything that has been going on recently with the Groom, I'm being paranoid. It's just a van, and everyone is on edge.

"Don't be stupid," I tell myself as I walk between the work van and my car. Stopping at my door, I twist my backpack to my front and unzip the front pocket to root around for my keys.

I hear it then. A smooth grinding of metal against metal, of a door sliding open behind me, and everything slows down. My fingers brush over my keys as I turn sideways. An odd smell surrounds me, and I open my mouth to take a breath, but I've already taken my last breath before I know it. A rough hand clamps down. Fear jolts up my spine as I'm pulled back. Another arm circles my waist, pinning my right arm. The odd bitter smell is everywhere, clogging my nostrils and throat, and I open my mouth to scream as my heart seizes in my chest. I lift my legs to fight back, but it's too late.

Too late.

"Don't fight me," he whispers in my ear. "Don't ever fight me."

Gasping for air, I jerked up into a sitting position, dragging in deep gulps of untainted oxygen as I scanned the dark, unfamiliar room. My heart thundered in my chest so fast I felt sick. For a moment, I didn't recognize where I was. It took me a couple of seconds to realize I was in my room, back in Berkeley County, above the Scarlet Wench.

"Just a nightmare," I whispered, forcing myself to lie back down. "That's all."

Nightmares would be common; at least that was what the therapist said. Probably have them for the rest of my life as my subconscious still tried to work everything out. I had them at least three times a week, but it had been a super long time since I had dreamt of *that* night.

There was no way I was falling back asleep now, so I stared at the ceiling as hours passed and dawn crept in through the small window across from the bed. By then, the nightmare was just that.

Doubting I'd beat Mom and make it downstairs before her, I took a quick shower, mostly dried my hair, and then twisted it up in a topknot. Grabbing a loose black sweater, since January was far colder here than it typically was in Atlanta, I paired it with a pair of checkered leggings that weren't the most flattering things on my thighs but were sure as hell comfy.

Covering my gaping yawn with my hand, I walked back into the bathroom and came to a complete stop. I frowned as I scanned the space. "Crap," I muttered, realizing I'd left the makeup bag in my tote, which was in the backseat of the car.

Damn it.

Spinning around, I walked over to the bench in front of the bed. Under it were my flip-flops. I toed them on, knowing Mom would side-eye the choice of footwear, but it was a habit I couldn't break, even when it snowed. I swiped my keys out of the purse and then grabbed the apartment key.

I headed out the back door instead of going out the front and using the staff staircase. I hunkered down when the cold morning air hit the still-damp strands of hair along the back of my neck. The flip-flops smacked the whole way down the stairs—stairs I would most likely bust my ass on at some point during the winter. As I crossed the veranda, I wiggled the house key onto the ring.

My breath puffed out misty clouds as I rounded

the side of the inn and cut across the yard. The wet grass poked at my feet, icy cold. I hit the cobblestone roundabout and made a beeline for the car I'd parked outside the carriage house, grateful none of the guests were early risers. Thinking I would have just enough time to put something on my face before it would be time to help Mom do the continental breakfast, I stopped in front of my car.

My mouth dropped open. "Oh my God."

I blinked, because I couldn't believe what I was seeing, but my eyesight was just fine. Stomach twisting and turning sour, I took a step toward the car. Glass crunched under my feet.

Glass that belonged *on* my car and not on the ground.

Every single window of my car had been shattered. Every one.

3

"I CAN'T BELIEVE this has happened. We haven't ever had a break-in or anything like that at all." Anger flashed across my mother's face, flushing her cheeks. "This is unbelievable."

We stood in front of my car, side by side. I wanted to pull it into the carriage house so the guests wouldn't see it, but she hadn't been too keen on moving the car until the police showed up. Plus, there was glass all over the seats, all over everywhere, and I really didn't want to spend the day picking glass out of the cheeks of my ass.

Mom had been against waiting, but I wanted to get breakfast ready so the guests didn't have to wait and end up leaving crappy reviews on Yelp. The crappy reviews were probably going to happen anyway, because the couple with the redheaded toddler had already seen the damaged car and was now worried about their own property. Not that I could blame them for that, but it was weird that only my car had been damaged and none of the three much nicer vehicles.

Like the Lexus the parents owned.

Because seriously, if anyone was going to break into a car, why in the world would they pick the Honda Accord over the Lexus *and* the Cadillac?

The criminals in Berkeley County really needed to get their priorities straight.

"Mom . . ." I shook my head as I folded my arms across my chest, knowing we weren't going to have to wait much longer. The police station was down the street. Like literally right down the same street. "I'm so sorry. The guests don't need to see this and worry about their cars—"

"Why in the world are you apologizing?" She frowned as she placed her hand on my shoulder. "This isn't your fault unless you got up in the middle of the night and did this to your own car. If so, then we do need to talk."

Despite what happened, my lips twitched into a grin. "It wasn't me," I replied dryly. "But I really wished I'd thought to park it in the carriage house."

"Why would you have thought that?" She folded an arm around my shoulders. "We don't have a problem with theft and vandalism here. In other parts of the town, yes, but nothing like this has ever happened before."

Of course, with my outstanding luck, the very first night back home, some douchebag would vandalize my car.

I stepped away from my mom as I reached up and tucked a strand of hair that had slipped free behind my ear. Part of me wanted to pick up one of the landscaping rocks and throw it at the car out of pure frustration. I had insurance, but this wasn't on my list of things to deal with today.

It was a damn good thing I hadn't picked up a rock and thrown it, because I caught sight of the white-and-blue cruiser coming up the driveway. Probably wouldn't look good if the city police officer caught me lobbing a rock at the car.

"I hope the officer is cute," Mom said.

I whipped around, brows raised as I stared at her.

"What?" She smoothed her hand over her wavy hair as she grinned. "I do love a man in a uniform."

"*Mom.*" My eyes widened.

"And if I remember correctly, you also had a thing for the boys in blue," she continued as she tugged the sides of her cardigan together, and my eyeballs about fell out of my head. *Oh my God, did Mom seriously just go there?* She rose on the tips of her toes, eyeing the cruiser as it coasted to a stop behind my car. "So maybe you'll have a thing for this one."

I was going to die.

"I can only hope. I'd love to see you happily married before I'm six feet under," she went on.

Heat crept into my cheeks as I gaped at her. Was she now drinking in the mornings?

"Oh." Disappointment rang out in Mom's voice. "He's very attractive, but a little young. Well, I guess you could always date younger. I mean, that's in style, isn't it? He—"

"Mom," I whispered, eyes narrowing.

A look of innocence crossed her face, and I took a deep breath, turned around, and saw the police officer. My jaw unhinged once again.

Surprise flickered over the cop's face on his approach. His steps slowed as my heart lurched in my chest. The cop . . . he looked so much like the boy from econ class—the guy who my mom had referenced only a few seconds before.

It couldn't be him, but . . .

The resemblance was uncanny.

Same light brown hair buzzed close to the skull on the sides of the head and styled into a trimmed fade. Broad shoulders—door-busting shoulders. Even with the dark blue uniform and vest, I knew there was a defined chest hidden underneath. Same exact build, down to the tapered waist and muscular thighs.

The similarity went beyond the body. Those eyes—*oh my God*—those pale blue eyes were a blast from the past and the square jaw was only a little gentler.

He looked so much like Cole Landis.

I took a step back as my heart kicked around in my chest. I almost couldn't do it—couldn't look at him, because all I saw was Cole.

But it wasn't him. This cop was too young, and Cole had been two years older than me when we met at the tail end of my freshman year. He had to be thirty-two now, and this guy was barely pushing twenty-five.

The police officer glanced at the car as he walked past it. "Mrs. Keeton?"

"That would be me." Mom stepped forward, smiling as she let go of her cardigan. "I was the one who called this morning, but the car belongs to my daughter, Sasha."

Confirmation replaced the look on the officer's handsome face. "Sasha Keeton?"

I stiffened as if invisible strings grabbed my spine. I now understood the surprised expression he wore. Even though this cop had to have been in high school when everything had gone down, *everyone* in this town who was breathing back then knew who I was.

Because I was the one, the only one, who'd escaped.

Panic blossomed in the pit of my belly, rising through me so swiftly acid churned in my stomach. Newspaper headlines flashed before me. The Bride Who Lived. The One Who Brought Down the Groom.

I shouldn't have come back here.

Instinct kicked in, and instead of spinning around and hiding in my room like I wanted to, I took a deep breath like my therapist had instructed many, many times before. Pushing the panic down, I lifted my chin. I was not going to run. I had nothing to hide. Not when I'd spent the last ten years hiding and losing all this time with my mom.

I could do this.

Second by second, the panic eased off, relaxing the vise circling my neck until I was able to speak. "Guess you know who I am, but you have me at a disadvantage. I don't know who you are."

The officer opened his mouth and then closed it. A moment passed. "I'm Officer Derek Bradshaw," he said, turning his chin to the right. "And I'm going to go out on a limb here and assume you didn't do this to your car."

Some of the tension seeped out of my shoulders as I shook my head. "Nah. I sort of liked the windows in my car."

"Understandable." He twisted sideways as he reached into his front pocket and pulled out a small notebook.

The door to the inn opened. Mr. Adams stepped out onto the porch, one half of the elderly couple. "Mrs. Keeton? I'm sorry to interrupt, but the TV in our room isn't working. We tried calling the front desk, but there was no answer."

"I'll be right there," Mom yelled and then turned back to me. "I'm sorry, but I have to take care of this." She paused, winking at Officer Bradshaw. I closed my eyes briefly and started counting again. "Even though I'm sure the TV just isn't plugged in," my mom added in a hushed voice.

Officer Bradshaw chuckled, and again, I was hit with a weird sense of familiarity. He laughed like Cole. A deep, sexy chuckle. "That's okay."

I felt like I needed to thank God for the interruption. I waved my mom off as I focused on the officer.

He was bent at the waist, looking inside the car. "Did you notice anything stolen, Miss Keeton?" He turned his head toward me. "It is miss, right?"

I nodded. "Not married."

"Interesting," he murmured.

My brows flew up. Interesting? There was nothing remotely interesting about that. I crept closer to the car. "I honestly haven't checked. I found it this way this morning—oh!" Remembering why I'd come out in the morning, I walked around the back of the car. "I left a tote in the car last night and

I'd come out this morning to get it. That's when I noticed the windows broken out." Bending over, I peered in the car. Surprise shot through me. "It's in there! My bag. Right on the backseat. There's no missing that."

"Yeah, you can't miss it. Even in the dark, I'm sure the fuchsia would stand out," he commented dryly as he peered over my shoulder.

I started to reach for the car, but stopped. "Can I open the door?"

He nodded. "I'm going to be honest, for something like this, we probably won't be dusting for prints unless something major was stolen out of the car."

I wasn't insulted by the honesty. It was just a car and no one was injured. Opening the door, I reached in and carefully grabbed the straps of the tote. Glass pinged off the seat as I lifted the bag and stepped back from the car.

As Officer Bradshaw walked around the front of the car and along the other side, I opened the tote, hoping no one had stolen my makeup. If I had to make a trip to Ulta to replenish my stock, I'd be leaving with at least two hundred more dollars' worth of makeup than what was stolen.

Biting down on my lower lip, I pried the tote open. "What the . . . ?"

"Yes?" Officer Bradshaw straightened and looked at me over the roof of the car.

"My MacBook is in here! With my makeup. I left both of them in the car." Stunned, I touched the laptop just to make sure it was in there. Then I touched the makeup bag.

Officer Bradshaw headed my way. "Anything else that was left in the car?"

Shaking my head, I stared in the bag. "I forgot I'd even left that in here," I murmured, lowering the tote. I turned to him. "Why would someone break into my car but not steal a laptop? The makeup bag I understand, but the laptop?"

"That is fairly uncommon." He scribbled in his little notebook as static crackled from his radio. "But that's usually a sign that the vehicle wasn't broken into."

I lifted a hand and gestured at the car. "Uh . . . ?"

"If there is damage but nothing stolen, especially valuable goods, then it's usually a case of vandalism." His pale blue eyes met mine. "You just arrived yesterday, right?"

A wiggly feeling returned to my stomach. "Yes."

"And you've been gone about ten years?"

The stiffness started to seep back into me. "Yeah. Just about."

"Did anyone know you were returning to town?" he asked, his gaze holding mine as a woman's voice spoke from his shoulder radio. "Besides your mother."

Brows pinching, I slowly shook my head as my mouth worked. "I . . . just my friend Miranda—um, Miranda Locke. I don't think she told anyone." I nibbled on my lip as I held the tote close to my chest. "My mom would've told the staff."

He nodded as he scribbled into the notebook and then he flipped it closed, shoving it into his front pocket. The pen followed. "Is it possible that someone would want to damage your car?"

My lips parted. "Like on purpose?" That sounded stupid. Of course he meant on purpose. "I mean, as in someone who came out here and did this because of me?"

"It's possible." He held up his finger as a code was called out from his radio and then he pressed a button on the radio. "This is Unit 59. I'll be 10–8 from the Scarlet Wench in a few minutes." His gaze pierced mine. "There's no polite way of saying this, but you have a history in this town."

Anger flushed my system like a swarm of angry fire ants. "A history that wasn't my fault."

"Of course," he quickly added. "I didn't mean it like that, and I apologize if it came across as that. What I meant is that you're . . . well known and for reasons that might make some people uncomfortable."

"Uncomfortable?" I repeated as my head cocked to the side. Thank God my mom was not outside to hear this conversation. "Other than me, I have no idea why it would make other people uncomfortable."

"I get what you're saying and I don't think you have a reason to feel uncomfortable, because like you said, what happened wasn't your fault." Officer Bradshaw got some brownie points for that statement. "I honestly don't think it has anything to do with what occurred back then, but it is something we have to take into consideration. Just to keep in the back of the head kind of thing, okay?"

I wasn't sure how to feel about that as I scoped out the yard. Yesterday I'd felt like someone had been watching me. I'd chalked it up to my imagination and mostly forgotten about it, but what if someone had been out here watching? What if someone was pissed enough that I was back in town that they'd vandalized my car?

No. That didn't even make sense. Nothing that had happened a decade ago had been my fault. Or any of the victims' faults, so why would someone have a problem with me coming back home?

"Most likely this was just a case of random vandalism," he said. "Probably some kids bored with nothing better to do with their time and everything else is coincidental."

I nodded absently.

"But if you have any more problems or think of anything related to this, please call us and ask for me," he said. "I'm going to file a vandalism report, so make sure you let your insurance know. Okay?"

"All right. Thank you."

Officer Bradshaw nodded and then walked back to his cruiser. He stopped at the driver's door. "Wish it could've been under different circumstances, but it was nice meeting you." He gripped the car door as he twisted toward me. Our gazes locked, and a cold shiver raced down my spine. "But I'm sure we'll be seeing each other again."

AFTER CALLING THE insurance company and setting up a time for an inspector to come out the following week, I cleaned up the glass the best I could and then moved the car into the carriage house.

I managed to do this all without ending up with glass sticking out of very sensitive places, so I considered that a win.

With James coming in shortly to begin work on the evening dinner service, I helped the blonde and bubbly Angela Reidy tidy up the reserved rooms.

Angela was several years younger and an adorable chatterbox. Immediately, I got why Mom thought she was flighty. She'd talk about one thing, stop in the middle of a sentence and switch topics. She talked about how she was taking night classes at the community college in nearby Hagerstown. She wanted to become a teacher, focusing on pre-K. Angela had a boyfriend named Ethan. They'd been together for three years.

I liked listening to her even though I didn't get a word in edgewise. Letting Angela take full rein of the conversation as we moved from room to room stopped me from dwelling on what happened this morning. I might as well give myself the break since my imagination was going to take it to the worst-case scenario as soon as I had the downtime.

And that would be that someone targeted my car.

Didn't make sense to me, but I knew crazier things were possible.

Finishing up the elderly couple's room, we walked into the laundry room, which used to be a bedroom. I grabbed an armful of warm towels out of the dryer and dumped them onto a clean worktable.

Angela grabbed the dirty sheets, humming under her breath as she shoved them into the washer. "There is only one thing I hate in this world and that's folding sheets."

I grinned as I started folding the towels. "It's because folding sheets is impossible."

"So true." Angela grabbed a bottle of detergent and measured out a cup. "How does it feel being back here?" she asked after a moment.

Creating a small stack of white towels, I shrugged. "Not sure. I mean, it's good. I've missed . . . this."

"Really?" Doubt colored the younger girl's tone as she moved on to the fabric softener. "You've missed picking up after people and doing laundry?"

I laughed. "Not exactly, but this is my family's legacy and . . ." I looked up as my hands smoothed across a towel. "I was originally going to do this, the whole follow-in-the-family's-footsteps kind of thing. I *wanted* to do that." And that was true.

When I was younger, it had been my dream to take over the inn. That dream had changed—no. That dream had been *stolen*. "I liked doing what I did in Atlanta, and this—folding towels—isn't exactly exciting, but this, all of this, belongs to my family—to me, and it's hard to explain, but it feels right."

Angela studied me for a moment and then smiled. "That makes sense. Kind of how I feel about teaching the little ones." She screwed the lid back on the softener and then stretched up, placing the bottle on the shelf above. After turning the washer on, Angela practically bounced her way over to where I was. She picked up a towel. "It had to be so hard coming back here after what happened. I don't think I could do it."

My gaze shot to the younger girl.

Angela was focused on her own pile of towels. "Every time I head down Route 11, I drive right past the old water tower and it's all I think about." Angela shuddered, and acid churned in my stomach. "It's horrible to think about, but I didn't live it like you did. I can't even imagine what you've gone through—"

A towel slipped from my fingers, hitting the floor. "Shit," I muttered, swiping it off the floor. Straightening, I shook the towel out. "Can we talk about something else?"

Angela's brown eyes widened as a pink blush zipped across her face. Clutching a towel to her chest, she looked seconds away from bursting into tears. "Oh my gosh, I'm so sorry! I wasn't even thinking."

Closing my eyes, I took a slow, even breath and then forced a smile. "It's okay."

"No, it's not. I talk without thinking. My mama is always telling me it's going to get me in a world of trouble. Ethan says the same thing," Angela said in a rush. "And she's right. I am so sorry. That was totally inappropriate of me."

I inhaled deeply and opened my eyes. "It's really okay." Folding the towel, I ignored the tremor that curled up my spine. "You said your boyfriend works in Frederick," I said, redirecting the conversation to much safer grounds. "What does he do again?"

Even with the topic of conversation going in a different direction, the atmosphere was strained as we replenished the towels and switched the sheets over to the dryer. Afterward, I went downstairs and plopped down at the registration desk. Flipping open the leather-bound reservation book, I tugged the bobby pin out of my hair. Strands of hair fell over my shoulders as I scanned the reservations for the upcoming week. I really needed to get my hands on the accounting to see where they were with the profits and the losses. Turning to the month of December, I picked up a pen—

Hands slammed down on the desk, causing me to shriek and jump back in my seat. Heart thundering against my ribs, I lifted my gaze as I clutched the pen, prepared to thrust it through someone's eyeball.

"Surprise!" Miranda Locke shouted as she waved both hands.

"Oh my God, you gave me a heart attack." I dropped the pen on the desk and shot out of the chair. Reaching across the desk, I smacked Miranda's arm. "Seriously."

"Shut up." Humor danced in Miranda's dark brown eyes as she flipped a rope of long skinny braids over her shoulder. "You should be hugging me right now, because you love and miss me."

"That's the only reason why I'm not stabbing you with a pen right now!" Rushing out from behind the desk, I threw my arms around Miranda's shoulders and all but tackled the slimmer, taller woman. "Oh my God, it's been too long."

Miranda squeezed me tight. "It's been—what? Two years?"

"Way too long." Drawing back, I clasped the arms of my best friend since sophomore year in high school. We'd met in gym class and had immediately bonded as we sat side by side on the bleachers and our extraordinarily attractive gym teacher strolled into the gymnasium. We'd both started drooling.

Miranda was a stunning dark-skinned woman and had the personality to match her beauty. She'd always been there for me—even when I bum-rushed out of this town and didn't want anything to do with anyone, Miranda had refused to be kicked to the curb.

Standing in front of her, it struck me with the force of a speeding freight train how much Miranda had done to maintain the friendship. "I've been such a shitty friend."

Miranda's head cocked to the side. "What?"

Dropping my hands to my sides, I stepped back and leaned against the desk. "I've just been a crappy friend. When I left here, I didn't even tell you."

Dark, elegantly shaped brows rose. "Yeah, that was pretty shitty."

"See!" I shook my head. "And you called and

called. I never answered. Other friends gave up, but you didn't."

"Of course not." She planted her hands on her hips. "Friends don't give up on one another, especially after they've been through a traumatic-as-hell event in their life. And those friends who did give up? Screw them. They should've known you were going through things and been there for you. They should've done what I did. Given you a couple of months and then got their ass on a plane and gone wherever you were."

And that was what Miranda had done.

After I had been . . . after I'd been released from the hospital, I'd been a mess—a physical and emotional disaster. Mentally checked out for *weeks*. Obviously no one blamed me. When my head had finally pieced together, I'd decided that I couldn't stay here. Not when the few times I had stepped out in public, people stared. People whispered. They pitied me. And then there was the media.

Freaking vultures circling prey.

I'd holed myself up through the fall while researching colleges far, far away and it was only when I'd picked Florida State that I'd told my mom about my plans to finish college away. Mom had hated it, but she'd understood.

I hadn't told anyone else.

"I'm glad my mom told you where I was all those years ago," I said with a faint smile. "And I'm glad you got your ass on that plane and found me."

"And I'm glad your ass is finally back home. I love you," Miranda said, tone serious. "You're my sister from a different mister."

"Ditto," I replied softly, and then took a shaky breath. "You look great."

"It's because I have no boyfriend, so I spend my free time in a gym instead of in the bed."

Tipping my head back, I laughed. "I was talking about the hair. It's new."

"You like?" She patted her braids. "I had to drive over an hour to find someone who knew what the hell they were doing. Not like I was trusting anyone in this town to touch my hair. That was the only good thing about you living in Atlanta. Salon options were limitless whenever I visited you."

I giggled. "Want to get something to drink and go out back? It's not too cold outside. I was just up here checking out the reservation book."

"Has your mom made her sweet tea? If so, then it's a yes," Miranda returned. "Her tea is like crack— the good kind of crack that doesn't rot your teeth or make you pick your face."

I laughed again. Damn, I missed how often Miranda made me laugh. The sparse in-person visits and weekly phone chats were so not the same thing. "She always has a pitcher of sweet tea ready."

James was in the kitchen, fussing with two rotisserie chickens he had in the oven. The lemon and herbs smelled something wonderful, but when Miranda said so James grumbled something inaudible back to her.

Mr. Jordan was not much of a talker.

"Is there anything I can help with?" I asked as I placed the pitcher of tea back in the fridge.

James grabbed an oven mitt. "Best you can do is stay out of the way."

Miranda's dark eyes widened, but I grinned. "That we can do," I said, starting toward the back door that led to the old kitchen.

"You been down in the basement?" James asked, stopping me.

"No." I glanced at Miranda, frowning. "Why?"

"Light was on down in the wine cellar when I came in," he replied. "Make sure you turn it off. Those wires are old."

I didn't bother telling him again that I hadn't been down in the cellar, so I nodded and then pushed open the door. The room was full of the old furniture, most covered in white sheets, and it was much cooler than the rest of the house. Along the back wall was a corkboard with several keys attached. On the other side of the long, narrow room was a door that opened onto the old staircase that led down to an old wine-and-root cellar that always smelled like rich soil. Only part of the basement was in use. The rest was just packed dirt and bare stone. The ancient tunnels that used to run from the cellar out into the backyard had long since been sealed off.

As I opened up the door to the veranda, the keys on the corkboard rattled. "He's a lovable fella."

"Seems like it." Miranda wrinkled her nose. "Personality must not be a requirement to work in the kitchen."

"Pretty much cooking skills is the only requirement," I replied.

As we walked across the vacant veranda, I told her about what happened to my car. Even though it was January, it was unseasonably warm for the area, pushing into the midfifties. With the sun so bright, it would be comfortable for at least another hour or so, I decided as we sat at the glass table in the Adirondack chairs.

"The car thing is really weird." Miranda twisted her wrist, knocking the cubes of ice around in her drink. "Like really weird."

"I know. When Officer Bradshaw started asking me if I knew anyone who might be bothered by me being back here, it kind of freaked me out." With my glass on the table, I sat back in the thick-cushioned chair and folded my arms across my belly. "I mean, I'm sure it was just some kids bored and completely random, because I don't think my mother told a lot of people and then there's just you."

"Well . . ." Miranda drew the word out and then took a drink.

I waited for her to continue. "Well what?"

"I might've told someone," she said, crossing her legs. "But it wasn't like a random person. It was Jason."

"Jason? Oh my God, he's still around here?" Jason King went to college with us. The three of us had met during orientation and had shared several classes the one and a half years I'd been in attendance. Jason was a good, fun guy from what I remembered. My age. Nerdy in a cute, boy-next-door kind of way. A whiz at math and statistics, which I could respect.

And I'd seen him after I got out of the hospital. He'd been the only one who had gotten past the news reporters and my mom. The last time we'd talked he held me while I sat on my bed, held me while I sobbed, and the last thing he ever said to me was that I was safe now.

I left him behind too.

Nodding, Miranda eyed me over the rim of her glass. "Yep. Like me. You know how it is. If you don't leave this damn town by the age of twenty-one, you don't ever leave."

"I don't think that's true," I replied, stretching over and picking up my glass. "You can leave whenever you want."

"Uh-huh." Dark eyes rolled. "Anyway, he graduated college and ended up opening his own insurance agency about two years ago. He stayed even though he never found his father. Do you remember that?"

I nodded. Jason's mother and stepfather had passed away tragically in a house fire when he'd turned eighteen. From what I remembered, it had been during a cold snap and they'd been using a kerosene heater to thaw out their pipes. Their deaths had been what spurned Jason to find his real father. "Yeah, he came here because he'd been told his real father was from Hedgesville. So, he never did find his dad then?"

"Nope. You would know that if—"

"I know. I know." I sighed. Jason had tried to get in contact with me before I left, but the calls had stopped when I changed my number.

Jason hadn't been the only person who'd done all of that. Cole had come to the hospital. He'd called and come to the inn.

And I'd done the same to him.

My gaze lowered to my glass as I pressed my lips together. Regret was a bitter tang on my tongue. Looking back, I knew I could've handled everything differently, but I did what I believed I had to do then.

"I did tell him you were coming back. He was really excited about that. Wants to see you when you're ready." Miranda paused. "I hope you're okay with that. He *was* your friend."

"I'm okay with that." And once I said it, I discovered that I was. "We all should get together sometime this week for dinner or something."

"Oh! That would be perfect." She sipped her tea. "My evenings, weekends, and summers are free."

"Except when you're doing lesson plans, working overtime tutoring, or when you're working part-time during the summer because you're worried about being laid off," I corrected.

"You're such a bummer." Miranda flashed a bright white smile. "Alas, the life of a teacher."

Miranda had been teaching at our old high school the last two years. It had taken her that long to find a full-time permanent position. Ironically, she was now the coworker of the gym teacher we'd drooled over all those years ago. According to Miranda, Coach Donnie Currie was still hot as hell.

Life was weird.

Speaking of weirdness, I thought back to the police officer who'd arrived this morning. "Want to hear something weird?"

"I love weird." Miranda finished off her tea. "Well, none of that weird paranormal crap. Like if you saw some damn ghost in this place last night, I don't want to hear about it, because I would like to sleep again."

I barked out a laugh. "Yeah, no. That's not where I was going with that statement."

"Okay then." She flicked her wrist grandly. "Please continue."

"Thanks for your permission." I arched a brow when Miranda got all squinty-eyed with me. "The officer who came out this morning, he looked . . . Miranda, he looked so much like him."

"*Him?*" she whispered as her lips parted. "As in the . . . the Groom?"

"Wait. What? Oh my God." My stomach dumped to my knees. "I don't mean *him*. I meant the officer looked like Cole."

"Cole?" Her voice dropped even lower.

"Do you remember him?" I asked, fingers tightening on my glass. "I know we haven't talked about him in forever, but—"

"Of course I remember him!" Miranda sat up straight. "I remember every extraordinarily hot dude."

"He was extraordinarily hot," I replied wistfully.

"Not as hot as Idris Elba."

"True," I laughed.

"Back to this officer. He looked like Cole? Wasn't Cole a cop?" Miranda refocused.

"He was a deputy, but it obviously wasn't Cole. The officer was way too young, but there was an uncanny resemblance. At least to me. Mom didn't say anything, but maybe she didn't see it." I shifted in the chair, knowing I probably shouldn't ask what I was getting ready to. "Do you . . . do you know if he's still around?"

"He stayed in college, but I didn't have any classes with him after econ. And he did ask about you often and was pretty persistent, but . . . you also know how that went down." Miranda knocked a braid off her cheek. "I haven't seen him in years. I'm pretty sure he's not a deputy any longer, at least not around here."

"Oh." A weird twisting motion lit up my chest. It felt like disappointment. Which made no freaking sense. Not like I came home expecting to rekindle a decade-old romance. Cole was probably long gone from here, married with a boatload of kids. At least he deserved that, a happily ever after. He was a good guy; the best kind.

Miranda eyed me intently like she'd done a hundred times, seeing right through me. "Do you still have his number? Probably the same. People don't change their numbers."

"I don't have his number. When I changed mine, I dumped all the contacts," I admitted, a little bit ashamed by that little factoid. "And even if I did, I so would not call him."

"Chicken."

I chuckled. "Come on, calling him after ten years would be super weird."

"You could just check out Facebook and see if he has an account." Miranda paused, lips curling up at the corners. "You so have checked it out to see if he has an account, haven't you?"

Heat splashed across my cheeks. "Maybe I have."

Miranda waited.

"Okay. Fine. Whatever. I did a while ago. Never could find one."

"Interesting," Miranda murmured.

Not really. Kind of just sad and a bit pathetic.

Miranda stayed for a little while longer, leaving

when dinner service was about to get started. I had just enough time to change into a pair of denim jeans. The flip-flops and sweater remained, and I'd taken a few extra minutes to let my hair down, run a brush through the waves and slather some lipstick on.

All the guests were in attendance for dinner, so we were constantly on the move. When the last guest packed up, it was close to eight, and all I could think about was face-planting onto my bed. Hopefully I'd actually sleep for longer than four hours.

With all the dishes cleared from the tables and the linens changed, I was replacing the tea candles on the table with new unlit ones when Mom returned to the dining room.

"Did you get a chance to grab something to eat?" she asked.

"Yes," I answered with a soft laugh. Mom. Always mothering. "I grabbed some chicken. Sort of feared for my life when James caught me."

"He's a little rough around the edges. You remember that." Taking two of the small candles from me, she placed them in the glass holder. "But he's a damn good cook and I love when . . ."

When she trailed off, I looked over at her as I placed the last candle on the table near the fireplace. The expression on Mom's face was odd. Like she was caught between wanting to pass out and do a happy dance. And I'd seen her do a happy dance before. Knees up. Arms out. It was something else.

Her gaze was fixed on something beyond my shoulders as she said, "Oh my word . . ."

Brows snapping together, I turned around and everything—*everything*—stopped. The entire world ground to a halt. My heart skipped a beat, possibly even stopped. For real. I lifted a hand, pressing the heel of my palm into the center of my chest.

A ghost from my past stood in front of me.

It was Cole Landis.

CHAPTER

5

THERE WAS A good chance I might be hallucinating. Perhaps I'd tripped over a chair leg, fallen and hit my head on the river-stone fireplace. That seemed more possible than Cole actually standing in front of me.

But I hadn't smacked my head off of anything.

He really was there, and it was unbelievable, and oh my sweet Jesus, the years had been extraordinarily kind to him.

I was struck by his rugged attractiveness.

Gone was the boyish handsomeness that had clung to his face the last time I'd seen him. In its place were sharper cheekbones and blue eyes even more piercing behind thick lashes. The proud, arrogant line of his nose was slightly crooked now, as if it had been broken at some point. Those lips of his . . . oh sweet Lord, those lips were still full. The hard line of his jaw was covered with stubble, adding to the roughness of his striking face. His light brown hair was buzzed into a messy fade, a little longer than I remembered.

He was . . . more, uh, *defined*.

His biceps stretched the worn cotton of the red flannel shirt he wore. The sleeves were rolled up to his elbows, revealing powerful forearms. The flannel was unbuttoned and underneath was a crisp white shirt. His waist was trim and it took no leap of imagination to know that underneath the plain shirt was anything other than plain.

"It's really you," he stated.

My world stopped for a second time. His voice. Oh my God, his voice had deepened and it was rougher, raspier, but it was his voice.

"I didn't believe it." Cole stepped forward, and every muscle in my body locked up. "Part of me didn't even want to believe it in case he was wrong, but he wasn't. It's you."

All I could do was stare as my heart slammed in my chest as if it was trying to beat its way out of me. I knew I needed to get my tongue to work, but I was shocked into silence.

Unfortunately, Mom wasn't.

"Well, this is a surprise," she said, announcing the obvious. "Isn't it, Sasha?"

I nodded slowly as Cole stared at me with those pale eyes. My throat dried. I *really* needed to say something, but I was thinking of my nightmare the night before, of the last time I saw him.

"I would've called the inn first." Cole's gaze flickered to Mom briefly before settling on me with an intensity that caused my entire body to flush hot. It had always been like that. He had such power in a single stare. Could send you running in the opposite direction or draw you right in like a magnet. "But I figured not calling was a better avenue to take."

Sucking in a sharp breath, I got what he was saying. He'd thought that if I knew he was coming, I wouldn't have been here, and the sad thing was, I couldn't say if that was the truth or not. Realizing that snapped me out of my stupor. "How did you know I was back?"

Cole's eyes widened slightly and those full, expressive lips parted, and it appeared he was the one now struck quiet.

"Well." Mom cleared her throat. "I'm going to go . . . do stuff," she said, and then pivoted around, hastily slipping through the pocket door.

Neither of us moved.

Alone and together for the first time in a decade, we stared at one another. The last time we we'd seen each other, he'd kissed me. He'd called me babe and said he would be waiting for me. I never called. Never made it home to do so.

It was Cole who spoke first. "Derek told me you were home."

Derek? It took me a moment to recall who that was. "The cop from this morning?"

"Yeah." He was staring at me like he'd never expected to see me again—like he'd hoped that he would but hadn't placed a lot of faith in that hope. "He's my cousin."

Well, that explained why I'd thought of him when I saw Derek this morning. Their family was rocking some powerful genes. But I didn't know why he'd immediately called Cole.

Or why he was here.

"And he called you about . . . about me?" I asked, folding my arms across my waist. It was that moment when I remembered I was wearing a sweater that most likely added twenty pounds to me. Nice. At least I'd brushed my hair earlier.

Cole nodded, started to step forward again, but stopped. "Do you have time to talk?"

Opening my mouth, I stopped myself a half a second before I said no. That was my first instinct. To shut down communication with him, because that was what I'd done before, what I always did when I felt even the littlest bit confronted by my past.

But Cole wasn't the bad guy.

He had never been the bad guy.

I drew in a shaky breath and then ran the tip of my tongue along my bottom lip. "Okay. I mean, yes. I have time." I gestured toward the opening with a trembling hand. "We can sit in there."

"Perfect." His gaze remained on me for a few moments, long enough to cause my cheeks to flush, and then he turned.

So many questions rose to the surface as we walked out in the sitting area. Did he still live here or had he driven in? Was he still a cop or had he made it to federal level, like he had planned in college? Did he get married and have kids?

My heart was still racing as I made my way to the wingback chair near the fireplace. As he sat across from me, my gaze dropped to his left hand. I didn't mean to. I had no control over it. I zeroed in on his ring finger. No wedding band or indentation indicating one was recently removed.

My stupid heart did Mom's version of a happy dance.

Okay. I really needed to not be concerned with any of that, because that was an extreme case of putting the cart before the horse.

Cole checked out the sitting room. "This place has really changed." His gaze settled on me. "I haven't been back here since . . . well, since you left."

"Me either." I mentally cursed. Of course I hadn't been here. He *knew* that. I was frazzled. Sitting across from one another was almost too overwhelming. Part of me wanted to get up and run. The other half was curious . . . and excited. My stomach dipped again.

Way too excited.

"You didn't come back, not even once?" he asked, rubbing the heel of his palm across his sternum.

Inhaling deeply, I shook my head. "No. My mother visited me. So did Miranda."

"Miranda." The corners of his lips tipped up and then quickly straightened out. "I remember her. It's good to know you did keep in touch with her."

He actually sounded like he meant that, and I found that strange considering I'd disappeared on him. I couldn't blame him if he harbored resentment. He'd done nothing wrong and I—well, I had been a mess.

I started to respond, but I couldn't believe he was actually sitting here in front of me. Those thick lashes lifted, and our gazes collided. I quickly averted my eyes, focusing on his shoulder as I clasped my hands together. "So, um, why did Derek contact you?"

He dropped his hand to the arm of the chair as he laughed or coughed under his breath. I wasn't sure. "Derek was young back then, but he knew you and I were seeing each other. He remembered who you were."

"Oh," I whispered, shifting my attention to the fireplace. Looking at him was . . . God, it was hard, too hard. He represented a future that never came to fruition.

"He remembered how much I was into you," he continued. "Everyone in my family knew it."

Whoa.

Wow.

He just put that right out there.

The gas-created flames rippled behind the glass as I tried to figure out how to respond to him. Guessing it wouldn't be cool for me to admit I tried to Facebook stalk him one or twenty times with no success over the years, I decided it was time to change the subject. "So, he's a cop like you?" I peeked at Cole, finding him watching me intently. I wasn't sure he'd taken his gaze off me for longer than a few moments. "Or are you not a cop anymore?"

"I work for the FBI now," he explained.

My smile wasn't forced as it raced across my face. "That's what you wanted to do. Congratulations."

"Back at you." He slid a long-fingered hand along the teal arm of the couch. "You're finally doing what you always planned."

I blinked, jolted by the fact he remembered this piece of information about me. "Yes. I . . . I am." Our eyes met again, and I coughed out a laugh. "I'm sorry. I'm just—I didn't expect you."

"That's understandable. I probably could've waited a day, but when Derek told me you were here . . ." He trailed off, dipping his chin as he looked up at me through his lashes. "I didn't want to wait. I had to see you. After so long, I had to see that you were really . . . okay."

See if I was okay.

Oh man, my heart swelled and deflated at the same time, and I didn't even know what to make of those conflicting emotions. His concern was as sweet as a warm spring day and it was as suffocating as an itchy blanket.

"You look amazing," he said, and then he laughed as my eyes widened. "That was awkward, wasn't it? I don't care. It's the truth. You're as beautiful—no, more beautiful than I remembered."

My entire face burned as my lips parted.

"Are you involved with anyone?" he asked, catching me off guard. "That also came out of nowhere, huh?"

"No," I answered without thinking. "I mean, I'm not seeing anyone."

His answering smile was slow, and damn it, it caused my chest to pitch in the most delightful way. "Me neither."

I'd guessed that earlier when I'd been checking out his ring finger. "Thank you—for the compliment." My fingers ached from how tightly I was clenching my hands together. "You look amazing too. Better than before." I winced. "I mean, you looked good then too, but now . . . I'm just going to stop."

That half grin appeared and his blue eyes warmed. "Don't stop on my account."

I needed to stop, so I refocused. "Um, so do you still live around here?"

He nodded. "Yep. In Falling Waters. Have a home there."

"That's nice." And I meant it, but a second later, I stalled out on what to say. Talking to Cole had never been hard, not in the past, but now I found my words stilted and cautious. I just didn't know what to say or do.

Cole didn't appear to notice. "Is everything all right with your car? Derek told me your windows were busted out."

"I called the insurance company and they're sending someone out. They're going to cover everything." I paused, looking down at my hands. My knuckles were bleached white. "It was so strange. They broke out the windows, but didn't take my laptop, which was right on the backseat."

"Sounds like a few kids with too much time on their hands," he replied.

"That's what your cousin said," I murmured, lifting my gaze.

His chest rose with a deep breath. Several seconds passed. "Are you okay, Sasha? Really okay?"

Oh God, there it was again. *That* question. The question everyone who knew who I was always ended up asking, and hearing that question come from Cole was what I had been avoiding for the last ten years. That was obviously why he was here. My spine stiffened. "Yeah, I'm okay."

Those eyes moved over my face as if he were memorizing every inch. Another stretch of tense silence rolled out between us, and I wondered if he even believed my answer. How could I be okay? I knew that some people couldn't understand how I could be okay after what had happened and they treated me like I was some kind of broken creature. It was why no one I met outside of this state ever knew about my past.

"I thought about that night." His voice carried a heavy weight. "A lot."

"Cole—"

"Should've walked you to your car that night," he continued, gaze unwavering. "Biggest damn regret of my life right there."

Oh God.

Leaning away, I pressed into the back of the chair. I wanted to run from the room, from what he was saying, but it was too late. His words were burned into my brain, and I didn't want them there. I didn't want him to feel that way. "You shouldn't feel that way," I said, squeezing my hands together. "What happened wasn't—"

"It wasn't my fault. I didn't do what he did. I know that." He exhaled heavily. "Doesn't change the fact that I should've walked you to your damn car. We all knew what was going on and—"

"And if he hadn't gotten me that night, he would've gotten me later." The fine hairs rose along the nape of my neck. It had been so long since I'd talked about it. "And we all knew that he'd been—" My breath hitched in my throat. "He'd been watching me. Like he'd watched all the others. He would've gotten me eventually."

Cole broke eye contact then and his voice was low when he said, "Yeah."

Uncomfortable, I shifted in my seat. "I'm . . . happy to see that you're doing well, but it's late and it's been a really long day."

"All right." Cole's eyes came to mine. "But I've got one more question for you."

I waited, prepared to take flight as soon as I could.

"Will you have dinner with me?"

My jaw dropped open. Okay, that was not what I was expecting.

"I want to catch up with you, but I get that it's late and I've surprised you. So maybe we could restart this conversation when you've had a little time to prepare."

God, I'd totally forgotten how straight to the point Cole was.

"What do you think?" he persisted when all I did was stare at him.

"I . . . I don't know about that," I whispered, almost immediately regretting my answer. I took a deep breath as part of my mind threw its arms up in disagreement while the other clapped its hands in approval. Dinner with Cole was not a good idea. Other than him needing to see that I was of sound mind and body, I didn't get why he'd want to.

One side of his lips quirked up. "Got to admit, not surprised to hear that."

I arched a brow. "And why is that?"

He tilted his head to the side and a moment passed. "It's been a long time, hasn't it?"

"Yes, but . . ." But that wasn't an answer, or was it?

Cole studied me in the intense way that was familiar yet different now. "It's okay."

Confused, I did what I felt like I'd been doing

since I saw him in the dining room. I simply gaped at him.

He scooted toward me, stopping just short of his knees touching mine. Our gazes locked, and I held my breath. "I'm going to leave you my number." He tilted his hips to the side and reached around, pulling out his wallet. A business card appeared. "This has my personal cell and my work cell. You change your mind, call me. Anytime."

Untangling my fingers, I went to take the card from him, when our hands brushed. I swallowed a soft gasp as a shivery-hot sensation radiated up my arm. It always had been like that, an electric combustion whenever we touched, no matter how chaste the gesture. *Shocked* didn't even cover how I felt when I realized that it was still there, at least for me.

"Okay?" he urged gently.

"Okay," I repeated.

"Good." Cole rose and then he was right there, his hands planted on the arms of the chair, caging me in. He lowered his head, and a moment later, I felt the brush of his lips against the curve of my cheek, the touch soft and fast. "I'm glad that you're back," he said, and I squeezed my eyes shut against the rush of messy, wet emotions. "Call me, Sasha. I'll be waiting."

CHAPTER

6

"YOU TOLD COLE NO?" Miranda sounded like I'd just told her the Ghost of Christmas Past had visited me Saturday night. "Are you completely out of your damn mind?"

There was a good chance that I was, because nearly two days later there was a part of me that wondered if I'd dreamt up Cole's sudden appearance.

Except the business card I obsessively stared at whenever I was in my apartment proved that he had been here.

"I don't know," I said with a sigh, picking up a pillow. "I was just so caught off guard by his appearance."

Miranda watched me fluff the pillow. It was Monday and she'd come straight from school as soon as she could. We were supposed to have dinner tonight with Jason, meeting at one of the restaurants down the street. "I can understand that, especially after we were just talking about him, and poof! He's right in front of your face."

That was kind of like how it felt.

"But this is Cole," she continued as I grabbed the dirtied linen off the floor and balled it up. "You were all about Cole, Sasha."

"That was ten years ago," I pointed out as she followed me into the hallway. Stopping, I closed the door behind us. "That was a very long time ago."

"So? Give me one good reason why you can't go out to dinner with him," she challenged in what I'd deemed was her teacher voice, which was an impressive combo with her demure black sweater and fitted slacks.

Easy. "I didn't come home to get into a relationship."

She rolled dark eyes. "And Cole asking you out to dinner to catch up signifies a relationship to you?"

I shot her a look as I headed down the hall. "You know what I mean."

"Yes, I know what you mean." We walked into the laundry room. "But you know what? You're right. You didn't come home to find a guy, even if that guy is extremely hot and told you he thought you were beautiful," she said as I shoved the linens into the washer and grabbed the detergent. "You came home to start living your life."

My hand jerked as I poured the detergent into the washer. *You came home to start living your life.* She was right, so damn right. I hated it when she was right.

Closing the washer door, I faced her. "I'm going out to dinner with you and Jason tonight—"

"And that's awesome. I know seeing him is going

to be hard for you," Miranda cut in. "But you've got to step up your game. You can't come home and live in the shadow of the past."

"Besides the fact I just got home, like a few days ago, I'm trying."

Miranda planted her hands on her hips. "I know, but I think trying harder would mean you'd take Cole up on his offer—and why are you doing this right now? Watching you wash laundry makes me feel like I should be helping or something."

I smiled as I turned on the washer. "I'm done now."

"Thank God," she muttered. "My stomach is about to eat itself and I was actually about to fold some of those towels over there."

Laughing, I led her out of the laundry room. We headed down the narrow staircase and by the time we hit the kitchen, tiny balls of nerves had formed in my stomach. "What time are we supposed to meet Jason?"

"In about twenty minutes." Miranda placed her hand on my shoulder and squeezed. "You're going to have a good time."

I straightened the hem of the sweater I'd changed into before Miranda showed up. "Do I look like I think I'm not going to have a good time?"

"You look a little pale." She smiled faintly. "Like you may need to sit down."

"Geez," I murmured as we walked out to the front of the inn. Darkness loomed beyond the glass panels in the front door. The sun had already gone down.

"Your hair looks amazing though. It's so pretty when it's down." Miranda winked when I looked at her. "It's okay to be nervous. You haven't seen Jason in a decade."

"It's not just seeing him. I mean, I am a little nervous." I walked over to the chair near the desk and plopped down. "I haven't been to a restaurant in this town in a very long time. I haven't even gone out in public."

"I told her earlier that no one would even pay attention to her," Mom announced. "That she had nothing to worry about."

I looked up to see Mom coming down the main staircase, her hand trailing along the railing. "I know I have nothing to worry about and I'm being irrational, but let me have my irrationality."

Miranda arched a brow in Mom's direction. "How about that makes no sense?"

"Whatever," I muttered, checking the phone. No messages. "I might drink an entire bottle of wine with dinner."

"I don't have a problem with that. I'm driving." Miranda grinned. "Plus the place is like a mile, if that, down the street, so we both can drink and stumble our way back here."

"Sounds like a plan," I said as I reached into the drawer and pulled out my purse. I checked my phone, making sure it had good battery life. "Also good if I want to leave and you can—"

"First off, you're not going to want to leave until you've finished the thick, juicy rib eye that they serve and ordered their chocolate lava cake," Miranda stated, and my stomach grumbled in anticipation. "Secondly, if you want to get out of there early, I'm going to leave with you."

"She's not going to want to leave." Mom leaned against the desk. "She's going to go, eat that steak, the dessert, drink the wine, and enjoy herself."

Taking a deep breath, I smiled as my mom stared at me as if she could will her faith into the very core of my being. The nervousness I was feeling was understandable, but it was the razor-sharp edge of the unease that tasted a little like panic. That feeling had been building all day, and it *was* ridiculous. It *was* irrational, and I totally knew that. Which was why I was going out tonight like a normal, well-adapted twenty-nine-year-old.

"I want you to do me a favor," Mom asked of Miranda as I stood, sliding the strap of my bag up my forearm. "Convince her to call—"

"Mom," I snapped.

"—Cole," she finished, ignoring me. "Because I can't believe my daughter has that man's phone number and isn't making that phone call."

Oh my God.

Miranda's eyes glimmered. "So, he *was* really hot then?"

"Oh yes. I'm half tempted to get that card and call him myself," Mom said. "You should've seen how he aged, Miranda. That boy is now a man."

Oh my God.

Miranda laughed loudly. "I really need to see what he looks like now."

Smoothing a hand over her hair, Mom nodded.

"Oh yes, you do need to see him. He was wearing this flannel shirt, and while that's not an attractive article of clothing on most men, it made—"

"All right. It's time for us to leave." I came around the desk and kissed Mom's cheek. "Do you need anything while I'm out?"

"Just for you to have a good time," she replied.

I pulled back, smiling. Damn, I was so lucky to have her as my mom. So damn lucky. Saying goodbye, I followed Miranda out into the chilly evening air. Her red Volkswagen Jetta was parked where mine had been before someone decided it needed a glass renovation. After the insurance agent came out, I figured my car would be back to the way it should be by the end of the week.

Climbing into Miranda's car was like stepping back into the past. Me in the passenger seat. Her car smelling like crisp apples thanks to the scent diffusers. I glanced over my shoulder as she rounded the front of the car and grinned. An entire week's worth of cardigans and ponchos covered the backseat.

Just like before.

Miranda was oddly quiet as she pulled out of the driveway and coasted to a stop at the end of the drive. "You know we're giving you a hard time about the Cole thing, right?" she said, and I looked over. Her eyes were squinted as she focused on the road. "Of course your mom and I would love to see you reconnect with him, but we understand why you'd be hesitant."

I swallowed as I nodded. "I know."

"I know you've dated," Miranda said, and there

was a long pause before she continued. "But I also know you never really allowed those relationships to go anywhere serious."

Flipping my gaze to the road, I bit down on the inside of my cheek as Miranda pulled out into traffic. I'd dated and those relationships had progressed to sex. The first time after . . . after the Groom had been my senior year at Florida State, and it was a disaster—I'd been a complete emotional mess afterward, but the hang-ups faded as the years moved on. Miranda was right though. The dates never really went beyond a month. I wasn't sure why.

"I've thought about Cole's offer all day yesterday and most of today," I admitted.

I'd thought about it so much I was driving myself a little crazy, but seeing Cole had thrown me off. Truthfully, thinking about him wasn't something new, but the idea of talking to him, seeing him again, had been a pipe dream, a silly little fantasy that I entertained late at night when I couldn't sleep.

And when I did let my mind wander there, I imagined that we'd talk about our careers and discover that we still had a connection. He'd kiss me, and I wouldn't . . . I wouldn't think of *him*. In other versions, we'd meet and he'd be happily married with kids, and I'd be sad but satisfied that he was doing okay. It never had been a real possibility, and now that it was, when there was a chance to talk about our careers and what the past ten years had meant for us, I couldn't wrap my head around it.

"And?" she queried when I didn't continue.

I sat back in the seat. "And I . . . part of me, a very big part of me, wants to have dinner with him."

Miranda didn't immediately respond as we came to the first of what felt like five hundred stoplights. "But?"

"But . . ." I dragged my fingers over the strap of my bag. But . . . hell, it was hard to even finish the thought, but Cole scared me. He'd scared me back when we first met, because I'd never felt anything like what I had when he would simply look at me. Like there was no one else in the world and he only saw me. When we talked, we never ran out of things to say, and when he had kissed me? I still remembered how crazy he made me feel with just a kiss, as if he was lighting every cell in my body on fire. Being with Cole had made me feel like I was on the edge of a cliff, more than willing to fall off. I'd never felt anything like that again. Not even a smidgen.

He terrified me.

Because he symbolized everything I should've had but didn't.

I couldn't admit that out loud, because I was afraid of not explaining it correctly. "I don't know," I said finally, easing my grip. "Maybe I will call him."

"Maybe," she murmured, but it was obvious she didn't believe me.

THE STEAKHOUSE HADN'T been here when I'd been around and it was surprisingly busy for the notoriously vacant downtown. Our table was in the back of the narrow first floor, a dimly lit seating area near a staircase that led to the second-floor private dining area I doubt saw a lot of action.

The skin along the back of my neck tingled as

our waitress, a blonde woman in her late twenties, poured water into glasses. She introduced herself as Liz. No one seemed to be paying any attention to us, so I ignored the sensation, and told myself to stop being stupid.

Miranda glanced at her phone. "Jason should be here any minute."

Slipping my fingers under my hair, I rubbed the nape of my neck as I glanced around. There was a table of men in business suits catty-corner to ours. All of them middle-aged. None of them looked familiar. All of them were focused on the dark-haired man at the head of the table. Whoever he was, he gave the impression of being important. "The place is really nice."

"Opened up about three years ago," Miranda said, glancing at the menu. "It's lasted longer than most nonchain restaurants."

"Do you come here often?" I asked just as the man at the table looked over. Our gazes connected. His eyes widened as he reached up and adjusted his red tie. Caught staring at them, I looked away.

She shook her head as she flipped over the menu. "Not really, but now that you're back and you live so close, I plan on making you meet me here at least once a week after work."

I grinned as I looked up again. Unable to focus on the menu, my gaze drifted across the restaurant and past a tall man wearing a white button-down and dark coat, then shot back to him. My brows rose as I lowered my hand to the table.

Took me a moment, but I recognized the man striding toward us. His hair was darker and he wasn't wearing glasses, but it was that cute boyish face all grown up.

"Jason?" I pushed back from the table.

His lips split into a smile as I rose. "Sasha, look at you."

Emotion clogged my throat as I stepped out. I hadn't expected to feel so much seeing him, but I squeezed my eyes shut as I wrapped my arms around him. He tensed a little and then stiffly hugged me back.

Oh man, that was Jason. Always all kinds of awkward, even when he'd held me while I cried last time.

"You look great," I said, pulling back as I looked up at him. "No glasses?"

"Lasik," he said, dipping his chin. "And you look amazing, Sasha. The years have . . . they have been kind to you."

I laughed as I stepped back to my chair, feeling a bit wobbly in the knees. "Thank you."

"Why don't I get a hug?" Miranda pouted.

Jason chuckled as he shrugged off his jacket and draped it over the back of his seat. He had a wiry, tall frame and that hadn't changed. "Maybe because I see you like twice a week and I haven't seen Sasha in a decade."

"Whatever. I should get a hug every single time you see me."

He shook his head as he folded his hands on the table. My gaze dropped and I saw a glimmer of a gold band. He was married? His brown eyes coasted over my face. "I almost can't believe you're sitting here. Wow. It's been too long."

"It has." I wet my lip, deciding I needed to get over the hard part. "I just want to say I'm sorry for the way . . . for the way I left things after everything that happened. You were my friend. You tried to be there for me, and I—"

"It's okay." He waved his hand. "You don't need to apologize."

"No," I insisted. "I do."

Jason looked over at Miranda. "Tell her she doesn't need to apologize."

"She needs to apologize," she replied.

"I'm sorry," I offered again. "Sincerely."

"I don't think it's necessary, but I accept." Jason looked up to his left as our waitress appeared. After placing an order for a bottle of white wine, he turned back to me. "So Miranda was telling me you had some problems with your car. If you have any questions once the adjuster shows up, call me. I can help you out."

"I'll do that." I paused when the waitress appeared with the wine and took our orders. "So, I see a wedding band. When did you get married?"

"Oh boy." Miranda moved his glass closer to him. "Probably should've told you about that."

I frowned.

"This?" He looked down and he smoothed his right hand over his left. "I got married about six years ago. I don't think you ever met her. Cameron wasn't from around here," he explained. "We're actually separated right now. She's been visiting family in Ohio."

"Oh! I'm sorry . . ." Trailing off, I slid a sideways glance in Miranda's direction. She was studiously sipping her wine. *That* would've been great information to have on hand. "I didn't know."

"It's okay." Jason shrugged it off, but I wondered if that was true. He'd been a quiet and kind boy in college. Not overly sensitive, but he was someone who I pictured was in it for the long haul when he got married. "Anyway," he said, clearing his throat. "What about you? Was there anyone you left behind in Atlanta?"

"No." I picked up my wine. "No one I was serious with."

"Cole stopped by and visited her Saturday night," Miranda announced.

"Miranda," I sighed, flipping my gaze to her.

Surprise flickered across Jason's face. "Really?"

"Yep. He invited her out to dinner. She said no." Miranda raised her wine glass at me. "I told her she should reevaluate that decision."

What happened to her understanding if I didn't want to go out with Cole? I guessed that hadn't lasted beyond her first sip of wine.

"Huh." Jason sat back, folding his arms loosely. "I had no idea Cole was still around here. Haven't seen him in ages."

I didn't know what to say.

"He was a good guy, right?" Jason set his glass down. "And you seemed to really like him back then. Might be good to catch up with him. Not like it could hurt anything."

I opened my mouth, but what could I say to that? He was right. Having dinner with Cole couldn't hurt anything. I'd just needed to check the irrational fear, which was easier said than done.

A shadow fell over our table, and I looked up. The man from the other table, the one with the red tie, stood there. Up close, I pegged his age as midfifties. His face was losing its definition, softening at the jowls, and his brown hair thinning at the peak. His gaze, slightly beady, darted around our table and he nodded at Jason. "Hello, Mr. King and Ms. Locke." His stare landed on me. "Miss Keeton?" he asked, his tone pitching high on my last name.

Who was this man?

I glanced over at Miranda, who eyed me over the rim of her wine glass. No help there. "Yes?"

He smiled tightly. "You don't recognize me, do you? Understandable. It's been a long time."

My helpless gaze swung to Jason. He shifted to the side, away from the man. "This is Mark Hughes—*Mayor* Mark Hughes," Jason explained.

"Hello." I had no idea who Mark Hughes was, but he was the mayor, so I figured I should smile, and I did.

Mayor Hughes buttoned his blazer. "When you lived here, I owned the hardware shop in town. Still do, but a little busy these days to actually be running it."

I did vaguely remember the hardware shop, but his face was pretty much still pulling up a blank, so I continued to smile as I nodded, and hoped my rib eye arrived soon.

"Such a surprise to hear that you were coming back to town. Your mother mentioned it when she was at the chamber of commerce meeting last week," he explained, and I couldn't fathom how or why that would've come up during a conversation with the mayor, but I guessed Mom had just been excited. "I'm hoping there won't be any . . . issues with your return."

"Issues?" I repeated, glancing around the table. "I'm not sure what kind of issues you're referencing."

"Well, you're kind of a celebrity around these parts. At least to the media you are." Mayor Hughes' shoulders squared while I replayed what he'd just said to make sure I'd heard him correctly. "After all, you are this sensational real-life survivor story and I'm sure once some realize you're here, they'd like to capitalize on that." There was a pause. "Maybe you'd like to capitalize on that."

Miranda cocked her head to the side, lowering her glass; it looked like she'd almost dropped it.

"Excuse me?" I said with a shocked laugh. The back of my neck tingled again, but it was a different feeling than nervousness. It was a wave of irritation.

"Mayor Hughes," Jason started, placing one hand on the table. "Sasha isn't—"

Raising a hand, I cut Jason off even though I appreciated his attempt to step in. I didn't need someone speaking for me. "Nothing about what I experienced is what I'd consider sensational nor something I would want to relive, even if I were to profit from it."

Mayor Hughes' hollow cheeks flushed. "I'm sorry if I've offended you."

I met his stare, because yes, he had offended me, and I wasn't feeling very forgiving at the moment. Not when my stomach was grumbling.

He lowered his voice as he looked around. "I just

don't want the past being dragged back up, Miss Keeton. I think you'd appreciate that."

"You're doing a fine job at not dragging the past up yourself," Miranda pointed out with a sarcastic smile. "Just want to throw that out there."

Mayor Hughes ignored her comment. "Our town suffered greatly with the whole Groom business—"

"The town suffered?" Another weird laugh was bubbling up my throat.

"And it took years to erase the stigma and fear," he continued. "I don't want to see us losing ground because of one wrong well-meaning conversation with the wrong person."

My mouth dropped open. Did he honestly believe that I'd speak to anyone in the press about what happened when I hadn't given one interview in my entire life?

"I'll leave you all to your dinner," Mayor Hughes said, backing away. "Have a nice evening."

Miranda raised her middle finger when he turned his back but chirped happily, "You too!"

"Jesus," I muttered, picking up my glass. I downed half the wine in a nanosecond. "That guy's a dick."

"He's normally pretty laid-back, but I think he's a little overstressed right now," Jason commented. "Especially after what happened this morning."

"Jason," Miranda warned in a low voice.

I frowned as I glanced between them. "What?"

"Nothing." He cast his gaze to his wine glass.

"What happened this morning?" Sitting forward, I plopped my elbows on the table. "Come on. You have to finish what you're saying."

"I don't know." Jason arched his brows as he ran

his finger down the stem of his glass. "Miranda might smack me."

"I might smack you anyway," she shot back with a shake of her head.

"What, Jason?" I persisted, ignoring the familiar teasing tone between them.

Sighing, he looked up at her as she pursed her lips. "She's going to hear about it anyway," he said. "You know that."

"But it doesn't mean she needs to hear about it right now." Miranda picked up her glass and downed the contents. Placing the glass on the table, she met my stare. Dread crept down my spine. "Especially after all of that."

"Actually," I said slowly, getting more irritated, "I want to hear about it right now."

"A woman went missing out of Frederick at the beginning of the month," he explained, repeating what I'd already heard on the radio. "Did you know about that?"

I nodded. "Not a lot but I heard about it."

"Well, there was an update, and I only heard about it because the boys—the troopers—always get coffee at the Grind. It hasn't gone public yet. Probably will by tonight or tomorrow, but I told Miranda when she had a lunch break today. I thought you needed to hear it before it hit the news." Jason's brown eyes met mine, and the dread increased, unfurling in my stomach like a noxious weed. "They found her . . . her body early this morning."

"Oh God." I pressed my hand to my mouth.

"Right now they think it was someone she knew. I mean, that's what it normally is," Jason continued, but the wry glint to his eyes warned me there was more.

I stiffened as I lowered my hand to my lap. "What aren't you telling me?"

"It's probably just a coincidence," Miranda said softly.

My heart tripped up. "What?"

"It's where they found her body, Sasha. It was off of Route 11," Jason said, and I jerked in my seat. "Back near the old water tower, where the . . . the Groom used to leave the bodies."

CHAPTER 7

I'M SLOW TO wake up. *It feels like I've been asleep for days and it takes time to pry my eyes open. The room is dark, so dark I can't see anything. Not even an inch in front of my face. My throat feels terrible, like sandpaper, and my head is pounding. Confusion swirls inside me. I'm cold, too cold. There's a draft rolling over my skin, bare skin. Where am I? I start to sit up, but my arms and legs don't move.*

My heart kicks up as I try again, realizing that something is holding me down—down on a mattress. It hits me then. I remember! Walking to my car. Seeing the van. Hearing the door open—

Panic explodes inside me, clamping down on my chest and throat. I struggle against the bonds. Something metal—the bed frame—rattles. Pain spikes along my wrists and ankles, but I don't care. I have to get out of here. I have to find a way—

"You're awake." A voice carries out from the darkness. "I was beginning to worry."

I stop breathing as I stare into the nothing that surrounds me. Ears prickle as I hear soft movement. The bed shakes and dips. My eyes widen and my heart beats faster than it ever has.

A hand touches my cheek, and I shriek at the contact, pushing away, but getting nowhere. Oh no. No, no, no.

"Don't," he orders. "I don't want us to fight. It's the last thing I want."

Fear digs in deep with its claws, taking hold of me, and only one hoarse word gasps out of me. "Please."

The hand slides into my hair, the touch oddly gentle. Approving. "That's my bride."

I didn't go back to sleep after having another nightmare. This time I didn't even stay in bed. I went out into my living room and turned the TV on. Some late-night infomercial about a food processor that could apparently save the world was on, but I wasn't really paying attention as I sat on the couch, wrapped in the soft throw.

I was thinking about the Groom.

He's dead.

If he weren't, he would be in his sixties now. That didn't mean he wouldn't be able to continue doing what he did, but I imagined that as he grew older, it would be more difficult.

I never saw the Groom's face the entire time I was with him. It was either completely dark in the room or he blindfolded me. I'd only seen what he looked like when I was recovering in the hospital and the federal agents brought in a picture of him for me to look at. I avoided all media surrounding him and me, and I only saw his face once, but his image was cemented in my memory.

So when I dreamt of my time with the Groom, he sometimes had a face even though I never saw it while I was with him.

I shivered as I tucked my knees against my chest. Deep down, I knew that this poor woman's fate had nothing to do with the Groom, but I couldn't stop where my thoughts were going, especially after the pretty and super skinny brunette news anchor had gone there. What had she said? *The body was found in the infamous location used by the Groom to dump the bodies of his victims.*

Dump the bodies.

Closing my eyes, I pressed my lips together. There were only a few phrases I hated more than that one. Like someone was out dumping trash along the road. These were innocent women—six innocent women who were sisters and daughters, friends and lovers. They weren't something, even in death, that could simply be dumped like an empty fast-food bag.

But what happened to this woman wasn't because of the Groom. He was dead, because I wasn't. Knowing that also meant that it was a coincidence that this poor woman's body was found in the same location favored by the Groom.

But that didn't make me feel any better.

I opened my eyes and let out a shaky breath. Rising from the couch, I walked over to the window overlooking the front lawn. I pulled back the curtain and pressed my forehead against the cool window.

The run-in with Mayor Hughes replayed as I stared out over the dark grounds. Did he really think I'd talk publicly about what happened with the

Groom? I couldn't understand how anyone would even think that was a possibility—

A shadow blurred across the lawn, disappearing into the hedges. I jolted back from the window as my stomach pitched. The blanket slipped off my shoulders. Then I jerked forward, yanking the curtain back.

My heart raced as I scanned the still grounds below. What had I seen? I wasn't sure. The shadow had appeared person-sized, but it was so fast that I couldn't be positive. I couldn't be certain that I'd seen a thing.

I stood at that window for several minutes, waiting to see if anything moved, but other than branches from the oak trees lining the driveway, there was nothing.

"God." Dropping the curtain, I turned and bent down, picking up the blanket. Now I was seeing things.

Was coming back here a mistake?

"No," I whispered to the room. Coming back here had been the right thing to do; the only thing.

Walking past the couch, I picked up the remote and turned off the TV. I went into the bedroom and flipped on the nightstand lamp. Sitting down on the edge of the bed, I picked up the small rectangular card.

I'd looked at it so much that I practically knew the words and numbers by heart.

Smoothing my thumb over the card, I thought back to what Miranda had said about me coming home. She probably hadn't thought twice about the words, but they were simple and powerful.

She'd said I came home to start *living*.

The photo of the woman they found started to form in my thoughts. It was the photograph used for her hospital ID. She had been young, early thirties, maybe late twenties. Light brown hair highlighted with blond streaks. She'd been pretty. Her smile was hopeful. The gleam to her eyes eager. She'd been alive until someone decided to take that away from her.

This woman I'd never met was not going to have a second chance. She wasn't going to spend years in therapy overcoming whatever was done to her. Her story had ended midsentence, in the middle of a chapter.

Exhaling roughly, I placed the card on the nightstand.

There were two types of death. Actual death, like the kind this poor woman had suffered, where the body and soul and everything was gone. Then there was the second kind of death—where the soul was stripped away, but the body continued on, going day to day, just existing in a shell of what once was.

I stood up and started to walk toward the living room, but realized I had no idea where I was going or what I was doing. I placed my hands over my face and held my breath.

I'd died ten years ago.

Not from the injuries and all . . . all the damage. I died from everything else, and I'd just been *existing* since then. That knowledge was nothing new.

My throat started to burn.

Leaving here hadn't fixed me. All it had done was give me time to deal. Not necessarily heal 100 percent, but to . . . deal. My therapist had pointed that out about one or five hundred times. Again, this knowledge wasn't new.

My lungs were burning.

Coming back here was almost like starting over. Doing what I'd intended to do. I was going to help Mom with the inn and then eventually I would take over, like I always planned. I was reopening that chapter of my life.

Tiny bright spots were dotting my vision.

My life before the Groom had included Cole. I had no idea where our relationship had been heading, but *something* was there, *something* amazing. Maybe we would've stayed together, finding our very own happily ever after. Maybe we would've drifted apart and found someone else. And maybe none of that mattered now, and if I picked up that card and called him, we would have dinner and never speak again. But if I did call him, I would finally be reopening that chapter of my life.

And maybe if I did that, I wouldn't see the Groom in harmless shadows on the grounds or the veranda. Maybe I wouldn't feel bodiless eyes on me. Maybe the nightmares would stop. Maybe I would finally start *living*.

Opening my mouth, I exhaled deeply, letting the cool air soothe the burn in my throat and lungs. I dropped my arms and turned back to the night-stand.

Maybe it was time to reopen that chapter.

"IS THERE ANYTHING else I can do before I head out?" Angela asked as she bounced into the kitchen.

I looked up from the leather-bound old-school

accounting books Mom had kept. I'd been spending the bulk of the afternoon bringing the Scarlet Wench's business side into the twenty-first century and my poor little fingers were aching. I also wanted to stab myself in the eyeballs, because committing numbers and receipts into a spreadsheet was about as fun as scraping off wallpaper with a nail. A lukewarm coffee cup sat next to my laptop.

"We're good," I told her, reaching around and rubbing at the kink forming in the back of my neck. "You have an exam tonight, don't you?"

"A paper," she said, smiling as she smoothed a blond curl back behind her ear. "I finished it last night, but I should probably look over it again."

Right now I'd prefer to do a paper than what I was doing. I picked up the highlighter. I'd gone with baby blue. "Well, good luck. Not that you need it."

"Thanks. I'll see you later." Angela hesitated at the door and then popped back around. She bit down on her lip as she eyed me.

I waited. "Is there something you need, Angela?"

"Not really," she said, shoving her hands into the center pocket of her pink sweater. "I just wanted to ask if you're okay."

I wanted to pretend like I didn't know what she was referencing, but I wasn't a fan of making myself look like an idiot. By earlier this afternoon, the discovery of the woman's body had really hit the public. It had been splashed across the morning paper. Mom had turned the TV off during the local news-at-noon broadcast when I'd walked into the kitchen to get started. She turned it off even though I told her it was okay.

It had to be okay.

I couldn't spend my entire life hiding from random violence. Though I was sure there were a billion other people who wished they could.

"It's all a little freaky," I admitted finally, rolling the fat highlighter between my palms. "But I'm okay."

"It is really freaky." She glanced down at her sneakers for a moment. "When I heard the news, I thought of you."

"Don't think about me. I'm fine. Think of that woman and her family," I said, placing the highlighter down. "But I do appreciate where you're going with it."

Her gaze lifted. "I know. It's just that . . . it has to be hard considering everything you went through. I know it's a huge coincidence, but still. There's just . . . something wrong about it."

My brows knitted. "I can think of a lot of things wrong about it."

"Me too," she said, shifting her weight from one foot to the next. "But for someone to use the same place that . . ." She swallowed hard as she opened her purse. "There's just something epically messed up about that."

The laptop screen flickered and started to fade into hibernation mode. "Maybe the person responsible didn't know about that place's history. It is possible."

"True." She reached into her bag. "It could've been someone who didn't know the area, but . . . you know how they always say it's someone the victim knows?"

Saying nothing, I nodded.

"I heard on the news this afternoon that she and her husband's family are from the tristate area. They had to know what that area was," she explained.

The screen on my laptop went black. "Maybe it was an acquaintance of hers who isn't from this area."

She raised a shoulder. "They haven't said how she died."

Acids in my stomach churned. "They won't for a while. Or they may never say how." It had taken weeks before the news had said how the first victim of the Groom had died. "I guess the police release that kind of info when they're sure it won't hurt their case."

"Makes sense." She shook her head and then forced a smile. "I'm sorry. I know you don't want to talk about this and—"

"It's okay." I wished I hadn't reacted the way I had the first time with her. "It's human nature to want to talk about these kinds of things." I paused, taking a sip of my now-cold coffee. Yum. "Back then, everyone talked about what was happening, even before people realized the cases were related. I talked about it. It's normal. Don't apologize for it."

Her smile wasn't forced this time. "Thanks." She took a step back. "Well, I got to go—damn it." Frowning, she withdrew her hand from her purse. Her eyes rolled. "I forgot my keys."

Remembering what my mom had said, I smiled as she darted across the kitchen and entered the back room, returning a few seconds with her keys in hand and an accomplished expression on her face. "Found them!"

Wiggling my fingers, I watched her leave. Before my mind started thinking about everything she'd said, I hit the mouse pad on my computer and got back to work.

An hour later, Mom stuck her head inside the kitchen. "You have a guest."

Before I could scrutinize the wide smile on her face, she pushed the door all the way open, revealing said guest.

Air caught in my throat as I sat straighter.

Cole stood beside her.

My first thought was damn, he looked amazing in dark trousers and a white button-down. No jacket, and it was pretty cold outside. My second thought was that even though I'd decided to contact him, I hadn't done it yet.

"Hey," he said in that deep, rough voice of his that sent the very right kind of shiver down my side.

Over his shoulder, Mom opened her mouth and eyes wide as she jerked her thumbs up.

Dear Lord.

She closed the door halfway as Cole stepped into the kitchen. "Hi," I said, shutting the laptop. A hundred butterflies fluttered in my stomach and chest—a hundred carnivorous butterflies by the feel of them.

He walked across the kitchen, stopping at the island. His gaze coasted over my face, and it was at that moment I realized that I didn't have a speck of makeup on and I hadn't showered. I'd planned to—at some point. My hair was up in a messy knot, and I was definitely the kind of woman who benefited from some blush, mascara, lip gloss, and an entire face full of makeup.

"I know the last time I left, I gave you my number, which can easily be assumed meant I was leaving it up to you to contact me, but—"

"I was planning to contact you," I blurted out, flushing. That sounded genius. "I mean, I was going to do it later this evening."

"You were?" The half grin appeared, replacing the quick flicker of surprise, and my stomach tumbled in a pleasant way.

I nodded. "I was."

"Well." He chuckled as he propped his hip against the kitchen island. "That does make me feel a lot better about busting up in here two times already."

My lips twitched into a grin. "Glad to hear that." Lowering my lashes, I checked him out, because . . . well, because I kind of couldn't help myself. Those slacks looked really good on him. "You don't work today?"

"I don't keep normal work hours, but I had court this morning and then I was heading back home." He glanced at the door. "So, you were going to get in touch with me tonight because . . . ?"

I exhaled softly, feeling my cheeks heat. "I was going to take you up on your offer to catch up over dinner."

Those intense eyes brightened. "I really like the sound of that. Do you have any place in mind?"

Thinking about what happened yesterday, I bit down on my lip. "Can we do takeout?" The moment I asked that question, I immediately wanted to take it back. Holy hell, that was a damn weird thing to ask considering everything and really sounded like I was—

"How about I make you dinner instead," he asked, not missing a beat. "I don't know if you remember, but I like to cook."

Our gazes collided. I remembered. I wanted to scream that *I remembered*. "At . . . at your place?"

"If that's okay with you."

My pulse was thrumming unsteadily. Was that okay with me? Going to his house was intimate, but I was the one who made the suggestion about not going out. I smoothed my palms over my thighs. "That will work."

"How about tomorrow night?"

Oh. Oh wow. That was quick. Nerves hit me. "I . . . I think it will be okay. I just need to make sure Mom is good with running the—"

"I'm good," she yelled from the other room. "Been doing this by myself for about ten years."

Oh damn it.

"Thanks, Mom!" I smiled tightly.

Cole's half grin spread as I blushed. He bent his head, his eyes glimmering with humor as he said in a low voice, "I forgot how much I liked your mom."

"It appears I am free tomorrow."

"Perfect." His gaze didn't waver for a second. "It's a date."

She wanted to believe that it would all be okay, that poor Mrs. Banks was just a victim of random violence. Everyone wanted to believe that, but *she* was nervous.

No hiding that.

Could *she* sense it? Ripe and violent vengeance, righteous retribution, lingering just outside the inn, waiting for the perfect moment to strike? She'd pulled the curtain back, the light in the apartment outlining her form. *She'd* sensed it. Of course she had.

She just didn't want to see it yet.

The front doors of the building opened, and there a slight body appeared. The young woman cleared the sidewalk, her bag thumping off her hip as she eyed the device in her palm. Not paying a damn bit of attention to her surroundings. She crossed into the parking lot, heading toward her car. A fucking tanker could plow right into her at this moment and she wouldn't see it coming.

People needed to be more aware of their surroundings. Weren't there enough *20/20* specials highlighting the importance of vigilance and personal safety? Apparently this little one thought she was invisible. They all did.

A horn blew in the distance, and she still didn't look up, didn't seem to hear the footsteps only a handful of feet away. So close, the apple-scented shampoo wafted into the air as the wind played with the blond strands of hair.

This one . . . this one was going to be really special but required a bit more patience. Not tonight. But soon.

She would see this one.

IT REALLY WASN'T a date.

That's what I told Miranda when I spoke to her Tuesday evening. That was also what I told Mom every time she brought it up, which was around a hundred times. And when Jason stopped by Wednesday during lunch, bringing a plate of cookies an employee had made and which he was obviously trying to unload on us, I told him the same.

Apparently Miranda had gone to Jason with an update.

Angela snatched a chocolate-chip cookie off the plate as she walked past the island, carrying an armful of clean dishtowels. "It sounds like a date to me."

I was eyeing the plate, but was trying to behave myself. "How do you know about this?"

"Your mom," she replied, popping the cookie into her mouth.

Jason watched Angela shove the towels into the

drawer. When she pivoted around, he hastily faced me. "I think it's a good idea."

"It's a great idea." Angela all but skipped past us, snatching another cookie. "These are delicious. Thank you, Jason."

"Y-You're welcome," he stammered.

Angela smiled brightly as she headed out of the kitchen, appearing oblivious of Jason's gaze latched onto the sway of her hips. I arched a brow when he finally managed to drag his attention back to me.

"What?" Jason asked.

"Nothing."

He grinned as he folded his arms on top of the island and leaned over, slightly bent at the waist. "I'm only a man."

"Uh-huh."

"I did have another reason for coming over here that had nothing to do with cookies or checking out Angela."

"Good to hear," I replied dryly.

Jason winked. "Did the adjuster for the insurance company get out here yet?"

I shook my head. "One is coming out tomorrow."

"They should've gotten here quicker or had you get the appraisal. You should let me look at your stuff. I bet I can get you better rates and better service."

"I do need to update my insurance." I continued to eye the plate of cookies. "I can get you the stuff later."

"Great. Give me your email address and I can send you the list." He smiled. "Eat a cookie."

"A cookie is the last thing my ass needs," I told him as I grabbed a pen and a Post-it note from the counter. I scribbled my email address down and handed it over.

Jason chuckled. "So how are you getting out to Cole's then?"

"I'm using Mom's truck." I really did want a cookie.

"Sounds good." He pushed away from the island. "Don't forget if you need any help with the insurance claim to ask and to get me that info."

"Will do." I smiled at him. "Thanks for the cookies."

"No problem." Jason started to turn but stopped. His shoulders tensed. "I am glad you're back, Sasha."

"Me too," I admitted softly.

"I just hope you don't regret it."

My gaze flew to his. "What?"

"I . . . I keeping thinking about that woman and what the mayor had said," he explained. "I don't want it all to stress you out, because it had to be hard for you to come back here, and for this to happen? It's messed up."

I relaxed a little. "It won't stress me out. I'm not going to regret coming back here, Jason."

He smiled, but something about it didn't feel right—didn't seem real—and I knew right then, he didn't believe me.

GETTING READY FOR dinner with Cole felt like I was getting ready for a date. Half my clothes were strewn across my bed. I'd changed no less than three times, finally settling on a pair of questionably slimming dark denim jeans I wasn't sure I could sit comfortably in and a sheer black sweater that required a camisole underneath. I paired the outfit with my knee-high gray boots, which were my absolute favorite.

I went for the whole natural, not-trying-too-hard look, which equated to thirty minutes of applying a face full of *natural* makeup and about forty minutes of waving my hair.

My heart raced the entire time I was getting ready, and I couldn't recall feeling this way before the dates I had in the last couple of years. Sure, I'd been fairly excited about them, but this was different. I felt like my heart was trying to throw itself out of my chest.

Luckily Mom was busy with the couple that was checking in, and I was able to slip out without having to witness her happy dance. Mom didn't necessarily trust me with backing the truck up and not taking out a family of four in the process.

Grinning at that thought, I unlocked the door and climbed in, dropping my purse on the seat next to me. I turned on the car and doubt seized me with blunt, heavy claws, digging in and locking up every muscle.

Was I doing the right thing?

"Crap," I whispered and then reached over, rooting around in my bag until I found my phone. I called Miranda.

She answered on the second ring. "Yo."

"What are you doing?" I asked, my voice sounding strained to my own ears.

"Leaving the school, and I'm either going to go

to the gym or Burger King," she said, and I smiled. "And you should be on your way to Cole's."

"Well . . ."

"Sasha!" she shouted. "You better be on the way to his house or I'm seriously going to kick your ass."

A laugh burst out of me, but I quickly sobered. "Am I doing the right thing?"

There was a pause. "Oh, honey, I think you are, but only you can answer that."

I exhaled heavily as I stared out the windshield, watching the blue hues of the sky deepen. "I think I am."

"Let me ask you three questions," she said. "Are you excited?"

"Yes."

"Do you want to see him?"

I didn't hesitate. "Yes."

"And do you think you're going to regret it if you don't see him tonight?" she asked.

I knew I would, and I also knew that there was a great chance that Cole wouldn't be as forgiving this time. The fact that he was so forgiving over the way I left last time still blew me away. "I would regret it."

"Then I think you know the answer, babe."

I did. I was just being a big freak. "Okay. I'm going."

"Good," she replied. "This is good. Trust me. You don't want to look back on this moment and regret you didn't go to him."

Something in the way she spoke said she had personal experience with that kind of regret. "You okay?"

"Yeah. Why wouldn't I be?"

I nibbled on my lip. "I don't know. Anyway, you

should go to the gym and then go to Burger King. Best of both worlds."

Miranda laughed. "I love the way you think. Now go have fun."

As soon as I hung up the phone, I got on the road so I didn't give myself any more time to freak out. Cole hadn't stayed long yesterday, but he'd given me his address before leaving.

Taking the interstate, it took about fifteen minutes to get to the other side of the county, and the directions for the exit took me about five minutes down the road and into a newish-looking subdivision that overlooked the Potomac River.

I clenched the steering wheel as I crept down the street, peering at the houses. He'd said it was the seventh from the entrance, on the left. There was a lot of green space between each home, at least an acre and maybe more. Squinting, I emitted a low squeak when I spotted what had to be his home.

Cole had a ranch-style house that sat a decent distance from the road. Focusing on each breath, I pulled into the driveway that led up to a two-car garage and killed the engine. I couldn't sit out in the car for an eternity like I had when I first arrived back in town. I got my hopefully slimmed-down ass out of the front seat.

A motion detector kicked on, lighting up the grounds. The front of his house was nicely land-scaped with trimmed bushes and a dark reedy plant I was unfamiliar with.

Reaching the front porch, I inhaled the earthy wet scent of the nearby river and stepped up. The porch light snapped on and the front door opened.

Cole was suddenly in the doorway, a red-and-white checkered dishtowel in one hand and a soft grin on his striking face. "Come on in."

I smiled as he stepped aside and did as he requested. The door opened up into an entry with a vaulted ceiling.

"How was traffic on the way up?" he asked.

"Not too bad." I glanced around, curious. Everything straight ahead was open concept. A large living room flowed into the kitchen. "Only took about twenty minutes."

"Perfect." Cole stepped ahead of me, and my gaze dropped. The worn jeans cradled his ass perfectly. "Would you like something to drink? I have wine, beer, and soda."

"Wine would be fine." The living room looked like only a guy lived there. An oversized sectional separating the kitchen appeared to have the ability to house an entire soccer team. A huge TV was mounted to the wall, above a stone fireplace. There were two coffee tables. A gray area rug broke up the hardwood floors. Very minimal. Very masculine. I assumed the hallway off the living room led to the bedrooms and the guest bathroom. "Your house is lovely."

"Thanks. I got it two years ago." He dropped the towel near the stove where a most savory scent was coming from. "It's more space than I really need, but I got a hell of a deal on it."

Checking out the kitchen, I tried to shed the nervousness building in my system. The kitchen was outstanding. White cabinets. Gray countertops.

Stainless-steel appliances. Several barstools sat in front of a wide island. I placed my purse on the counter.

"I don't normally have wine in the house, but I picked up pinot grigio at the store," he said as he walked to the fridge. "Is that okay?"

"That's good." I sat on the barstool.

"Thank God. I had to ask my mother what kind of wine to pick up." He pulled the bottle out.

I stared at him as he walked over to the cabinet and reached up, causing the hem of his shirt to ride up and expose a thin stretch of taut muscle along his lower back. "You called and asked your mom?"

Casting a sheepish grin over his shoulder, he shrugged. "Yeah. I'm a beer-and-whiskey man. Wine is not something I know shit about."

For some reason, picturing this grown man calling his mom to ask about advice on what kind of wine eased the knots of tension cropping up over my body. It was sweet of him. "I'm not picky when it comes to wine."

He popped the cork like a pro, facing me. "I'll keep that in mind for the future."

For the future.

I got a little giddy as I grinned. "So what did you cook?"

He poured the wine and walked over to the island, placing the glass in front of me. "I remembered that you're a meat girl. Hopefully you haven't turned vegan."

I laughed. "Absolutely not."

"I made pot roast, complete with potatoes and

carrots." He pushed up the sleeves of his shirt and leaned against the island, drawing my gaze to his arms. "Should be ready in about twenty minutes."

Realizing I was developing some weird kind of fixation for his arms, I took a sip of my wine, welcoming the bite. "Thank you for doing this—the cooking dinner and everything."

One side of his lips kicked up. "I always welcome the chance to cook. Thank you for giving me one."

"Do you still find it relaxing?"

He nodded. "Until I try to pan sear something and want to burn the whole fucking house down."

I laughed. "Pan searing is a bit hard-core."

"One of these days I'm going to master it." Winking, he pushed away from the counter and walked to the fridge, grabbing a beer. "So, Sasha," he said, popping the lid of the bottle. "Tell me what you've been up to."

I watched him walk over to the island, and my heart skipped a little beat when he took the stool next to me, thighs spread. He angled his body toward mine, leaving very little space between us. Cole was like that before. Always close. He liked the physical closeness and contact.

I found that I still liked that.

"It's not very exciting." I sipped the wine. "Kind of boring."

"Doubt that." He took a drag of his beer. "Nothing about you is boring."

I laughed softly. "You may change your mind."

"How about we do tit for tat then?" He raised his brows. "You tell me one thing and I'll tell you one thing."

Our gazes met. "We've done that before."

"On our first date," he finished, leaning one arm against the counter.

"Yeah," I whispered. Our first date had been after class, and we'd gone to a small café. We sat there for hours, and I ended up missing my afternoon class.

It had been one of my best days.

"We can do it again," he said, pale eyes intense and focused as he lifted the mouth of the bottle to his lips. "Can't we?"

"We can." I watched his throat work on another swallow. "I went to Florida State and graduated with a degree in business."

"I graduated from Shepherd with a BS in criminal justice."

Running my finger over the wine glass, I smiled. "While living in Florida I realized that I could never stay there, because it's so damn hot. There's only like three months when you don't feel like you're on the cusp of hell. Even in Tallahassee, where you actually have all four seasons."

"Haven't been there," he said, tipping his head back. "Let me see. I've lived here. Don't really have any plans of living elsewhere."

"I then moved to Atlanta, where I was an executive assistant," I said, taking a drink. "I traveled a lot, all around the States, once to England and one time to Japan. I pretty much was in charge of his schedule, which was a lot." I lowered the glass and looked over at him, flushing when I found that he'd been watching me. "I liked the job, but I don't . . ." Lowering my gaze, I took a deep breath. "I don't think I was really happy. I mean, it was good but it wasn't what I wanted to do."

"Running the inn was what you wanted to do," he said quietly, and I nodded. He set the bottle on the counter. "I continued to work as a deputy while I was in college, spent another two years in the cruiser, and then I applied to the FBI. I started with them six months later and have been working in the Violent Crimes Unit since."

"Wow. That's impressive. I didn't know there was a department like that around here."

"There isn't." He paused as a buzzer went off and slid off the chair. "I work in Baltimore."

"Can I help?" I popped off the stool.

"Sure." He showed me where the plates and silverware were, and I got to pulling them out. "My schedule is all over the place. I'm rarely home when there's a case, but I'm not out on the street."

"Are we eating in there?" I asked, noticing a dining room beyond French doors. "Or at the bar?"

"I haven't eaten at that table yet." Grabbing oven mitts, he said, "Don't plan on starting tonight."

I laughed. "Works for me." I placed the plates on the island. "So what do you mean about not working on the streets?"

"I'm not undercover and my department does more than just focus on gang activity." He paused, sending a sly grin in my direction. "I'll tell you more, but it's your turn to tell me something."

My stomach grumbled as he placed the steaming pan on the counter. "Okay. Well, this is where my life is pretty boring compared to yours. Um, I tried to pick up a hobby while living in Atlanta. So

I took up a painting class. I was so bad I got kicked out."

He paused, silver prongs in hand. "Seriously?"

"Seriously." I sighed. "The instructor felt I wasn't trying and I was taking up space. He hauled out all my poor paintings just to prove that I wasn't improving." I grinned as Cole transferred the meat and the sides to a platter. "I can remember staring at a painting that was supposed to be of a house—I didn't remember it was supposed to be a house until the instructor reminded me."

"What did it look like then?"

"It actually looked like . . . a shoebox with windows."

Cole laughed deeply, and my stomach wiggled. His laugh . . . it was deep and sexy. "I would pay good money to see these paintings you were working on."

"Ha." We took our seats, and I picked up my knife. I cut off a piece of the roast beef and the moment it hit my tongue, my taste buds exploded. It was a perfect mix of spices and tenderness. "Wow. This is so good."

"Did you doubt that it would be?" he teased, sending me a sidelong glance.

I shook my head. "You in for a career change? I could hire you as my personal chef."

"Anytime you want me to cook for you, babe. I'm your servant."

Flushing, I liked the sound of that way too much. I took another bite and then tried the potatoes. Perfect. "So what do you do in your department?"

"We focus on major theft and different types of

violent crimes," he explained. "Usually we're called in by state or local authorities."

Cutting into more of the roast beef, I put two and two together about his job. "When you say violent crimes, you mean things like what happened here." I swallowed, focusing on my plate. "Those kind of crimes?"

"Sometimes but very rarely. There are more specialized units within the FBI that would be called in for cases where they believe there is a connection."

"I remember those agents." I continued cutting up my roast. "They came while I was in the hospital and afterward. They'd been here after, what? The third or fourth death? I never saw them in person though. Not until they came into the hospital. I remember thinking at first that it was stupid that they had so many questions." I placed the knife and fork on the plate. "The Groom was dead. What did they need to know? I didn't realize until later those agents were also collectors—collectors of information. I . . ." Trailing off, I let out a shaky laugh. "Wow. I really ruined that conversation. Anyway—"

Two fingers pressed under my chin, guiding my gaze to Cole's. Air caught as his gaze latched onto mine. There was something in those blue eyes I couldn't quite place. An emotion that was raw and unfettered. "You didn't ruin anything, Sasha. Ever. If you want to talk about those agents, we can. If you want to talk about something else, we will. Just let's talk. Okay?"

My gaze searched his and after a few moments, I nodded. "Tell me . . . tell me about your mom. Is she still working at dispatch?"

Cole didn't answer the question immediately nor did he drop his hand. Maybe only a second passed before he dragged his thumb along the curve of my jaw, eliciting a shiver that effectively scattered my thoughts. He lowered his hand. "Mom retired five years ago. She and Dad are both enjoying their golden years."

"That's nice." I refocused on my plate, and even though my stomach had soured, I couldn't let this delicious food go to waste. That would be a crime. "I want that for my mom. I don't want her to be working up to the day she dies even though I think she wouldn't have a problem with that."

"Your mom has always been one hell of a worker," he said.

As we finished dinner, the tit for tat faded off, and the knots of uncertainty from earlier were back and multiplying like damn Mogwais fed after midnight. Why had I brought up the Groom? I was sure that was the last thing he wanted to talk about, no matter what he said. It was the last thing I wanted. And now I couldn't unsee what I'd seen in his stare as I helped him clean up, wondering how we were doing this. A hundred questions started racing through me.

How were we talking and sharing dinner like there hadn't been ten years between us? Like I hadn't walked out on him? What was the point of this? For him to make sure I was emotionally stable after everything or for me to see that he was doing well after all these years?

I fell quiet as I helped place the leftovers into questionable-looking Tupperware. Once done, Cole opened the fridge door while I stood in the middle of the kitchen, my heart racing again. "Would you like a refill?" he asked.

Yes, I did. I wanted to go back to playing our game. I wanted those blissful moments where I wasn't thinking about the Groom and everything I'd left behind when I fled this place. But I couldn't go back and I wasn't sure how he could pretend to.

As I lifted my head and looked at him, I didn't see Cole. Not really. I saw the Cole from ten years ago, the last time I'd seen him. He had been staying behind to meet up with a study group for another class, but he'd walked outside with me, and we'd kissed. Oh God, no one had kissed like Cole. Each time had outdone the last and each one had been perfect.

How could we be here like none of that happened?

"What are we doing?" I blurted out.

Cole turned around slowly, one hand on the fridge door and the other empty. "Well, I was hoping we'd share another drink, talk some more."

"That's not what I meant." Folding my arms across my chest, I willed my heart to slow down. "Why are you okay with this? I never answered your calls. I wouldn't let you see me. I left town without saying a word to you. Why would you even want to see me now?"

He stared at me a moment and then closed the fridge door. "That's a good question."

I exhaled heavily. "And that really isn't an answer."

Cole walked over to where I stood, stopping a foot from me. I'd forgotten how tall he was, and I had to lift my chin to meet his stare. "I don't know if you want to hear the answer to your question."

It hit me then, something I really hadn't considered but made total sense. It would explain why he'd showed up as soon as he heard I was back in town. It explained what I saw in his stare. My stomach sunk. "You . . . you pity me, don't you? This is what tonight is about? You feel sorry for me."

Horror and embarrassment rose swiftly. Why didn't I figure this out the first night he stopped by? I took a step back, bumping into the counter. Once upon a time something great and damn near magical, but now we just had years, a hundred what-might-have-beens between us, pity and remorse. That was it.

A pink flush crawled up my neck and splashed across my cheeks. That look crept into those beautiful eyes. The same I'd seen before. I couldn't deal with it. I pushed away from the counter, then hurried around it, snatching up my purse. "Thank you for dinner," I said, not meeting his stare. "It was amazing—"

"What?" Cole barked out a short laugh. "I didn't want to have this dinner with you because I feel sorry for you. Is that what you think tonight is about?" He thrust his hand through his messy hair. "Seriously?"

"—and I'm glad we got the chance to catch up," I continued, swallowing down the sudden knot in the back of my throat.

His hands closed into fists at his sides. "I don't know why you think that I had you come over for dinner because—"

"Why wouldn't that make sense? You know what happened. God, *you* more than anyone know what happened," I said, my hand tightening on my purse.

"We can't sit and eat dinner, pretend like there hasn't been ten years between us."

His eyes flared. "I'm not pretending that."

"And we can't . . ." I said, sucking in a sharp breath as my chest burned. In the back of my head, I knew I was being too hard on this situation, on him, but I couldn't seem to stop myself. "We can't pretend that nothing happened."

"I do know what happened and I sure as hell am not pretending that what happened to you didn't," he said, lips thinning. "Fuck, Sasha. It was all I thought about for years. For *years*. But it is not what I think about when I see you standing in front of me. It's not what I—"

"Don't," I said, hand up and voice shaking. "I need to leave. Okay? I just need to go." Without waiting for an answer, I turned around and headed for the front of the house. He called out my name, but I kept walking.

I knew when I got home, when I had a few minutes to really think about what had happened, I was going to want to throat punch myself, but the flight response was in high gear.

The night air rushed to greet me as I stepped out onto the porch, closing the door behind me. I was halfway down the walkway when the door reopened behind me. Hell, he was fast.

"Sasha."

I kept walking, nearly breaking into a run. I didn't care. Not like I could be any more embarrassed than I already was. I just had to get out of there.

"Sasha, please stop." He was only a few steps behind me. "Damn it, don't run from me again."

Don't run from me again.

God, those words hurt, because they were true. That was what I was doing, and I couldn't seem to stop myself. Grabbing the handle of the truck, I threw open the door. The dome light came on, and it immediately hit me. I staggered back from the open truck, dropping my purse. The *smell*. Oh God, my stomach immediately revolted. The smell was raw and metallic. Rotten. There was a loud buzzing sound. Flies. I glimpsed brown and white fur matted with red before I whipped around.

Cole stopped at my side. "What the . . ."

Bending over, I placed my hands on my knees and tried not to gag. No luck. My chest and stomach heaved.

He stepped around me and stalked up to the open door. "Holy fuck," he grunted, and whipped around. A nanosecond later, he grasped my upper arms, forcing me up straight. "I think you need to go back into the house."

My wide gaze met his as my knees went weak. "What is that in the truck?"

His jaw was locked down, as hard as a diamond. "Let me just get you back in the—"

"What's in there?" I demanded.

"You don't—"

I wrenched free, surprising him as I bolted to the right. He grabbed me, circling an arm around my waist, hauling me back against his chest. But it wasn't quick enough. I saw. A scream rose in my throat, but shock choked it back down, silencing me.

I saw what was in my mother's truck.

CHAPTER 9

PRESSING MY HANDS over my face, I counted until the urge to vomit all over Cole's hardwood floors passed. No matter what I did or what I tried to focus on, what I saw in that truck appeared in my mind, in all the gory details.

It reminded me of the only time I hadn't been in the dark while I was . . . with the Groom. It had been during one of his moods, and he had a lot of them, almost as if he were two separate people. One moment he was almost . . . kind and gentle, as revolting as that still was. Other times he was violent and unpredictable, and breathing would set him off. It had been during that time, after being dragged out of that room to use the restroom, after my face and stomach burned from his fists, he'd shoved me into the room, blindfold off. It was then, as my knees had cracked off the floor, that I learned the lights were controlled from the outside.

He'd turned the lights on then, and it had taken

several moments for my eyes to adjust to the brightness, and when they had . . . I'd thought I knew fear. I'd believed that I couldn't have been terrorized any more than I was.

I'd been so wrong.

I saw everything in flashes, one after another, as if my brain was too overwhelmed to process it all at once.

Rusty red blood had dried in splatters all over the hardwood floor, most likely seeping through the subfloors. There were cuts in the floor, nicks I didn't understand then. Fresher blood—my blood—was on the bed. And the walls—Oh God—I could still see those walls. Dried blood arced across the section above the bed, and I knew someone had lost their life right there, but it was what hung from the walls across from the bed I'd normally been chained to.

Bloody white wedding gowns.

Six of them.

Something hung from them by a thin piece of wire. Something I couldn't even begin to process. Something that had taken years for me to accept.

A finger had hung from each dress.

And I knew then I was going to die in that room, like so many others. I'd screamed and screamed until my hoarse voice went out, until—

"Drink this."

Lowering my hands, I looked up in time to see Cole place a cup of fizzing water on the end table beside the couch. He'd disappeared down the hall for a few moments and had returned with the cup. My hand shook as I reached over and picked up the cool glass. "Thank you."

He stood there a moment. "We got . . . it out of the truck."

Shuddering, I started to sip the Alka-Seltzer and then chugged it. The front door opened and I looked up. Through the front windows, blue and red lights flashed. Cole had called the police. I wasn't exactly sure what the police could do in this situation, but state troopers had showed up about twenty minutes ago.

The trooper walked into the living room, his green uniform starched and pressed. He was an older man who looked like he'd seen weirder shit than what was found in my truck.

He looked over at Cole before speaking. "I have a few questions to ask."

I nodded as I held the empty glass.

"Cole was telling me this truck belongs to your mother—Anne Keeton?" When I nodded once more, he asked, "Who knew you were using your mom's truck besides her?"

"My friend Miranda knew. So did Angela. She's a young woman who works as a housekeeper at the inn." I paused. "And Jason knew. He stopped over at lunch. But none of them would've done that."

"Jason . . . ?" Cole cocked his head to the side.

"Yeah. Remember him? He was in our econ class. He's an—"

"Insurance agent now," he finished. When he saw my expression, he said, "He has a billboard over by Route 9. Haven't seen him in person in years though."

"I know him," the trooper said. "Pretty good man. Gets coffee every morning down at the Grind."

My eyes met Cole's. "I don't know who could've done that or why."

"Cole had mentioned your car was vandalized on Friday while it was outside the Scarlet Wench," the trooper said. "Have you been having any problems with anyone recently?"

Shifting on the couch, unease filled me. "No. I haven't even been in town long enough to tick someone off. I don't understand this."

The trooper didn't have much to add after that. What law was broken tonight? Without a suspect or any idea of who could've done that, I wasn't sure if this was a case of vandalism or harassment or something more sinister. Another call came in, a vehicle accident on the interstate, and it sounded way more pressing than what was happening here.

"Can I talk with you real quick?" the trooper said to Cole.

He eyed me and then said, "Sure."

I rose and walked the empty glass over to the sink and washed it out as they went outside. Then I stood there, staring at nothing as I tried to grasp what just happened. I clenched the rim of the sink and took a deep breath, seconds away from freaking out. Like the kind of freak-out that would put the earlier one in the kitchen to shame.

I should've been home right now, sitting on my couch, eating a gallon of ice cream while mentally kicking myself. Who would've thought I'd prefer that?

I had no idea how long I stood there, but I heard the front door open again. Turning, I saw as Cole walked through the entry that the flashing lights were gone outside.

"He's filing a report," he said, glancing down at his cellphone before he slipped it into his pocket. "That's the best they're going to be able to do right now."

Nodding, I leaned against the sink and folded my arms. "I don't know why you called them."

He stopped at the edge of the kitchen island and raised his brows. "Someone picked up a deer that looked like it lost a fight with a Mack truck and placed it inside your truck."

I flinched as my stomach turned. Yep. That sounded about right. And that poor deer had been dead. For a while.

"There needs to be a report of that," he finished.

A weird taste coated the sides of my mouth. "I don't even . . . I don't know what to say right now."

Cole didn't respond to that as he walked into the kitchen. I tensed as he passed me and headed for the fridge. He pulled out two bottles of water. Facing me, he handed one over. "Are you okay?"

I nodded.

"I want to hear you say it," he said, voice gentle but firm.

I opened my mouth and then gave a little shake of my head. I wasn't okay. I shivered. This was totally messed up. "That's my mom's truck. What in the hell am I going to tell her? She's going to flip out."

He took a drink of the water. "I got a buddy in town who does car detailing. I called him while I was outside and filled him in on what happened. The deer is out of the truck, and he'll come by tomorrow morning and get to work on it. He'll have it like new by tomorrow afternoon. It will be like nothing happened."

That was good to hear, but there was also a good chance I'd never get in that truck again no matter what was done. I glanced at him, letting out a harsh breath. "You didn't have to do that."

"But I did."

Resisting the sudden need to run over to him and face-plant into his chest, I looked up at the ceiling. "Thank you. Just let me know how much it costs and I will take care of it."

"You don't need to thank me."

"But I did," I parroted back.

One side of his lips briefly turned up.

Taking a deep breath, I squeezed the bottle until the plastic crinkled. "I'm not telling my mother."

Cole went silent and eyes sharp.

"She'll be just like me. She'll never be able to get inside that truck again. It's not like she can go out and buy a new car," I reasoned, putting the bottle of water aside. "And I don't want her to worry."

His jaw tightened. "Maybe she needs to be worried."

My heart lurched. "Why . . . why would you say that?"

"I'm not trying to scare you. I hope you realize that, but something isn't right here, and I think you know that." Cole finished off the bottle of water and tossed it in the trash. He faced me, and anger was etched into his striking face. "Your car was vandalized the first night you were back in town and someone put that deer in the truck with some kind of intention. That's not something a bored kid does."

"If that was something a bored kid did, someone needs to see a child psychologist stat," I commented.

His lips twitched into a wry grin. "I agree."

I smiled at him, but I felt sick. I wasn't naive or stupid and from the moment I sat on the couch while Cole dealt with the stuff outside, I knew what was done had been on purpose. I just didn't understand why. "I still don't want my mother to know."

"Sasha, she should know so she can be careful."

"Careful of what? A dead raccoon in the mailbox? Or a run-over cat that might be dropped off on the front porch?" I pushed away from the counter and tucked both sides of my hair back. "Look, I understand what you're getting at, but she's been through a lot, Cole. *A lot.*"

"So have you," he reminded me, tone gentle.

"Yeah, but I was able to leave. I got to hide from what happened and from this town. She didn't. I don't want to put this on her unless I have to."

His face softened. "Sasha . . ."

"Don't look at me like that," I warned, sucking in a soft breath. I could barely deal with him when he looked at me normally, but like this? With his handsome face softening and his cool eyes warming? It was too much.

"Like what?"

Like he wanted what I had wanted earlier. To cross the distance between us and wrap his arms around me. While I wanted to run to him in this moment, I couldn't do it.

Closing my eyes, I took several deep breaths and reopened them. "Until I know what's happening here, I don't want her stressing out. And this has nothing to do with her. No one has been bothering her. It's . . . it's about me."

Cole looked like he wanted to argue further, but inhaled roughly. "That's your decision. I just want to go on record to say I don't agree with it."

"Duly noted."

"I know the trooper asked who knew you were driving your mother's truck tonight, but I have another question for you."

"Ask away."

"Is there anyone you can think of in particular that would be upset with you?"

I immediately knew where he was heading with this. "You mean upset enough with me to vandalize my car and leave a dead deer in the truck? No. I don't know anyone who would want to do that."

He lifted a hand and clasped the back of his neck. My heart did a stupid little flip, because that was a habit of his I remembered from before. I used to be fascinated with that act. Truthfully, I still was. "Maybe a boyfriend—"

"I told you I wasn't seeing someone," I reminded him, cheeks flushing.

"An ex-boyfriend?" he corrected, lowering his hand.

I didn't want to answer the question, but felt like I needed to. "None of the . . . relationships I've been in have been serious enough for someone to get upset with me."

The skin around his eyes pulled taut. "That sounds hard to believe."

"Why? Actually, don't answer that. There is no guy in my past upset enough to travel here."

He raised a brow. "What about your boss?"

I shook my head. "He was . . . disappointed to lose me, but he got over it in about five minutes when he saw the twenty-five-year-old redhead I was interviewing to replace me."

His lips twitched briefly. "I want you to think about it, Sasha. I don't care if it's someone you ticked off three years ago while at the grocery store. I want you to really think about who could be upset with you. You don't have to answer it now. Take a day or two."

I didn't need to take a day or two. While living in Florida and Georgia, I mostly kept to myself. Went to work. Sometimes had drinks with coworkers. Every so often met someone who wasn't looking for more than a few good nights.

Now that I thought about it, what in the hell had I been doing these last ten years? Pretty much nothing. Frustrated, I walked over to where my purse sat on the barstool. I reached in, pulling out my cell.

"It's something—what are you doing?"

I looked up from my phone. "Getting ready to call Miranda. I need a ride home."

"I can do that."

Of course he would offer. He'd made me dinner because of—God, I didn't even know why anymore. My earlier freak-out seemed like hours ago, but I didn't need him doing anything more for me. "That's not necessary."

"Sasha," he said, tone firm. "I'll take you home."

I stared at him a moment and then nodded, suddenly too weary to argue over something so pointless. "Okay."

We didn't talk as we headed out into his garage

and I climbed into his truck. I couldn't head toward my mother's truck even though the deer wasn't in there anymore.

So many questions plagued my mind, but mainly why would someone do something so disgusting? Why would someone break out the windows in my car? The answer was right in my face. It had to be because of my past, but the why was what didn't make sense.

I was freaked out though. Thoroughly. The vandalized car was one thing but this . . . this was ratcheting things up to a whole new level. They felt like . . . like *warnings*, and I knew to some that would seem irrational but the thing was . . . after everything that had happened ten years ago, I spent many sleepless nights, still did, obsessing over if there had been signs. If there had been warnings about what was about to happen to me that I'd blindly ignored.

And I felt that way again.

Halfway home, something occurred to me as I glanced at Cole. His profile was pretty stoic, jaw a hard line and steely eyes focused on the road. "Can I ask you something?"

"Of course." Not a moment of hesitation.

"It's about your job," I clarified, holding my purse in my lap.

"If I can answer it, I will." He glanced over at me. "What do you want to know?"

I took a deep breath, not sure if I wanted to know the answer. "Are you working on the case of the . . . the missing woman who was found near the old water tower?"

"The FBI hasn't been called in on the case yet,"

he answered after a moment. His hand tightened on the steering wheel. "But I know the department head has been in talks with both the Maryland and West Virginia State Police."

Turning my gaze to the window, I watched the dark blur of the trees zooming by. "Do you . . ."

There was a heartbeat. "Do I what, Sasha?"

I swallowed hard. "Do you think it's weird that her body was found there, of all places?"

Cole didn't immediately answer. Not until I found myself looking at him again did he say, "Yeah. I find it weird."

"I'LL WALK YOU to your door," Cole said as he turned off the engine.

Before I could tell him that wasn't necessary, he was already out of his truck. Sighing, I opened the door and climbed out. He walked me to the porch and started toward the front door. "I'm not going in that way."

He stopped, then turned toward me. "You're going in the back entrance?"

I nodded. "There's a private entrance to the apartments in the back." I could easily just go in the front door, but I hadn't come up with a good reason to why I had Cole drive me home and I didn't want to risk running into my mother. "You don't have to do this. I'm home."

"I'm doing this." He started walking toward the side of the house and I sighed. "Do you guys lock the door at night?" he asked.

Frowning, I nodded as I stepped off the porch. "We usually make sure all the guests are back."

"And what do you do if the guests aren't back?"

"The doors are locked at ten o'clock, no matter what. Guests have to use the keys they're given upon check-in if they stay out later," I explained.

Cole moved ahead of me. Motion detectors kicked on, lighting up the path. As we rounded the back of the house, I stepped around him and headed for the flight of stairs hidden behind the tall oak. Of course, Cole was right behind me. Once we were in front of my door, I already had my key in hand.

"Thank you for the dinner and for helping out with the whole . . . truck thing," I said as I opened the door, keeping my voice low just in case Mom was in her apartment. "If you could just text me and let me know when I could pick it up, I'd appreciate—"

"You're not getting rid of me that easily."

Stopping, I turned around and faced him. The balcony light cast deep shadows along his cheek-bones. "What?"

Cole stepped inside my apartment, forcing me to take another step back. "I'm staying here."

I blinked, knowing I didn't hear him right. "What?"

Crowding me in, he grabbed the door and closed it behind us. There we stood near the kitchen, my mouth hanging open in what was probably the most unattractive manner. "I'm staying here."

My hearing must be experiencing technical dif-ficulties. "Why?"

"There are a couple of reasons." He paused, squinting as he glanced around my apartment. I'd left the lamp on by the sofa, and since the room wasn't large, it was fairly lit up.

I stood my ground. "How about you start ex-plaining those reasons?"

Busy checking out my apartment, which I thought was a totally cute space, but nowhere near as nice as the house he owned, he stepped around me. Dumbfounded, I turned toward him. "Can I help you?" I demanded, dropping my purse on the small table by the door.

He faced me, one side of his lips kicked up, and the look on his face was nothing like the way he'd looked at me earlier. It was teasing and mischievous. My belly flip-flopped. "That is a loaded question, Sasha." He tossed his keys onto the kitchen counter. "There are a lot of things you could help me with."

Our gazes met, and a tremble coursed down my arms. Was he . . . flirting with me? I sucked in a sharp breath, needing to focus on the fact that somehow Cole had ended up in my apartment. "Why do you think you need to stay with me?"

"I think it's pretty obvious." He turned and walked toward the couch, and I stood there, sort of shell-shocked as he sat down . . . in the center. "Someone is messing with you."

The words sent a very different kind of shiver over my skin as I walked over to the couch. "That might be the case, but that doesn't explain why you think you need to be here."

He tipped his chin up, staring at me as he scooted forward. "I don't like you being here alone when someone is messing with you."

I opened my mouth, but there were no words, because okay, that was sweet of him. That was actually very sweet, but he couldn't stay here. "You being here is unnecessary."

"How is it unnecessary?" he challenged as he

reached down, lifting the hem of his shirt. What was he doing? Undressing? I didn't know if I should tell him to stop or just let him continue. My heart rate kicked up until I realized he had a gun holstered at his right hip. Had it been there the whole time? I needed to be more observant.

"Because I'm not alone," I whispered-yelled. "Obviously. I live above an inn, and my mother is literally a room or two away."

He smiled, and my heart did another jump. Perhaps a cartwheel, because damn it, he was so incredibly hot just sitting there and breathing, but when he smiled, he was beautiful. "Let me ask you a few questions."

I crossed my arms and waited.

"Are all your guests in the hotel?"

My brows knitted. "I don't know. I haven't been here."

"Correct. So it's entirely possible that anyone could've come into this inn while you were gone, hidden away until everyone is asleep, and then have free rein of the hotel."

I locked up as my stomach dropped. "Oh my God, do you think—?"

"I don't think that's happened, but it's a possibility."

I gaped at him.

"My next question for you is do you have an alarm system?"

"We have one—"

"I know you have one for the inn, but what about for your apartment?" he corrected, unhooking his holster.

I shook my head. "No, but—"

"But you need to get an alarm in here stat, and I have a friend who installs them and owes me a favor. I'll call him tomorrow."

There was a good chance my face was frozen with my mouth hanging open. Getting an alarm for the upstairs made sense. The way the main one was wired, it would be cheaper setting up a separate one than adding to it. We'd need a brand-new system for the upstairs, a wireless one. "I don't even know what to say to you."

"Thank you?"

A surprised laugh burst out of me. "Those are not two words I am thinking of right now."

"I can imagine what those two words are," he said dryly, placing the gun on the coffee table.

Was this really happening?

Part of me wanted to grab him by the arms and drag him out to the door, but I knew there was no way that was going to be a successful endeavor. The other half just couldn't believe this was happening, but there was a small part of me, a stupid and completely irrational part of me, that was secretly thrilled that Cole was here, sitting on my couch.

There was also a part of me that was terrified, because his insistence made me feel like I wasn't safe, and neither was my mother. If I was being honest, I already knew that, but since I couldn't figure out why, it all seemed too surreal.

I shifted my weight from one foot. "Should I . . . I be worried about all of this?"

Cole's eyes met mine, and then suddenly, moving unbelievably fast, he was up and right in front of me. Then he was touching me, his hands carefully cradling my cheeks, and my heart was definitely doing cartwheels now. "Whether or not you should be worried about it isn't the deal here. You *are* worried about it."

Lies formed on the tip of my tongue as I stared into crystalline eyes, but I spoke the truth in a whisper. "I am freaked out about it."

"Anyone would be," he said, his voice just as low. "Even if they didn't have . . . well, if they didn't have your history."

I flinched, and then closed my eyes as he swept his thumb along my right cheek, chasing away the reaction. I don't know why I admitted what I did next. "Sometimes I wonder if I missed things before. You know? Like there had been signs that the Groom was coming after me and I missed them?"

"Even if there were signs, you wouldn't have known that was going to happen." His voice was as gentle as his hold. "And I'm not saying that these things are signs now, but I'd rather be safe than sorry."

Swallowing the lump in my throat, I opened my eyes. "If I hadn't . . . if my past wasn't what it was, would you insist on doing this now?"

A muscle worked in his jaw. "Sasha—"

I pulled away, slipping out of his grasp and putting space between us. Disappointment filled me, like it had while I'd been at his house. I didn't want my past driving his actions, and it was absolutely silly of me to think that would ever be a possibility.

The knot in my throat expanded. "You don't have to do this because you feel sorry for me, Cole."

His head tilted to the side as his brows drew tight. "I don't feel sorry for you."

I almost laughed. "And you don't need to do this because you feel some sort of obligation to me, because of what happened."

Understanding flashed across his face. "You know, there are things we still need to talk about. One of them being all that crap that went down in my kitchen before you ran out of my house."

My spine stiffened. "We don't need to talk about any of that. What you need to do is—"

"Oh, we're going to talk about that, but it's going to wait, and in the meanwhile, you can get angry and you can tell me I'm being unreasonable, and you can come up with any number of crazy reasons why you think I'm doing this, but I'm not leaving. No way in hell," Cole said, eyes flashing, "am I leaving you again."

CHAPTER 10

COLE DIDN'T LEAVE.

And I also didn't stand in the living room of my cute-but-not-as-amazing-as-Cole's-house apartment and argue with him. I'd stormed into my bedroom, only to remember that my bathroom was outside the bedroom.

So after pacing for several minutes, chafing at the idea that Cole felt he needed to be here to protect me from some unseen threat that probably didn't even exist, I threw open my bedroom door and stomped back out into the short hall. I didn't see Cole, but he'd apparently found the remote to the TV.

Cole was literally sitting in my living room, watching TV.

I couldn't believe it.

Quickly completing my nightly routine, I stormed back into my bedroom and managed to resist the urge to slam the door shut behind me. I needed to talk to Miranda.

Except I'd left my phone in my purse on the kitchen counter.

And I refused to go back out there.

Undressing, I grabbed the first thing out of my drawer and I slipped it on over my head. My bedroom door didn't have a lock on it, and the last thing I needed was to be standing around half naked if Cole decided to roam into the room for some reason.

I all but threw myself onto the bed. It wasn't late, and normally I wouldn't be anywhere near bed at this time, but I was trapped.

Okay. I wasn't trapped. It was by choice that I was hiding in my bedroom. *Hiding* yet again, and as I lay there, I knew he was doing what he thought was the right thing. He wanted to make sure I was safe, and I could appreciate that even though it annoyed me greatly. I wasn't a damsel in need of protection. Not that I didn't recognize what Cole could do if I was threatened. I wasn't stupid. He had a gun. I didn't, but I didn't . . . I didn't like feeling as if I couldn't take care of myself. For ten years, I'd been doing just that. I'd beat back that fear and I'd been fine.

But Cole was here because of what happened to me before. And I didn't need a PhD in psychology to know that he felt like he hadn't been there for me before. In a way, he was atoning for what he believed he had failed at.

Or maybe, just maybe, I was making up a lot of reasons and deciding they were true without even talking to him, because I just couldn't deal.

The last thought sounded way too rational to be the truth.

"I'm a mess," I said to my ceiling.

My ceiling had no response.

And my thoughts drifted to what had happened when I tried to leave Cole's house, and I shuddered under the covers as the memory of the stench of death and decay nearly swallowed me whole.

Curling onto my side, I folded my hands under my chin and stared at the small window across from the bed. I closed my eyes, not wanting to think about the deer or my vandalized car. I didn't want to think about anything, but for the next several hours, I did, and whenever I heard movement outside my bedroom, I would go stiff and hold my breath, ears prickling as I tried to figure out what he was doing. Would he come in here? He had no reason to. Would he still be out in the living room in the morning or would he leave once the sun came up? I didn't even know if he had to go to work, but I did know that couch was not big enough for someone as long as him.

I wasn't sure how long I lay there, and I'd given up tracking how far the moonlight reached across the floor by the time I slipped into that half-awake stage. I was floating there when I felt it, the featherlight brush along the curve of my bare shoulder.

My heart rate kicked up. What was Cole doing in here? I held my breath as his fingers coasted over my skin, spreading a wave of tiny goosebumps along my flesh. His fingers slipped under the strap of my nightie, slowly dragging it down my arm.

I needed to stop him. Hell, I needed to be pissed about him sneaking into my room and touching me, but I . . . I *liked* it. Oh God, I did like it, and I could lie here, pretending I was asleep.

His hand drifted over my shoulder and danced along the blade until he reached my spine. I let out a shaky breath. He dragged his hand down the center of my back, the pressure heavy and—

"*Sasha . . .*"

Pressure twisted in my chest. The hand at my back. It was too heavy, too rough. Too familiar. Too cold.

I twisted, flipping onto my back. My eyes widened as I stared into the darkness, knowing I couldn't see his face. I'd never see his face, but I knew, oh God, I knew this wasn't Cole. A scream built into my throat, ripping free, and my ears burned from the sound. I heard it then, the high-pitched laugh. The laugh that signaled pain was on its way, because when he *touched* me like that, when he *laughed* like that, he wasn't just the Groom anymore. He was more than a monster.

"Sasha!" Pressure tightened on my arm, and my scream intensified. "Sasha! Stop. You're okay. You're safe. Stop."

You're safe.

Two words the Groom would never speak.

Jackknifing up and to the side, my flailing hand hit air and I tumbled to the left, right off the bed. I didn't hit the floor.

Cole was fast, wrapping an arm around my waist and hauling me back onto the bed, *against* him. Chest to chest. Skin against . . . *skin? What?* The nightmare faded like wisps of smoke as I slowly became aware of everything. Cole was holding me to him, his breath warm against my cheek, and he'd taken his shirt off at some point, and now my heart was racing for a whole different reason.

"You with me?" he asked.

I was *so* with him.

The room was dark and I couldn't see anything, but all I could feel was him, and it was at that moment that I realized what I'd thrown on before getting into bed. It was a spaghetti-strapped nightie and had a heart-shaped bodice; the kind of nightie made of soft cotton that only reached the midthigh and was most likely completely see-through in bright light. A very thin nightie that made it feel like there was almost nothing between our bodies.

And his chest was warm, actually felt hot against mine, and the denim of his jeans was rough against my inner thighs. It was then when I also realized that somehow I wasn't just in his lap, I was *straddling* him. I had no idea how that happened, but his shoulders were also smooth and hard under my hands.

"Sasha." His voice was deeper as one hand folded around the nape of my neck, bunching up my hair. "Are you with me?"

My throat was dry as I gasped out, "Yes."

"Good." He didn't let go, but his hand tightened, as did his arm. "Does this happen often?"

"Does what happen often? This?"

His chuckle was throaty. "The nightmares, Sasha. Do they happen often?"

Oh. I closed my eyes as I gave a little shake of my head. "Not often."

"Why do I have a feeling you're not being exactly honest?" His breath coasted over my forehead.

"I don't know why." I should lift my hands away, but they felt like they were weighted against his skin with lead.

"There's something you're forgetting." He shifted suddenly, and I gasped as I slid toward him. My legs spread wider, and now my belly was pressed against his much harder stomach. "I know you. I'm not a stranger."

"You don't . . ."

"I don't what?" His voice dropped to a whisper.

Maybe it was the darkness. Maybe it was the nightmare and the almost-surreal nature of him holding me like this. I don't know but I answered his question. "You don't know me anymore."

The muscles under my hands tensed. "I still know you, Sasha."

Shaking my head, I let my hands drop to his chest. "You don't. Ten years have passed, Cole. You don't know me anymore."

"The Sasha I know is still in there. I've seen glimpses of her tonight while we had dinner. You are still her," he insisted, his voice rough and firm. "And I still know you."

"You—"

"I know you're not telling me the truth about the nightmares," he continued. "You have them often, don't you? Not every night, but enough that you don't sleep well."

My breath caught. He was dead on.

"I'm right, aren't I?"

Cole was right, but he didn't need to know that. He didn't need to know anything else that would make him feel even sorrier for me. I struggled to keep my voice even. "It was just a nightmare. Not a big deal." I started to climb off, but he held me in place. "I'm fine now. You can let go."

"I'm not fine."

Tilting my head to the side, I looked at him, wishing I could see his expression. "Why are you not fine? Did you have a nightmare?"

"No. But hearing you scream like that was like having a nightmare." His tone was dead serious. "It woke me out of a dead sleep. I thought . . ."

I stiffened in his arms. I didn't want to know what he thought, because I had a pretty good idea already. "I'm okay. You should go back to sleep. Actually, you should leave. I'm—"

"Why are you shutting me out?"

His question caused me to jerk. "I'm not—"

"Yes, you are."

Not wanting to have this argument in the middle of the night, in my dark bedroom with me in his lap, on my bed while I was wearing next to nothing, I pushed against his chest.

Cole didn't budge.

"Let me go," I said.

"I will." Cole didn't. "But I have something to say first."

I pushed again, ignoring how . . . wonderfully smooth and hard his skin felt under my palms, like silk stretched over steel. "You can say what you need to say while not holding me."

"Nope."

"Cole," I snapped.

The hand at the nape of my neck slid up and his fingers splayed across the base of my skull. A shiver followed, spreading out over my shoulders and down my front, and it was the good kind of shiver. I felt my nipples harden, and was at once grateful that it was dark.

"You've got walls up. I get it. Can even understand why you would, and I bet that's why you haven't had a single damn serious relationship in the last ten years. And I can get that too. I understand." He guided my head toward him, stopping when I felt his breath against my lips. "But I'm not some random guy you just met. I'm not someone who doesn't know that what's at the core of you is worth working at, breaking through those walls for."

Oh my God.

"People don't get second chances often, Sasha, but we got one, and I'm not going to let that pass us by."

"A second chance?" I repeated dumbly. "For us?"

"That's what I'm thinking."

Stunned, I was quiet for a moment. "What if I don't want a second chance?"

He laughed. "Oh, you want a second chance."

My mouth dropped open. "And what makes you think that, Mr. All Knowing?"

Those lips of his coasted over my cheek, causing me to gasp. "Yeah, *that* right there tells me you want a second chance, and I've seen the way you looked at me today, but you know what else?" He paused. "Those hard little nipples pressed against my chest tell me you want a second chance."

Oh my *God*.

"And there are no walls I can't break through.

Teflon? Barbed wire? It's not going to stop me from getting through."

All I could do was stare at him in the dark, and I wasn't even sure I was breathing at that point.

"I meant what I said earlier, Sasha." Cole's lips brushed the curve of my cheek, causing me to shiver. "I'm not leaving you. Not again."

CHAPTER 11

"OKAY. THAT'S HOT."

I narrowed my eyes at Miranda. We were sitting in the kitchen the following afternoon. She was on her lunch break and had about ten minutes before she had to get back to the school, which was within walking distance. She looked glorious, as usual, wearing a deep purple sweater dress that was a perfect match for her dark skin. If I wore something like that I'd look like a purple people eater. Now she was scarfing down a salad that smelled like it had overdosed on Italian dressing. "He wouldn't leave," I reminded her.

She pointed her leafy-green-speared fork at me. "He wanted to make sure you were safe."

"From what?"

Leaning forward, Miranda whispered, "From crazy people who would leave roadkill in your mother's truck."

I glared at her and then sighed, dropping my

chin. "You have a point there." I'd told Miranda everything. Well, I didn't tell her about the hard nipples, because seriously, I doubted she wanted to hear about that. Needless to say, she was freaked out about the deer thing. Who wouldn't be? When it came to everything else, she was of the mind that everything Cole did and said was utterly hot.

"What did you tell your mother?" she asked as she glanced at the open kitchen door.

"I told her I drank too much wine last night and Cole drove me home." I fiddled with the cap on my Diet Coke bottle. "She didn't question it. She was just happy to assume I had a great time, and I'm pretty sure she's already thinking of grandbaby names."

Miranda laughed—she threw her head back and cackled like a hyena.

"It's not funny."

"Oh yes, yes it is," she replied with a grin. "None of the other stuff is funny, but that is. I can see your mom doing it too. She's probably already knitting a genderless onesie."

I groaned, because I could totally picture my mom doing that.

"So what's happening with the truck?" she asked, stopping in front of the trashcan.

I leaned back in my chair. "Cole texted about an hour ago." For some dumb reason, my heart flipped. It did it every time I said his name, and I'd been ignoring the stupid little motion in my chest. Well, I'd been failing at ignoring it, obviously. "He said the car will be ready this afternoon."

Miranda dropped her plastic fork into what was left of her salad. "Does she know he stayed the night?"

I shook my head. "I don't think so. If she does, she hasn't said anything."

Grabbing her take-out container, she closed the lid and rose. "I want to talk all about everything Cole said to you last night, but the whole deer thing . . ."

"I know." I watched her dump the container in the trash. "I don't know what to think."

"Have you thought about what Cole asked?" She picked up her purse, slinging it over her shoulder. "A list of people who could be upset with you?"

Pushing up, I stretched my arms to work out the stiffness in my upper back. After the nightmare and everything Cole had said, I hadn't fallen back to sleep. He'd left the bedroom and returned to the couch to sleep, I guess, while I stayed awake, my body unnaturally stiff. I'd used that time wisely, thinking of possibly anyone who could be upset with me. I normally didn't sleep well anyway, but spending the wee hours of the night thinking about people who could potentially be angry with you wasn't exactly the best bedtime thing to obsess over.

Lowering my arms, I rocked back on the heels of my flip-flops. "I have thought about it. I just . . ." I trailed off as I heard footsteps.

Mom drifted in, frowning as she glanced around the kitchen. "Have you seen Angela?"

I raised a brow. "I haven't." Folding my arms, I said, "I figured she was upstairs cleaning."

"She hasn't showed up or called," Mom said, the skin tightening around her pursed lips. "That is very unlike her."

"She might be sick," Miranda said, heading

toward the dining room. We followed. "There's a nasty bug going around. Mrs. Chase, the tenth-grade history teacher, got it last week and was up all night, and barely was able to call in sick in time for the school to bring in a sub."

"Oh no. Maybe I should bring her a bowl of soup," Mom was saying as we crossed the sitting area.

I glanced at the phone on the registration desk to see if there was a message that I might've missed earlier. There wasn't. Luckily, we only had one room booked, with two more coming in tomorrow. "I'll head upstairs and take care of the Mattersons' room. Tidy up the rest."

"And then you'll call me," Miranda added as she opened the front door. "Because we still have a lot to—whoa. Oh my God." She laughed, stepping back to the side. "I almost ran you over."

Turning, I saw an unfamiliar man standing in the doorway. He was middle-aged, hair a light brown. He wore a dark brown button-down sweater and his tan khakis were pressed to the point I doubted they ever wrinkled.

The man smiled at Miranda as his gaze flickered over to me. "Miss Keeton?"

Unease blossomed in the pit of my stomach. "Yes?"

The man's smile became a big one, displaying all his ultra-bright, ultra-straight white teeth. "Hi, I'm David Striker, but most call me Striker. I'm a freelance journalist working with the—"

"Oh hell no." Miranda cocked her head to the side as my stomach sunk all the way to my toes. "Whatever you want, she's not interested."

Striker's smile started to fade. "But you don't even know what I want."

I stiffened.

"Like I said, whatever you want, she's not interested." Miranda glared at the man. "Do I need to spell that out for you?"

The smile was completely gone now. "No." His dark brown eyes narrowed. "Miss Keeton, I only need a few minutes of your time."

Miranda opened her mouth, but I stepped forward. "You need to get back to work," I told her. "I can handle this."

"And by handling this, she means that no matter what your questions are, she's not going to answer them." Mom used her Mom voice—the voice laced with authority. "Now, if you would—" She'd stepped forward as she spoke and had caught the open door and started to close it.

Striker's hand flew out, blocking her. "You know the body of the woman who disappeared out of Frederick was found in the exact same location that the Groom left his victims. You know that, right?"

The dread exploded like buckshot, spreading throughout my system. Mom tried to close the door again, but Striker wasn't going anywhere. Neither was Miranda, and while my stomach was churning and a huge part of me wanted to dash upstairs, I didn't want her to get into trouble. This was my problem. Not hers. Not my mother's.

"Miranda, please go. I've got this," I said, meeting her angry gaze. I smiled at her reassuringly. "It's okay. This was bound to happen. Go."

The press of her lips told me only an act of God

was keeping her mouth shut, but she nodded curtly and then stepped around Striker, sizing him up with a dismissive curl of her lips.

I watched her cross the porch and then disappear around the corner before I focused on Striker.

He went on like we hadn't given him an indication that we weren't happy to answer his questions. "Mayor Hughes gave a press conference this morning on the discovery of the body and he's saying—"

"I know you're just doing your job and that is the only reason why I'm going to *kindly* tell you that I have nothing to say."

"So, you need to leave and I need to close the door, because we're letting all the warm air out," my mom added, moving to close the door again. "And I'm asking that kindly."

Striker's foot jutted out, joining the battle along with his hand. "I know this is a sensitive topic for you and I understand that you'd be reluctant, but it is entirely too convenient that the same place was used to leave the body."

I curled my hands into fists. "It *is* convenient and it also has nothing to do with me."

"But doesn't it concern you at all?"

I almost answered the question. My nails were digging into my palms. "Why would it concern me? This has nothing to do with—with what happened?"

He bit down on his lip. "Look, I just want—"

"I don't care what you want," I shot back as the welling irritation gave way to anger. "What happened to me isn't some story to run in the Sunday paper to entertain people. It's *my* life. It has *nothing* to do with what happened to this poor woman and it's disgusting to even attempt to sensationalize what happened to her."

Striker widened his stance, and I knew then he wasn't planning to go anywhere; I knew by the change in his expression, the sudden hard jut of his jaw, he was going for it. "Is it true that the Groom was planning to kill you when you escaped—that you escaped during the attempt itself?"

Oh my God.

Blood rushed so fast from my head I felt dizzy. I stepped back, bumping into the desk. He knew. How did he know that? Were those kind of records available? There hadn't been a trial. There hadn't been a need for one. The Groom had died, and even though a lot of info had leaked to the press, that hadn't.

I gasped. "How . . . did you know that?"

"I'm a reporter, Miss Keeton. It's my job to know things."

"That's enough," Mom snapped before Striker could answer. She pushed on the door again. "I'm giving you ten seconds to get off my property before I call the police."

"That won't be necessary," a deep, rough voice said, and my heart did that unsteady flip again. Over Striker's shoulder, I saw Cole stalk through the entryway, and he looked furious. He clapped a hand down on Striker's shoulder and spun him around, away from the door. "He's leaving now."

Striker stumbled to the side, his eyes widening when he came face-to-face with Cole. Surprise flickered over his face. "I know who you are."

Cole smirked. "Then you should know that you better be getting the hell off this property."

"I'm not breaking a law," he challenged. "Surely not a federal one."

"Actually, you will be breaking a law. This is a private property, and they've asked you to leave." Cole stalked toward Striker, forcing him back. "You don't leave, that's a law you're breaking."

The center of Striker's cheeks flushed red. He opened his mouth as if he were about to say something but then snapped his jaw closed. He glanced over at me and then pivoted around, hurrying off the porch. Cole closed the door.

"Thank you, Cole," Mom gushed while I was still standing practically petrified in front of the desk. "I was seconds away from picking up that floor lamp and beating him over the head with it until he left."

Cole's lips did that twitch thing that said he was fighting a smile. I slowly looked over at my mom. "That would've been a damn shame too. I purchased that lamp from Wayfair after searching for months for the perfect one," she added.

My gaze darted to the floor lamp in question and I frowned. There was nothing special about it. It was a white lampshade on a gray pole.

"Well, I'm glad I saved the floor lamp." He reached into his pocket and drew out a set of keys. "Your truck is parked outside."

Remembering the truck and everything else, I snapped out of it. "Thank you for bringing it back. You didn't have to do that."

His cool gaze drifted over to me. "But I did."

Those three words again. They were haunting

me. So were those eyes. Cole had left this morning before I stepped out of my bedroom, but not before turning on my coffeemaker and letting it brew so it would be ready for me.

So damn thoughtful.

Our gazes met in an instant, and I drew in a shaky breath. He was several feet away from me, but it felt like he was standing right against me. I swore I could feel the warmth of his body. Though there were a ton of things that I needed to be focused on, all I could think about in that moment was what Cole had said to me last night about second chances and breaking down walls.

And I so needed to get a grip.

Focusing on my mom, I said, "I'm sorry about that."

Her brows knitted together. "Why are you apologizing, honey? That's not your fault."

"I know, but what if one of the guests were here to hear that?" I crossed my arms. "That's not exactly something that will help us book rooms."

"Still isn't your fault, babe," Cole said.

Babe?

"Is that the first time he's been here?" Cole asked.

"Yes," Mom answered, smoothing a hand over the hem of her loose sweater. "Back after everything happened, it was a very frequent occurrence, but that was the first time he showed."

"If he does again, you let me know," Cole offered, folding his arms. He was wearing a black henley, and this time I noticed the gun holstered at his hip, tucked under the hem of the shirt. "I'll make sure he gets the message."

"Hopefully we won't continue to have that problem." Mom plastered on a smile I wasn't sure was real. "I think he just caught us off guard."

As I listened to Mom and Cole, something the reporter said started to nag at me. I pressed my lips together as I replayed what Striker said. Then it hit me.

"The mayor," I whispered.

Mom turned toward me. "What, honey?"

I blinked as Cole's gaze sharpened. "Nothing. Just thinking out loud."

Cole did the hand thing with a head tilt this time, reaching back and clasping the back of his neck as he eyed me.

Mom glanced back and forth between us. There was a pause. "I'll take care of the Mattersons' room."

I turned at the waist. "I said I would do it."

"It's okay." She was already at the stairs. "You go ahead and chat with Cole." She beamed at him like he'd invented flying cars. "Thank you again for making sure my daughter was responsible last night," she said, and I barely was able to resist rolling my eyes. "And thank you for getting my truck back to me."

"No problem, Mrs. Keeton." One side of his lips kicked up. "I will always make sure your daughter is responsible."

I snorted under my breath. Totally ladylike, but I couldn't help myself.

"Did you say something, babe?" Cole asked.

I looked up, arching a brow. "Nothing." I paused. "And don't call me babe."

"Cute," Mom said, with one hand on the railing. "So cute."

My eyes narrowed as I watched her climb the stairs. Her steps were a little slow, and I wasn't sure if something was paining her or if she was just taking her sweet old time, hoping to overhear Cole and me.

Probably the latter.

I waited until Mom was out of sight and then turned to Cole. Before I could say a word, he crossed the short distance between us, and I leaned against the desk, angling his body toward mine. I had to tip my chin up to meet his eyes.

"I was being serious earlier. If that jackass shows up again, you let me know," he said, voice low. "I'll make sure he fully understands."

I started to tell him that wasn't necessary, but then I realized I'd told Cole that about a dozen or so times since he walked through these doors. It struck me then, as I stood beside him, close enough to touch him, that I didn't want to tell him that.

What he offered was necessary.

Even though I knew pity and a twisted sense of obligation drove him to be here and to do everything he'd been doing, I wanted to ignore all the many reasons behind it and I wanted him here. The spreading warmth in my chest told me I was glad he was here. "Thank you," I said, lowering my gaze. "For taking care of my mom's truck and for running off the reporter."

"You don't need to thank me." His hands folded around my arms and he gently uncrossed them, drawing my gaze to his. He held on to my arms, and a rapid flutter started deep in my chest. "I know that reporter showing up here had to have bothered you."

There was no point in denying that. "He's looked into me, Cole. He knew . . ." I cleared my throat. "He knew that the . . . Groom was trying to kill me when I escaped."

A muscle spasmed along his jaw. "Shit."

"How did he know that?" I whispered. "Are there records of what happened that people have access to?"

"Not easily." He slid his hands to my upper arms and then down to my elbows in a soothing slide he repeated. "But he's a journalist, babe. They make friends with cops and detectives. Favors get called in. Rub my back, I'll rub yours kind of thing."

"Jesus," I muttered. I knew there was a mammoth-sized file on me. I'd had to talk to the police and the federal agents, and I had to tell them *everything*. I wasn't even sure how much Cole knew, but I imagined it was enough, since he'd been a deputy back then, but this was different. Knowing that someone, a complete stranger who had no business reading any of that, could get access to the file sickened me.

His hands slid down again, rubbing my arms. "I wish there was something I could say that would change that."

A weak smile formed on my lips. "This was bound to happen. It'll probably happen again. I should get used to it."

"You shouldn't have to."

My gaze lifted to his and I inhaled softly. His eyes searched mine as his hands continued to move over my arms. It would be so easy to just stand there and forget about everything for a few blissful seconds, but there was something I remembered that I needed to talk to him about.

I bit on my lip and glanced at the stairwell. Mom would be busy for a little bit. "Can you . . . stay for a couple of minutes?"

His eyes warmed. "Of course."

The next breath I took was shaky, and I stepped away, slipping out of his grasp to lead him to the sitting room. I sat near the fireplace and he took a seat next to me. I kept my voice low as I talked, just in case my mother or the Mattersons roamed into the room.

"You asked me to think of anyone who might be upset about me returning home, and I've been trying to think of someone, but I've been coming up empty-handed," I told him, and he shifted toward me, one arm resting on the arm of the chair. "But it was something the reporter—Striker—said that made me think of someone."

"Okay." His body was on alert. "That's good. At least that asshole was useful for something."

Despite the topic of conversation, I grinned. "Mayor Hughes."

Cole's brows flew up. "Come again?"

"I know it sounds crazy, but this whole thing is crazy. Every part of it." I slid my hands over my knees. "Miranda and I went out to dinner Monday night with Jason. Mayor Hughes was there, and he came up to me. He wasn't exactly rude, but you could tell he wasn't thrilled with me being back here. He made some kind of comment about me talking to the press and basically was worried I was going to drag back up everything that had happened."

"Did he say anything else to you?"

I shook my head. "Nothing except he did know I was coming home. Mom apparently mentioned it at a chamber of commerce meeting."

He rubbed the back of his neck. "That also means anyone at that meeting could've overheard your mom telling the mayor you were coming home."

"True." My hands stilled. "Or it could mean we're reading way too much into this, and both things were freaky occurrences."

Cole dropped his hand. "Do you really believe that, Sasha?"

God, I wanted to, so very badly, but instinct was telling me a different story. "I—"

Cole suddenly held up his hand and then twisted in his seat, toward the front of the inn. I followed his gaze, and a second later, Cole proved he had supersonic hearing.

A young man walked in, his hands twisting the bill of a baseball cap. The flannel he wore was wrinkled and his brown hair disheveled, appearing as if he spent hours shoving his fingers through it. "Excuse me," he said, his brown eyes darting around the room. "I'm looking for Mrs. Keeton."

"She's busy right now." I rose, realizing Cole had already done the same. "I'm her daughter. Can I help you?"

His fingers stilled, knuckles bleached as white as his complexion. "My name is Ethan—Ethan Reed. My girlfriend works here."

The name was familiar. "Angela?"

He nodded. "Is she here today?"

I shook my head. "No, she didn't show up for work. We thought maybe she was sick."

Ethan's fingers started moving again, twisting the stiff material of the cap. "She's not sick. At least I don't think she is, but she didn't come home from class last night," he said, the words coming out in a rush. "She hasn't been home at all. Angela's missing."

CHAPTER 12

SHE'S MISSING.

Those two words were haunting, the worst kind of thing for someone to hear. You immediately wanted to spring into action, start scouring the whole entire state, checking every back road and busting down every door, but the enormity of the situation was a punch in the gut, leaving you feeling utterly helpless.

It was the first time I'd heard the words spoken about someone I knew personally, but I knew what it was like to be on the other side.

The one who was missing.

Seeing the turmoil on Ethan's face, watching him pace, his fingers continually twisting around the bill of his cap, I knew it wasn't easy not knowing what had happened to your loved one.

All I had to do was talk to my mother or Cole to confirm that.

"She's never not come home or missed work." Ethan flinched as he spoke the words. "I've called her and called her, about two dozen times. She'd never not answer."

Cole immediately took charge of the situation, asking Ethan, "Have you contacted the police?"

He shook his head. "She hasn't been gone twenty-four hours and—"

"There's no waiting period when someone is missing and you have reasonable belief that they are, in fact, missing. You can thank poorly researched movies for that shitty misconception," Cole answered as he reached into his pocket and pulled out his cellphone. "I'm going to call it in. The local police are going to ask a lot of questions, so be prepared for that. It'll help if you have a picture of her available."

"I . . . have one in my wallet," he replied, pulling his ball cap on over his head before reaching into his back pocket. "It was taken a year ago. It was just a stupid selfie that she took on her birthday, but it was beautiful and I . . . I made her get it printed out and . . ." Trailing off, he stared at the small photo he held in his hand.

My chest squeezed as I listened to him. "Why don't you sit down and I'll get you something to drink," I offered, wishing there was more I could do.

His unfocused gaze swung to me and he nodded absently, sitting down in the chair. Cole was on the phone, talking in a low voice. His eyes came to mine before he turned, clasping the back of his neck with one hand.

I hurried into the kitchen, startled to find James was in there. "I didn't know you were here."

He was placing a large pot on the counter when he looked up. "Been here for a while."

"Angela's missing," I blurted out.

His aging face, full of deep grooves, seemed to pale by several shades. Dark eyes widened on me as his hands stilled on the handles of the pot.

"Her boyfriend is out there," I explained, forcing myself to get moving. I went to the fridge.

"Damn," he said gruffly. "That girl ain't missed a single day of work. Not even last year when she got that damn flu bug goin' around."

I grabbed the pitcher of fresh tea, realizing that despite everything Mom and I had been through, we hadn't assumed the worst when Angela hadn't showed for work. I wasn't sure if that was a bad or a good thing.

"Damn," James muttered as I poured a glass of tea. "That's some rough news."

"Yeah," I whispered, lifting my gaze to his.

He walked the pot over to the sink. "That's some familiar news."

"Yeah," I repeated.

I couldn't let myself focus on that last fact as I left the kitchen. By the time I got back out to the sitting area, Mom was downstairs, kneeling in front of Ethan. Her worried gaze collided with mine as I placed the glass of tea on the small end table. Cole wasn't in the room, but I heard him speaking from the front of the inn.

"Thank you," Ethan murmured as he picked up

the glass. "I haven't eaten or slept. Been surviving on coffee." He took a drink and then looked at my mother. "Do you think . . . ?" His voice filled with anguish. "Do you think she's okay?"

"Of course, honey." Mom rubbed his bent knees. "Of course."

His gaze lifted to where I hovered. He didn't say anything, but he didn't need to. The pained glaze to his eyes was mingled with horror.

"She'll be okay," I told him, wanting and needing to believe that myself, because I couldn't picture otherwise. I couldn't fathom how bubbly and happy Angela could be anything else but okay.

"*You* really think that?" he asked, and that was a hit to the chest.

My mouth dried. I knew what he'd meant by that question, because he knew, just like anyone who had lived in this town ten years ago, that sometimes when people went missing, there wasn't a happy ending.

Ethan took several long sips, the glass shaking in his hand. "I checked at the college, you know, to see if her car was there. It . . . it wasn't. I even left a message with the professor to see if she made it to class."

"She was here yesterday," Mom explained, rising slowly. "She worked her shift."

I nodded, thinking of how she was bouncing around the kitchen just yesterday, eating the cookies that Jason had brought.

Cole returned, everything about him on alert. I imagined this was how he was while at work. He hung up the phone. "You have your car, Ethan?"

The young man nodded, setting the glass aside. "Yeah."

"Okay. We're going to drive down to the police station together," he said as he crossed the room. "They know you're coming in to file a report."

"Is there anything we can do?" I asked.

"Anything," Mom repeated.

"There is." Cole stopped in front of me, and before I could do anything, he lowered his mouth to my ear and said, "Please stay in tonight. That's something you can do for me."

I found myself nodding and agreeing.

He drew back, his eyes coming to mine. "We'll talk later."

And once again, surprising me, he dipped his chin and kissed the curve of my cheek. Then he was at Ethan's side, placing his hand on the younger man's shoulder, guiding him out.

I watched Ethan and Cole leave, then looked over at my mom, not surprised to see her eyes fixed on me. She didn't comment on what Cole had just done, which was the only surprising part, as she leaned into me, wrapping her arm around me. I didn't know what to say, and she seemed to understand that, like she always did.

Mom squeezed my waist. "I know."

THE INSURANCE ADJUSTER showed to look at my car that afternoon. Shortly after he left, a tow truck arrived to cart it off to a body shop about ten minutes down the road. I chatted with one of the guys at the garage. They figured they'd have my car finished by Tuesday.

I did as Cole requested. I stayed in, mainly because I had no reason to go anywhere. I spent the rest of the afternoon completing what Angela normally would do while hoping to hear something about her whereabouts, something good.

News about Angela's possible disappearance spread fast even though the town wasn't that small. After dinner was served to the Mattersons and they retired to the room they'd rented, Miranda showed up and then Jason. They joined Mom and me in the kitchen.

Miranda was sitting on the kitchen island, legs dangling off, and it was a good thing James had already left, because he would've kicked her butt if he saw her on the counter.

Not minding where Miranda's rear end was, Mom sat at the table with Jason, and I stood near Miranda. All four of us had fresh coffee in our cups. There'd been nothing on the news about Angela, which was frustrating, but I imagined someone like Striker would be all over it come morning. At least, I hoped he would be spending his time on something more useful.

"I can't believe this is happening," Miranda stated, and it was probably the fourth time she'd said it, and like all the times before, she trailed off before saying what we all were thinking.

Everyone was avoiding saying it because I was there, so I went ahead and said it. "I can't believe this is happening *again*."

She sucked in a shrill breath as Mom pressed her lips together, casting her gaze out the window, onto the dark veranda.

"That's what everyone is thinking, right?" I said, placing my cup on the counter behind Miranda.

"The woman in Frederick was missing and they . . . found her body, and now this has happened."

"Doesn't mean these two things are related," Jason argued, bending forward and resting his arms on his legs. "I heard that the cops were really looking at the Frederick woman's husband."

"That's what they did before," Miranda interjected quietly. "When the first woman disappeared, they swore it was her husband. Didn't they actually arrest him?"

Mom nodded and her voice sounded distant when she said, "They did. It was Becky Fisher's husband. Held him for several days until they released him, because they didn't have any evidence."

"And because Jessica Rae disappeared," I said, rubbing my hands over my arms, chilled. "That was before people realized that when another woman disappeared, the other one was already dead, but everyone figured it out pretty quickly after that."

Twisting toward me, Mom said, "Sasha."

I bit down on my lip. "This is just too—"

"Coincidental," Jason cut in, and my gaze went to him. "Look, all I am saying is that we might be jumping the gun here, assuming the worst. Not that anyone could blame anyone for doing it, but if Angela really is missing and that's somehow tied to the woman from Frederick, then we're dealing with a . . ." He took a deep breath. "Then we're dealing with another serial killer, and what is the likelihood of this area having not one but two serial killers?"

I jolted, seriously unnerved. It wasn't because of Jason, but what he said. Two serial killers. Pushing away from the counter, I snagged the mug and went to the sink.

"It's probably not related, and Angela will show up tomorrow." Miranda smiled, but it didn't reach her eyes. She didn't believe it.

And I didn't think any one of us did.

Conversation moved to some kind of drama Miranda was sensing at work. She didn't know the details, but there'd been a lot of closed-door after-school conversations taking place. It started to get late, and Miranda and Jason moved to leave.

"I'll see you later." Jason leaned in, giving me a stiff one-armed hug that made me grin, because he was pretty terrible at hugs. "Walk you out?" he said to Miranda.

"Normally I'd tell you that wouldn't be necessary, because I can kick ass." Miranda hopped off the counter. "But I'm officially freaked out, so you can totally walk me out."

"Be careful," I told them. "Both of you."

Miranda saluted me. "Yes, ma'am."

"Sometimes I wonder if you're a closet drinker," muttered Jason.

"I'm an in-your-face drinker," she replied, and Jason just shook his head as he walked her out of the kitchen, his hand on her lower back. My brows lifted. Was there something going on between them? If there was, I imagined Miranda would've said something. Why wouldn't she?

I stood there for a moment. "I'm going to lock up behind them since the Mattersons are here."

"Okay, honey." Mom rose from the table. "But

please come back. I want to talk to you for a moment."

Nodding, I left the room and went to the front door with my hands pressed against the cool wood.

Two serial killers.

The air in my throat caught, and I opened up the front door, staring out over the lawn. The porch light and the lamp cast a soft glow that did nothing to chase away the shadows. Tiny bumps raced across my skin and the fine hairs at the back of my neck rose. Stepping back, I quickly closed the door and locked it like there was an ax murderer racing up the drive.

Mom was back at the table when I returned, all the coffee mugs washed out and placed in the dishwasher. She patted the table, and I walked over, sitting across from her. "How are you hanging in there?" she asked.

Biting my lip, I shook my head. "Tomorrow marks one week back home, and . . ." I lifted my hands helplessly before dropping them to the table. Talking about how I was dealing felt wrong when one woman was already dead and Angela was missing. "This isn't about me. You shouldn't be worried about me."

"Honey, I know that." Reaching across the table, she folded her hand over mine. "But I am worried about you."

"I'm okay." I was unsettled. Freaked out. Worried about the whole deer thing and my car, but I *was* fine even though I sounded a little desperate when I asked, "Do you think Angela will turn up?"

"I don't know. I'm hoping and praying that's the case. Angela could be flighty, but she never missed work. She wouldn't just run away." She squeezed my hand. "But there's something else I want to talk to you about."

I didn't need to take a wild guess to figure that out. "Cole?"

A soft smile appeared on her face. "His truck was outside this morning when I got home."

Oh geez. I was so hoping he'd managed to leave before she woke up.

"Now, I'm not looking for details, but I'm guessing something good went down between you two based on the way he was acting this afternoon."

Was that just last night? Felt like an eternity ago. "He drove me home and then he stayed the night—on the couch," I added. "It was late."

Her head tilted to the side. "I don't know if I should be proud of you or disappointed that you had that fine-looking man sleeping on your couch when I know that bed of yours is more than big enough."

My mouth dropped open and I gasped, *"Mom."*

"What?" she laughed. "I may be getting up there in years, but I can still fully appreciate a good-looking man." She sat back. "Especially a man who cared for my daughter once before and seems like he still does, and I also know you cared for him deeply once before too. What I want to know is if you care about him still."

I tipped my head back and stared at the ceiling lights until the brightness was burned into my retina. "It's . . . I don't know how I feel."

"I'm not sure I believe you."

Sighing, I lowered my chin and rubbed my eyes until the burn went away. Mom knew me too well sometimes. "It's complicated."

"I'm of the mind that anything worth a damn in life, anything fun and joyous, will always be complicated," she said. "If it's easy, it's probably not exactly worth it."

"True, but I think . . ."

"Spit it out, honey."

"Fine," I groaned. "I think he feels sorry for me and he came back here out of some messed-up, twisted sense of obligation."

Mom's brows inched up her forehead and several moments passed before she spoke. "And what exactly has he done that would make you think that? Not what you think he has done, but what has he done?"

I opened my mouth, prepared to point out the reasons why I believed this based on our few times together since I returned, and I couldn't find anything actually concrete—anything that wasn't my perception of what he'd done. I snapped my mouth shut.

"I'm going to be honest with you, honey, like I've always been."

Mom's brand of honesty and truth could either be really hilarious or downright awkward. I had no idea which way she was going to go with this.

"You've been through things that no woman should ever have to go through. You've survived things that no one should ever have to face. You are strong. You have the real strength that's important. Up here." She tapped on her head and then her chest. "And here. You picked your life up and pieced it back together. I'm proud of you, honey, so damn proud."

The back of my eyes burned as I listened to her.

"But that doesn't mean you're seeing everything right. People are going to feel bad for you. I feel bad for you. It's human nature for others to feel that way, and I bet Cole does feel that way," she explained gently. "But that doesn't mean that's driving his actions. That doesn't mean he asked you out to dinner, drove you home, and stayed on your couch because he pities you or feels like he had to."

I stared at her.

"All I'm saying, maybe even asking, is that you judge him based on what he is doing," she finished. "Not on what you think he's doing. Okay?"

"Okay, Mom," I whispered.

Her smile reached her tired eyes. "Good to hear that." She rose. "Now I'm going up to bed. If you happen to hear anything about Angela, please let me know."

"I will."

Mom headed upstairs from the in-house stairs, and I double-checked the doors again. As I did so, something occurred to me. Heading back into the kitchen, I walked into the old room, and flipped on the overhead light. I walked over to the corkboard, searching out the keys until I found the one Mom had mentioned before.

Angela's house key.

Hers hung at the bottom, next to an extra set of keys to Mom's truck. Her key had one of those pink caps, and a black marker had etched *AR* on it. I reached out, running my fingers over the key, hoping that it would be reused again by Angela.

Sighing, I turned around, hit the light, and then entered the stairwell, making my way up to my apartment. Since it was almost ten, I washed my face and pulled my hair up in a bun. Then I changed into a pair of flannel pants that were nowhere near as sexy as the nightie I'd grabbed the night before.

My gaze zeroed in on the bed as I pulled a pale blue cami on. What Mom asked of me replayed over and over in my head.

Judge Cole on what he did, not on what I thought.

Such a simple idea, but it wasn't easy when I got caught up in my head, thinking the things that I thought.

I walked over to my bed and picked up my nightie, folding it before taking it back to the drawer. Dinner yesterday did feel like forever ago, and if I was being honest with myself, I'd freaked out with Cole when I started to think about the Groom.

I grabbed an oversized cardigan, slipped it on, and padded back out into the living room. I was about to pick up the remote when there was a knock on the outside door.

I spun around, my heart leaping into my chest. I could think of only one person who'd use that access this time at night. Gathering the sides of my sweater together, I darted over to the back door and flipped on the porch light before pulling the blinds aside.

It was him.

The leaping heart started pumping wicked fast in my chest as I let go of the blinds. With a shaky hand, I unlocked the door and opened it.

Cole stood outside. Our gazes met. He didn't say a word, and neither did I. *Judge him for what he has done.* I wasn't sure I was of the right mind to be judging anyone at the moment, but I also knew the answer to Mom's question, the one I said I didn't know.

I still cared about Cole.

I don't think I'd ever stopped caring for him, and I knew it sounded crazy, because there were ten years between us, but I believed that sometimes you cared so deeply about someone that no matter what happened, you never really stopped.

Because of that tiny truth I kept close to my heart, I stepped aside and let Cole in.

CHAPTER 13

COLE'S GAZE MOVED over me, from the top of my messy bun to the tips of my bare toes, and when his eyes finally made it back to mine, one side of his lips quirked up in his familiar half grin.

"Cute," he murmured, reaching down and unhooking the holster at his hip. It and the gun went onto the counter.

My hand flickered to my hair. "What is?"

"All of it." He closed the door behind him, and the click of the locks turning into place made me feel oddly nervous. "Though I did like what you were wearing last night. That was also very . . . cute."

Heat swept across my cheeks and filled my veins as I dropped my hand. "Let's not talk about that."

The kick to his lips spread to the other side as he tossed his keys on the kitchen island. "I'll try not to bring up the lace I could feel but couldn't see, but I won't make any promises."

The lace wasn't the only thing he'd felt. Clutching the sides of my cardigan, I wished it had buttons, because I didn't have a bra on underneath the cami, and I wasn't the kind of person who could get away with not wearing a bra. "Would you like something to drink?"

"Not that I'm complaining, but you're actually not going to ask why I'm here and demand that I leave?" he inquired, eyes gleaming in the light.

"Not yet," I replied, dipping my chin. "But I won't make any promises."

Cole's chuckle was deep and sexy.

The heat was now washing over my belly. "Why . . . are you here?"

"You forgot already? I told you my ass was going to be here until I get an alarm on this door and, come to think of it, your mother's. Didn't get a chance to talk to my buddy today, but I'll do that tomorrow."

Seconds away from pointing out I didn't need a person acting like a real, live, breathing security system, I stopped myself mainly because I wanted him here. I also seriously doubted he'd be here every night until an alarm was installed.

"So, what do you have to drink?" he asked.

"Not much." Pivoting on my bare feet, I walked over to the fridge. "I have some of my mom's sweet tea, a couple of bottles of water, and Diet Coke. No alcohol. Sorry. I haven't had a chance to run to the store yet."

"Tea works for me." He followed me into the narrow kitchen. "Got to work in the morning."

"Maybe you shouldn't be up late then," I said, grabbing the tea. I turned, sucking in a soft breath when I discovered he was right behind me. The kitchen was small, but not that small. His closeness made me nervous again in that weird way. Not a bad way. Not unpleasant. Just in a way that made me feel hyperaware of anything about him, because there was this innate knowledge that he didn't need to be this close. He was because he wanted to be.

I cleared my throat. "I mean, I figure you have a long commute."

"My schedule doesn't necessarily have a start time," he said, angling his body so that we were feet to boots. "I can take care of myself. I'm a big boy."

That he was.

Cole plucked the small pitcher of tea from my hands. "Where're your glasses?"

"The cabinet above the sink."

"Would you like some?"

"Sure," I whispered. How he ended up being the one to do the serving in my house I had no idea. He grabbed two glasses and got to pouring while I got busy watching the way his muscles moved under the henley. When he turned, handing me my glass, I averted my gaze, but not before I caught sight of his knowing smile. "So . . ." I drew the word out as I walked into the living room. "Is there any news on Angela?"

Cole brushed past me and made his way out to the living room. He sat on the couch. "Not a lot."

I followed him, then took a seat next to him. The couch wasn't a large one, so that left very little room between us. "But something?"

"While I was at the station with Ethan, one of the local detectives—Tyron Conrad—was able to get in touch with Angela's Wednesday-evening professor. She was in class. The professor said everything appeared normal with her, and he assumes that she left campus after the lecture." Pausing, he took a drink. "Ethan said he'd checked the campus in Hagerstown and didn't see her car. Tyron contacted the state police in Maryland, and they have her vehicle information. As far as I know, they were double checking just to make sure her vehicle isn't there."

I let that sink in as I sipped my tea. "If her vehicle isn't there, that means something happened to her on her way home or when she got home."

"Or she left after class and didn't tell anyone. I know that sounds unlikely but at this point, anything is possible." Leaning forward, he placed his glass on the coffee table. "What I'm about to tell you needs to stay between us," he explained, angling his body toward mine. "Okay?"

"Yeah. Of course."

He watched me for a moment. "Ethan said they had a fight while she was driving to class. He wasn't very open about what the fight was about, but they argued."

"That could be a good thing or a bad thing. I mean, she could've just needed time to get away, clear her mind. Completely irresponsible but that's better than any of the other options." I pressed my lips together. "That also means Ethan is probably a suspect?"

"It's really not anything personal against him. When anyone turns up missing, those who know the person are the first anyone is going to look at, especially if there was an argument," he explained. "A missing person's report was filed, and all nearby agencies have the description of her and her vehicle. Hopefully something will turn up."

"Hopefully," I murmured, lifting the glass to my lips. A tremble coursed down my arm. "Do you think that's what happened?"

"Honestly?" Reaching over, he took the glass from my hands. My eyes narrowed as he placed it on the coffee table beside his. He rose as he said, "Lived here my whole life, and the only time we had more than one woman disappear, it was because we had a serial killer on our hands."

My stomach churned at what he said and my pulse quickened because he was standing in front of me. "You think there's another serial killer?"

"I didn't say that. Could be two completely unrelated cases, but anything's possible."

"Anything—" I gasped as he knelt and wrapped his hands around my arms. "What are you doing?"

"Talking to you," he replied.

"This isn't talking—" Air whooshed out of me as he lifted me up. In one smooth action, he sat back down with me in his lap, my side pressed against his chest and my legs stretched out on the couch. Stunned, I was frozen stiff like a mannequin as I stared at him. We were face-to-face until he shifted me down a few inches so I was now at eye level with his throat. "This is *not* talking."

He grinned at me. "Yeah, it is. We're just talking very closely."

My mouth worked but no words came out for several seconds. I was surrounded by him, by his warmth and the citrusy scent of what was his aftershave or cologne. I was guessing it was his cologne, because as close as I was, I could tell he hadn't shaved in at least two days. "It's not—"

"It's totally necessary," he cut in, reading my mind. He circled one arm around my waist. "And you know what?"

I lifted my gaze to his. "What?"

"You haven't tried to get away."

Damn it. He was right. I was sitting all comfy in his lap. My nose scrunched. "Maybe because I realize it would be a fruitless endeavor."

"Uh-huh." His grin went up a notch, and it was nice when I wasn't sitting in his lap, and stunning when I was. "Back to what we were talking about. Anything is possible. We both know that, but I keep telling myself that two serial killers hitting up this same area seems improbable to me."

Worrying my lower lip, I lowered my gaze back down his throat. Jason had said the same thing, and it did seem improbable but it also wasn't impossible. No matter what, even if Angela showed up tomorrow, a woman was dead, and it was frightening.

"Hey." The hand on my hip squeezed, and I looked up to find him watching me. "What are you thinking?"

I let go of my lip. "I was thinking . . . that this is familiar. Like it was before, sitting around and hoping that someone was going to show up and be okay."

His hand left my hip and ran up my back. It was a comforting gesture. "Yeah," he murmured. "It is familiar."

As the seconds passed, my body relaxed without me having to force it. I was leaning into him instead of sitting stiffly. My hands slowly unclenched. Neither of us said anything for what felt like a long time, and the quiet wasn't uncomfortable. There was something actually peaceful about it, and I imagined if I laid my head on his shoulder, it would be bliss.

Then Cole broke the silence with something that was shattering in many different ways. "I do feel bad about what happened to you."

My head whipped around. "What?" I started to scoot off.

Cole's arm flexed around my waist and his other hand came down on my hip. "Let me explain, okay?"

Instinct demanded that I break his hold, but I remembered what my mother had said earlier, and truthfully, if I didn't want to hear him out, why did I let him in my apartment?

Why was I sitting in his embrace?

I drew in a shallow breath. "Okay."

His eyes searched mine. "I do . . . I do feel bad. I don't know everything that happened to you." He splayed his hand along the center of my back when I tensed. "I only know what I learned about the other cases, heard about you, and what I suspected. I don't need to know every detail to feel horrible for what was done to you."

I closed my eyes.

"And I struggled with guilt for a long time over that night. Still do," he admitted quietly, and my eyes flew open. He continued before I could speak. "I'm also angry. When you disappeared, and damn,

Sasha, we knew almost immediately that the Groom had you, I never felt such rage and helplessness."

A knot formed in my throat, choking and bitter. "Cole . . ."

"I wanted to kill him myself," he said, voice razor-sharp. "I swear to God, I would've if I could've gotten my hands on him. I would've torn that son of a bitch apart, skin and bone, because of what I knew he'd done." The hand on my hip lifted to my cheek. "For what he took from you."

Oh God, I couldn't look away and I couldn't stop him from saying what he was.

"For what he took from me," he added, his cool blue eyes latched onto mine. "So, yeah, I feel bad and I still feel guilty at times, and I sure as fuck still want to murder that dead SOB, but what I feel about that night and how I feel about what happened to you is not why my ass is sitting here with you in my arms. It's not why the damn moment I heard you were back in town, I got my ass over here as soon as I could."

The knot in my throat was expanding, threatening to claw its way up.

Cole's thumb smoothed over my jaw as he said, "None of that is why I had you over for dinner, and I'm going to let you in on a little secret here. While I am worried about you being here unprotected, I'm also using that fact to my advantage. It's a damn good excuse to get you to spend time with me that I'm not going to waste."

I stared at him, my lips parted on a soft inhale. I heard what he was saying and I got it, but I . . . I couldn't believe it. Or maybe I wasn't ready to believe it. "Why?"

His brows flew up. "Why?" he repeated with a slight shake of his head. "You know, I was going to take this slow with you. Get comfortable with each other again, however long that takes. Maybe make it to one more date."

Date? Dinner at his place *was* a date?

Everyone else was right.

As usual.

"I know I have to take it slow with you," he continued, his blue eyes vibrant behind his thick lashes. He stared at me more and then said, "Fuck it."

Cole slid his hand into my hair, gathering it in his fingers as he tilted my chin back. A heartbeat passed and then his mouth was on mine.

CHAPTER 14

COLE WAS KISSING ME.

For a handful of seconds, I was shocked and completely unprepared, but that surprise quickly faded into the background. In an instant, I wasn't thinking of anything other than him and what was happening at this very moment.

Every part of my being focused on the arm at my back and the hand in my hair, and on his lips against mine. Every sense became hyperaware of how soft and yet firm his lips were. This kiss was sweet and all too brief.

He lifted his mouth just enough that when he spoke, his lips brushed mine. "Does that kiss tell you that I pity you?"

"No," I whispered, eyes closed. A shiver started, spreading out of control.

"Good." His voice was even raspier. "Because that is the last thing I'm feeling right now."

My pulse was pounding throughout my body,

heavier and faster in certain points. My hands were still in my lap, but they itched to touch him. Maybe this was too soon, too quick, but I could remember the last time I kissed someone. Eight months ago maybe? His name was Greg. We'd met at a charity function Mr. Berg was hosting. I remembered Greg kissing me, but I couldn't recall a single detail other than that. But this? This soft brush of Cole's lips would be something I knew I would never forget, and I . . . I wanted more.

I needed more.

Giving in to the rising tide of sensations, I unfolded my arms and lifted my hands, placing them on his chest as I leaned in and closed the tiny distance between our mouths. I slid my hands to his shoulders and my fingers dug in, curling around his shirt.

I kissed Cole back.

He drew me tight against his hard chest and stomach, and the kiss . . . there was nothing brief or soft about it this time.

Cole tasted amazing, and everywhere our bodies met, heat flowed out, invading my muscles and veins. A deep, rumbling sound radiated out from the back of his throat and felt wonderful against my chest. The tips of my breasts tingled, and the kiss went deeper. My lips parted, and he kissed me like . . . like he never expected that he would do it again. And I might've dreamt and fantasized this, but I never expected it to happen.

The hand at my back slipped to my hip and his hold tightened. I shifted, wanting to get closer, and he seemed to be of the same mind, because at the same time I squirmed, he dropped both hands to my hips. He lifted as I moved, and then I was straddling him, a knee planted into the couch on either side of him. There wasn't a break in kissing. My hands were sliding, my fingers sifting through the silky strands of his hair.

A moan curled its way out of my throat as his hips lined up with mine. Holy wow. I could feel *him* and that definitely was not pity. That was a whole lot of arousal. My heart rate sped up, and I melted into him, into the kiss.

"Fucking hell," he groaned against my mouth. Both of us were breathing heavy when we came up for air. "I forgot this."

My thoughts were spinning as I opened my eyes. "Forgot what?"

"How this felt." He slid his other hand down my throat to the nape of my neck as his hips jerked under mine. "How *you* felt."

Oh my God.

He rested his forehead against mine. "How one fucking kiss makes me feel like a sixteen-year-old boy who's never even been close to a girl."

Oh. My. God.

"Did you?" he asked after a moment. "Did you forget?"

My eyes fluttered shut. "No," I admitted. "I never forgot."

The hand along the back of my neck clenched. "Does it make me an ass to admit I'm glad to hear that?"

I grinned. "I don't think so."

His head tilted slightly and he kissed the corner

of my mouth. "I'm going to be up front with you. Okay?"

Kissing me seemed really up front, I thought, but I nodded anyway.

"I told you that the moment Derek said you were here, I didn't think twice. I had to see you. Heading here, I honestly don't remember what I was thinking." He tipped his head in the other direction and kissed the other corner of my lip. "I didn't want that side of your lip to get jealous."

I laughed, feeling a hundred pounds lighter.

His lips curved into a grin. "When I got to the inn and I saw you . . . well, some things about my life suddenly made real fucking sense to me."

And that made absolutely no sense to me.

Cole dragged his hand down the center of my back, causing me to shiver. He drew away and placed his hands on my hips again. Without warning, I was on my back and he was hovering above me, one hand by my waist, an elbow pressing into the cushion by my head.

Stunned at his strength, my hands went to his chest. I didn't push him away. "What . . . what made sense to you?" I asked.

He lowered his head instead of answering, and his mouth moved over mine, coasting softly until he urged my lips open. His tongue touched mine, and the kiss deepened. It was different like this, with me on my back and him above me. He shifted his body down again, slowly, and only until I could feel a little of his weight, a little of him.

I was kissing him back, and I wanted more. Fingers balling into his shirt, I tried to pull him down, but he resisted, controlling how much he was giving me. "Cole," I whispered, feeling like I was on fire, burning from the inside in the most delicious way. It had been a long time since I felt this way. Too long.

"We have ten years' worth of stuff to talk about," he said against my mouth. "There's still a lot we need to say."

"I know." I wanted him closer, so I curled my left leg around him. Biting down on my lip, I lifted my hips just the slightest, pressing into his. He made that sound again and dropped his head to my neck.

Cole kissed me there, just below my pulse. "Still trying to take this slow, babe. That's the smart thing to do."

I dragged my hands up to his shoulders, restless. "I . . . I can do this."

A moment passed and Cole lifted his head. Heated blue eyes met mine. Warmth invaded my cheeks. "I've had sex since . . . since then," I told him. I'd been a virgin when the Groom came into my life. I hadn't been afterward, and it took years with lots of therapy and failed dates for me to go there with my body and to trust another person in that way, but I had. "I'm not scared . . . of sex."

"Babe," he murmured, kissing me softly. "I'm relieved to hear that you've moved on in that way, but I still don't want to rush it."

"I appreciate that, but . . ."

Those remarkable eyes were fixed on my mouth, and I liked that. A lot. Heat was pounding through my veins, and I wanted to rush things, because I knew there wasn't always a next time. There wasn't always a promise of tomorrow, and we were two adults who wanted what we wanted.

Instead of speaking, I cupped his cheeks and drew his mouth back to mine. This time when I kissed him, I threw everything I wanted into the kiss, and I curled my leg around his once more, lifting my hips to his. *Oh*, he wanted this as badly as I did. Cole made that sound again, and things . . . well, they spiraled beautifully out of control.

He glided his hand down my throat and over my shoulder, brushing the cardigan aside, and heady awareness followed. I gasped into his mouth as his palm coasted over the top of my breast. The material was so thin it was like there was nothing between our flesh. My nipple pebbled, and he groaned. Air hitched in my throat, and every cell in my body waited. He didn't let me down.

Cole slipped his hand under the cami, and I jerked. His fingers skimmed the side of my stomach, and my eyes flew open as a tiny bit of heat faded. He was near . . . a scar—a scar that had long since healed, but was still raised and rough, and weirdly sensitive. But he didn't touch it. Oh no, those fingers found the tip of my aching breast as his kiss took on a different strength, becoming demanding. He caught my lower lip, and I let out a little breathless moan. Everything about him invaded me— the taste, his smell, the way he felt. The liquid fire burning in my core was too potent to ignore, and I shivered when he spoke in a deep, rumbling voice.

"What do you want, Sasha?"

Him. Everything. "Touch . . . touch me."

He moaned. "I can do that, baby. I can do that."

And he did.

His hand left the tip of my breast, deftly slipping under the hem of my bottoms and the band of my panties. He lifted up slightly, supporting his weight on his left arm. His eyes were on fire. "Open your legs for me."

Doing as he asked, I held my breath as his fingers made their way over the mound between my legs. My heart was in my throat as he dipped his chin, watching his hand under my clothes. A finger skimmed, barely touching me, but my entire body jolted with sensation.

"Damn," he said as he gently explored, and I breathed like I'd just run the entire flight of stairs in the inn. "I want to see you, all of you, but we don't have time for that."

"We don't?" I whispered, hips twitching.

"Oh no." Thick lashes lifted as his thumb pressed against the little bundle of nerves, causing me to whimper. "You're too ready to wait for all of that."

He then increased the pressure until my hips were moving, rocking against his hand. A fierce heat rose, building and building until I feared I'd combust right here on the couch. He ran a finger down into the gathering wetness. Tension coiled as I pressed into his hand and then his finger slipped inside.

"Oh God." My fingers tightened around his shirt, bunching the material. "Cole . . ."

"Damn," he grunted out again. "Love the way you say my name."

There was this rhythm he started, and it was perfect, and too much, and not enough all at the same time. My hips thrust up, meeting his hand as my body twisted with sharp spikes of pleasure. Another finger slipped in, and I cried out, a fine tremor coursing throughout me.

I wanted to feel him, the hard planes of his chest and stomach, but all I could do was hold on to him as his name became a plea. The pounding tension inside me expanded as his fingers pumped. Groaning, Cole pressed his erection against the side of my hip and swirled his thumb in the right way, in the right place. The whirling force of the orgasm hit me hard, crashing over me. Crying out, I tensed as my back bowed. Spasms racked my body, seeming to go on forever.

"That was beautiful," he murmured against my mouth, easing his hand out of my bottoms.

"I think that was supposed to be . . . my line." My voice caught as a tight aftershock hit me. This wasn't the first time I'd had an orgasm, but damn, it blew every one of them away.

"Mmm." He kissed me.

My heart was starting to slow a little, but I wanted to give him what he gave me. I lowered my hand. My fingers brushed his belt when he reached down and gently grasped my wrist, lifting my hand back to his chest.

"You don't have to do that," he said, his eyes taking on a sexy, hooded quality.

"But I want to."

He shuddered at my words. "Sasha."

"And what you did was just . . . it was amazing." Those were the truest words I'd spoken. "I want to make you feel that way."

Cole shifted slightly. "Babe, watching you come on my fingers was enough for now. Hell." His lips brushed mine once more. "I was really trying to go slow here."

"I like our pacing."

"Yeah." His hand coasted over my breast on the way up to my cheek. "Yeah, me too."

Something in my chest swelled, and it felt a lot like my heart. I was still breathing heavy, but my pulse was starting to slow down. I closed my eyes as I loosened my death grip on his shirt. "Do you . . . want to play tit for tat now?"

He chuckled in the way that made me shiver. "I want to kiss you again. I want to peel those pants off you and get in between those thighs with more than my hand," he said, voice low, and a fire swept through my veins as he spoke. "I remember kissing you. I remember holding you in my arms. I remember touching you that one time." He dropped his forehead to mine. "You remember that?"

"Yeah," I whispered. How could I forget? It had been the first time I'd gone to his apartment he shared with another deputy. We'd hung out in his room, watched a movie, and one thing led to another. His hand had worked its way inside my pants and mine had done the same thing.

It had been as amazing as tonight.

"Never got to feel you like I want to though." He tilted his head, and his nose glided over mine. "Never got to know how you taste. So, that's what I really want to do."

I bit down on my lip to stop from moaning. At the moment, I liked the idea of him discovering all those things. *Really* liked the idea, and maybe slowing down was smart. Both of us obviously were feeling something, and going too fast, jumping back into this or into something we hadn't shared in our past, could blow up in our faces.

My fingers splayed across his chest. "But you're not going to," I said, opening my eyes. I looked up at him, and I took a deep breath, really let myself be right where I was, and where I was gave me one of the best views of a lifetime. His handsome face open and warm, within grasp. And I could touch him, because he was actually here and this wasn't some fantasy I'd concocted over the years, so I touched him. I lifted a hand from his chest and ran the tips of my fingers over his cheek, memorizing the feel of the short, rough stubble. "So we should . . . talk more then."

A half smile appeared. "I don't think tit for tat is going to cover it."

My heart fluttered when he turned his cheek and kissed my fingertips. That was new, something he hadn't done in the past. "Probably not."

"But it's late, and I do have to get up early to head into Baltimore." Thick lashes lowered, shielding his eyes. "I'm not going to get back until late tomorrow, but do you think you can manage to do dinner Saturday night?"

Doing dinner again when Angela was missing didn't seem right, but if I'd learned anything from my past, it was that life doesn't pause, no matter what terrible or even wonderful things are happening. Life keeps ticking on. So I nodded.

"Perfect." Dipping his head, he kissed me, and

then he was sitting up between my legs. Catching my hands, he pulled me up into the sitting position. "You want me to cook or are you up to going out?"

I was a little dazed, so it took me a few moments to gather my thoughts. My first response was to say he could cook, but that was also another way I'd be hiding. "We can go out. It'll have to be later," I said before I changed my mind. "After I help Mom with dinner service."

Cole smiled at me. "That works for me."

Straightening my sweater, I managed to get my feet on the floor. I stood, pressing my fingers to my still-tingling lips. I turned, discovering that he was watching me, still grinning. Flushing and feeling like I was almost a decade younger, I dropped my hand. "Is there anything I can get for you? A heavier blanket or . . ." Why was I making him sleep on this couch? It was a nice, comfy couch, but he was a long guy and the fact he'd slept on it last night was insane. Two nights in a row was unnecessary.

"I'm fine, babe."

My mouth dried as I stared at him. "You can . . . sleep with me."

His brows flew up. "I—"

"Not have sex with me. But sleep with me." I ignored the burning flush that was racing down my throat. "The bed is big enough. You saw that last night."

"Yeah." His voice did that dropping thing that caused my belly to do the same. "Yeah. I saw that."

My shoulders rose in a deep breath. "If you're insistent upon staying here, there's no reason you should sleep on the couch."

He shifted. "I can think of several good reasons why I shouldn't get in that bed with you."

Air caught in my throat and that warmth turned heavier, spreading out across my chest. I tugged the ends of the cardigan together. "We're both adults. We can sleep in the same bed and behave ourselves."

"You have a lot of faith in us."

I narrowed my eyes. "It's not like we're going to slip and fall on one another."

He smirked. "I do hate when that happens."

I rolled my eyes, but my lips twitched. "Look, the option is there. I can handle it. If you discover that you have the willpower, the door will be unlocked."

Cole's head cocked to the side, and I held his gaze for a few moments before I murmured goodnight and then all but dashed into the bathroom. He was still out in the living room when I closed my bedroom door.

He wasn't going to come in here.

A weird mixture of disappointment and relief swirled inside me as I stripped off my sweater and climbed into bed. Stretching out, I started to turn off the nightstand lamp. My bedroom door opened and Cole came in. I froze.

"This is probably a bad idea," he said, walking to the other side of the bed. "Or maybe I'll surprise myself." His gaze flickered over to me. "You're not wearing that nightie, so that's a plus on the whole behaving-myself side."

I might've stopped breathing.

Cole placed his gun on the other nightstand as he toed off his boots. "But you're right. Sleeping on that couch sucks and this bed looks amazing."

"It is," I murmured.

"Mainly because you're in it," he added, reaching back to the nape of his neck with one hand. He pulled his shirt over his head and then off. He tossed it to the bench in front of the bed.

And I really did stop breathing for a little bit then.

It had been a long time since I'd seen him shirtless and even though I could feel all the gloriousness under his shirt, it was nothing like seeing it for real. His pecs were defined, as were his abs. He wasn't overly muscular. He had the lean, cut body of a runner. He also had those indents on either side of his hips.

His hands went to the button on his jeans. There was a noticeable bulge there. One I'd felt earlier. "You keep staring at me like that and every good intention I have is going to go out the damn window."

Cheeks flushing, I twisted onto my side, away from him, and squeezed my eyes shut. Pants hit the floor. A second later, the bed dipped and the covers shifted. Then he rolled, reaching over me. My eyes flew open. "What are you doing?"

"Turning off the light," he answered, and did just that. The room plunged into darkness. He didn't move away though. I could tell he was raised on one elbow. His hand found my blanket-covered hip. "Everything is locked up."

My heart was pounding. "Thank you."

"I might be gone before you get up."

"I . . . don't know about that," I said, turning my head to look over my shoulder. I could only make out an outline of his face. "I don't sleep well."

The hand above my hip moved a little. "I know."

Obviously, he remembered the nightmare from last night. Even then, he knew better. "Maybe tonight will be different."

I wasn't so sure of that, for different reasons than normal, but I stayed quiet as Cole settled in behind me. Like right behind me. The hand at my hip slid forward, over my stomach, and then he hauled me back against his chest.

Oh gosh.

We hadn't done this before. And I hadn't done it with anyone that I . . . that I had wanted to. The men I'd been intimate with never stayed the night. Never. This was new. I was *cuddling*. Or was it spooning? His leg moved against the back of mine, and then shifted. His hips pressed into my behind. Oh man. He was still . . . aroused. So was I.

"I . . ."

"What, babe?" he murmured.

I wet my lower lip. "I've never done this before. I mean, not with anyone I chose to be with."

Cole didn't respond for a long moment and then I felt him brush my hair off my shoulder. His lips pressed against the skin there.

"It's nice," I admitted, and maybe I did because it was dark and we couldn't see each other.

His arm tightened. "Yeah. Yeah, it's nice."

I let out a shaky breath. "And I'm sorry about freaking out on you yesterday at dinner."

"You don't need to apologize." He shifted, easing his leg between mine.

"I do. I was . . . I don't even know what I was doing." I paused. "I ruined dinner."

"Babe . . ."

"I did," I whispered.

His lips coasted over my shoulder again. "You didn't ruin dinner. A dead deer in the truck did."

My lips kicked up at the corners. "Good point."

"I'm always right." His voice sounded heavier. "I know there's been a lot of time since we've been apart, but how could you forget that?"

I rolled my eyes. "Whatever."

He chuckled deeply. "You'll start remembering that soon enough."

In the dark, I didn't fight the smile. It spread across my face. Several moments passed. "Cole?"

"Mmm?" he muttered.

I could tell he was half asleep. "Nothing."

"What?" His arm squeezed my waist. "What, Sasha?"

"When I woke up this morning, I never thought . . . I didn't think this would happen," I said. "But I'm glad it is happening."

That got me another arm squeeze. "Me too."

After that, I stayed silent, and the warmth of his front against my back had the strangest effect on me. As cliché as it sounded, as completely unbelievable, I was out before I knew it, falling asleep in Cole's arms for the first time.

COLE WAS UP and gone before I woke up, proving that he had been right about today being different. And today did feel different. It wasn't that my head was in the clouds or that I forgot everything else that was going on, but by Friday afternoon, I realized that maybe the difference was because I was letting Cole in, and it wasn't so much about him, but more about the act itself.

I was opening up.

And that meant I was living.

I just hoped that somewhere, Angela was doing the same.

We had guests checking in, the first a young couple who appeared to be really into the history of the Scarlet Wench and the surrounding area. They were adorable—adorably nerdy. As I helped them carry their bags upstairs, I gave them directions to the nearby battlefield. They'd booked one of the suites.

"This room is gorgeous." Mrs. Ritchie dropped her bag on the four-poster queen-size bed. She looked around the room. "It's like stepping back in time."

That's one way of putting it, I thought as I reached into the pocket of my jeans. "Ah, I forgot to grab an extra key for you," I said. They'd requested two at check-in. "I'll go grab that key for you now."

"Can you leave it at the desk?" Mr. Ritchie asked, his eyes on his wife. "We may be . . . a little busy for a while."

Oh dear.

His wife giggled.

I smiled as I walked back toward the door. "I can hold it at the desk for you." I stepped out into the hallway, closing the door behind me. "Have fun."

Mrs. Ritchie's giggle turned into a happy squeal, and I turned away from the door, walking toward the end of the hall at the back of the inn for the staff staircase. I was going to have to move my laptop out to the front desk and work from there since I couldn't just leave their key there.

Opening the door, I entered the narrow, much cooler staircase. It smelled like mothballs no matter how many times anyone sprayed air freshener in here, and it creeped me out. The smell was most likely because the stairs continued all the way to the cellar. I hurried down, my hand trailing along the old wooden rail. Rounding the second-floor landing, I took the steps two at a time and reached for the door at the same time it swung open.

I couldn't move back quick enough.

The brass handle caught me in the stomach, the force knocking me back. My arms flailed out as I let out a surprised shriek. All I saw was a white shirt with a logo on it that was vaguely familiar and a black baseball cap with the same emblem—a gray *something*. I grabbed for the railing, my fingers slipping around the wood, catching myself before I tumbled down the set leading to the cellar.

"Shit," a man grunted at the same second a loud crack thundered through the narrow landing. For a horrified moment I realized it was the railing breaking, giving way under my weight.

And then I was falling backward into the air.

CHAPTER 15

THE FALL WAS fast and brutal, all happening so quick. One minute there was nothing behind me and then I was slamming into the hard, uneven floor. I cried out sharply as pain exploded and the air punched out of me.

Agony flared along the side of my head and arced across my left shoulder, deafening the sound of approaching footsteps. Confusion beat at me. I tried to sit up—-I knew I needed to get up—but my stomach churned viciously. My arms . . . they didn't seem to work. They were useless at my sides.

Suddenly, a hazy image of a man formed, bending over me. I saw the black baseball cap again. I squinted, because I saw two hats. Two men?

I tried to get my mouth to work, to ask for help.

"*Shit*," he grunted, and there was a creaking sound of old hinges, and a rich, earthy scent surrounded me.

Then there was nothing.

Skin damp and chilled, my knees press into the hard, cold floor. He's behind me, sitting on the edge of the bed, combing my wet hair. I want to vomit, but my stomach is empty and my sides already hurt too much. I don't want him touching me. I don't want to listen to him talk as if I want to be here.

The comb stills, and I sense the change in him. He stiffens. My fingers curl inward, blunt nails digging into my palms.

"Don't move," he says, rising and stepping around me. He leaves the room, and I hear the door lock in place.

I don't move.

I remain on my knees, shivering and straining to hear anything, but there's nothing but the muted sound of cows. If I listen hard enough, I will hear a horse.

A door slams shut somewhere.

My chest aches and the shivers turn into trembles, but I don't move. I don't dare move. Heavy footsteps thunder. Something crashes. He's in a mood again. Oh God, he's in a mood, and I'm going to die—no.

No, this isn't real anymore. This is a nightmare. Wake up. Wake up!

I woke up.

"I should've gotten those railings fixed a long time ago." Mom fretted, pacing in front of the small window like a nervous bird. "You could've cracked your head open."

Shifting my gaze to the dull drop ceilings, I slowly turned my head to the left. A dull spike of pain flared. "My skull is too thick for that."

The way-too-young-looking doctor at the foot of

the bed smiled as she scribbled in my chart. "You're actually lucky."

"That means I get to go home?"

"No." She hooked the chart at the end of the bed and slipped her pen into the front pocket of her lab coat. "You're here for the night."

Frustration rose. "But—"

"You lost consciousness, and even though you currently don't have signs of a serious concussion, we want to monitor you for the next twenty-four hours just to make sure everything is okay." She moved over to the pole where what I felt was a very unnecessary IV bag was hooked up. "If everything checks out fine in the morning, you'll be free to go home."

"Sorry." Mom drifted to the bed and started fiddling with the thin blanket draped over my legs. "Sasha isn't very good with the whole hospital thing."

"Not many people are." Her cool fingers checked the IV as her smile turned absent. "The nurses will be in here in about thirty minutes to check on you. If you need anything, you know where the call button is." The doctor turned as the curtain parted. "Perfect timing."

My gaze flickered over her shoulder, and I wanted to sink through the bed when I saw who was parting the sea-green curtain.

Officer Derek Bradshaw, of course. He must be the only cop on duty in the entire world.

His brow rose as he stepped around the doctor. "Small world," he murmured, approaching the bed. "Cole know about this?"

I squeezed my eyes shut briefly. "Haven't exactly

had the chance to fill him in," I said. "He's at work. I don't want—"

"You're in the hospital. He's going to want to know and that's not a bother to him. Ever." He glanced over at my mom. "What's going on?"

"A man pushed her down the steps of the staff staircase," Mom answered. "She almost fell *through* the cellar door! God knows how long she would've lain there if poor old Daphne hadn't found her. Nearly gave her a heart attack. Thought I was going to have to call two ambulances."

His gaze sharpened.

"That's not exactly what happened." I rose onto my elbows, but a dull thump spiked along my temples, so I decided almost at once that lying on my back was A-okay. "I mean, the door opened quickly and I couldn't move out of the way. That's what technically knocked me down the steps."

Officer Bradshaw frowned as his shoulder radio crackled. "I need some clarification on this. Were you pushed or was it an accident?"

"Don't downplay the situation," Mom warned as she dropped into the really uncomfortable chair next to the bed. "This is serious."

"She's right, Sasha." Officer Bradshaw shifted closer. "I need to know exactly what happened."

Biting on my lip, I let out a ragged sigh. "I was coming downstairs to get the Ritchies their extra key, and when I reached the main-floor landing, the door to the old kitchen swung open so fast I didn't get a chance to move out of the way. The doorknob caught me in the stomach." Using the IV hand, I gestured at my stomach. "I fell back and my foot slipped on the step. I grabbed the railing to steady myself and it broke. That was how I fell."

"Should've gotten the railing fixed," Mom muttered.

"Mom," I sighed.

"So you weren't pushed?" Derek asked.

I shook my head and winced. "No. I think it was an accident. He cursed twice, like out of surprise, but . . ."

Mom clucked her tongue. "But if it were a true accident, he would've stayed with you or gotten help. He wouldn't have just left you lying there."

There was that.

"We also don't know who the man was," Mom continued. "It wasn't James, and he's the only man who has any business being back in the old part of the kitchen."

There was also that. "I don't *think* I know who he was," I clarified. "I didn't exactly see him. Like I said, it happened so fast, all I caught a glimpse of was a white shirt and a black baseball cap. There was something on it. A gray emblem of some sort." My brows knitted together. "And I think he was white—no, I'm sure he was white. Other than that, that's all I saw of him."

Derek had pulled out that notebook of his and was scribbling away again. "And it's not possible that it was a guest who checked in?"

"The only male guest who was in was Mr. Ritchie," I explained, swallowing as I lifted my hand and gingerly touched the side of my head. There was a nice little knot there. "There was no way he made it downstairs."

"Anyone else who could've been in the inn?" he asked.

Mom answered, "No."

I shifted slowly as I thought back to the hazy moments after I hit the floor. "I think . . . I'm not sure about this, but I think he stepped over me before I passed out. I thought I heard a door open behind me—the main cellar door."

"You think he went out through the cellar and not back out the other way?" Derek asked, looking over at my mom. "Can you get out of the inn from the cellar?"

Mom glanced at the ceiling, her nose scrunching. "There used to be a tunnel that ran out to the old family cemetery—the one that's way at the end of the property."

The old creepy cemetery that used to be overgrown until my father cleared it out while I was in middle school. The team that did the maintenance on the yard also took care of the cemetery.

"Those tunnels, they were used to get people in and out of the house when it was used as a part of the Underground Railroad," Mom explained. "But my husband closed off that tunnel years ago."

"Are you sure about that?" he asked.

"Well, of course . . ." Her nose scrunched again. "I haven't been out to the cemetery in a long time, but I can't imagine how the tunnel would've reopened."

His familiar eyes came back to me. "I want to check that out. How can I find the entrance?"

"Look for the creepiest thing in the entire cemetery and you'll find it," I said, and he grinned. "It's in the mausoleum. Looks like a cellar door, but that's what Dad had bricked up, right, Mom?"

She nodded. "You just head out the back of the inn, keep walking past the alley, and you'll hit the cemetery."

"Is there any reason why either of you think someone would be in the inn who shouldn't be there?"

I looked over at Mom. She frowned. "Other than someone getting in there to steal something, no."

Derek's gaze held mine. He didn't say anything, but my stomach started churning. "Mom? Can you see if I can have something to drink? Like a soda?"

"Of course, honey." She was already on her feet. Leaning over, she brushed her lips across my forehead. "It may take a few minutes. I'm also going to check in with Daphne. She can handle things, but I don't want her stressing out."

"Okay, Mom." I smiled. Once she was gone and the curtain stilled behind her, I turned my head toward Derek. "Did . . . did you talk to Cole?"

"I talk to Cole a lot." Looking behind him, he grabbed the only other chair and dragged it over. He sat on the edge. "I know he's been spending time with you. And I know about the issue with the truck."

My chest rose with an unsteady breath. "I . . . I don't know why someone was in the inn. I don't know why the thing with the deer happened or with my car." I took another deep breath. "Has there been any news on Angela?"

Derek shook his head after a moment. "I'm going to check out the tunnel, make sure it's still blocked.

Whoever was in that stairwell could've gone back out the normal way. I'll head over there now to check it out."

"Okay," I whispered, shifting my gaze to the dull ceiling.

He reached over, finding my hand. "You got your cellphone here?"

"I don't think so." I'd been kind of out of it after Daphne started shrieking and I'd barely managed to climb the steps to the old kitchen without vomiting. Everything had been funhouse hazy from that point to when the EMTs arrived and brought me here. I had no idea if my mom had grabbed my purse or cell.

"I'm going to call Cole." When I opened my mouth, he squeezed my hand gently. "He needs to know you're in the hospital and that you're okay before someone else gets part of that info to him."

"Oh, all right," I murmured. "Please make sure he's not worried. I don't want him to do that when I'm okay."

Derek rose. "You fell down the stairs. Accident or not, you could've been seriously injured and you are hurt. Being alive doesn't always mean you're okay."

I didn't know how to respond to that, so I said nothing. Derek left. Mom hadn't returned yet, so I closed my eyes, and I tried to figure out what the hell had happened.

It was quite probable that someone got into the inn through either the front door or the back entrance to look for money or items to pawn. This county had a major drug problem, but on the flip side, nothing like this had happened before and the drug problem around here, all the thefts and robberies, weren't anything new.

But what was new was me.

I'd only been home for one week.

CHAPTER 16

EYES FLUTTERING OPEN, it took a couple of moments for my brain to catch up to what my eyes were seeing. I was staring at the hospital ceiling and my mouth was still incredibly dry. What was it about hospitals that always made you feel like your throat had turned into the Sahara Desert? During my only other much longer hospital stay, it had been the same every time I woke up. Strange.

I inhaled, expecting the bitter and weird scent, a mixture of cleaning products and sickness of the hospital, but I caught a clean, citrusy scent that so did not belong anywhere in a hospital. My heart skipped, and I shifted my gaze to the left.

And I fell in love.

Right then and there.

I fell in love.

Sounded absolutely crazy and some might believe it was the pain meds I'd been given after Derek had left, but I knew the swelling in my chest, much like an overinflated balloon, was not a result of whatever it was the nurse had shot into my IV. It wasn't the much-needed nap I'd gotten after Miranda and Jason had visited. As soon as my eyes settled on Cole, I knew what I was feeling was real, and the intensity of that swelling brought tears to the back of my throat.

Truthfully, I'd fallen in love with him ten years ago and never fallen out of it.

Cole was sitting in the narrow, uncomfortable hospital chair. His feet were propped up on the edge of my bed. He had on dark trousers again. Work pants, I guessed. He had a black leather jacket, a dress shirt underneath. One arm was folded across his lower stomach; the other was jabbed into the arm of the chair, and his chin was resting in his open palm. The position he was in had to be uncomfortable, and I had no idea how long he'd been there, but the sky was dark outside the small square window, and the hospital, other than the beeps and clicks, was relatively quiet. His hair was rumpled, like he'd dragged his fingers through it many times. Cole, even with his long legs up on the bed, was cramped in that chair.

And he was the most beautiful thing I'd seen.

He didn't have to be here. Though I wasn't surprised that he was, since I knew Derek called him, but he didn't have to do this, and in that moment, everything he had been doing really hit me. It had started to make sense after talking with my mother, but now I truly realized that he really wasn't doing any of this because he felt like he had to. It was always because he wanted to.

Apparently it took a fall down a set of stairs to see things clearly.

I inhaled a ragged breath, and Cole's eyes snapped open. Our gazes connected, and a moment passed before he straightened, dragging his feet off the bed. They hit the floor with a heavy thump.

"Hey," he said, voice rough with sleep as he leaned forward.

"Hi," I whispered back.

A half grin appeared. "How you feeling?"

"Perfect."

That grin spread as he caught a strand of my hair and carefully tucked it behind my ear. "You're in the hospital after hitting your head. How is that perfect?"

"You're here," I admitted in the same whisper.

His brows flew up and then everything about his gaze softened. The hand dropped to my cheek and his thumb swept along my jaw. "Is this a drugged-up Sasha talking? Because I kind of like her."

I laughed, ignoring the dull flare of pain. "I'm not that drugged up."

"Yeah?"

"Yeah."

His gaze coasted over my upturned face. "Want something to drink? They have some water in here."

When I said yes, he got to pouring me some into a plastic cup while I figured out how to get the bed into a somewhat sitting position so I didn't spill water down my front. He handed it over, and the cool liquid soothed the dryness in my throat. I started to gulp it down, but he caught my wrist, slowing me down.

"You might want to take that easy," he said.

He was probably right. I lowered the cup to my lap. "What time is it?"

Glancing down at his watch, he said, "A little after midnight."

My eyes widened. "How are you in here?"

He lifted his gaze to mine and raised an eyebrow. "Flashing an FBI badge has its benefits. Plus my charming smile goes a long way." He grinned. "And nothing was keeping me out of this room."

My heart did a little tap dance.

Cole got closer and lowered his head, brushing his lips along my forehead. I closed my eyes at the sweet gesture. "Terrified."

My brows snapped together. "What?"

"I was scared as hell when Derek called and said you were in the hospital," he explained, pulling back just enough that I could see his face. "Even when he said you were going to be okay, even after he explained what happened, still terrified. Was the whole way here."

"Cole . . ."

"Had to see for myself that you were okay." His thumb made another swipe, this time below my lip, sending a shiver down my spine. "Don't like seeing you here."

"Don't like being here," I admitted, finishing off my water.

His eyes searched mine as he took the empty cup and placed it on the little tray by the bed. "Guess it's a good thing I didn't see you in here last time."

Last time I'd looked a mess. Blackened eyes. Shattered jaw. Bruises in places I didn't even know could bruise. And then there were the bandages over my stomach and chest.

Cole picked up my hand, threading his fingers through mine. The hospital bracelet dangled. "Derek told me what went down."

A cold draft moved through me. "Did he find anything out?"

His lashes lowered, and a moment passed before he said, "How about we talk about this tomorrow. It's late. You need your rest—"

"He found something, didn't he?" My fingers tightened around his. "I want to know."

A muscle flickered along his jaw, and for a moment, I thought he wasn't going to answer. "He checked out the inn twice. Came back when your mom returned just to make sure nothing was taken. Your mom didn't find anything missing."

Not that I expected anyone would.

"When he went there the first time," he continued, "he checked out the old entrance to the tunnel. The bricks were down."

I sucked in air. "Really?"

He nodded. "The thing is, he doesn't know if the bricks came down naturally or not. Your dad put them up there, right?"

"Yeah. It was a long time ago."

"Could've fallen down or they could've been brought down, and no one knows how long they've been like that. Your mother said it's been years since anyone has been inside the mausoleum." He turned my hand in his and moved his thumb along the center of my palm.

I had a feeling there was more. "But?"

Thick lashes lifted and his eyes met mine. "But the doorway that led to the door from inside the cellar was open."

"Oh God." I turned my head, thoughts racing. "I mean, the door down there could've been open for a while, but . . . someone could've come into the inn through the tunnel and gone back out. The question is, why would someone go through all that trouble? Most of the time, they could come right in through the front door."

His thumb kept moving along my hand. "Because they don't want to be seen. Someone goes to that trouble when they don't want to risk it."

I pressed my lips together. "If you know anything about the history of the inn, you know about that tunnel." I thought about the mayor, the only person on my not very helpful list of those who possibly weren't thrilled about my return, but why would he be in the inn?

Why would anyone be in the inn?

My gaze lifted to Cole, and I found him watching me carefully. For some horrible reason, I thought of my time with the Groom and I knew if I hadn't shut Cole out, he would've been sitting right where he was now ten years ago. The rarest thing happened in that moment. For the first time, I wanted to talk about what happened. He continued to hold my gaze, and the words sort of tumbled out.

"I didn't think I was going to survive, that I would die in the windowless bedroom," I whispered, and understanding flared in his eyes. "I wanted to die so many times, and I know that sounds weak, but I couldn't . . . the things he did. And he saw nothing wrong with it. He was in search of the perfect bride." Closing my eyes, I turned my chin to the ceiling. "That's what he wanted—for his brides to want to be with him, to enjoy it. I guess you already know all of that. I heard some of the details were in the papers, but . . . he was like two different people. One minute he was almost kind. He was sick and twisted in the head, so freaking disturbed, but then, when he got into these moods, it was like a different man, one that thrived on pain and hurting others. Those moments were the worst."

Cole said nothing, but every part of him was focused. His thumb had stilled, but he held my hand tight. The silence allowed me to keep talking.

"He told me once, after I . . . I made him happy," I said, shuddering, "why the other brides had displeased him. They'd all fought back. So did I. It wasn't because of that. He insisted that he could've trained them, would train me to be *obedient*." I spat the last word out. "But it was normal things, you know? One wasn't a real blonde. She dyed her hair, and for that, she wasn't *perfect* enough. Another had told him that she couldn't have children. I don't even know if that was true or not, but he ended her life because of it. There was another who . . . who got too thin for his tastes. Too thin because she wouldn't eat her food." I swallowed hard before continuing. "He killed one of them because she cried too much. As if he weren't the reason why she was crying." Revulsion twisted my stomach. "The one before me, he killed her because he decided suddenly that she was too old. He had to have known her age before, because he stalked them—us. It was like no matter who he picked, they would never be good enough. He'd find some flaw. Something. And that would be it."

The next breath I drew was shallow and it burned all the way to my soul. "I know I couldn't have been the only one who told him what I did, but he eventually decided it was the reason why I could no longer be his bride, and when he told me that, I knew what that meant. I was no longer good enough in his eyes."

I opened my eyes, but I really didn't see the ceiling. "I knew when he put me in that gown, blindfolded me, and led me outside, I knew he was going to kill me. I can remember those moments like it happened seconds ago. The dress was so thin, nothing more than lace, and I could feel the warm breeze on my skin. I could taste the fresh air, and I could smell fresh rain and the faint scent of manure. I knew I was outside. I knew that was *it*. It was going to happen." A tremble coursed through my body and Cole squeezed my hand. "He cried, Cole. He cried while he escorted me outside. Sobbed, and I . . . I begged him. I pleaded with him, and oh God, I said everything and anything, because when I knew that I was going to die, I didn't want to."

A knot in my throat almost choked the next words off. "He stopped crying, and he'd let go of me. I didn't know where he was, but I tried to run. I didn't make it very far when he slammed into me, knocking me to the ground. He flipped me onto my back, and I felt it, this horrible burning sensation in my stomach, like I was being ripped apart. He'd stabbed me."

Cole remained silent, but the tension rolling off him was a third entity in the room, a heavy presence of righteous fury.

"He hadn't bound my hands. He was that confident of handling me, and I . . . I don't know exactly what happened next. All I know is that I fought back. There was this fire-type pain again here," I said, waving my hand over my breasts. "We were struggling on the ground, and he dropped the knife at some point. He had his hand on my throat, choking me. I got ahold of a rock. Dumb luck," I whispered. "That's what saved my life, dumb luck. I hit him on the head, and he let go. I remember jumping up and running, tugging off the blindfold at some point, and I just kept running until I reached that farm . . ."

The farm that had the horses I could hear. Dumb luck had also sent me in that direction, and a round of extremely good luck had Mr. Mockerson, the older owner of the farm, out mending a fence around his cattle.

Turning my head toward Cole, I drew in a deep breath. "If he had killed me, he would've cut off my ring finger. He would've stripped me out of the gown, put me in a new one, and that gown . . . and my finger would've hung in the room with the rest of them." I blinked slowly. "I don't know why I told you all of that."

A muscle flickered along his jaw. "I'm glad you did."

Some of the ten-year-old tension seeped out of my muscles. My therapist had touted the therapeutic benefits of opening up about what had happened, and I hadn't really believed her. I'd been wrong, because the next breath I took was cleansing.

"Got a few things to say though. That wasn't a damn bit weak," he replied quietly. "There is nothing about you that is weak. You survived hell and it wasn't just dumb luck. You fought back and you survived. You're a survivor. You earned that title, baby. You *own* it."

A faint smile pulled at my lips. "Own it. I like that." I paused. "You know, I never knew what he looked like until afterward. He always kept his face hidden. Either I was in a dark room or he blindfolded me. I don't know why he did that, but when I finally saw a picture of him, I was blown away. Messed me up in the head a lot, because he . . . he looked so normal. Like he could've been teaching one of our classes at college. He was someone you saw in the grocery store behind you or you smiled at when you saw them on the street."

"That's how they usually look," he said, raising his hand and mine. He kissed the back of my knuckles, each of them. "Serial killers tend to look like the guy next door, someone you wouldn't judge as unsafe based on appearances."

"Everyone was surprised, weren't they?" I asked.

Cole nodded. "Not a single person who knew Vernon Joan suspected he was the Groom," he said, and I flinched at the sound of his name. "None of his neighbors or his coworkers down at the plant. He didn't have any family around these parts. Don't think he had any alive."

Vernon Joan.

The Groom.

Serial killer and rapist of at least six women. Some people believed there could've been more, but it was unlikely that anyone would ever find out. My escape had led to his arrest. Even as bad off as I was, almost dying on the way to the hospital, I managed to tell them what I knew, and it had been enough to lead the authorities to his home at the base of the Appalachian Mountains. Instead of being arrested, he'd taken the hunting knife he'd used on me and slit his own throat in the room that I and many other women had been held in.

I didn't know how to feel about that, probably never would. Part of me wanted him to go to trial, to answer to the families and loved ones of the lives he robbed from them. The other half was simply glad he was dead.

My eyes came to his again. There was something else I hadn't shared with Cole. "I told him that I was in love with someone else."

The skin around his mouth tightened. "What?"

"That's what I told him—the Groom," I clarified. I hadn't used his real name and I wouldn't start. I wouldn't give him that. "I told him that I was already in love with someone else."

For a few seconds, all Cole did was stare. Those pale, frosty eyes warming by several degrees. When I'd told the Groom that it had partly been me pleading with him, trying to get him to see me as a human being that people loved and would miss—as a person who would miss those she loved. In a twisted way, it had worked, enabling my escape, but it hadn't been far from the truth. I'd been falling in love with Cole back then, maybe even in love with him.

Just like I was now.

Cole's eyes drifted shut and he lowered his forehead to where our hands were joined. He didn't speak. I didn't know what he was thinking, but as I lay there watching him, I knew what I felt upon waking and seeing him sitting there was true. How he felt wasn't going to change it.

I was in love with Cole Landis.

COLE STAYED THE night in my hospital room, and I was guessing that badge and charming smile really went a long way with the nurses. I was discharged in the morning and Cole drove me home.

He didn't bring up what I'd told him last night, but it wasn't like what I shared was hanging between us. It was just there, now out in the open, and it changed me, how I was around him. I don't think it was noticeable, and it wasn't like I wore a sign on my head that announced I'd done the whole sharing-is-caring thing, but it was different for me. It felt . . . good.

I didn't regret it.

Mom insisted on making him breakfast and fawning all over him while she heaped fried bacon and sausage onto his plate. The grin said he liked the attention, and I liked watching him receive the attention. After breakfast, I followed him out to the entryway.

"I'll be back soon," he said, placing his hand on my hip. He angled my body toward his. "Got to take care of a few things. Shower being one of them, and I've got to pack a bag."

"A bag?" I inquired.

The half grin appeared. "Staying the weekend here with you."

"Really?"

"Yep. Figured we still had dinner plans, but we'd change them so you're not out running around. Yeah, I know you're okay," he said, stopping me before I could actually say that. "But we aren't going to push it."

I raised a brow.

"Not going to be gone long." He cupped my cheek with his other hand. "Promise me you're going to take it easy."

"Promise," I murmured, a little lost in those blue eyes.

A knowing tilt to his lips appeared and then he lowered his mouth, kissing me softly and a little too briefly. I didn't want to let him go, and that was a strange new feeling for me, one I pondered as I walked back to the kitchen. The scent of fried bacon lingered.

Mom had already cleaned up, and even though I'd promised to take it easy, that didn't mean I was going to sit around all day. There was only a dull ache in my temple and head, manageable without taking anything for it, and there was something I wanted to see.

I grabbed a flashlight and my peacoat-style jacket out of the back room, shoved my arms through it, and then slipped out the back door. I crossed the veranda, zipping up my jacket as I dragged in a deep breath of cold winter air. It smelled like snow. Not a lot of people thought that incoming snow had a smell, but to me it was always signaled by a fresh, airy scent.

Frozen grass crunched under my boots as I passed the bare trellis. A low stone wall appeared. It had been here since the house was built, and I imagined it marked the original property line. I passed through the opening and crossed the narrow, unused alley before hitting a patch of dying grass. Several yards ahead was another stone wall, this one waist high. A lone mausoleum stood in the center.

My stomach tumbled as I approached the old cemetery. I couldn't even remember the last time I'd been here, as I'd avoided it like it was full of flesh-eating zombies when I was a kid.

Heart thumping in my chest, I entered the tiny cemetery. There were only five headstones. The cement was crumbling, and the epitaphs were indistinguishable, having long since faded.

A horn blew in the distance, causing me to jump. I was a grown damn woman, but the cemetery still creeped me out. We were in the middle of the town, the cemetery within eyesight of many homes, but as I walked to the open door of the mausoleum, I felt like I was a hundred miles away from civilization.

The opening of the mausoleum was dark and yawning. At one time there had been a door, but for as long as I remembered, it had been missing. Taking a deep breath, I stepped inside and flipped on the flashlight.

The creepiest part about the mausoleum was the fact there were no tombs inside. There used to be tombs in here, but they'd disappeared long before Grandma Libby had purchased the mansion and property. No one knew why or where they went, and something about that just freaked me out.

Moving the flashlight, I cast light along the floor, immediately finding the old cellar-type doors. One side was closed, and the other was in shards next to the entrance. Half of the brick wall was down, falling into the blackness of the tunnel. A small pile of red-and-white brick was next to the boards. I wasn't a crime scene expert, nor did I have any experience in construction, but I couldn't tell if the bricks had been torn down or had caved in.

During breakfast, Mom had told me that she'd already contacted someone to come out first thing next week, which was roughly around the same time Cole's buddy was also coming out to install the alarms on the apartments.

Someone had gone in there and entered the house. You couldn't pay me a million bucks to go down there. The amount of spiders alone gave me nightmares.

But Derek had been right. That wall was down, and the first thing I was doing when I got back was finding some boards, nails, and a hammer. The cellar door was going to get boarded up.

I backed out of the mausoleum, stopping abruptly when I heard a snapping sound behind me. A cold chill snaked down my spine and the hair along my neck rose. I turned sharply, hand tightening on the flashlight. I half expected to find someone standing behind me, but there was no one there.

Twigs snapped to my left. I twisted toward the sound, but I still saw nothing through the bare low-hanging branches. My gaze darted around the cemetery, beyond the stone wall, and across the yard that led to one of the nearby homes. Nothing moved, but tiny bumps spread across my skin.

Anyone could be out here.

Anyone.

Unnerved, I turned off the flashlight and high-tailed my behind out of the cemetery. Once inside the house, I closed the door and locked it behind me.

After placing the flashlight on the counter, I shrugged off my jacket and my gaze coasted over the corkboard. I draped my jacket over the hook and started to leave when I whipped back so fast my head started pounding.

I ignored the pain as I walked toward the cork-board, scanning it more closely. There were the extra room keys, labeled clearly. Another was an extra set to the inn doors. Another set for the carriage house. There were Mom's truck keys, and then the next spot was empty.

But it wasn't supposed to be.

Angela's house key was missing.

She'd come so close, so incredibly close to my secret, so close I could almost reach out and touch her.

And she had no idea.

I wanted to laugh.

I wanted to wrap my hands around her neck and watch the life seep out of her eyes.

Even right now she had no idea I was there, watching her lock the door behind her, like that could help her. A smile curved up the corners of my lips. I could gain access to her anytime I wanted. I *always* could. Close up the tunnels outside. Lock the doors. I could get in.

Because I've always been here.

I bit my lip as she walked over to the corkboard by the door. Her brows pinched together as she studied it. Right now, I could take her.

No one would ever know what happened to her.

Like it should've been the first time.

But I could take her.

I'd almost done so when she lay unconscious, could've easily taken her, but that would've been too easy and this would've been over too quickly.

And I wasn't ready for that.

Because I still wanted to play.

SNATCHING MY CELLPHONE off the counter where it was charging, I immediately called Cole.

Luckily he answered on the third ring with an amused "Babe, I'm standing here naked and dripping. You miss me already?"

Naked *and* dripping?

"Sasha?"

Okay. That effectively distracted me for a couple of seconds. I blinked away the fantastic image of him. "Angela's house key is missing."

"What?" All amusement was gone from his tone.

"Her house key is missing." I walked to the pocket door and peered out into the dining room, making sure it was still empty. "She kept an extra key to her house here, and I know I saw it yesterday morning before the whole stair incident."

"Shit. You sure?"

"Positive," I said, turning from the door. "That key

was there and now it's not. I haven't asked my mom if she did something with it, but I doubt she did."

"Yeah," he replied. "I'll be over in about an hour. Do me a favor and don't touch anything in that room from here on out, okay? Make sure no one else does."

"All right."

"I'm going to get on the phone with some people. One of them is the detective working on Angela's case. He may show up before me. You good with that?"

"Of course." I tucked a few strands of hair behind my ear.

"Perfect." There was a pause, and I sort of wondered if he was still naked. Not the best thing to focus on, but I couldn't help myself. "That's very good of you to remember."

I smiled. "Thank you."

"I'll be there soon."

Hanging up, I laid my cell on the table and left to find Mom. She was upstairs in the laundry room, and when I told her what I discovered, she was more than a little unnerved, but relieved that Cole was sending someone over. In her mind, he had it handled.

"The man you saw was in here to get Angela's key?" She stated it even though I hadn't. "You sure it wasn't Ethan?"

"I'm pretty positive it wasn't him, but if it were, do you think he would've just left me to lie there?"

She shook her head as she placed a flat sheet on the bench. "I didn't know that boy well, but that doesn't sound like him."

"Plus, wouldn't he have a key?"

"You'd think." She folded one end of the linen over.

I thought about what Cole had said, that Ethan and Angela had a fight that day. "How was Angela and Ethan's relationship?"

Her brow puckered as she continued folding the sheet. "Seemed good to me. She talked about him a lot. Granted, Angela talked a lot about everything." Her brief smile faded quickly. "Why do you ask?"

I shrugged. "Curious." Knowing I could trust her with the bit of inside knowledge, I said, "Cole learned that they had a fight the day she . . . disappeared."

"Goodness." Her hands stilled as she squeezed her eyes shut. "I don't know what to think. The boy seems like a good one, but you never really know people."

"True," I murmured, thinking of all the people who'd known the Groom in real life. Like Cole had said last night, no one would've ever suspected him of such atrocious crimes.

Mom sighed as she lifted her gaze from her sheet. "How are you feeling?"

"Fine."

"Honey, why don't you go work the front desk," Mom suggested when I bent over to pick up a pile of laundry.

I frowned. "You could use the help."

"I can take care of this myself, but you're looking a little pale, and with everything going on, the last thing I want to worry about is you passing out on me." She dropped the linen on the workbench. "Listen to your mama."

A dull ache had started behind my eyes, some-thing the doctor advised would be common, so I decided not to argue. Walking over to her, I kissed her cheek and then started downstairs. I was passing through the dining room when I heard the bell ring from registration. Picking up my pace, I made my way to the front.

Every muscle tensed when I saw who was stand-ing in front of the desk.

Mayor Hughes.

He was dressed more casually today, in a pair of blue jeans and a button-down moss-green shirt. His smile was just as tight and fake as I recalled.

"Hello," I said, clasping my hands together. "What can I help you with, Mayor Hughes?"

"Heard you've had a busy couple of days." He leaned against the desk, propping one arm upon the surface, rattling the vase of white orchids. "Wanted to check in on you."

Why in the world would he check in on me? I schooled my expression blank even though surprise shot through me, stiffening my spine. "I'm not sure what you mean."

That smile went up a notch, but didn't reach his eyes. "Miss Keeton, I'm the mayor of a small enough town that I hear all kinds of gossip. Such as the ongoing property dispute between Mrs. Dawson and her much younger neighbors, the Rogers family. You see, the Rogers have a teen-age boy, and you know like every family that has a teenage son, they have a basketball hoop up in the driveway that is partially shared with Mrs. Dawson. That does not make the latter very happy.

Apparently it's the constant thumping of the basketball that bothers her."

I had no idea why he was telling me this.

"So when someone like you moves back to town, has her car vandalized not once but twice, and then suffers a fall that lands her in the hospital, I hear about it." He paused, the smile fading. "And then there's the tragic situation with Miss Reidy, who happens to work at your inn."

My mouth moved, but there was no sound. At first, I didn't know what to say, but then I focused on one part. "My mother doesn't know about her truck. I haven't told her yet," I said, voice low. "Please do not speak to her about that until I have the chance."

He inclined his head. "And why didn't you tell her?"

"I don't want her to worry needlessly."

"Looks like she should be worried," he replied.

Unease flooded my stomach. "Why would you say that?"

His dark brows rose. "Your mom has single-handedly taken care of this inn for ten years with no help from you. You left. That was your right. But your mother talked about you a lot, every chance she got. Missed you, but I'm sure you know that. She was able to do it all without you being here, without any . . . drama, but now you're back."

"And now there's drama?"

"I didn't say that."

"But that's what you're insinuating," I stated, struggling to control my tone. "I didn't vandalize my own car or my mother's. I didn't fall down the steps on purpose, and what is going on with Angela has—"

"Nothing to do with you," he finished. "That is very correct, but all these things have happened since you've returned. Perhaps the world," he said, circling his right arm, "is trying to tell you something."

Seconds from losing my temper, I crossed my arms over my chest. What was it with this man? I didn't get it. "And what is that?"

"That maybe you shouldn't have come back here."

I stared at him as he pushed away from the desk. Anger flashed brightly inside me. "What is your problem with me?"

"I don't have a problem with you. Nothing personal," Mayor Hughes protested. "It's all about business."

"How so?" I asked, genuinely curious, and still ticked off—very ticked off.

His gaze flickered behind me as he said, "You show back up in my town, I got one dead woman and another missing. Doesn't that sound familiar?"

I gaped at him.

"The thing is, I know those two horrific tragedies have nothing to do with you, but when people think of what has happened recently, they'll think about what happened before. The past will get dragged back up, and that's the last thing this town needs, Miss Keeton. Now, I need to get going, but you think about what I've said."

What exactly was I supposed to think about? I turned away once the door closed behind the mayor, furious and thoroughly confused. I could understand the whole town not wanting me to do interviews about the Groom. It was a small town, and bad press was not good press, but come on. What exactly was I going to do that would have that much of an impact? There had to be something else, something more behind why he was so unhappy with my return.

I'd made it to the sitting area when I heard the door open once again. Head now thumping, I pivoted around to see a tall man walk in. A very tall, *handsome* man, which made my headache seem less painful.

It was like God was rewarding me for dealing with the mayor.

The man appeared to be half white, half African American, and he had cheekbones for days. Features angular and striking, hair buzzed close to the skull, combined with the dark suit he wore, he looked like he'd walked off the pages of a men's magazine.

Or a hot police calendar.

The badge clipped to his belt flashed out from his jacket as he strode forward. His dark eyes settled on me. "Miss Keeton?"

"Yes?"

"I'm Detective Tyron Conrad," he said, stopping and extending a hand. He took my hand in a firm grip. "Cole contacted me earlier."

"Thank you for coming out."

He let go of my hand. "No problem."

Trying not to stare at the man, I stepped aside. "If you don't mind, could we go into the kitchen? I don't want any guests to overhear us."

"Lead the way." He flashed a heart-stopping smile.

Oh dear.

"Got a question for you, Miss Keeton," he said as I led him toward the kitchen. "Did I just pass the mayor on the way out?"

I fought the urge to punch something as I slid open the pocket door. "Call me Sasha. Yes. He was . . . checking on the inn," I explained, weighing my words. I doubted the detective would take too kindly to me spewing less than flattering adjectives like I wanted to.

"Interesting," he murmured.

"Would you like anything to drink?" I offered, changing the subject.

"I'm good but thanks for the offer," he replied, glancing around the kitchen. "Cole said you discovered something missing that might pertain to Angela Reidy?"

"Cole didn't give you the details?" I leaned against the counter.

"He did, but I want to hear them from you."

"Oh." Taking a deep breath, I knocked my hair back over my shoulder. "Angela keeps an extra key here. From what my mother explained, she had a habit of locking herself out. The key was here yesterday morning. I remember seeing it. I actually touched it," I told him, clutching the counter behind me. "I don't even know why I did that. I saw it and thought of Angela, and then I fell down the stairs."

"I looked into that." He reached into his pocket, pulling out a small notebook like Derek had. "I want you to tell me about that."

I quickly told him what had happened yesterday morning and then moved on to how I discovered the missing key. His gaze sharpened when I explained that I'd gone out to the cemetery. I ignored the look. "That's when I discovered the missing key. My mother didn't take it, and the only other person who has been here is Daphne, and she would have no reason to pick it up."

"Can you show me the room?"

"Sure." I took him to the door and pushed it open, shivering as we stepped down into the chilly room. "This was a part of the old servants' kitchen. That door there leads outside." I gestured at the exit that opened up under the stairs that led upstairs to the apartment balcony. "I don't know if it was locked, but we normally keep it that way. Staff has keys. The other door goes to the staff stairway—the one I was coming down yesterday."

"And you can get to the cellar from there?" When I nodded, he asked, "Can you give me a few minutes?"

"Sure. I'll be in the kitchen."

Smiling, he nodded. "Thank you, Sasha."

He walked toward the corkboard and I saw that his back was just as attractive as his front. Wow. Back in the kitchen, I made a fresh pot of coffee, and I'd just poured myself a cup when the door opened. Detective Conrad was back, hands empty. "Would you like a cup?" I felt like I had to offer again.

"Trying to lay off the caffeine," he replied.

"That sounds like a sin."

He grinned. "It hasn't been easy, that I will admit." Stopping in front of the kitchen island, he said, "I'm going to have forensics come out here. Just going to be one guy, have him dust for prints and take some pictures. If you want, he can come in through the back and the guests won't even know he's here."

"That would be good." I took a sip of the coffee. "I would like for the guests not to be aware of any of this."

"That is easy to do." Leaning at the waist, he propped his elbows on the counter. "I can have a guy here in about an hour. Make sure he stays out of everyone's hair." He paused. "Got to say, I appreciate the fact you're observant."

"I've learned to be," I admitted, cradling my mug with both hands. "Do you think the missing key is related to Angela's disappearance?"

"Not sure, but we're checking all avenues until something turns up."

Reading between the lines told me that all the avenues they've searched so far had turned up zilch. Unsettled, I took a sip of my coffee. "How can someone disappear without a trace?"

"Happens more than people realize," he remarked, eyes meeting mine. "I think you know that."

"True," I murmured, lowering my cup. "I do know that. Probably more than anyone, but sometimes I forget."

"That's human nature." A few seconds of silence stretched out and then he shocked the hell out of me. "I went to the academy with Cole."

"E-Excuse me?"

"Wasn't in law enforcement around here. I was up in Morgantown when everything was going down. Didn't realize you and him had a thing back then until I transferred down here and took a city position. That was about a year after the Groom business."

"Oh," I murmured, lifting my mug. "I . . . I didn't know that."

"Didn't think you did. He talked a lot about you back in the day. Told him more than once to track your ass down." Detective Conrad flashed a quick, very charming grin. "Even told him that marrying Irene was a mistake. His heart wasn't there, no matter how badly he wanted it to be."

My lips parted as I jerked my hand back, splashing coffee on my hand. I didn't even feel the warm liquid. What did he just say?

"Think he got respecting you confused with giving you space, but it all worked out again. Funny how life does that." He straightened, completely oblivious to the fact my jaw was on the floor. "Anyway, I'm going to call—"

"What did you say about Cole being . . . being married?" I asked, knowing—*just* knowing—I heard him wrong, because if Cole had been married, he would've said something. He *had* to have said something.

Detective Conrad's nostrils widened slightly as the skin between his brows creased. "Aw shit," he muttered.

I stared at him.

"Cole was married."

CHAPTER 18

COLE *WAS* MARRIED?

Those three words were on a vicious cycle despite the more pressing things going on—say, like the highly attractive detective currently calling a forensic specialist to come dust for prints.

My heart was thundering in my chest as Mom roamed into the kitchen. I numbly introduced her to the detective and then excused myself. I needed a few moments alone to really process what I'd just learned.

I walked through the dining room, rubbing my palm against my sternum. I didn't know what to think or how to feel. We hadn't seen each other for ten years, and I had been with other people. It wasn't like I had thought Cole was celibate and saintly, waiting patiently for my return. I figured he had been in relationships, and for the longest time I believed he was married, living out the happily ever after I'd wanted so badly to be a part of. But he hadn't said anything to give the impression that he'd been married.

How could Cole not mention that? Being married seemed like a super important detail when you were talking to someone about second chances and breaking down Teflon walls.

Then again, we'd only been back in each other's lives for a week.

Only a week.

Plopping down in the chair behind the front desk, I realized that we were moving way too fast—*I* was moving way too fast. Obviously, there hadn't been a lot of time for Cole and me to have multiple in-depth conversations, but being married was something major. Something I thought someone would bring up pretty quickly.

I tipped my head back and closed my eyes, the ache in my temple slowly receding. Mom's laugh carried from the kitchen, and I had no idea what the detective could be saying while investigating possible evidence related to a missing person that would make someone laugh. Otherwise, the inn was quiet. The guests were out, and in those moments, I realized what I was feeling wasn't so much disbelief.

It was hurt, and it was stupid, because I didn't think I had the right to be hurt over the fact that Cole had indeed moved on to the point that he got *married*. I'd left this town. I'd left *him*, and just because I hadn't moved on, I hadn't expected the same from Cole.

It hit me then, much like it had the night before when I woke up and saw Cole sitting there, that I didn't just love him, I never *stopped* loving him. He'd burrowed his way in, digging deep and carving out a piece of my heart just for him, all those years ago, and he was still in there.

That's why discovering that he was married from a virtual stranger hurt. That's why I was questioning what the hell I was doing when it came to him.

Screw the being-alone-and-sorting-things-out part. I needed to call Miranda and tell her what I'd learned.

Opening the desk drawer where I stashed my cell, I reached for it. Her phone rang and then went to voicemail. Knowing she hated voicemails, I hung up without leaving one.

Rising, I shoved my cell into the back pocket of my jeans as the door to the inn opened. I looked over, and my heart stuttered as Cole walked in.

It had started snowing, and sprinkles of the white stuff dusted his shoulders and hair. Grinning, he thrust his fingers through his hair, brushing the snow off as he said, "Hey, babe."

"Hey," I whispered, and the damnedest image formed in my mind. Cole in a tux standing at an altar as some faceless but most likely beautiful woman in white slowly approached him.

His brows creased together. "You okay?"

"Yo, Landis." Detective Conrad was in the sitting room. "Can we talk for a second?"

"Yeah." Cole's gaze remained trained on me. "You all right, Sasha?"

I wanted to blurt out the whole marriage business, but now was not the time, so I nodded and smiled. "Sure."

He studied me for a moment and then walked

over. Detective Conrad clapped a hand on Cole's shoulder. They headed toward the dining room, passing Mom on the way.

Her hair was pulled back at the nape of her neck in a low bun, but several thin wisps framed her face. She placed her hands on the desk and leaned over, whispering, "That is one attractive man, isn't he?"

My lips twitched. "Yes, he is."

"Such a small town," she said, glancing over her shoulder, "and I've never seen that man. I would've remembered seeing that man."

That made me laugh. "He went to the academy with Cole apparently."

Her gaze shifted back to me. "Is that so?"

I nodded, wanting to tell her about Cole being previously married, but before I could say anything, the inn doors opened yet again. This time it was new guests.

By the time we had them checked in and upstairs, James was banging around in the kitchen preparing the evening meal, and an older man had showed up from the police department. I caught a quick glimpse of him, and luckily he wasn't wearing anything that showed he was from a forensics unit. Cole and Detective Conrad were in the old kitchen with the investigator, and looking for things to keep my mind busy, I realized we hadn't grabbed the mail yet.

Slipping out the front door, I hunkered down in my sweater as the brisk wind circled around me. Snow fell in a fine sheet, dusting the driveway. For once, I actually had boots on instead of flip-flops, but I was wary of the icy spots. I reached the end of the drive, and stepped outside the stone wall, reaching the mailbox. Wishing I'd stopped to grab gloves, I opened the lid and quickly yanked out the contents. There were several bills. Of course. Something from Triple A, and a small package about four inches long and narrow.

As I walked back up the drive, I turned the package over. Surprise flickered through me. The little brown package was addressed to me. Having no idea who it could be from, I glanced at the sender's address.

"Where in the hell is your jacket?"

I glanced up at the sound of Cole's voice. He was standing on the porch, the corners of his lips turned down. "In the back room."

He prowled toward the steps. "Just in case you haven't realized, it's snowing."

"I didn't want to bother the investigator." And I also was sort of avoiding him. I climbed the steps. "Besides, I've been outside for like two minutes."

"It's snowing," he repeated.

"And I'm heading back inside now." I walked past him, but he cupped my elbow. "Wha—?"

His mouth cut off my words as his other hand circled the back of my neck. The kiss caught me off guard, and I almost dropped the mail, but within seconds, I wasn't thinking about what I held or anything other than the feel of his lips against mine. His kiss . . . damn, he always kissed like a man who believed he wouldn't get another chance.

It was mind-blowing.

Lifting his mouth, he gently squeezed the back of my neck. "We need to talk."

I believed that we needed to kiss again. I opened

my eyes. A gust of wind blew snow onto the porch. A second passed, and then I *remembered*. My eyes flew to his.

"I know Tyron told you."

I sucked in a sharp breath. "Cole—"

His pale eyes held mine. "I didn't want you to find out that way."

"How did you want me to find out?" I pulled free, putting space between us, because with him holding me, standing right there, it made it hard to be objective.

"With the words coming out of my mouth," he replied. "Let's take this conversation inside."

My heart was thumping, partially because of the kiss. "I have to make sure everything is good to go for dinner service."

A brow rose as he opened the door. "Your mother is in the kitchen with James, and I'm sure they have it covered."

Warm air greeted us as the door swung shut. "What about the detective and the investigator?" I asked, keeping my voice low. "Shouldn't you be with them?"

He cocked his head to the side. "I should be right where I am, talking to you. Don't shut me out."

I squinted. "I'm not shutting you out."

"You just found out that I was married from someone other than me," he said in a low voice, angling his body toward me. "We need to talk about that, but you're coming up with excuses to delay it. That's shutting me out."

Placing the mail behind the desk, I admitted he had a point. I glanced toward the sitting room.

One of the guests was resting in front of the fire-place.

"Okay. Let's go up to my apartment."

We didn't speak on the way up, taking the main staircase and hitting the staff one from the third floor. Once inside my apartment, I leaned against the closed door. Cole stood in the center of the room. He opened his mouth, but I spoke first. "Why didn't you tell me?"

"I was planning to. I know that doesn't mean much at this point, but I was. Do you remember when we had dinner and I said there was stuff we needed to talk about?"

My brain raced back to the dinner, and I did remember that. "Okay. So the dinner got way off track with everything, but we've seen each other nearly every day since then. That's kind of big news not to mention it."

"You're right." He stepped forward. "But a lot of stuff has been going down. Every time there seemed to be a right time, more shit went down. I have no reason to purposely hide that from you."

"I don't . . . I don't know what to think," I admitted, tipping my head back against the door. I let out a heavy sigh. "It's not like I believed you were single this whole time. There was even a part of me that accepted you had married. I wanted that—wanted you to be happy and in love. I really did."

"I know." He was another foot closer. "But I'm taking it you don't like actually knowing that I was married."

Hearing him say that made me want to cringe. "I

honestly don't know how I feel about it. I mean, it just really caught me off guard."

Cole was in front of me, and I didn't protest when he took my hands, tugging me away from the door. "Maybe you'll know how to feel about it after I actually tell you."

He led me to the couch, and when he sat, he pulled me down beside him. "Her name is Irene. I met her two years after you left. She's not from around here originally."

I dropped my hands to my lap and stayed quiet, because honestly, what in the world was I supposed to say to any of this?

"She's a teacher in London County," he explained, "and we met at the gym."

Of course she would be someone who went to a gym, while I'd forgotten what those things looked like on the inside.

Cole leaned back as he rubbed a finger over his brow. "We started off as friends, and I knew it was more for her even from the beginning. She even asked me out first, and we dated for about a year and a half before I proposed to her."

A horrible, completely irrational twisting motion compressed my chest. I left him, I reminded myself. I had no right to be upset or . . . or jealous of the fact he proposed to someone.

"We married six months later. Small ceremony," he continued, and I worked to keep my expression open. "Irene is a great woman. We still stay in contact. It's not often, but I always enjoy seeing her. She did nothing wrong in the marriage."

Genuinely curious, I asked, "Then what happened?"

A wry smile formed on his lips. "I worked a lot, so I was away from home quite often. She tried to be okay with that, really she did. And I kept telling myself the reason why I worked twelve-hour shifts was because I was new at the FBI. I had to put my time in. Then she wanted to start a family, and that . . . that was the last thing I wanted. God's honest truth, the moment she sat me down and said she wanted a baby, I didn't even think about it. Told her that wasn't happening. Felt like a huge dick, but that's what I did. She said she was okay with that, and I think she really wanted to be. Truth was, she wasn't, and I should've done the right thing then and ended the marriage."

Cole shifted forward, resting his arms on his bent legs. "Two years ago, she asked me if I loved her or the job more, and that was when we separated, then divorced. I messed up. I really did. I'm not perfect, Sasha. I should've been honest with myself and her. As horrible as it is to say this, I should've never married her. Doing so made me the kind of man I never wanted to be."

I sucked in a soft breath.

"She's moved on since. Met someone. A doctor, actually. They'll probably be married within a year."

Okay. I was way too happy to hear that last part, and that probably didn't say good things about me. "I . . ." I started to say I was sorry to hear that, because that was the natural response when you learned someone had divorced, but that sure as hell wouldn't be genuine considering he'd already given me one orgasm and how I felt for him. So I decided to be honest. "I don't know what to say, Cole. I want to say I'm sorry, but I'm . . . I'm not." Lifting my gaze to his, I ignored the warmth zipping across my face. "If you were still with her, then we wouldn't be sitting here."

His eyes softened. "Babe . . ."

"But I'm wondering if . . . if we're moving way too fast with everything," I admitted, and my pulse started skyrocketing again. "Everything has been crazy, and it's only been a week since we've laid eyes on each other and—"

"I haven't told you everything," he said.

I stiffened even though I imagined there was a lot he hadn't had a chance to tell me.

Cole smiled. "For the longest time, I'd convinced myself that it was the job that came between us—the job that made me not even consider having kids."

My brows snapped together. "It wasn't?"

"No, babe. It wasn't the job. As much as I love what I do, I never wanted it to be my life. I *made* it my life though. What came between Irene and me wasn't the FBI. It was you."

"What?" I jerked.

"You heard me right." He took my hand, holding it between his. "It was you. It's always been you."

Oh my God.

Oh. My. *God.*

My pulse was all over the place for a totally different reason now. "I . . ."

A thunderous series of raps knocked off the interior apartment door. "Cole? Sasha? Are you two in there?"

"That's Tyron." Frowning, Cole rose swiftly from the couch. I followed him. He opened the door, and over his shoulder I saw my mother standing behind the detective, her face pale and worried. "What's going on?" Cole asked.

My stomach knotted with dread.

"I'm sorry to interrupt you two, but this couldn't wait." The detective was holding a clear plastic bag, and inside of it was the package I'd gotten out of the mail. "This was behind the desk. Sasha, did you bring it inside?"

"Yeah," I answered, stepping to Cole's side. "Why are you asking?"

"I was on my way out when your mother picked up the mail from behind the desk," he explained.

"It was leaking," Mom added.

"Leaking?" I whispered. "Leaking *what*?"

"Have you opened it?" Cole demanded.

Detective Conrad shook his head. "I wanted to get her permission first."

"You have my permission," I told him, glancing at Mom. I noticed the guy from forensics was also in the hallway.

Detective Conrad turned, handing the bagged package over to the man. That's when I saw that the corner of the package was a darker color of brown. I reached out, placing my hand on Cole's arm.

The man reached inside with a gloved hand. Using a small knife, he carefully peeled one end open as Mom folded her arms. "Did you see where it was from?" she asked. "Who sent it?"

I shook my head. "I glanced at it, but I didn't really look at it. I got distracted and set it down . . ."

"Sasha," she whispered, and the dread exploded like buckshot.

The investigator eased out a black cardboard box the size of the package. It looked like a plain gift box to me. I held my breath as he opened it.

"Oh goodness!" Mom clapped her hands over her mouth and quickly twisted to the side.

"Holy shit," the man said, turning to Detective Conrad. "You're going to want to see this."

"What is it?" I stepped forward, but only got so far, because suddenly Cole was in front of me and out in the hall. "Mom—?"

Cole cursed as the detective planted his hands on his hips, and that horrible feeling spread like a noxious weed, choking me as I stepped out in the hall.

Cole shifted, trying to hide what the investigator held, but I got between him and the detective. My mouth dropped open as I jolted back, bumping into the wall outside my apartment. Disbelief flooded me.

"No," I whispered. "No way."

Cole faced me, and there was a different set of emotions etched into his features. He took a step toward me, but I held up my hand. I needed the space—a moment, because what was in the box was wrong on so many levels.

It was a finger.

A woman's finger.

CHAPTER 19

A DEEP NUMBNESS seeped in through my skin, right into my muscle and bone. There was a finger in a box sent to me. A woman's finger. The bubblegum-pink polish was typically a dead giveaway on that.

"Honey." Mom rubbed my arm. "Maybe you should go sit down."

Shaking my head, I leaned against the wall. I didn't want to go sit down or move. My eyes were glued to the three men. Detective Conrad was on the phone. Cole was bent slightly, eyeing the package the investigator held.

I dragged in air, but it seemed to go nowhere. There was a huge part of me that couldn't believe what I had seen. A part of my brain that absolutely just shut down and belly-flopped into denial.

This wasn't happening.

My throat dried. "There was a finger in that box," I whispered.

Cole's head swung sharply in my direction and

a heartbeat later, he said, "You hanging in there?" When I nodded, he glanced down at Mom. "Can you do me a favor?"

"Anything," she replied.

"Call Miranda and get her over here," Cole said, voice low. "Let her know what happened. Stress the importance of keeping that quiet."

I pushed off the wall. "She doesn't need to be here. I just need a few minutes to myself—"

"That is not what you need. This is some serious shit, Sasha. You're telling me you're fine. Maybe you are right now but that might change, and when that does, I want you surrounded by people who care about you instead of being by yourself."

"He's right, honey." Mom squeezed my arm. "Let me call Miranda."

About to protest again, I stopped. I nodded. Taking a few minutes seemed normal to most people, but for me, those few minutes could turn into years.

Mom hurried off down the hall while Cole took my hand and led me back into the apartment. He left the door ajar behind us as he tugged on my hand, pulling me toward him.

I went even though my first instinct was to pull away. He folded his arms around me, one hand on the center of my back and the other curling around the nape of my neck. He slid his hand up and down my spine.

Closing my eyes, I face-planted into his chest and welcomed the comfort of his warmth and touch. I took a shallow breath and repeated, "There was a finger in the box."

"Yeah, babe, there was." His tone was somber. "Tyron's going to need to talk to you again."

My fingers curled around his shirt. "That was a woman's finger."

He didn't respond to that, and he didn't need to, because I knew his thoughts had gone where mine had. The Groom always removed the ring finger of his victims. Always. For that—

I drew back, remembering that there was something about the package I didn't know. "What was the address?"

Cole's chest rose with a deep breath, but before he could respond, there was a knock on the door. "Yeah?" he called out.

"It's me," Detective Conrad said. "All right to come in?"

"Yes." I stepped back, and Cole dropped one arm but kept his other arm around my waist as the detective came in. He left the door open. "Detective Conrad—"

"Call me Tyron," he said.

"Okay." I tried again. "What was the address on the package? Did it say who it was from?"

He stared at me a moment and then his gaze flickered above me. Looking over his shoulder, he called out, "Chris, can you bring the package in here?"

Bile rose as the investigator came back in, and my stomach only settled a little when I realized the package was closed and back in the plastic bag.

"Show her the address," Tyron instructed.

Cole stiffened beside me and his hand slipped to the center of my back, but he didn't stop the investigator when he lifted the baggy and turned it over.

At first the words sort of blurred together, and

maybe I had recognized the name and address immediately but my brain refused to process them.

Because the address no longer existed.

And the name, the initials—I knew what *V. Joan* stood for.

Vernon Joan.

A sharp slice of panic lit up my stomach and my chest compressed. "Impossible." My gaze darted from Tyron to Cole. "That's impossible. That house was torn down and he . . ."

"The Groom is dead," Tyron finished for me. "But someone obviously is saying something with this package."

"But what could they be saying?" I looked at the baggy Chris held, and my mind went to the worst possible place. Only things nightmares were made of could be told with a package like that and with that address information.

"God." I placed my hand around my throat. "What is going on?"

There was no answer.

At least none any of us wanted to hear.

TYRON POSED THE same questions Derek and Cole had asked after my car had been vandalized and the deer had been left in my mother's truck, then he left, along with the investigator.

Cole remained, having already gone out to his truck and grabbed a gym bag. He deposited it on my couch and then turned to me. "It's time for you to tell your mom what happened with her truck."

Sighing, I closed my eyes. A moment passed. "This is insane."

"I know. I wish I could tell you something that wouldn't scare you, but this . . . this isn't looking good."

Wanting a glass of wine or maybe an entire bottle of it, I sat on the arm of the couch. I stared up at him. "What do you think is happening here? I want you to be honest with me and don't try to hide anything."

"My first thoughts?" Cole crossed his arms. "Someone is fixated on what happened here in the past. That package practically screams it, but this isn't a harmless fixation some idiot develops. That was a person's finger."

"And unless that finger belonged to the person who sent it and they willingly cut off their own finger, it belonged to . . ." Trailing off, I bit down on my lip. The worst possible thought popped into my head. Angela was missing. What if it was her finger?

Cole walked over to me and placed his hands on my legs. His eyes met mine. "I hate to say that and I don't want to scare you, but all of this is linking back to you."

There was no denying that. I shuddered. I wanted to ask why, but I knew it had something to do with the Groom. What exactly it was I didn't understand.

"Do you think what happened to Angela has something to do with me?" I asked, almost afraid of his answer.

He shook his head. "That I don't know. Could be unrelated, but it could not be."

"God," I whispered and exhaled roughly. "I wish I could've seen that man's face from yesterday."

Cole studied me. "Truth is, if that person really did take Angela's key and if he has anything to do with the other stuff, he's been in here. He knew how to get in here."

"So many people could know about that tunnel, Cole. It's on the historic registry, for crying out loud." Suddenly remembering I had a visitor today, I almost popped off the arm of the couch. "The mayor stopped by today. I totally forgot."

Cole frowned. "What did he want?"

"He'd heard about what happened yesterday, but he wasn't really checking on me to see if I was okay. He basically told me that I shouldn't have come back here."

"What?" His shoulders tensed. "What did he say exactly?"

I told him the best I could remember. "Isn't that weird? I mean, I get that if I went to the media, it would drag up the past, but seriously, what would be the big deal? There has to be more to this."

"There has to be." He squinted. "Got to admit, I didn't entirely dismiss him when you mentioned him the first time. I just doubt he had anything to do with the vandalism."

I wasn't surprised. "And now?"

"Still not sure. What could be the motive? That's the thing I'm not getting here."

"Ditto," I muttered. "I don't know who else could be behind this, but what happened—that thing in the box—that's a whole different level. This isn't someone fooling around. This . . . this is terrifying," I repeated.

In a way, it was even more frightening than

before, because I hadn't seen the Groom coming, but I saw this. There was no escaping it, no obliviousness.

"I'm not going to let anything happen to you," Cole promised, squeezing my knees. "I'm going to keep you safe."

I lifted my gaze to his. "I'm going to keep myself safe." I paused, and I was. I wasn't a fainting damsel in distress. I'd been through *the* worst, and I would protect myself. I also needed to stop being stupid when it came to accepting protection. "But I'll let you help."

His lips twitched up on one side. "That's my girl."

Placing my hands over his, I let out a shaky breath. A tendril of fear curled around my throat. "This is scary, Cole."

Taking my hands, he hauled me up and to his chest once more. His embrace was tight and full of strength. He bent his head, brushing his lips over my forehead. "We're going to figure out what the hell is going on." Pulling back, he said, "I'm going to make a few calls. Mind if I hang in here to do that?"

"Who are you calling?" I asked.

"My boss. I want to fill him in on this. Tyron would probably get pissed if one of our offices step in, but I'm not going to cater to jurisdiction bullshit while this kind of thing is going down and you're involved."

I figured it was only a matter of time before the Feds got involved. "Make yourself at home. I'm going to go talk to Mom."

Slipping around him, I started toward the door

when Cole snagged me around the waist and drew me up against him. Before I could take my next breath, he kissed me hard and deep. My pulse immediately pounded. When he let go, I was a little dizzy. I looked up, and our eyes met. I couldn't help it, but my thoughts tracked back to Irene. All of that had faded to the background along with the knock on the door, but now the knowledge that Cole had been married, that he'd said it had always been me, was still in the back of my mind.

"I'll be down shortly."

"Okay."

I left the room and by the time I found my mother, my heart had finally slowed. Dinner service was about to begin, so I took her into the old kitchen and tried not to think of the fact that the person who took Angela's key could've been the same person I'd run into.

Breaking the news about her truck to her had gone over surprisingly well with the exception of her being rightfully ticked off at me for keeping it secret.

"Don't ever do that again," she said, marching right up to me. She grasped my arms. "I get why you did, but you do not keep me in the dark. If something happens, you tell me. I'm a grown woman, and I can damn well handle it."

"I know and I'm sorry."

Mom's lips thinned as she stared at the closed door that led into the kitchen. "Part of me wishes you hadn't come home."

"What?" I gasped.

"Please don't take that the wrong way." She faced

me, eyes full of concern. "But I'd rather only see you once a year than you be terrorized or harmed."

Little knots of dread formed in my belly. "I'm not terrorized—"

She shot me a look that shut me right up quick. "You're strong, honey, one of the strongest people I know, but this is frightening. No one would fault you for being scared and nor do I believe for one second that you're not."

Mom. She knew me too well.

"I want you safe, Sasha, and I don't feel like you're safe here," she admitted, eyes gleaming in the low light, and if she started crying, I'd lose it. "I wish I didn't feel that way."

"I know." And I knew she really did mean that. She was beyond thrilled when I told her I was coming home. She wanted nothing more than for me to be here, but not like this.

Never like this.

Dinner service was a blur, and every smile and laugh felt brittle, but I tried. Miranda showed up during it, along with Jason, and I ushered them into the kitchen.

"Jesus, Sasha, someone sent you a finger?" Jason exclaimed the moment the door swung shut.

"Keep it down. James doesn't know about that." I cut Miranda a sharp look. "You weren't supposed to say anything."

"He needed to be here," Miranda stated. "He's my friend. He's yours. You're not shutting anyone out."

Had she been talking to Cole? And I also wondered if Jason was more than Miranda's friend. I really needed to find some time to talk to her.

Jason stepped to the side as James came in through the old kitchen, smelling faintly of cigarette smoke. He scowled in their direction as he shuffled to the sink.

"I wasn't trying to cut you out," I told Jason in a low voice. "I hope you know that. It's just that this is . . . well, it's kind of crazy."

"I know." He straightened his glasses as he smiled. "I don't take it personally. That's why I'm here."

"Thank you." I turned to the door. "Can you guys hang out in here—"

"And stay out of my way," James barked out.

"And do that while I finish up dinner service?" I asked. "Cole is around somewhere. He'll probably be down soon."

Once they were situated, I hurried back out to the dining room. My head was aching by the time Mom and I removed the last of the dishes with Jason's help. He'd even rolled up his sleeves and was putting away dishes.

Miranda was currently "managing" or something, sitting at the table with a glass of wine from a bottle she'd obviously helped herself to. Cole had come down at some point and he caught me after I placed a stack of white dishes near the sink.

"You're looking a little pale." A concerned frown pulled at his lips. "How's your head?"

"Hurts a little."

"Let me get you something," Mom said, dashing off into the back room and returning within seconds with a pain reliever. She handed it over. "Take these."

"Thank you." I walked over to the fridge and grabbed a bottle of water. Knocking back the pills, I faced the little group. "Shouldn't be much longer."

Jason turned from the counter. "How about you take a seat and I'll help Mrs. Keeton finish up."

"You don't—"

"Let me rephrase that," he said, walking past me. "Sit and I'll finish it."

Cole grinned. "Like that guy."

"Whatever," I sighed, moving over to the bistro table.

Miranda sat back. "I bet you wish you could have some wine."

"I do." However, a concussion, even minor, put the kibosh on that.

We didn't talk about anything until James left for the night. At that point, I'd moved from the table and was sitting on the counter. Mom had taken my seat, and Jason and Cole stood while Miranda was nursing her second glass of wine.

I'd checked outside earlier and seen that the snow had tapered off, and only a dusting remained.

Everyone was filled in on, well, everything. Miranda downed what was left of her wine. Jason was pacing. Cole was leaning against the counter I sat on.

"I'm going to be up front with you," Cole warned, and keyed into what he was talking about. "Press is going to hear about this soon. They have ways. You already know that. They're going to be all over this. Tyron and I can keep them away—"

"So will Jason and I," Miranda chimed, arms

crossed and looking like she enjoyed the idea of keeping journalists at bay.

I glanced over at them.

Jason nodded as he stopped to stand by Miranda's chair. "Of course. We'll be your anti-press guard."

"That's good, but those bastards are relentless." Cole pushed my water closer to me. "I just want you to be prepared."

Miranda watched Cole with a small smile and then she glanced over at me. I picked up the bottle and took a drink before she chimed in. "I am."

"When's the alarm going in?" Miranda asked.

"Tomorrow," Cole answered. "And the tunnel is getting closed up."

I looked over at Mom. She had been quiet as she sipped her glass of wine, but she still looked like she had when we'd been in the back room, as if she was thinking about packing up my stuff and sending me back to Atlanta. That coming home had been a mistake.

CLOSE TO MIDNIGHT, Cole and I returned to my apartment. Full of restless energy, I washed my face and slathered on lotion, my mind in a thousand different places.

I changed into a lavender nightie with fluttering cap sleeves and then pulled a cardigan on over it. Not the sexiest combo, I realized as I wandered into the bedroom.

Cole was standing by the bed. His shirt was off and his gun was on the nightstand. The button on his jeans was undone, and for several seconds, I got a little lost staring at him. Twenty-nine years old and

I'd never seen a stomach so defined. Come to think of it, I'd actually never seen a six-pack in real life. Up until this moment, I was beginning to believe they were like a unicorn.

A half grin formed as he eyed my getup. "That's cute."

"Only you would think that."

"I don't think that's true." His hands fell to his sides. He'd already taken off his boots and his toes peeked out from the hem of his jeans. "I know you didn't invite me back here, but I want to be in bed with you."

My breath caught.

"I want to hold you," he continued. "Today. Yesterday. Both days have been rough. You've learned a lot. So, I'm hoping you're not going to kick me out."

"I'm not." I moved to the edge of the bed and let the cardigan slip off my shoulders. I placed it on the bench, feeling his gaze travel over my arms and heart-shaped neckline. "I want you in my bed."

"Best words I've heard in a long time." His voice had deepened.

Biting down on my lip, I peered up at him. "I was shutting down earlier," I admitted. "Right after I saw what was in the box, I started to shut down. It was the easiest thing to do, but I don't want to do that."

He lifted his chin as a tense, aware energy poured off him.

"I want to feel." I made up my mind right then as I stared at him standing by my bed, so stunning and so strong—but more than that, he was *here*.

Drawing in a shallow breath, I walked up to him and placed my hands on his bare chest. His skin was hot under my palms, and I felt his sharp inhale in every cell of my being. I tipped my head back. "Stay with me tonight," I whispered. "Be with me tonight."

CHAPTER 20

THE BREATH THAT Cole inhaled was ragged as his hands closed into fists at his sides. "I'm here with you. I'm not anyplace else."

"I know." I slid my hands down over his hard stomach, marveling at the way his body jerked at my simple touch. He had those muscles on either side of his hip bone. They fascinated me. "But I want . . ."

His hands reopened at his sides. "You want what?"

"You." I lifted my gaze to his once more. "I want all of you."

"Christ," he groaned, lips parting as he raised his hands and touched my bare arms with just the tips of his fingers. "You have no idea how long I've waited to hear those words. Feels like an eternity."

I slid my hands to his sides and then stretched up, kissing him. His fingertips coasted down to my wrists, where he loosely wrapped his hands.

"A lot has happened today," he said, voice strained. "I don't want you—"

"I know what I want." I settled back and met his gaze. "I know what I'm feeling. This has nothing to do with today." My chest rose sharply. "I want you."

He lifted my hands back to his chest. "You have me, babe."

"Prove it."

His nostrils flared and he didn't move. He just held my hands to his chest, and I thought he was going to turn me down. He was going to use some rational excuse for why we shouldn't do this, and I was going to resort to desperate measures.

I had no idea what those desperate measures would be.

But then he moved, sliding his hands back up my arms. He lifted me up onto the tips of my toes and brought my mouth to his.

And his kiss told me he wasn't going to deny me.

I loved the way he kissed—how he tasted me with every part. My breath hitched and then sped up as one hand dropped. Circling an arm around my waist, he brought me against him, and I could feel him pressing against my lower stomach.

There was no going back from this moment, and I dove in headfirst. Need rose swiftly, and I was so lost for him, so hot with a need that spanned a decade. I'd waited so long for this. We'd both waited so long for this.

"Hurry," I pleaded.

He moaned against my lips. "You're going to kill me."

Sensual heat flowed through my veins as his other hand skimmed down my side and slipped under the hem of my nightie, ghosting up my thigh. He kissed me hard, dragging his tongue over mine. I gasped into his hot mouth when he cupped my rear and squeezed.

And then he let me go.

A cry of disappointment rose in my throat and then faded like smoke in the wind when his heated gaze locked with mine. The intense look in his pale blue eyes stole my breath and caused a series of shivers to skate all over my skin.

Cole's hands went to his zipper. The tinny sound of it coming down echoed throughout the room. Hooking his fingers into his jeans and tight black briefs, he swiped both off in one quick, smooth motion, and then he was completely nude.

I inhaled, at a loss for words as I stared at him. His body was beautiful. A work of chiseled muscles and lean length. A faint, light dusting of hair covered him, and his erection was thick and long, jutting out.

Cole was . . . he was not lacking in that department, and he was more than beautiful, and I . . . I wasn't. My body wasn't all long and lean lines. It was more lumpy and curvy. Actually, I was pretty sure some of the lumps had their own curves. It was far from flawless, and then there were the scars.

No one had seen me nude.

I swallowed hard and then turned, heading for the nightstand lamp he'd turned on when he came in here.

"What are you doing?" Cole asked, his deep voice raspy and about five hundred different types of sexy.

My cheeks flushed. "Just turning off the light."

"No."

I stilled. "What?"

He approached me slowly, cupping my cheeks. "I want to see you."

"No, you don't," I whispered.

His head tilted to the side. "There is nothing about you that I don't want to see. Nothing about you that doesn't turn me the fuck on."

Heart racing, I shook my head. "You don't know, Cole. I . . ."

"I know," he said softly. "I know what happened to you. I want to see you. Please give me that. Give me you."

Give me you.

Those three words shattered my defenses, and I found myself whispering yes. Still holding my gaze, he gathered up my nightie and carefully lifted it over my head. The material disappeared, and I was standing in front of him in just my pale pink panties. Not even sexy panties. Cotton ones. With pink and blue flowers, I believed.

Cole wasn't looking at my undies though.

His gaze was trained on my chest in a way that made me flush. I wanted to cover them and I wanted him to look his fill. The tips of my breasts tingled and hardened. I didn't think he was checking out the faint pink raised scar that had almost ended my life.

Before I lost all courage, I curled my fingers around my panties, drew them down, and stepped out of them. Then there was nothing between him and me. His gaze moved slowly over my body.

"Christ," he groaned again. He slowly shook his head. "You're so damn beautiful. Every part of you."

His fingers brushed over my shoulders and then down my front. I jerked when he touched the scar between my chest and then on my stomach. "These are beautiful to me, because it shows how incredibly strong you are. Never think you have to hide them from me." His hand slipped down to my hip. "Never think that this," he said, grasping his erection with his other hand, "isn't all for you. You have no idea what you do to me. If you did, you wouldn't be standing there looking at me like I'm crazy, but you're fucking beautiful to me. You drive me crazy. Don't ever forget that."

His words turned my muscles to mush, because even though I found it all hard to believe, I knew he believed every word he just said.

Anticipation swirled hotly. "Make . . . make love to me."

Cole drew me to him. Our thighs brushed. The coarse hair on his tickled mine. His hard chest brushed into my much softer one. Sensation thundered through me. "Do you have condoms?"

"Yeah. Yes. I have some in the top drawer of the dresser."

"Stay right there."

I wasn't moving, even if a giraffe walked into my apartment and tap-danced. My gaze was glued to the firm globes of his ass as he retrieved a condom. He tossed the foil package on the bed. The room was heavy was tension.

Then he was 100 percent focused on me. He took my hand as he kissed me, slowly turning me around and backing me up until I bumped into the bed. Gently he guided me down, folding his hands under my arms and lifting me up, depositing me in the center of the bed.

"Waited years for this." He lowered himself onto me, and the contact of his body over mine, with nothing between us, ignited a fire. "You know that though, don't you?"

"Yes," I whispered, touching his chest.

Cole rose onto his knees and grabbed the condom, tore it open, and started to slide it on. His gaze rose to mine. "You sure you're—"

"I'm a hundred percent ready." To prove it, I sat up and took over, loving his deep moan as I rolled the condom on.

"Hell," he groaned.

Since I was there, I wanted to explore his golden skin. I went for his hips, tracing those marvelous bands of muscles. I was reaching lower when I suddenly found myself on my back, his lips trailing a blaze of hot, fiery kisses down my face and lower and lower, until his lips and mouth closed on the tips of my breasts.

Crying out in pleasure, my fingers curled around the short strands of his hairs, holding him close as he sucked and licked. My hips moved restlessly against him, causing him to shudder as his erection nestled against where I wanted him. He shifted slightly and his hand was between my thighs, wringing another cry out of me as his fingers eased in.

Everything moved fast at that point.

My greedy hands were all over him. I was shuddering and shaking, and I almost came apart when I felt the first touch of him pushing in.

"Hell, Sasha, you're . . ." His voice choked off as

I lifted my hips and he thrust in, seated fully. The pressure and fullness was unbelievable. "You're fucking perfect."

This was what was perfect.

I wrapped my legs around his waist, and the only sound in the room was our breaths and gasps, and the sound of our bodies moving against one another. His hips rolled and pumped, and I followed, quickly becoming desperate as a tight tension built inside me.

Planting his elbow into the bed beside my head, he shoved his arm under my back and lifted me. Each stroke moved deeper, became more powerful. My body tensed around him and then a floodgate of pleasure built. We moved faster, our hips grinding together as our mouths clashed together. His tongue tangled with mine and then the tightly coiled knot of tension broke free. The orgasm was fierce, kicking my head back and lighting up every cell in my body.

Cole came as the spasms racked my body. He shouted out my name as his hips jerked and lost all rhythm. My hands glided lazily up and down his sides as one last shudder hit him.

Neither of us moved for a long time. Our hearts slowing down and our breaths becoming deeper, more even.

"God," he said, lifting his head. He kissed my swollen lips. "That was . . ."

"Perfect. Marvelous," I suggested. "Beautiful."

"Yeah." He rested his forehead against mine. "All three of them sound about right."

I smiled, feeling like I had no muscles left in my body. "I could come up with a few more if you want?"

He chuckled, lifting his hips and easing out of me. "I'm going to take care of this. Need anything?"

Shaking my head, I bit down on my lip as he slid off the bed and walked toward the door. God, I could watch that man walk around naked all day.

Even though there was a good chance I could fall asleep right there in the middle of the bed, I forced myself up and under the covers. I didn't even bother grabbing the nightie. I drew the covers up to my chest.

Cole returned, a look of approval etched into his striking face. "You sleep nude most of the time?"

I shook my head. "Not normally but I'm . . . too lazy to grab my clothes and put them on. That doesn't bother you?"

"What the fuck would be wrong with me if there was a problem?" He pulled back the covers and climbed in, stopping long enough to turn off the light. The room was flooded with darkness with only the faint moonlight streaming in.

Cole got an arm around me and drew me to his side. We were back to chest, his arm securely looped around my waist. There wasn't an inch of space between us. My rear was cradled against his hips and the front of his thighs pressed against the back of mine. "Thank you."

My brows inched up my forehead. "For what?"

"For . . . giving me you."

My heart swelled so quickly and fiercely I thought I'd cry. A moment passed and I felt his lips brush the back of my shoulder. I focused on taking several deep breaths, working the happy little messy knot out of my throat.

As I lay there in his arms, my mind wandered over the evening, all the way back to when he was telling me about his ex-wife. He'd been about to tell me something, but we'd been interrupted. I twisted onto my back. His hand slid to my hip, leaving a trail of fire in its wake. Silvery moonlight caressed the bridge of his nose. His eyes were closed, expression relaxed. "You still awake?"

"Uh-huh." He tipped his head down and kissed my brow.

I smiled as I closed my hand over his forearm. "You were telling me something about . . . about your marriage. You said it wasn't the job that caused it to fall apart. You said it was . . . was me, but I don't understand how."

He drew his hand away from my hip to the center of my belly. "You haven't figured that out yet?"

"Um, were there clues I missed somehow?"

"Yeah." He chuckled, sliding his hand up to rest between my breasts. "There's been a lot of clues."

"Want to help me out then?"

Cole's lips coasted over the curve of my cheek. "For a while I thought you were the one who got away. That one day I would somehow piece it all back together, but I was wrong. You were the one."

I might've stopped breathing.

He curled the tips of his fingers around my chin. "You *are* the one. Took me a long time to realize that. I kept telling myself that I was just focused on my job and that's why I was never really there with Irene. Then I told myself that I hadn't tried hard enough to make the marriage work, because it hadn't been her. She'd done everything right. It had always been me. Me and you."

"Cole," I whispered.

His thumb swiped my lower lip. "When you left, you were still here. Like a damn ghost haunting my every step and thought. I never really moved on. Wasn't going to. You had a piece of me."

I didn't know what to say, so I rolled onto my side and planted myself against him, burying my face in his neck.

"Irene didn't know about you and us. Never felt right telling her about you. That's why she believed it was the job, but it wasn't. Just was that a big piece of me was always with you."

"Oh God," I murmured, clutching his shoulder with the hand that wasn't wedged between us. Tears welled up in my eyes. "I . . . it was the same. It is the same for me."

Somehow he managed to circle both arms around me, and our legs tangled together. Cole held me tight, and as I lay there, sated and *happy*, something occurred to me that should've many years ago. With every man I'd been with since the Groom, I held them back, built up walls that no one had really tried to scale or to knock down. I'd always believed that I'd been open, but I knew I hadn't. Not until now. But Cole had seen that wall and he knocked at it until a crack formed, and that fissure spread, bringing that wall down. It was more than just him though. It was also me. I let him in.

I was ready.

The riot of emotions I was feeling were good, and

a small smiled tugged at the corners of my lips. I was finally *ready*.

It wasn't too much longer before I fell asleep and for the first time in a very long time, I slept without nightmares.

SUNDAY WAS A surprisingly normal day despite *everything* that had happened. Cole was up before me, and that meant he had coffee ready for when I stumbled out of the bedroom. For that alone, he was truly a keeper.

He became even more of a keeper throughout the day. He helped out around the inn, taking care of small maintenance issues Mom hadn't gotten around to hiring someone to fix.

After lunch—lunch he'd run out and grabbed for us—I found him in the bathroom of one of the rooms, half his body under the sink. One booted foot rocking to some unheard rhythm. Metal clanged off metal.

"What are you doing?" I asked, leaning against the frame of the door.

"Fixing a pipe." His foot stilled. "Your mom mentioned she hadn't been putting guests in this room because the pipe leaks after the water is turned on."

I bit down on my lip but it didn't stop my smile. "You don't have to do this."

"I don't mind," he replied. "Just a washer that needs to be replaced. Nothing major."

"That's sweet of you to do," I said, my gaze traveling over his long legs. He was wearing jeans that faded over his knees. "Thank you."

There was a pause. "Thank me later, babe."

I started to ask how and then I completely understood how he wanted me to thank him. My entire body flushed hot. Memories of last night flooded me. "I can . . . I can do that."

Cole chuckled from under the sink. "Oh yeah, baby, you can."

Needless to say I was distracted most of the day.

Cole's friend showed up in the later part of the afternoon, and he was there until the evening, wiring my apartment along with Mom's. Both of us got a new key fob out of the deal.

No press showed up, but every time I heard the door open, I waited for that shady journalist to pop back up or for Detective Conrad to come by. Tyron never showed to ask more questions. Later that night, I admitted to Cole that I'd expected the detective to be around, but Cole explained that was common. Tyron had asked all that he needed to at the time, and if he'd missed something, he'd be back.

Cole knocked all thoughts of the detective out of my head when we were in bed. First it was with his hands, his mouth, and then every part of him. Then afterward, when we lay in each other's arms, he did it again.

"I want you to meet my parents," he announced.

I was running my fingers over his hand, tracing the line of the bones from knuckle to knuckle. My hand stilled. "Come again?"

"You never got to meet them before," he continued. "And I want you to meet them."

"I . . ." I trailed off, because I had no idea what I was about to say.

He threw his long leg over mine. "You're not planning to go anywhere soon, are you?"

"No."

"Then I think it's a great idea for you to meet my parents."

Mulling that over, I agreed after a few moments. No actual plans were made, and it still felt a little weird thinking and planning for the whole meet-the-parents deal when I was receiving severed fingers in the mail, but I knew it was important to continue living. Not just existing like I had been immediately after the Groom or, in reality, how I'd existed the last ten years. So it was okay to make plans and to live.

Cole woke me up Monday morning, before the first light of dawn had begun to splash across the floors, with his hand between my thighs and his mouth on my breasts.

So I wasn't complaining.

Not when he flipped me onto my belly and lifted me up onto my knees with an arm around my waist—there was nothing but an excited gasp parting my lips. And when he entered me from behind, complaining was the last thing on my mind.

"Grab the headboard," he ordered in a rough voice.

Doing what I was told, I held on to the smooth wood. The fullness was insane. He started off with a languid pace, but then he gripped my waist. A moan slid out of me as he started moving fast and hard. My hips pushed back to meet his thrusts. He felt great. Amazing, actually. One hand reached around, swiping his thumb along the knot of nerves, and I came apart, the rippling sensations rolling over me. Grunting, he pumped his hips and then buried deep.

Cole brought me down to the bed, his weight half on me, and I didn't mind that at all as we both lay there, me on my belly, our bodies tangled together, being surrounded by his weight, his smell—everything. Completely sated, I was floating in that blissed-out half-awake state. His hand trailed down the center of my back and over my hip. "You okay?"

"I'm dead. But I'm dead in a good way," I mumbled.

He chuckled. "I'm going to head out. Got to head to work. I'll call you later, okay?"

"Mmm-hmm."

His lips brushed my shoulder. "You need an alarm set or anything?"

"Uh-uh."

"You going to sleep a little more?"

I gave my best impression of a nod.

Laughing the sexy laugh again, he rose over me and kissed my cheek, pulled up the comforter, draping it over my back, and then he was gone. Feeling a way I hadn't in a long time, I fell back to sleep just the way Cole left me, on my belly and with a smile on my face.

MY CELLPHONE RANG around ten o'clock Monday morning, while I was about two hours into book-keeping. When I saw Miranda's name appear on my screen, I more than welcomed the break.

"What's up?" I answered.

"Oh my God, girl, why didn't you tell me Detective Tyron is one fine-looking man?" she demanded.

I blinked. "What? How did you see him?"

"He was here, but I don't have a lot of time. I'm in between class right now," she continued. "But you're not going to believe what is going on and it has to do with why I now know that Detective Conrad will be the father of my future babies."

Grinning, I rose from the table in the kitchen and stretched out my back. Maybe I had misread the whole Jason thing. "Did he come talk to you about what happened?"

"No. He was here with another detective this morning. I just happened to be talking to Cindy—she's one of the counselors here, and I saw him talking to Coach Currie. You remember him, right? The hot coach we drooled all over in school? I told you he still works here."

I walked over to the island. "Yeah, I remember."

"Well, I figured the rumors about him having possibly inappropriate relationships with some of the senior girls was finally panning out to be true."

"What?" My brows flew up.

"But it wasn't," she continued like she hadn't just suggested that the coach was breaking what I assumed was more than one law. "Tammy, who works the front desk and literally can hear a cricket sneeze two rooms over, says they were here questioning the coach about Angela."

My back stiffened. "What?"

"I don't know any more details," she said. "But obviously Detective Hottie must suspect something."

"Yeah," I murmured, turning toward the door leading to the back room.

"I have to go, but I'll call you later."

Hanging up, I placed my cell on the kitchen island. Tyron was questioning Coach Currie over Angela? That was . . . absolutely unexpected, but there was something about that piece of news that nagged at me.

I walked around the kitchen island and slowly opened the door. Cold air swirled around my legs. What was the man who practically plowed me over wearing?

Opening the door to the staff staircase, I peered inside the dimly lit landing. Wasn't he wearing a baseball cap with some kind of emblem and a white shirt with the same kind of emblem? And I'd thought that emblem had been vaguely familiar.

My pulse pounded as I stared down into the shadowy cellar door. It was locked, and Cole had put a deadbolt on it, something we probably should've done a long time ago.

I shivered.

Coaches wear baseball caps. So did a lot of other people, like more than half the male and female population. It was a long stretch, but Tyron was questioning him.

Biting down on my lip, I closed the door and turned around. I needed to see Coach Currie. It had been forever since I'd seen him and when I pictured him, I did so through sixteen-year-old eyes that weren't very reliable, but maybe seeing him would jog a memory loose.

Short of camping out at the high school to catch a glimpse of him, I wasn't sure what to do. I hurried back into the kitchen. Mom was there, scratching out a grocery list at the kitchen island.

"Everything okay?" she asked.

I nodded absently as I sat at the table and took my laptop out of hibernation. Hitting up Google, I typed in the name of the high school and the city. The county website for the school was the first option. I clicked on it.

"The workers are out in the cemetery." Mom nibbled on the cap of her pen. "They're trying to get the entryway to the tunnel sealed up before it starts snowing again."

"When is it calling for more snow?" I scanned the menu bar, finding the athletics tab. I clicked on it.

"Late tonight." She frowned at her list. "Going to the grocery store with Daphne in a couple of hours. If you need anything, add it to the list."

"'Kay," I murmured, scanning the list of departments. What did Currie coach? Football.

I clicked on football and was rewarded with a series of images of the varsity, JV, and freshman teams. Clicking on the one that showed the coaches standing behind the team as they posed on the bleachers, I expanded the photo but was unable to recognize their faces. Or anything.

But they were wearing black baseball caps like the man in the stairwell.

Since Currie taught gym, I went back to the teachers tab and searched him down. Excitement rose when I saw his name, clicking on it, hoping it brought up a picture.

Nothing.

There was absolutely nothing under his name.

"Oh, come on," I muttered.

Mom drifted closer. "What are you doing?"

"Nothing," I said, and then glanced up at her. "Actually, Miranda called and said the detective at the school today was questioning one of their coaches. The rumor is that it was about Angela."

"Really?" She sat across from me.

"And I was thinking about the guy that was in here. He was wearing a baseball cap. I got online to see if I could look up a recent picture of the coach." Leaning back, I crossed my arms. "But there's nothing under his name and the football pictures aren't much of a help."

Mom's brows puckered. "Wait a minute. You said there was an emblem on the baseball cap and the shirt, right?" When I nodded, she said, "Was it a bulldog? I believe their logo or whatever you want to call it for their mascot is gray."

Stomach dropping, my gaze snapped back to the computer screen, and there it was, right at the top, on the right side. Jesus, if it was a snake it would've bitten me right in the boob.

"And I think the coaches wear white-and-black shirts with the same emblem," she continued.

Holy crap, she was right. Now that I was looking at the head of the bulldog, I got why I originally thought it was familiar. Everything had happened so fast and it hadn't been well lit in the stairwell, but now that I saw the mascot, I knew—I knew—that was what I'd seen.

And Coach Currie was homegrown. There was a good chance he would've known about the tunnel. A hell of a good chance. What if he had been the person who came in here and took her key?

But he couldn't have anything to do with the vandalism or the . . . the finger. My life had absolutely nothing to do with his. So maybe these two things, whatever happened with Angela and what was happening with me, were completely unrelated. That had to be good news, I thought. Not sure that I believed that, but it felt that way to me.

"Mom," I said, looking up at her. "You're a genius."

"I like to think that." A faint smile appeared. "What did you find out over there?"

I drew in a deep breath. "I think the guy who was in the stairwell might've been Coach Currie."

UNSURE IF I should take my suspicions to Detective Conrad, I called Cole, figuring he'd be able to tell me if I was wasting the detective's time or not, but his cell didn't even ring. Went straight to voicemail.

I tried to busy myself with the bookkeeping, but that lasted all of twenty minutes before I picked up my phone and went up to my apartment, finding the detective's card on the coffee table. There was a good chance that my suspicions could be helpful to them, and there was also the probability that it meant nothing, but a girl was missing. Better safe than sorry.

Typing in his number, I hit call and then waited. It rang several times and then also went to voice-mail. I left a quick message and then headed back downstairs.

The kitchen was silent, and I walked toward the front of the house, too restless to sit down at the computer. Exhaling roughly, I stood at the desk, staring at the reservation book, but not really seeing anything. I placed my phone on the top.

My mind wandered to this morning, and as I splayed my hands on the smooth surface of the desk, a small smile tugged at my lips. That had been beyond amazing. Actually, Cole was—

The inn doors opened, and my smile faded as I turned toward them. Two men walked in, both in matching dark trousers and black down jackets. They were middle-aged, their expressions serious, and I knew immediately they weren't here to check in.

"Sasha Keeton?" the light-haired man on the right asked.

I crossed my arms, glancing between the two. "Yes. Can I help you?"

"I'm Special Agent Myers," he replied, reaching into his jacket and pulling out the flashing badge with *FBI* written across it. "This is Special Agent Rodriquez. We need to speak with you about the murder of Angela Reidy."

"ANGELA'S DEAD?" I pressed my hand against my chest as I leaned into the desk, suddenly weak in the knees. Shock blasted through me, and I wanted to believe I hadn't heard the agent correctly. "How?"

The darker-haired Agent Rodriquez slid Agent Myers a sharp look. "I'm sorry. Typically we prefer to not announce such tragic news so bluntly."

Agent Myers simply raised a fair eyebrow.

I stared at them, but I really wasn't seeing them, because all I saw was pretty Angela standing in the kitchen, smiling as she nibbled on a cookie. All I heard was Angela chattering on about nothing and everything.

She wasn't going to smile anymore.

She wasn't going to ramble on ever again.

Horror sucked the air out of my lungs. This couldn't be happening.

"Oh my God," I whispered, swallowing hard. "I'm sorry. You've caught me off guard. I hoped that she would be found alive. I . . ." Trailing off, I shook my head.

"We all hoped that would be the case, but unfortunately that is not what has occurred," Rodriquez responded. "It is of the utmost importance that we speak to you in private."

My stomach tumbled. "Of course. We can go into the—"

"Not here," Myers cut in. "We need you to come with us."

Unease blossomed at the base of my spine. "Go where?"

Meyer slid his badge back in his jacket. "The station down the street has a room available that we can use."

"The police station?" My voice rose.

The other agent tried to smile reassuringly but failed a little. "It's just a formality and it's a secure location."

That made sense. I guessed. "I'm the only person at the inn right now—"

"It's imperative that we speak with you now," Myers interrupted. Again. "Is there anyone you could call in?"

Pressing my lips together, I turned to where I'd left my phone on the desk. Mom was in the middle of grocery shopping with Daphne, and I knew there was a good chance she'd left her phone in her car. She always did that whenever she was out. I could text her and let her know what was happening, but she wouldn't get it until she was done. Miranda was teaching.

"Let me try our . . ." I didn't finish that statement.

Calling James seemed suitable, but our chef was so not a people person. I don't even think he'd ever stepped foot out of the kitchen once since he worked here. That left Jason. "Let me call one of my friends."

The agents waited while I picked up my phone and hit his contact. I roamed away from the desk.

Jason answered on the third ring. "Hey, Sasha, what's up?"

"Um. I have a huge favor to ask," I said, voice sounding weird to my own ears.

"Yeah. Yeah. Ask away."

"I hate to ask this, but can you come down to the inn and watch over things until Mom gets back?"

"Sure." Not a moment of hesitation. He was such a good friend despite how terrible of a friend I was. "Is everything okay?"

I glanced over my shoulder, clearing my throat. I couldn't tell him about Angela. Not right now with the agents standing right behind me. He would find out soon enough. "Yeah. There's some agents here—federal. They need to talk to me."

"Shit. Is anyone there to go with you? Cole?"

"No, but I'll be fine." My hand shook. "Are you sure you can do this?"

"Of course," Jason replied. "Be there in ten minutes or less."

"Thank you," I whispered. "I owe you."

"It's no biggie. Be there soon."

I faced the agents. "One of my friends will be here shortly."

Rodriquez nodded. "We apologize for the inconvenience."

"It's okay." Coldness seeped into my bones. "How

can I be inconvenienced when someone . . . someone is dead?"

THE ROOM IN the police station down the street looked like the ones on TV. It was small, walls a plain white with fingerprint smudges at chest height. There was a small round table and four metal folding chairs that weren't particularly comfortable.

The ginormous SUV they'd driven me down the street in had extremely comfortable seating. Heated seats too. I didn't even know why I was thinking about seats, but it seemed a safer thing to focus on.

I really owed Jason. Right now he was sitting behind the desk at the inn, having no idea what he was doing, but he was sitting there until Mom returned. I'd texted her on the way to the police station. I also hadn't told her about Angela, because there was no way one could break that kind of news over text.

A shiver coursed over my skin.

Did Cole know I was with these agents? He was a federal agent himself. Wouldn't he know? Maybe that was a stupid thought. Not like the FBI had one giant hive mind.

My hands were chilled despite the fact I had them shoved between my knees. I'd been escorted through the back entrance of the police station, down a narrow hall, and then deposited in this room with a small bottle of water.

The door opened, causing me to jump. My chin jerked up. Both agents came in. They weren't alone. I relaxed when I saw Detective Tyron Conrad's familiar face.

"Hey," he said, taking the seat beside me. "Sorry about this. I didn't know the agents were coming to get you." His jaw hardened. "If I did, I would've been there to advise them that bringing you down here wasn't necessary."

"It was completely necessary," Myers retorted.

Tyron huffed a laugh out as he leaned back in the chair, planting an ankle on his knee. "Landis is not going to like this."

My eyes widened.

Myers stiffened. "This has nothing to do with Agent Landis." Skin crinkled around his eyes as he sat at the table. "Miss Keeton, we're going to be very blunt about what happened."

"I don't expect anything less," I replied, taking a deep breath. "Why am I being spoken to about . . . about Angela?"

Tyron opened his mouth, but Myers answered. "You received a severed finger in the mail on Saturday. We're pretty confident that finger belonged to Miss Reidy."

Acid churned in my stomach. I opened my mouth, but nothing came out.

Tyron placed his hand on my arm. "Angela's body was found this morning. The ring finger on her left hand was missing."

Pressure clamped down on my chest, squeezing tight like a vise. When I spoke, it sounded like I did so inside a tunnel. "Where . . . where was her body found?"

"I think you know the answer to that," Myers stated.

My gaze shot to him.

"Her body was found by the old water tower off Route 11," Rodriquez spoke up, voice gentler.

"Oh my God," I whispered, inhaling roughly.

Rodriquez rested an arm on the table. "She was found in the same location the victims of the Groom were discovered and in the same location—"

"The woman from Frederick was found there." I pressed my palm against my forehead. Bitter panic mixed with sorrow, increasing the pressure in my throat and chest. "I don't understand."

"I think you do," Myers retorted.

Tyron dropped his foot to the floor with a heavy thud and leaned forward. "What in the hell is that supposed to mean, Myers?"

Lowering my hand, I looked at the agent. He was sitting back, arms crossed over a puffed-up chest. "What I'm saying is that Miss Keeton seems like a bright woman. She can put two and two together. We've got a copycat on our hands . . . or we got someone trying to make it look that way."

Anger spiked, pushing down the horror. "Yes, I can put two and two together, but that sure doesn't tell me why you insisted on bringing me to the police station to tell me this."

"Because if it is a copycat, then you may be able to add some insight into our investigation," Rodriquez explained, his gaze steady. "You were the only victim of the Groom to survive—"

"I know that." My hands were trembling so I shoved them back between my knees. "I know that I'm the only one." The room felt like it had shrunk. I glanced at the door, wanting out of here so badly. I looked at Tyron. "What happened to Angela?"

Voice low, he said, "Current evidence suggests she was strangled."

"Oh God," I whispered, closing my eyes and immediately regretting it. I saw Angela but with horrible marks around her throat. The kinds of bruises that snuffed the life out of someone. "Was she . . . do you know if she was held captive?"

"There was evidence suggesting she was held," he explained, and I knew what he was referencing without him even elaborating. If she'd been restrained the way the Groom had held his victims, there'd be ligature marks on her ankles. Her wrists.

"Was she . . . was she sexually assaulted?" I asked.

"We don't know yet," Tyron responded.

The contents of my stomach shifted as I placed my elbow on the table and rested my forehead in my palm. "Does her . . . boyfriend know?"

"He and her family have been notified," Tyron told me.

The burn in my eyes increased. What they must be experiencing right now was beyond imagination.

"We have some questions we need to ask you," Myers spoke, and this time, the edge of impatience was gone from his voice. "Do you think you can help us?"

What I wanted to do was to get out of this room, go home, and have space, silence, and time to process what I was told. But I couldn't do that. I couldn't be that person anymore. It wasn't just cowardly. It was also selfish, because if I could somehow help Angela in death, I would, so I nodded.

"Good," Rodriquez murmured, and I heard the rustling of paper. "We're aware that there have been other instances outside of what happened on Saturday involving you since you returned. Can you please go over, in detail, what they were?"

Even though I'd already been down this road more than once, I told them everything I remembered, taking breaks to sip my water. It wasn't until I was finished telling them about discovering Angela's missing house key did I remember what I'd suspected from earlier.

"I think I might've figured out who took Angela's key. I could be wrong—"

"Let us be the ones to determine that," Myers said.

I glanced at the men. "I think it might've been Coach Currie. It's why I called you earlier," I said to Tyron. "The emblem that I'd told Derek—I mean, Officer Bradshaw about? I think it was the bulldog—the high school mascot. I know thousands of people could have that baseball cap and shirt, but . . . I heard he was being questioned this morning, and that was what triggered the fact the emblem on the hat seemed vaguely familiar."

Tyron arched a brow, but didn't, thankfully, ask how I knew Currie had been questioned. "Do you have any type of relationship with Coach Donnie Currie?"

"No. I mean, he was coaching at the school when I went there, but that's the extent of how I know him."

"But he was around during the time of the Groom," Rodriquez stated. "You haven't seen him since you returned, other than when you believe you ran into him at the inn?"

"I haven't seen him. At all. I've only gone out once really, and that was to a restaurant down the street with my friends."

"Which restaurant was that?" Rodriquez asked.

"The steakhouse a few blocks down," I explained, giving them the name. "That was a week ago."

Myers shifted in his seat. "Anyone else who you've talked with? Tyron here has told us you're seeing Cole Landis."

I nodded once more. "Yes. We . . . um, we dated before I left, and we just reconnected."

"You didn't stay in contact during the years you were gone?"

Looking at Myers, I shook my head. "No. I only stayed in contact with my mother and my friend Miranda."

"But you two are together so . . . quickly?"

The tips of my ears tingled. "Once he heard I was back in town, he came to see me and the rest . . ." The rest was really none of his business. "We reconnected."

"Huh," murmured Myers. "Just like that? Interesting."

Tyron's eyes narrowed.

My breath caught. "Yeah, just like that. What are you insinuating?"

"Not insinuating anything, ma'am." Myers moved on. "Anyone you've met that you might've thought was acting strangely?"

One person came to mind, and it was possibly the most awkward place to bring it up. "There has been someone, but it's going to sound crazy. When I went out to dinner, I ran into the mayor."

"Mayor Hughes?" Tyron questioned.

"Yes." I told them about the mayor's odd behavior and his second visit. "I know he's worried about me possibly stirring up the past, but it just, I don't know, feels like more than that."

The two agents shared a look and then Rodriquez said as he scribbled something on a piece of paper, "Anyone else?"

I shook my head. "There is no one else. I've thought about this. There isn't anyone else that I know of."

"How close were you to Angela Reidy?" Myers asked, suddenly shifting topics quick enough to give me whiplash.

"Not that close," I responded truthfully. "I'd just met her last week, but I know she's been working at the inn for a while."

The door cracked open and a younger officer stuck his head in. "Conrad, you got a second? There's something I need you in."

Tyron nodded and rose. "I think it's Miss Reidy's family. I'll be back as soon as I can."

"It's okay," I whispered, thinking I had it so much easier than what Angela's family was experiencing right now. I watched him leave and then faced the two agents.

Myers' dark eyes met mine. "Did you two have any arguments?"

"What?" Shock splashed through me, locking up my muscles.

"It's just normal line of questioning," he replied.

I glanced at Rodriquez. His expression was impressively blank. "I didn't know Angela well enough to have an argument with her. From what I know of her, she's really nice—*was* really nice," I corrected myself with a wince. "Actually, really sweet. She's someone I would call bubbly and talkative."

Myers cocked his head to the side. "So, you barely knew her, but she's dead and her finger—"

The door swung open with force and suddenly Cole was storming into the room, his eyes like glacial ice. Relief poured into me.

"What the fuck?" Cole demanded, walking around the table.

Rodriquez leaned back in the chair, dropping his pen on the table as Myers rose. "This is not even your department, Landis. You have no reason to be in on this interview."

"Doesn't have anything to do with me?" He stopped in front of Tyron's empty chair and planted a fist on the table. "You haul my woman into the damn police station to question her about a murder she just found out about?"

Myers' face flushed with anger. "It's protocol, and you damn well know that."

"I don't give a flying fuck if it's protocol or not, you have my number, you should've called me," Cole fired back, straightening. "I know how you work, Myers. That shit isn't going to happen here."

"Oh, you know how I work?" Myers snorted. "How about you go—"

"Finish that sentence and that's the last thing you'll be doing with your mouth for a while," Cole warned.

"All right. Everyone chill the hell out." Tyron appeared in the doorway. Over his shoulders, I saw a couple of blue uniforms. "No one needs this shit right now."

Cole drew in a deep breath as he pinned a stare on his friend. "This shouldn't have happened this way. You know that."

"And that's why I called you the moment I knew they were heading to talk to her," Tyron responded.

"Fucking A," muttered Myers, sitting back down.

Surprised, I glanced up at Cole, but he was still eyeballing Myers like he wanted to put him through the wall. I was sensing there was definitely a past between the two of them that was not friendly. Cole had to have sped like a demon to get from Baltimore to here.

Rodriquez lifted his chin. "You know we had to talk to her."

"And you know what she's been through," Cole shot back. "You do not pull her into the station like she's a damn suspect."

Myers pinched the bridge of his nose. "She's connected to this. You know that. I know that."

My stomach dropped, and even though I'd figured that out the moment they told me that they believed the severed finger belonged to Angela, I'd had literally no time to process this.

"We need to find out what the connection is," Rodriquez said, voice carefully even. "That's why we're talking to her."

"You don't do it this way," Cole responded. He turned to me, his hand curving around the nape of my neck. Our eyes met, and it was the first time he'd looked at me since bursting into the room. "You okay?"

"Yeah," I whispered, because I figured saying

something other than that would not be wise in the moment.

His eyes searched mine for a moment and then he looked over at Rodriquez. "Do you all need anything else from her?"

He shook his head. "We pretty much got what we need."

"Which isn't much," snapped Myers.

A muscle flexed along Cole's jaw and he opened his mouth to respond, but I beat him to it. "If I can be of any help, I will be. I've told you everything I know, and if that hasn't been of any help, then I'm sorry."

"So, nothing else?" Cole asked, tone hard as he slid his hand to my shoulder. When they didn't answer, he said, "Let me get you out of here."

Glancing at the agents, I grabbed my purse off the floor and stood. Tyron moved out of the doorway as Cole folded me into his side. We walked out of the room, and into the narrow hall.

Cole's arm around my shoulders tightened as we walked toward the back door. Tyron followed us out into the fading afternoon sun.

"Hold on a sec," Tyron said, waiting for us to stop. He glanced at Cole and then looked down at me. "I'm sorry that they pulled you in there. That conversation could've happened at the inn."

I folded my arms across my stomach. "It's over. It's whatever, but . . . someone really is copying the Groom, aren't they? That's what's happening here."

Tyron placed his hands on his hips. Wind stirred the white dress shirt he wore. "We aren't a hundred percent sure yet."

Cursing under his breath, Cole lifted his gaze to the sky. "What else would be going down? Someone out there is following in that dead son of a bitch's footsteps. And you and I both know what's coming next."

Tyron didn't respond, but he knew. So did I. If there was someone out there copying the Groom then that meant . . . that it was already too late for the next victim.

Because if this person knew enough about the Groom and was following the Groom's pathology, then the next victim was already taken.

The woman had no idea why it was her, why she was here in this cold place that smelled of dirt and death. Angela had known. She'd known the moment she'd opened those pretty eyes and seen where she was.

Angela had cried.

She'd begged.

Like they all did, and there was nothing wrong with that. If they hadn't pleaded for their lives, then what life did they have?

Angela had known who to blame. She'd known whose fault all of this was as the blade cut deep into her finger, severing it. She'd known when she took her last wheezing breath that she'd still be alive if *she* hadn't come back.

But this woman, in her plain white blouse and one-size-too-big black pants, had no fucking clue. It was perfect, really. Angela would be bad enough, but this one . . . oh yeah, this one was the icing on the fucking cake. This woman was someone who simply had the poor luck of crossing paths with *her*.

This one would prove no one was safe.

SNOW FELL, DOTTING the night sky and blanketing the ground below. From where I stood in my living room, looking out below, I couldn't tell how much was out there, and I had no idea when it would stop, but there was nothing more beautiful than freshly fallen snow. It was one of the things I'd missed most when I lived in the South.

When Cole and I got back from the police station, Mom had returned, and I told her and Jason what had happened.

It had been horrible.

Because I recognized the look in my mom's eyes as the news of Angela's fate processed, as she worked through the details of what had happened to the poor girl and what that meant. She had stared at me like she had when she said she almost wished I hadn't come home. Now I don't think she "almost" wanted that.

It was a definite.

Jason had sat down, his gaze far off, and he remained at the kitchen table; the only thing he'd said for about an hour was, "She was just eating cookies."

Here one moment, gone in the worst way the next.

Miranda had come over in the evening, and by that point, what happened to Angela had hit the evening news, and it was all the newscaster spoke about. We'd sat quietly, and then we'd tried to change the subject. Miranda talked about Coach Currie and the rumors flying around about him.

When we lapsed into silence again, I immediately jumped on another subject, wanting to hold back other darker, more troubling thoughts. "Can I ask you something?"

Her brows rose. "Uh. Yeah."

"Is there something going on between you and Jason?"

"What?" Her head whipped toward mine so fast I was surprised she didn't hurt herself. "Why would you ask that?"

"Well, you two seem really close." I nudged her arm. "Like I get you guys have stayed friends this whole time, but . . ."

"But what?"

"But there's just something there," I said, grinning when she sighed heavily. "I can't put my finger on it, but I—"

"We hooked up," she interrupted me, and when my eyes widened, she smacked her hands over her face. "It was a couple of months ago. We went out. Both of us were drinking. We weren't super drunk, but one thing led to another, and yeah, we hooked up."

I twisted toward her. "Wow. Okay. I suspected something, but wasn't a hundred percent sure."

She lowered her hands. "We haven't really talked about it. He's still technically married even though he's separated, but . . . yeah, it hasn't been weird or anything. And I don't think he's getting back with Cameron."

I processed all of that. "Do you like him, as in you want more than just that one random, not entirely drunk hookup?"

"I don't know," she said, untypically unsure. "I mean, I like him. I really do. We've been friends for a long time, and I don't know, there's just something cute about his nerdiness. And that man's got a body under those dress shirts and slacks."

Holding my hands, I warded all the info off. "I really don't want to think about Jason's body, because that would be weird for me."

Miranda laughed.

"Why don't you talk to him, be up front about wanting to see how things go?" I asked.

Her lips curved up on the corner as she tucked a braid back behind her ear. "Maybe I will, but I just don't want to ruin our friendship. I couldn't deal with that, you know?"

"Yeah." I pressed my lips together. "But I think you should think about it. He seems to really be into you and you seem to really like him more than just a friend."

She nodded slowly, but I had a feeling that she wasn't ready to broach that conversation with Jason. I didn't blame her for that.

Miranda had left before it got too late, and I made

her text me when she got home. She hadn't balked at the idea, and I'd relaxed when I got the message from her saying her "ass was in bed."

Tugging the ends of my heavy cardigan together, I shifted my weight to my other foot. It was late, well past two in the morning, and I'd long since given up on trying to sleep. The respite from the restless nights hadn't lasted long, because even with Cole slumbering next to me, I couldn't sleep. Not wanting to disturb him, I'd slipped out of the bed and made my way out to the living room. I watched the snow fall, my mind caught up in the twisted memories of the past and the horror of what was happening now.

I couldn't stop thinking about Angela and her family. This shouldn't have happened to her. This shouldn't happen to anyone, but it had to her, and I knew deep down it had also happened to the poor woman from Frederick.

Should've known better than to believe in coincidences.

Now a nightmare from the past was back, and I had to *believe* this was happening. Someone was out there and they'd already killed one woman, most likely two, and I knew that if the person was following the behaviors of the Groom, he already had someone else.

Stomach churning, I closed my eyes. It could be anyone. Not necessarily even someone who'd lived here ten years ago. You could find anything on the Internet, including sites dedicated to serial killers, where they were talked about as if they were celebrities. Their sick predilections discussed with enough information that you could recreate every murder down to the last detail. Someone from anywhere in the world could've decided they were going to introduce the world to the Groom, round two.

But why—why the Groom out of all the serial killers with higher body counts and who were more well known? Why did it start when I returned? Actually, it had started right before I returned with the woman from Frederick. Did it—

So caught up in my thoughts, I gasped when I felt strong arms circle my waist from behind.

"Sasha." Cole's deep voice rumbled in my ear. "How long have you been out here?"

I relaxed into his embrace. "Not too long. I didn't want to wake you."

"Babe." His chin dragged along the side of my neck. "If you can't sleep, you wake me. I'll help you get back to sleep. You talk to me about what's on your mind that's keeping you awake, and if that doesn't work, then I can get creative."

That last part brought a smile to my face.

Lifting his head, he rested his chin atop mine. "What's on your mind?"

"A lot of things."

"Tell me."

I sighed. "Cole, it's late. You have to work in the morning. You should be asleep."

"Yeah, I got to work, but my girl is standing in front of a window in the middle of the night watching the snow with her mind most likely full of terrible shit," he said. "And that's more important than getting a full night's sleep."

My girl. Those two words. I loved the sound

of them. They also made me think of what Agent Myers had said. "Do you think it's . . . weird that we're . . ."

"We're what?"

"That we're here right now. That ten years have passed and we're this close after a handful of days?"

He didn't answer for a moment. "It's uncommon. Doesn't mean it's weird. But you know what it does mean?"

I leaned my head back against his chest. "What?"

"What I said before. We're lucky."

I liked the sound of that better than the weird part. "I'm not sure we're so lucky right now."

"We will be." Lowering his head, he kissed my cheek. "We will get through this."

He'd said that with such confidence, I almost had to believe him. The only hang-up was that I knew life didn't care about how much confidence you had or how badly you wanted to believe in something.

"Did someone say something that's got you asking a question like that?" Cole asked.

I raised a brow, wondering if he'd developed some kind of mind-reading ability. "That agent—Agent Myers said something."

He cursed under his breath. "He's a dick and doesn't have a clue what he's talking about."

"You two don't get along, do you?"

"Not particularly." His arms tightened around me and then he loosened them, sliding his hands to my hips. He turned me around so I was facing him. "He used to work in my department. When I was a new recruit, we had a case that came across our desk because the perp had gang ties. Was just a kid, only sixteen, but already deep in the streets," he explained. "But the crime he'd committed had nothing to do with the gangs or running drugs. He'd shot his father."

"God," I whispered.

"He'd shot his father because that bastard was beating the shit out of him and his mom," Cole added, and that was even worse to hear. "Myers didn't give two shits that it was an act of desperation. Don't get me wrong, not like I'm saying violence is the answer to violence, but you can understand how someone eventually snaps. Everything is black and white with Myers, but the world doesn't operate that way. We didn't see eye to eye on that case."

I cocked my head to the side. "What happened to the boy?"

"Went to prison." He took my hand. "Got life."

My brows knitted. "You didn't think he deserved that?"

One shoulder rose. "The kid was a product of a shitty home and streets that suck them in. He grew up in an environment where violence is answered with more violence. Where a bullet to the chest is the end-all. That's all the kid knew. Sometimes people do wrong and they need to be punished for it, but there are times when you can understand what drove their actions."

"True," I murmured. "You see a lot of stuff that isn't black and white, don't you?"

"Sometimes." Cole led me over to the couch and when he sat down, he pulled me into his lap so I was sitting sideways. "But most of the time it is black and white." He paused. "You up thinking and not sleeping because of Myers?"

I had a feeling that if I said yes, it wouldn't end well, and the truth was, it wasn't just because of Myers. "Do you think it was a mistake that I came home?"

"Hell no." Not a moment of hesitation.

I smiled as I placed my hands on his chest. "Mom said something like that. She meant it from a good place and a bad one—a bad one full of worry. She's scared for me."

"Sasha . . ."

Fear trickled into my blood like drops of ice. "What if me coming home caused this?"

"Babe." He grasped my cheeks as his eyes came to mine. "Nothing you've done has caused this. You aren't responsible for what is happening."

I gripped his shoulders. "I get what you're saying, but indirectly—"

"Indirectly or directly, you're not responsible." He slid his hands back and his fingers gathered my hair back from my face. "You've already given up ten years of your life to that bastard."

"I—"

"You know you did," he stated firmly, and damn it, he was right. "And you're not going to give up more of life to some nameless, faceless monster. No more."

God, what he said was so damn true.

"I can't . . . I can't help but feel like we're on the verge of repeating history," I whispered, giving words to the fear that had been building inside me. "That it's going to happen all over again."

"It's not," he was quick to respond. "The past is not going to repeat itself. There is no way I'm going to let that happen."

I wanted to ask how he thought he could stop it, but there wasn't going to be an answer. There couldn't be.

"You belong home," he said, guiding my head toward his. "You belong here, with me, like you should've been this whole time."

Some of the pressure in my chest eased off. "Yeah," I whispered as I sifted my fingers through the short, soft strands of hair at the base of his neck.

"Sleepy?" he asked.

"No." I lifted my chin. "I'm thinking about the whole get-creative part you mentioned earlier? I'm really interested in that."

His eyes took on a hooded, heavy quality. "I'm always interested in that."

I pressed my forehead against his. "What exactly would those things entail?"

"I could tell you." His hands dropped to my hips and then suddenly I was in the air. Cole lifted me up as he rose, and my legs circled his waist out of instinct. "But I prefer to show you."

Holding on, I laughed softly. "I think I like the idea of you showing me."

"Good, because that's what you're going to get."

Cole's mouth was on mine as he walked us back to the bedroom, one arm securing me to him, the other hand at the back of my head. The strength he had was unbelievable as he lowered me to the bed without breaking contact. I by no means was a small woman, and I was surprised he didn't drop me.

Then I wasn't really thinking about any of that, because his mouth and hands were everywhere, shucking off my cardigan, and easing down the straps of my nightie, exposing my breasts to the cool, night air. The tips of my breasts beaded under his hot breath and then his mouth. The skirt of my nightie came up, the flannel bottoms he wore came off, and then he was between my thighs, and my knees were pressed into his sides.

The way he rocked his hips, the way each thrust hit the right spot each time with startling precision, took me farther and farther away from everything that had kept me awake and haunted me during the day.

Muscles started tightening in the most delicious way and Cole braced his weight on one arm. His lips glided over mine, and it was such a soft kiss, a sweet one, and it broke me.

I cried out, calling his name, and he was right behind me, his powerful body shuddering before half his weight hit me. He was heavy, but I didn't care. I wanted him there.

Kissing his bare chest, I slid my hand down his back as my pulse slowed. "Guess what?"

"Hmm?" His head was buried against my neck.

"That was an amazing sleeping aid," I told him. "I'd like one of them every evening, please."

Cole chuckled against my throat. "I can do that for you and then some."

MY CAR WAS finally ready for pickup on Tuesday. Since Cole had to head into Baltimore and someone needed to be at the inn, Jason picked me up during lunch and took me to the body shop down the road.

"Thank you for doing this," I said as we coasted down the street.

Jason smiled as he straightened his glasses. "It's really no problem. I own my own agency, so I can pretty much come and go as I please."

"Still awesome of you." Snow-covered lawns blurred. "Especially yesterday."

"Got to admit, I hope I don't get a call from you in the future to watch the inn because of something like that again."

I glanced over at him. "Me too."

Jason slowed as we neared a red light. "Have you seen the newspaper this morning?"

Shaking my head, I said, "Do I want to?"

His lips quirked. "No."

I sighed. "What does it say?"

Jason's hand tightened on the steering wheel. "It's about Angela—well, a little bit of the article is about her. The rest is about the . . . the Groom, and how we might have another serial killer on our hands."

"Yeah." I tipped my head back. "I'm not surprised to hear it."

"Miranda called me this morning about it. She wanted to go get every newspaper and burn them all."

My lips curved up. "I could see her organizing that."

His fingers tapped along the steering wheel. "How's your mom hanging in there?"

"Okay, but I know it's getting to her. I think . . . well, I know she's really worried and she's scared." I stretched out my legs, sighing. "I just hate that she's having to go through this again."

"And you," he pointed out. "You're having to go through it again."

Biting down on my lip, I didn't say anything. It was easier focusing on my mom and everyone else than myself, because when I did allow myself to really think about it, it scared the living hell out of me.

"You're lucky to still have your mom around," Jason said as he turned left. "I miss mine every day."

I thought about how he'd lost his mother and stepfather. A horrible, tragic accident. "Are you still looking for your father?"

His fingers stilled as he said, "Not anymore."

"I'm sorry."

Slowing down as we reached the body shop, he pulled into the parking lot. Gravel crunched under the tires. "It is what it is. Had to make peace with it."

Sometimes you didn't have any other option than to do that.

It took about fifteen minutes for me to get the keys to my car, and when I walked back out, Jason was there, standing outside of his car with his hands shoved into the pockets of his wool coat.

"What are you still doing here?" I walked up to him.

He tilted his head to the side. "Just wanted to make sure you got your car and everything starts."

"In other words, you're playing bodyguard."

Jason grinned. "Pretty much."

"That's sweet." Stretching up, I kissed his cheek. "You don't have to follow me back to the inn."

"Are you going straight back there?" he asked.

I nodded. "Thank you again." I started to turn as he headed for his driver's door. I stopped. "Have you talked to your wife recently?"

Jason blinked. "Random question."

My cheeks heated as I twisted the ring of keys in my hands. "I know, but I realized I haven't really asked about you and her. I didn't even know about it, and I'm trying to not be such a crappy—"

"It's okay." Jason laughed. "I talked to her a couple of days ago. She might come home for a visit."

"That's good news, right?"

"Yeah." His nose scrunched. "I think so."

"That's good." I glanced down at my keys. "I better get back."

He nodded with a grin. "Call me if you need anything. Serious."

"I have been, haven't I?"

Laughing, Jason climbed into his sedan, and I turned, walking toward my poor car. Happy to see it with windows again, I unlocked the door and climbed in. The coldness of the seats seeped through my jeans, and the air had a certain chemical smell to it, something that vaguely reminded me of a new car.

The trip back to the inn was uneventful and it felt amazing to be behind the wheel of my own vehicle again.

And I was so not parking it outside.

When I got back to the inn, I saw a UPS truck parked out front. Letting the car idle outside the carriage house, I jumped out and went around to the front, unlocking the large barnlike doors. They opened, inch by painful inch.

Making a mental note to get a quote on replacing these things with an automatic garage-door opener, knowing it would probably get turned down by the historic society, I climbed back into my car and eased it in beside Mom's truck.

Once parked, I turned off the car and patted the steering wheel before grabbing my purse and climbing back out. I closed the car door, hitting the lock button on my fob as I turned and looked. Sucking in a quick breath, I saw someone standing at the entrance of the carriage house, the bright sun blocking out their features and turning them into a tall, broad shadow.

Hairs along the back of my neck rose as I jerked back a step, surprise flashing through my system and quickly giving way to fear that felt like slush in my veins.

I clenched the keys, my mouth and throat drying. "Hello?"

The form—a man—stepped forward, out from the brightness of the cold January sun and into the dimly lit garage. The unease multiplied and spread, gluing my feet to where I stood when I saw who it was.

Coach Currie stood before me. "I need to talk to you."

CHAPTER 24

INSTINCT SPRUNG ALIVE. My heart jumped in my chest as I quickly realized several things at once. If Coach Currie was here, then he might know what I'd told the investigators, and that couldn't be good. I also realized in that moment that we were alone, very much so, in a carriage house, and no matter what his intentions were or how deeply he was involved, I could not be in here with him.

My gaze darted behind him. "I'm sorry, but I need—"

"I didn't mean to knock you down the stairs. That was an accident," he said, coming forward. "I didn't mean to do that. You have to believe that."

"Okay," I said, deciding to agree with him at this moment was the best possible practice. "I believe you, but I can't talk right now. I have to go. Maybe we can set up a time—"

"I would've stayed and helped, but I freaked out."

Outside, a truck turned on, engine churning loudly. "But I didn't do it on purpose. I swear."

"It's okay. I'm fine." I forced my voice to remain level as I shifted my weight. I was stuck between the two cars, only able to go backward, farther away from the doors, and he was too close, way too close. "But I really can't talk—"

Currie lurched forward, grabbing my arms before I could move back. I gasped as his fingers dug in. "This can't wait."

My heart ended up in my throat. Fear rose as my purse slipped from my grasp and hit the ground. "Please let me go."

"I didn't have anything to do with what happened to Angela. God, I would never do something like that." His brown eyes were wide. "We were screwing around and I'd left one of my jackets at her place. I just didn't want it to get out. My wife would leave me and it would be all over this goddamn town. I knew she left a key here in case she locked herself out. I thought I could grab it and get out without being seen. That's why I used the tunnel—"

"You need to let go of me." I tried pulling free, but his hands tightened. A hundred different scenarios flashed before me, nearly all of them involving me kicking him between the legs. "You need to let go of me."

"But I had nothing to do with what happened to her or—" Coach Currie's body jolted forward as his hands let go. I jumped to the side, bumping into Mom's truck as Currie's eyes rolled back. He fell forward, smacking into the floor.

My head jerked up, and I saw Jason standing there between my car and Mom's. He was holding a wrench. Wide eyed, he stared down at Currie. "I just remembered I left my gloves here yesterday, behind the desk. I was coming back to get them when I saw the doors open."

I almost laughed out of relief. "Oh my God."

"It was him? He was the one responsible for all of this?"

"I . . . I don't know," I whispered.

"Are you okay?" he asked, stepping around the prone body of the coach. "I heard you telling him to let you go, and I—I just reacted. I picked up the wrench that was on a shelf and I didn't think."

"I'm okay." I reached out, placing my hand on his arm as I stared down at the coach. "I think we need to call the police."

Jason lifted the wrench and swallowed hard. "And maybe an ambulance."

"YOU DID THE right thing." Derek stood next to Tyron, inside the lounge area. Luckily our guests were out, and I hoped the police would be gone before they returned.

Jason had his glasses in his hands and was fiddling with the arms as he sat in one of the chairs. "Is he . . . going to be okay?"

"The paramedic said he should be fine." Tyron folded his arms. "You're not in any trouble."

That was a relief to hear.

"I'm going to head to the hospital." Derek turned to the detective. "You coming?"

"In a few."

Derek said his goodbyes and left, probably getting tired of showing up here. I turned my attention to the detective. I'd already given my statement, and the ambulance had carted off Coach Currie.

"Do any of you have any questions before I head to the hospital?" Tyron asked.

Mom stood behind the chair I sat in, her hand resting on my shoulder. "Was he responsible for what has been happening?"

"We don't know that yet, Mrs. Keeton," he replied. "But hopefully we'll find something out once he awakens."

I watched the flames ripple behind the glass. A huge part of me didn't believe that he was the one who killed Angela and sent her severed finger to me, unless what he'd been saying outside had been a complete lie. I guessed that was plausible, but why lie about that?

"It has to have been him," Jason said. "He was grabbing Sasha and he admitted to messing around with Angela. Maybe he did the whole finger thing to throw people off."

That was also a decent theory.

Mom murmured under her breath as she pushed away from my chair and sat in the one closest to the fireplace. "Do you think that's possible, Detective Conrad?"

"Anything is possible." His phone rang from inside his jacket pocket and he pulled it out, glancing down at it. "I've got to go. Anything else?"

I shook my head.

"You better call Cole before he finds out," he said as he walked away.

I sighed. "Was planning to!"

Jason scooted forward in the chair. "Well . . . today has not gone as planned."

"I don't think any day recently has gone as planned," Mom said.

I laughed dryly as I slid down in the chair. "That is the truest thing spoken."

He smiled wryly. "I better get going."

Pushing myself up, I stood. "Thank you again for everything."

"Stop thanking me. I'll get a complex." He let me hug him even though he was as awkward as ever when he patted my back. "Stay out of trouble, okay? For like the rest of the day."

"I'll try," I promised, then said goodbye. He waved at Mom and then made his way out.

"Angela was sleeping with Donnie Currie?" Mom shook her head as she stared up at the ceiling. "I don't believe it. She was so in love with Ethan."

I remembered the first time I talked to Angela, all she talked about was Ethan. "I guess you really don't know someone."

Mom sighed. "People only show you what they want to be seen, but something about what that man was telling you is fishy. Anyway, you better call Cole," Mom said, and I looked over at her. She placed her hand to her sternum. "You don't want him to get worried."

"Mom?" Concern blossomed and not for Cole. "Are you feeling all right?"

"What? Oh," she said, glancing down at herself. She dropped her hand. "Yes. Just indigestion. I forgot to take my heartburn pill this morning."

I came to her side and knelt down. "Are you sure that's it? Maybe you should call your doctor. I'm sure—"

"Honey," she laughed. "It's just heartburn. I'm okay. You do not need to worry about me right now."

"But I do," I said. "There has been a lot of crazy stuff going on in a short period of time. It's been stressful."

"I'm okay, honey."

I stared at her, wondering if the skin had been creased between her brows before, and I just hadn't noticed it. "I . . . I don't know what I would do if something . . ." I couldn't even bring myself to finish the sentence.

Smiling at me, she leaned forward and patted my knee. "I'm not going anywhere for a long, long time. You're stuck with me."

I hoped—no, I prayed—that was the case.

"You better call Cole," she said, gripping the arms of the chair. I stood, giving her room as she rose. "And let's hope that what happened today is . . . the end. I feel terrible for saying that, but if it was him, then it's over."

Mom kissed my cheek as she passed me, and I turned at the waist, watching her head toward the kitchen. Was it over? Had it been Coach Currie, the man Miranda and I drooled all over when we were in high school? The man who apparently had been sleeping with Angela, who we all believed was madly in love with her boyfriend Ethan, hoping for an engagement? Mom was right. Something didn't add up, I didn't think we had the whole story, and I didn't think it was over.

UPDATING COLE VIA phone had not gone exactly well. He'd been pissed that he hadn't been here, as if he was my personal bodyguard and had failed somehow. Then he was relieved to know that Jason had been there, and the call ended with him saying that once he could get out of the office, he was coming straight here.

After that, I took care of a minor housekeeping issue. More towels were needed in one of the suites, and once that was done, I was planning to spend the rest of the afternoon finishing off the bookkeeping. It was possibly the only thing that required my 100 percent focus, and I really needed that right now.

I came back down the main staircase, and when I reached the main landing, I cursed under my breath. Today just . . . it sucked.

Leaning against the desk was the reporter named Striker. His brown hair was messy, but he wore the same neatly pressed clothes I'd seen him in before. He lifted his gaze and smiled faintly when he saw me.

I clenched the railing. "I so do not have the patience for this today. You need to leave."

Pushing off the desk, he lifted his hands. "I know I'm probably the last person you want to talk to."

"The very last," I agreed, coming down the steps. "And I will call the cops to have you removed. And I will also file a restraining—"

"I know that Donnie Currie was over here and he got taken to the hospital due to a little blunt-force trauma."

Reaching the bottom of the stairs, I resisted the urge to pick up the vase and swing it over his head. "Are you even supposed to know these things?"

He ignored my comment. "Donnie Currie is a cheater with an eye for younger women and then some, but he's not the type of man to cut off a finger and mail it to the only known survivor of a serial killer."

My mouth opened, but there were no words.

"Yes, I know all about that too."

"And you haven't plastered that all over the front page?" I challenged.

A wry smile formed. "Only because I just heard about that."

Irritation prickled my skin. "But I guess I know what's going to be the headline tomorrow, then?"

"Even I have my limits," he replied. "That's not particularly something I'm willing to put into print."

I wasn't sure if I believed that or not.

"The mayor is convinced that Donnie Currie is the very bad man who killed poor young Angela Reidy, and the people need to realize there is absolutely no evidence supporting that."

"If there's no evidence then it doesn't matter what the mayor thinks or says."

"That would be true if the power of public opinion didn't outweigh the power of common sense, but if the people knew that we most likely have a copycat serial killer on our hands, they'll be prepared and therefore safe."

I almost laughed. "Oh, so your motives are altruistic then?"

"Not really," he admitted with another smiie.

"This—all of this—makes you happy, doesn't it?" Disgust rose.

He rolled his eyes. "Not happy. Eager? Yes. It's my job. I love digging things up and pulling back the veil. My job is to report the truth and sometimes expose it."

"You know I'm not going to give you information about the Groom. So why are you here?" I asked.

Striker was quiet for a moment. "Aren't you frightened?" he asked quietly. "You know what kind of horror a person is capable of, and you received a severed finger in the mail. Whoever is behind this knows you're here. That finger is a message of some sort."

My eyes narrowed. "Yes. I am frightened. Who wouldn't be? But again, that has nothing to do with you."

"Look, I know we got off on the wrong foot, but I'm not here to do a story on what happened to you. That's not why I came here in the first place. I'm hoping you can answer one question for me."

I said nothing, partly because I didn't believe him and I was also curious what his one question could be.

"Can we sit?" He gestured at the chairs in the lounge area.

My eyes narrowed but I nodded. Walking over to them, I sat and he did the same. He shifted to the side and reached into his pocket, pulling out a tiny recorder. I stiffened.

"It's not on. I wanted to show you that." He also pulled out his cellphone and showed the home screen. "I don't have this recording either. This conversation is off the record."

I smirked. "Am I really supposed to believe that?"

"I can't make you believe that, and while I do think people want to hear your story of *survival*, I'm not here to report on it." Striker bent forward, resting his elbows on his knees. "I was just out of journalism school when the Groom hit this town. I didn't cover the story. It went to one of the more veteran reporters, but I followed it closely. Even after you escaped and he was dead, I read everything I could on it. You can say I became a couch expert on him and other serial killers."

My upper lip curled. "That must be something to be proud of."

He smiled. "There's something . . . fascinating about a person who understands right and wrong, but does not operate on any social norm and has their own moral compass."

"More like terrifying," I corrected.

"That too." His head tilted to the left. "Anyway, I've read everything there is on Vernon Joan. I know what he did to the other victims. I know what he was planning to do to you when he led you out of the house. I know everything except one thing. That's why I'm here."

I took a deep, even breath as an idea formed. "I'll consider answering your question if you answer one of mine."

Striker tensed. "What do you want to know?"

"You seem to know a little bit about everyone," I said, choosing my words wisely. "How well do you know the mayor?"

Interest piqued in his eyes. "Probably more than the average citizen. Why?"

This could be a huge mistake. Tomorrow morning he could write up a story where I pin suspicion on the mayor, but I was willing to take that risk. "The mayor has been really worried about me . . . talking to someone like you and dragging up everything that has happened."

"And you're wondering why he would be so adverse to something like that?" he asked.

I nodded. "Obviously, he's not the kind of person who believes any press is good press."

"Oh, he is that kind of person. Except when the bad press might have to do with him."

My brows snapped together. "What does that mean exactly?"

He studied me a moment. "You don't know?"

"Know what?"

"Huh. Well, I guess a lot of people didn't hear about it. After all, people with money have a way of making sure things aren't widely known."

"I'm going to need a little more detail," I said.

One side of his lips tipped up. "Mayor Mark Hughes is the grandson of Bobby Hughes, who sold a whole lot of acreages to developers back in the eighties. Made their family very, very wealthy. Now, Bobby's boy, Robert Jr., is Mark's father. Junior owned a lot of the businesses downtown. The rest of the businesses were sold off before Junior passed away. Mark took over ownership of one of them—a hardware shop."

"I know about the hardware shop."

"But I bet you didn't know that Bobby had a sister named Cora, who had a baby out of wedlock. That was a big no-no in the day. Cora had a daughter who married a man who used to work at the corning plant. His name was Victor Joan."

I stilled.

"And I can tell by the look on your face you just connected the dots. Victor Joan was the father of only one son. Vernon Joan."

"Oh my God," I whispered. "The mayor was related to the Groom."

"Yep." He laughed under his breath. "That's the family's dirty little secret. It got out briefly in the aftermath of the Groom, but was virtually swept under the rug."

"Holy crap." Stunned, I shook my head. "How has that not been all over the place?"

"Like I said, people with money have a lot of pull. Mayor Hughes is probably worried that someone who values their job a little less than me will dig that up if you started giving interviews on the Groom." A wicked sort of amusement filled his eyes. "You sure you don't want to give an interview?"

Staring at him, I shook my head.

"Now it's my turn."

I wasn't sure I could focus on whatever he was about to say after a bomb like that was dropped, but I nodded.

"There was always something that didn't make sense—something that the profilers with the FBI never really addressed." He pressed his hands together. "It's actually something you said to them."

I gripped the arms of the chair. "What?"

"In the reports, you said at times that the Groom was almost kind and at other times he was extremely violent. That he had severe mood shifts and swings."

My stomach churned as thoughts of the mayor slipped away. "Do I even want to know how you read any of that?"

Striker said nothing.

"The Groom was a sociopath. Of course he had mood swings."

He scooted forward. "But the way the report read, you said to the agents that it was like you were dealing with two people. The Groom who was sick and twisted, but almost gentle, and the other side of him that was beyond cruel and violent."

Acid rose. "Yes, I did say that."

"Would you go as far as to say, one side of him was patient and the other not?" he queried softly.

Feeling sick, I nodded.

"Is it possible . . . that there were two of them?" Striker asked.

At first, all I could do was stare at him. What he was suggesting was absolutely insane.

"He kept you in the dark, didn't he? Made sure you never saw his face. That's correct?"

"Yes, but . . ." But I trailed off as I thought about it, really considered what Striker was suggesting. A numbness poured into my chest. "Are you saying that you think the Groom was actually two men and not one?"

"It's not impossible. There have been instances of more than one serial killer working together. It's not even that rare," he explained. "So my question is, do you think it's possible that there were two—"

"And that the other one is back, targeting other women?"

"If that's the case, then you know he's got another woman."

Squeezing my eyes shut, I hated that he'd said what I already believed. "A copycat would follow—"

"Yes, a copycat would follow the same pathology. Agreed," he said. "Can you answer the question?"

I wasn't sure I could. I opened my eyes, but I didn't really see the journalist. All I saw was the shadows of the room I was kept in. All I heard was *his* voice and the heavy slide of *his* hand.

Sometimes the Groom had been talkative, but when he was mad, when he used his fists and his feet, he never spoke. Thinking back, I realized, the Groom never spoke when he was angry. Not until the last day, when he took me outside, when he cried and then tried to kill me.

Exhaling roughly, I met Striker's gaze. "Why do you want to know what I think on this?"

"Curiosity," he answered. "It's something that's plagued me for ten years. Going to be honest with you. Vernon Joan wasn't an extraordinarily bright man. I never believed he could've pulled it all off by himself for so long without getting caught."

I couldn't believe what he was suggesting, but as horrifying and—and as sickening as it was to consider, that there were two men and not one, it wasn't impossible.

"And it's more than that," Striker continued. "Because if there was another one working with Vernon Joan, he got away. Not only that, there's a good chance he's been here this whole time, living among the families of the victims. No one would even take my theory seriously. Not until now. Do you think it's possible?"

Bile was sitting in the base of my throat. "It's . . . it's possible."

Striker's shoulders rose with a deep breath, and the look that settled over his face was equivalent to him being told he won the lottery.

From the table, his cellphone rang, startling me. "One sec," he said, and then answered the phone while I sat there floored.

The mayor was related to the Groom. I remembered once hearing that psychopath level of crazy could run in the family.

Holy crap.

"Damn." Excitement gleamed in Striker's eyes as he rose, snatching up the recorder and shoving it in his pocket. "Are you serious?" There was a pause as he placed a fist on his hip. "Yeah. Yeah. I'll be right there." Striker quickly hung up, his gaze finding mine. "It's happened again."

I felt the chair shift below me. "He's taken someone else, hasn't he?"

Striker nodded as he rose. "Liz Chapman, a waitress just down the street, was just reported missing. Her mother hasn't seen her since Sunday night."

CHAPTER 25

THE PICTURE OF twenty-three-year-old Liz Chapman was in the middle. Her photo was flanked by two smaller images of Tania Banks, the nurse from Frederick, and Angela Reidy.

It was hard to look at them.

It was also hard to not see the uncanny similarities between the women. All were in their twenties. All were pretty in a common, girl-next-door type of way. All were a version of blonde.

And they all faintly resembled me.

Just like I faintly resembled the Groom's victims ten years ago.

The most horrifying thing, and most likely why Miranda was downing wine like water, was the fact that we'd briefly met her.

She had been the waitress at the steakhouse we'd gone to.

When I'd seen a picture of her earlier in the day,

I'd immediately called Tyron and told him that I had recognized her. Ten minutes after I got off the phone with him, Agent Myers called.

He was as friendly as he was the first time I met him, but I told him what I told Tyron. Liz had been my waitress at the steakhouse, and even though no one said it out loud, I knew. They knew.

It was yet another connection.

"I think I need a bottle of wine," Miranda said, glancing down at her glass. "Your mom only picked up one bottle?"

I smiled faintly. "Only one."

"I'm about to obliterate it and totally regret it in the morning," she replied, and then downed the contents before she rose.

Jason raised his brows. "Nice."

We were sitting in my apartment. Cole was beside me on the couch, one arm around my shoulders and one leg propped up on the coffee table. I was tucked against his side, and Miranda had been sitting on my other side. She was now at the counter, pouring herself another glass of wine.

Mine sat on the coffee table, precariously close to Cole's foot, and virtually untouched.

Jason had brought the chair in from my tiny kitchen and had set it on the other side of the end table. We'd all had dinner in the kitchen together while I tried not to watch Jason to see how he acted around Miranda, and then Mom had retired to her apartment, and at first, when we sat around the TV, we all pretended like this was a normal Tuesday evening. That lasted about five seconds.

"This is just absolutely insane." Miranda stood by Jason, her wine glass full once more. "They're saying we have a copycat."

I wasn't too sure of that anymore.

Miranda looked over at me. She opened her mouth to say something, seemed to change her mind, and then took a drink instead.

I hadn't had the chance to tell any of them what I learned today, and I figured now was a good time. "Striker stopped by."

She lowered the wine glass.

Cole leaned to the side, and without even looking at him, I could feel his stare. "He's the journalist," I explained.

"Yeah, I know who that is." Anger thickened his tone. "You should've said something earlier. I don't want him—"

"He wasn't trying to get a story. Not really," I said, and held up my hand when Miranda opened her mouth again. "He was just asking questions. I didn't tell him anything, but he did say something that was super interesting."

"What?" Jason asked, leaning forward.

"You guys know how the mayor hasn't been happy with me being here, and I thought it had to do with more than just the possibility of me giving an interview?" I crossed my legs. "So I asked Striker if he knew why the mayor would be so unhappy about it."

Miranda sipped her wine. "Because he's a giant dick face?"

I smiled. "He was related to the Groom."

"What?" Jason sat back, eyes wide.

"For real?" Cole's brows furrowed.

I nodded. "Apparently, the mayor comes from a really wealthy family—"

"I knew that." Miranda frowned. "Everyone knows that."

I shot her a look. "The Groom was his grandfather's sister's son or something like that."

"I'm surprised that didn't get out and blow up like a gas station in an action movie," Cole said.

Miranda snorted and laughed.

"It didn't because I'm guessing the mayor used his wealth to keep that quiet," I explained. "Anyway, I think that's why he's worried about me talking about what happened. That people will start asking questions again and it's something he doesn't want brought up."

"Then maybe he does have something to do with what has been happening." Jason pushed his glasses up to his head, and tufts of brown hair stuck up. "Messed with your car—your mom's."

"And killed two women?" Miranda leaned against the kitchen island. Or possibly staggered against it. The bottle was looking awful empty on the counter. "Because that's not going to bring unwanted attention on yourself."

"Hey," he said, holding up his hands. "No one ever said killers and liars were smart."

"He has a good point there," I said, folding my hands in my lap. "But it also really wouldn't make sense."

"Well, someone is doing what the Groom did." Jason tossed an arm along the back of his chair.

"It's not the same as the Groom," I said, looking

up at the screen. The newscasters had moved on to the weather.

Cole placed his hand on my knee and squeezed reassuringly.

After Striker had left, I'd spent the better part of the day thinking about what he'd said and what I knew about the Groom. What was happening now was similar but not. "The Groom kept his victims for days and even weeks in some instances. Angela went missing Wednesday evening—maybe. Thursday by the latest. She was dead by Monday, maybe even earlier than that. The Groom didn't lose interest . . . or patience that quickly. Whoever this is, he doesn't have the patience."

"Or the control." Cole settled back against the cushion. "To keep someone as long as the Groom did, you'd have to have a lot of control."

"And be a total freak," Miranda muttered under her breath as she finished off her wine glass in record time.

I looked over at Cole, wanting to share my suspicion but wary of doing so, because . . . saying it out loud made it so much more real. Saying it out loud also sounded a little crazy.

He leaned over, crossing the tiny distance between us and brushed his lips over mine. "You still here?"

Blinking, I didn't realize how long I'd sat there staring at him. "Yeah."

"You guys are so cute it makes me want to squeeze both of you to death." Miranda sighed. "It also makes me want to have a boyfriend I can be all cute with."

Flushing, I looked over at her. She saddled up to Jason's side. "Want to hook up?"

I choked on air.

"This just got real interesting," Cole murmured under his breath.

Jason whipped around in the chair so quickly I thought he might break his neck. "What?"

Miranda giggled as she draped her arms over his shoulders. "I'm just kidding. Geez. I know you're saving yourself just in case your wife comes back." She reached up, tweaking his cheek. "Plus, I like my men a bit darker in the skin." Pausing, she lifted her gaze to Cole. "Which brings me to the fine-looking Detective Conrad. Is he single?"

Cole grinned. "I believe he is."

"You should introduce us," she said, straightening. "Actually, you should call him right now. I'll give you—"

"And I think it's time for you to go home," Jason announced.

Miranda pouted. "You're no fun, but you're correct." She shimmied around Jason and bent over, clasping my cheeks. "I don't like this at all," she whispered.

"I don't either," I whispered back.

Her lower lip trembled. "I'm still glad you came home though."

"Me too."

She stared at me a moment and then patted my cheek. "I might be a little tipsy."

"Did you drive?" I asked, frowning up at Miranda.

Jason laughed. "No. I drove her here."

She rolled her eyes and then pulled away, snatching up her jacket. "He sounds so happy about that."

He ignored her as he slipped on his gloves. "I'll make sure she gets home."

"Thank you," I said. "Love you guys."

"Love you more," Miranda called back.

Cole walked them out and once he returned, he locked the door behind him and made his way back over to me. He sat on the edge of the couch, his body twisted toward mine. "Striker seriously wasn't here to do a story?"

Exhaling softly, I tipped my head back against the cushion. "Yeah. He didn't want to do a story, Cole. He wanted to ask me one question."

His eyes flashed. "Journalists lie, Sasha. They'll say anything to get information out of someone."

"That might be the case, but damn, he had a point, Cole. He really did."

He studied me for a moment. "What did he say?"

"Striker is kind of obsessed with the . . . the Groom. Or maybe serial killers in general, and besides that being incredibly creepy, he picked up on something I'd told the agents while I was in the hospital." I slid my hands along my thighs. "I think I even said it to you. That at times it seemed like the Groom was two different people." My gaze shifted to Cole. "I don't know a lot about who *he* was. I purposely avoided learning anything, but Striker didn't and he said that he'd always believed that the Groom hadn't pulled it off by himself."

His brows creased together. "None of that means that there were actually two of them working together."

"But it sort of makes sense. There were times when it was like I was dealing with two separate people," I told him. "And I never saw *him* while I was held. Not once, and when he was angry, he didn't speak. So let's say there's two of them. The Groom I knew was more patient and the other more violent. That would explain why the victims this time don't last very long."

"Sasha."

"It is possible," I insisted.

He looked away, a muscle flexing in his jaw. "I know it's not impossible, but it's also not very likely."

"It's about as likely as there being another copy-cat serial killer, isn't it?" I replied, sitting forward and snatching my wine glass off the table.

"But there would've been evidence of another person. No matter how careful someone is, they always leave trace evidence behind. Hair. Skin cells. Fingerprints," he explained. "There had to have been something."

I considered that as I took a much smaller sip of wine. "How hard did they look for additional evidence?"

He opened his mouth.

"Evidence of there being another person? They never suspected that and I . . . I never gave them any real concrete evidence seriously suggesting it." His eyes came back to mine. "And they thought they got him. What do you think they did?"

Lifting his hand, he thrust his fingers through his hair and then clasped the back of his neck. "I wasn't a part of that investigation. Because of our relationship, I was out."

I glanced down at my wine.

"They probably bagged everything they could and then they would've filed it after combing through it," he said. "They would've scanned for fingerprints, but nothing is a hundred percent. They were probably looking for prints to match the victims, but I would think they'd come across something."

"None of that means it's impossible."

Cole was quiet while I took a huge gulp of the wine, wincing at the slight bitterness. "No. It's not impossible."

I lowered my glass to the table as I lifted my gaze to his. "What if it is the case? What if there were two of them, and I never realized that?"

His gaze sharpened as it shot back to mine. "Don't do that."

"Do what?"

"Put the blame on yourself."

"I'm—"

"Yeah, you are. You're thinking that you missed something and if you had figured it out, you would've been able to warn the agents. There was nothing you could've done, Sasha. And you don't even really know if there were two men." He curled his hand around my neck and forced my gaze to him. "Don't put that kind of guilt on yourself."

Biting my lip, I nodded the best I could with his hand on my neck.

"I'm serious, babe. I know what that kind of guilt does. Fucking eats you alive," he said in a low voice. "You have no idea how many times I lay awake at night asking myself what if I'd just walked you to the car—"

"No. We talked about that." I placed my hands on his chest. "There was nothing you . . ." Trailing off, I sighed heavily. "I see what you did there. You can't blame yourself. I can't blame myself."

His eyes softened. "No, you can't."

"Neither can you," I whispered.

He brought his forehead to mine. "That will always be a work in progress no matter what."

I closed my eyes. "I hate hearing that."

"I hate knowing that you've got to go through this shit again."

Sliding my hand to his shoulder, I tugged on him. He came, wrapping an arm around me and gathering me close. "It's just not me who's going through this again."

"You're all that matters," he replied, his lips brushing my cheek.

I turned my head, unable to shake the questions Striker had raised. "If Striker is right, you know what that means."

Cole didn't respond, but his arm tightened around me.

"He's probably been around this whole time. Living here. Interacting with people and . . ." Something occurred to me. "But there haven't been any murders, have there?" I pulled back. "Before the woman in Frederick disappeared?"

"There've been murders, but nothing like this. Nothing unsolved."

I rose, picking up my wine glass. "Here's the thing. If this is a copycat or someone who was working with the Groom before, they either haven't been abducting women for ten years or they've done a damn good job at hiding it until now."

"Until you came back," he said, scooting back to the edge of the couch. "So this person knew you were coming back or the Frederick abduction is a coincidence."

"Either way, I doubt someone just up and decides to copycat a serial killer, right?"

"I don't think there's really a playbook on that, but I can check the NCIC—it's a database that tracks crimes," he explained. "See if there's been any suspicious murders or kidnappings that have been reported in the tristate area."

Placing my wine glass on the counter, I stood there, running my palms over the edge of the counter. Being told I shouldn't feel guilty was totally different than actually feeling that way. Truth was, my return had tripped something. Either ignited a murderous rampage or exposed it.

"I want to run something by you," Cole said, and when I looked over, he was standing by the coffee table. "How about you stay with me for a couple of days."

I faced him. "Cole—"

"I know it's hard with the inn, but I would just feel better if you were at my place. There aren't a hundred different points of entry, the possibility that someone could sneak in there during the day and wait until everyone is asleep. I don't have to worry about someone losing a key and this fucker picking it up and getting in here," he said, and I shivered. "Nor do I have to worry about some asshole showing up and scaring you, like Currie and Striker. You'll be safer at my place."

God, going to Cole's house and hiding out sounded amazing. "I can't do that. My mom—"

"She can come too."

My heart tripled in size as I walked up to him. "That is so sweet of you, but we have guests who have somehow not realized what has been happening. We can't ask them to leave. It's not like we're making a ton of money, and we can't risk bad reviews. Bed-and-breakfast places live and die by word of mouth."

He did not look happy with my answer. "How far are you booked up?"

I rested my hands on his sides. "We don't have a break anytime soon. I'm sorry. I appreciate what you're offering. I think you're wonderful for it, but I can't."

His shoulders rose with a heavy sigh. "Didn't think you were going to go for it. But I'm going to be honest with you, if something else happens, I'm going to throw you over my shoulder and cart your ass out of here."

Despite everything, I smiled. "I just pictured that, and there is something oddly hot about it."

"Well, the image did involve me, so . . ."

I laughed. "You definitely don't have any modesty issues, do you?"

"Nah."

Our eyes met and held. "Everything is going to be okay."

"Yeah," he murmured. Cole folded his arms around me, and I turned, pressing against him. He was all warm strength, and in his arms, it was easy to believe that everything would be okay.

It was easy to pretend.

THINGS WERE SORT of normal on Wednesday. Miranda called me in the morning, and she was only slightly hungover from a wine headache. Cole was at work, but my mind was not far from him.

Last night, we slept. His arms wrapped around me, a leg thrown over mine, and I stayed asleep until he woke me in the way I was growing incredibly accustomed to, his hand and then his mouth between my thighs. He got me off that way, and then I got him off in the shower.

The shower thing had been a first for me.

I'd never showered with a man before, and I sure as hell had never gotten on my knees in a shower either.

I decided I wanted every morning to go like that.

Sipping my soda, I sat at the front desk while Mom started to work on a light lunch. Not much of a cook, the moment I tried to help her, she shooed me out, so it was back to the endless updating of spreadsheets. I figured I'd be done sometime in the next five hundred years.

It was hard to sit at the desk when I knew Cole was currently combing through the database he had mentioned. I wanted to be out there, helping to figure out who was doing this, but I wasn't a detective. I wasn't a grown-up Nancy Drew. There was little I could do other than keep myself safe.

So my butt stayed in the chair.

I looked up at the sound of steps. The Wilkins couple was coming down the staircase. They'd checked in earlier. Both were from Upstate New York. They were road-tripping to Florida, which I was in awe of. There was no way in the world I could ever be in a car for that kind of trip.

Except maybe with Cole.

I bet we could make that interesting.

"Hi," I said as Mrs. Wilkins approached the desk, her strawberry-blond hair falling in curls over her shoulders.

Her smile was more of a grimace. "I hate to be that guest who immediately has a complaint."

"No. It's okay," I reassured her as her husband walked to the doors. "What can I help you with?"

She twisted a pink fuzzy winter cap in her hands. "There is this really weird smell in our room. We thought maybe it was just our imagination at first, but it's not. I think it's coming from one of the rooms next to us," she said. "I don't know what it is, but it's pretty rank."

"Oh no, I'm sorry to hear that." I rose from the desk. "I will check on that immediately."

"Thank you," she said, pulling on her cap. "The inn is really lovely, by the way."

"I'm glad to hear you say that." I stepped around the desk. "You said it was room seven, correct?"

She nodded and then joined her husband at the door. Cold air rushed in, along with some flurries. Smiling at them, I shoved my hands into the pockets of my sweater and walked toward the kitchen. My stomach rumbled at the scent of pasta. Mom was at the counter, cutting peppers.

"Hey," I said, heading toward the back room. "Room seven and five haven't been booked, right?"

"Nope." She paused, looking up. "Seven's the room that had the leaky sink. The one that Cole fixed. Why?"

"Strange." I opened the door. "The young couple who booked room six said that there was a bad smell they thought might be coming from one of the nearby rooms."

Mom frowned. "That's really odd."

"I'm going to check it out. Cross your fingers that it's not a dead mouse or something," I told her.

"Better not be."

Snatching up the keys to the rooms, I headed to the staff entrance. My first stop was the Wilkinses' room. After stepping inside, I left their door open.

I inhaled deeply, and all I smelled was perfume—vanilla perfume. I walked past the bed, to the wall that bumped up to room five, and I still didn't smell anything. Wondering if they were imagining things, I headed to the opposite side of the room, and opened their bathroom door. A faint scent of aftershave and fruity body wash clung to the small room, but as I stepped in further, I did smell something under those scents. I inhaled again, nose wrinkling.

There was definitely a scent. Not sure what it was. Sort of reminded me of something spoiled?

Why in the world didn't she say you could smell it in the bathroom? That meant it was either coming from inside the walls—please God, no—or it was from the bathroom in the other room.

Oh no.

The sink.

What if the sink broke again and had flooded the damn room. Granted, I doubted it smelled like that. I hurried out of their room, locking it behind me. I went to room seven and unlocked the door. The moment I opened it, heat washed over me along with a stronger scent that was not . . . pleasant.

"What the hell?" I muttered, turning to the right. The heat in the room was jacked up to eighty.

A knot of unease formed in my stomach. We kept the rooms set to sixty-five if they weren't filled for a ton of obvious reasons, so I could not understand why this was up to eighty. It hadn't been like that when we were in the room before.

And the smell . . .

I placed my hand over my mouth as I walked farther into the room. The stench was powerful, and it was vaguely familiar. I neared the bathroom, realizing it smelled like spoiled meat.

The dread grew as I opened the bathroom door. It creaked as it slowly drifted to the side. The smell slammed into me, and I clamped my mouth shut to stop the gag as I reached out, smacking the light switch. I flipped it on. As if in a daze, my eyes traveled across the floor to the bathtub.

Horror seized me, reaching in deep and locking up my muscles. Something was in the tub. Something gray and pale in the dank water that filled the tub. Fingers—fingers connecting to an arm, dangled lifelessly over the side. It was her left arm and hand. There were only four fingers. Splotches of brown marred the skin. Her hair was limp and blond.

I stumbled back. "Oh my God."

A dead woman was in the tub.

"I'M SO SORRY," Mom said for probably what was the hundredth time as she followed the Wilkins and their luggage to the front door. "If there—"

"You've done enough," Mr. Wilkins said. "You helped us find a new hotel. You've done all that you can."

I hadn't heard Mrs. Wilkins say a word, but I'd seen her with her husband when they first appeared in the entry. Her face was leeched of all color, and I knew she was thinking that what she'd smelled in her room was a dead body in the next. That was pretty horrifying. Seeing it would be yet another image I would never erase from my mind.

That poor woman . . .

I'd seen her face.

Her eyes had been open, wide and fixed. Her face frozen in horror, gaping in a silent scream.

I closed my eyes as I leaned against the wall just inside the dining room. I could hear Mom at the desk now. The Wilkinses were gone. She was calling incoming guests and cancelling. I tried calling James to tell him he wasn't needed for the next couple of days, but he hadn't answered. All I could do was leave a voicemail.

There was no other choice. The inn was a crime scene. A body was still upstairs, in the bathtub, and even once everything was gone, we couldn't allow people to stay here. Not when it was obviously unsafe.

Tyron was here, as were the FBI agents. I'd already given them my statement. Cole was on his way back from Baltimore. He'd mentioned something about taking leave, but I didn't remember the specifics.

I heard my mom apologizing again.

Moving to one of the dining room chairs, I sat down and placed my head in my hand. I should be the one out there dealing with the fallout, because this—all of this—was because of me.

There was no denying it.

This wasn't an "everything is about me" party. This was the reality. There was a dead woman, a woman who briefly served me dinner, upstairs in a bathtub, beaten and bloody.

"Sasha."

I looked up at the sound of Tyron's voice and lowered my hand to the table.

"You hanging in there?" he asked, approaching slowly. When I nodded, he stopped behind a chair, gripping the back of it. "Cole's on his way?"

I nodded again.

"Coroners are on the way," he said quietly.

"They're going to remove the body, but that's the extent of what they're going to do. Okay? I went ahead and contacted a company that specializes in biohazards for you. The earliest they can come is tomorrow morning. I'd suggest you just keep that door closed until they arrive."

"Okay." I sat back, folding my hands in my lap. "Do you . . . do you know if she was killed here?"

"It doesn't appear to be that way. With the kind of wounds she suffered, there'd be more blood if she was murdered here." Pausing, he sat down in the chair. "She was stabbed, Sasha."

I bit down on my lip. "How long do you think she was here?"

"What's left behind is mostly fluids from decomp. Time of death right now is going to have to wait on the autopsy. With the heat jacked up in the room and her body partially submerged, it's going to make it hard to determine, but we think she's been in that bathtub for at least a day or two."

Acids in my stomach churned. She'd been in that bathtub for a day or two. Oh God, I couldn't . . .

"I know you're dealing with a lot right now. You're probably feeling numb, but I need to ask you a couple of more questions, okay?"

Swallowing, I nodded for a third time. "I understand."

He leaned forward, resting an arm on the table. "What we're guessing is that someone moved the body in here at night. You have an alarm. Who knows the code?"

"Not many. My mom," I said. "James Jordan— our chef. So did Angela and Daphne. But that's it."

"Do you think there is a chance that someone moved her in here before you set the alarm?" he asked.

"It's . . . it's possible. We don't watch the entrances, but I think we'd hopefully notice someone carrying in . . . in a body through the front doors." I reached up, tucking my hair back. "The only other way would be through the back entrance. Someone could carry someone in that way, up the back stairs, and not be seen, but we keep that door locked and the tunnel leading into the cellar is closed off."

"Is it possible that someone could've gained a key to the back entrance?"

My first response was to say no but it wasn't impossible. "Nothing is impossible."

"You keep extras with the rest of the keys in the back room?" he asked.

When I nodded, he patted the table and told me he would be back down. Tyron made good on his words when he walked back through the dining room with another officer and the forensic investigator who'd been here before.

Then I was alone, and I didn't know for how long. All I could think about was the fact that someone had been in here again without our knowledge, but this time they weren't just snatching a key. They were carrying a body upstairs.

Could it be Currie?

He'd been here yesterday morning. Maybe he grabbed a key and made a copy at some point. God knows how many times he'd used that entrance before I'd run into him. He could've taken her upstairs, found an empty room and left her body there, jacking up the heat before leaving—leaving and coming to me.

If it wasn't him, then was it the mayor? Killing someone and leaving their body here was enough to make me want to leave, but again, his involvement made no sense.

Footsteps snagged my attention, and I lifted my head.

Cole appeared in the doorway, his jaw a hard line and eyes icy. He said nothing as he stormed forward, brushing Myers aside. I hadn't even realized the agent had entered the room. How long had he been there?

I honestly didn't care about him at the moment.

I rose and went to Cole, meeting him halfway. His arms came around me, his fingers digging deep in my hair.

Pressing my face against his chest, I felt the burn in my throat and behind my eyes, but the tears didn't come. No matter how tight Cole held me or how hard I squeezed him back.

But I wasn't numb.

I was *scared*.

"I WANT YOU to pack a couple of days' worth of clothes." Cole was standing in the center of the kitchen. Twenty minutes ago, the FBI agents had filed out. "Same with your mom. She can stay in my guest room. Tomorrow, when the cleanup company is scheduled to come over, I'll meet them here."

I nodded slowly, this time not arguing. I didn't want to stay here. Even with the . . . the body gone, this place, as terrible as it was to admit, was tainted for me. I knew, or at least I hoped, it would fade one day. It had to, but right now, I needed the distance.

So did Mom.

"She's not going to be happy with it," I said, placing the salad Mom had been making in the trash. "But I agree. We both need to get out of here."

"It'll do you both some good." He leaned against the island while I grabbed the cutting board and took it to the sink. "But it's more than that, Sasha."

My stomach tightened as I added the board to the bowls and turned on the water. "I know."

He was quiet for a moment. "I don't want to scare you."

Swallowing, I looked over my shoulder. "I'm already scared. You can't scare me anymore."

The skin around his lips tensed. "Sasha—"

"I know." I turned back to the sink and picked up the sponge. "I know what is happening," I said, scrubbing at the bowls. "I know that Angela and the woman from Frederick suffered horrible deaths. I know that the woman—that Liz—died in a horrific way. It doesn't matter if it's a copycat or if it's someone who was working with the Groom ten years ago. They all died in horrible ways."

"Stop," he said quietly.

Turning the bowl over and running it under clean water, I kept going. "And I know that whoever is doing this is going to come for me. I know." My throat dried. "Or maybe he won't. Maybe he's just doing this because—"

"Sasha."

"Because I got away." My voice cracked as I

picked up another bowl. "Maybe this is punishment. Maybe—"

"Stop," he said, closer. "Stop and look at me."

"I need to clean these dishes," I told him, clearing my throat. "I don't want to come back to a bunch of dirty dishes. And I don't want Mom—"

"Babe . . ."

Inhaling slowly, I squinted at the bowl. Was that a seed stuck? I started scrubbing again. "I'm almost done and then I will go pack—"

Cole reached around and turned off the water. Then he took the sponge from my hand and tossed it into the sink. "These bowls can't get any cleaner."

I stared at the bowls. He was right. They were pretty clean. My hands fell to the rim of the sink.

He turned me in his arms. Two fingers curled around my chin, and he lifted my gaze to his. "This isn't punishment."

A knot was at the base of my throat. "It's not?"

"No."

"Can you really think that?" My voice was hoarse. "Let's be real with each other, because I need to be real with myself. This started when I decided to come home, or maybe someone was doing this all along, but they've changed their pattern. They are making it known now. They're making sure I know they are here. Why else would this be happening now? It has to do with me and the only reason I can think of—"

Glass shattered from the dining room, and I spun around. Cole beat me to the door first, shoving it open, and I was right behind him. An anguished cry tore free as I saw my mom on the dining room floor.

Cole was immediately at her side, whipping his phone out of his pocket.

"Mom," I cried out, dropping to my knees beside her. My heart pounded sickeningly fast as I reached out and felt her skin. It was cool and clammy. "Mom!"

Her face was incredibly pale, a sickly shade, and there was no response. Nothing. There was nothing.

TWISTING MY HANDS together, I squeezed my eyes shut until I saw tiny sparks of light.

A heart attack.

Oh God, she had been having a heart attack and she was in surgery for what felt like forever, but had only been an hour or so.

Cole's hand slid down my back. He'd been doing that on and off this whole time, and it was the only thing keeping me from having a legit mental breakdown in the middle of the hospital.

I couldn't lose my mom.

If I did, I wouldn't—

The doctor stepped out of the doors and called my name. "Miss Keeton?"

I rose, heart thumping in my chest. Cole was right beside me. "Yes?"

He smiled as he approached me. "Your mom is awake and in her room. She is recovering fine."

"Oh thank God." My knees felt weak as I clutched

Cole's arm. "Oh my God, I want to hug and kiss you."

The doctor glanced at Cole. "That's not necessary," he replied wryly. "We were able to stop the heart attack with an angioplasty." He continued to explain the procedure, mentioning words like *balloon* and *stent*. Finally, he got to what I wanted to hear. "You can go up and see her now, but I would suggest to make the visit brief. She needs a lot of rest, but the good news is that she should be released in twenty-four to forty-eight hours."

I mumbled my thanks about a dozen more times before Cole got the room number and carted me off, up to the room.

I stumbled when I saw her in the bed, her body so small and frail looking, and too pale. Not as bad as when I saw her on the floor, but still so incredibly void of color.

Rushing to her bedside, I picked up her hand as Cole moved to the other side of her bed. "Mom," I whispered.

Her smile was faint. "Don't squeeze my hand like I almost died."

"Mom," I laughed, sniffling. "You scared me half to death."

She slowly turned her head toward Cole. "She's been a wreck, hasn't she?"

"She's been holding it together," he replied, grinning. "Though she almost started a fight earlier."

I frowned at him. "What?"

"She said she was going to kiss your doctor," he explained, and I rolled my eyes. "Wasn't having that."

"Of course not," Mom replied, her words slow. "Not that . . . she would want to ever kiss another man when she has you—"

"Mom." I shook my head.

Her gaze slid to me. "Honey, I might've had some crap shoved up my veins to stop a heart attack, but that does not mean I am . . . dead or blind."

Cole chuckled.

"Geez," I muttered.

It wasn't long before Mom's eyelids were lowering and it was taking longer in between each blink. Even though I wanted to camp out, it was time to leave. I glanced over at Cole, and he nodded. "I'll come back later," I told her.

She smiled tiredly. "Honey, you go home with Cole. Don't—"

"Mom—"

"Don't come back here. I'm going to be sleeping. Just go home with him and be safe," she insisted, her weary gaze fixing on mine. "Be safe."

I took a deep breath and then nodded. "Okay." Rising, I leaned over and kissed her cheek. "I love you, Mom."

"I love you too, honey."

It took me a couple of moments to make myself leave her bedside. Once out in the hall, Cole turned to me. "You want to come back later, after dinner?"

I smiled faintly. "Yes."

"We can do that after we pick up your clothes and get some food in you."

Heading toward the elevator, I dug out my phone and hit the screen, quickly scanning texts. "Miranda and Jason are waiting for us at the inn."

"They're inside the inn?"

"Seems so." I slipped my phone back in my purse. The elevator doors opened. "I don't think I locked up afterward. I was in such a panic." And honestly, what was the point? Someone already had a key most likely.

Snow was starting to fall again, dusting the parking lot and freshening up the snow already on the grass.

Cole's steps slowed as his truck came into view. Tyron was waiting beside it, a black skullcap pulled low. "Would've called but heard you two were at the hospital," he said. "How's your mother?"

"They were able to stop the heart attack." I took a deep breath as Cole tucked me into his side and ran his hand down the center of my back. Even with a jacket on, the gesture was comforting. "The doctor said it was minor compared to how bad it could've been. They're going to keep her for a few days, but she should be okay."

"That's great news. Glad to hear it." Tyron glanced between us. "And I think I have even more good news for you."

At this point, I figured almost anything was good news.

Cole dropped his arm and reached down, finding my hand. "What's going on?"

"Just heard from a unit who's over at Mayor Hughes' house." Tyron stepped forward, voice low. "This isn't the good-news part, but looks like he committed suicide earlier this afternoon. Left a note. That's the good-news part. He admitted to *everything*."

COLE CURLED AN arm around my shoulders and hauled me forward, against his chest. We stood at the front doors of the inn a few hours after we left the hospital. The crime scene unit had just been leaving when we arrived. I imagined they'd combed the entire house. The room upstairs was still closed off, probably would be for several days.

"You're going to be okay," he said, folding his other arm around my waist. "Your mom's going to be fine."

Wrapping my arms around him, I rested my cheek against his chest. I tried to smile and failed. Too worried about my mom and unable to shake a wealth of nervous energy, I felt absolutely horrible for the mayor's family. No matter what evil that man had done, I couldn't imagine what his family was going through.

But there was something else nagging at me. I . . . I couldn't help feeling like we were missing something—that I was missing something.

"It doesn't make sense," I said, opening my eyes. "Why would he do that to hide his secret? All it did was draw attention to what happened. I don't get it."

Cole didn't immediately respond as he threaded his fingers through my hair. He knew what I did. That the mayor's wife had found him in the office of his home with a single gunshot wound to the head and a suicide letter on the desk. According to Tyron, he admitted to not just the vandalism of our vehicles, but the murders of the three women and to mailing Angela's finger to me. DNA hadn't confirmed that the finger had belonged to her, but from what I gathered, due to the state of her body, it most likely was hers. He'd given no reason other than he could no longer live his life with, as Tyron said, "the shame of his family."

It didn't make sense.

And Cole had been stiff and tense ever since. He wasn't saying it, but I knew he was thinking the same thing as me. The mayor had repeatedly showed his worry over me dragging up the past, and with the knowledge Striker had given me, that was understandable since very few people knew he was related to the Groom. His actions today didn't match his actions of the past.

"That's why I'm heading over to his house with Tyron. It's not my case or jurisdiction, but he's going to get me in," Cole finally said. "I want to see this for myself."

I drew back, lifting my head. The crime scene was as it had been found, secured by the FBI and local law enforcement. "And you're not going to get into trouble?"

"Myers will be pissed to see me, but he can't do shit." He cupped my cheeks. "Miranda and Jason are going to stay here until I get back. Or at least one of them," he said, kissing my forehead. "I won't be gone long. Okay?"

"'Kay," I whispered.

His eyes searched mine and then he lowered his mouth. Cole kissed me, and there was nothing soft or slow about it. It was deep and rough, and all too brief. When he pulled back, those beautiful pale blue eyes were full of fire.

"I'll be waiting for you," I promised.

"Better be." His hands lingered, almost like he

didn't want to let go, and honestly, I didn't want him to. He brushed his lips over mine once more and then he did step back.

As he walked away, the urge to say "I love you" flared so brightly on the tip of my tongue, but the words didn't come out. All I did was smile and give him a corny-ass finger wave that caused him to give me a crooked grin. And those words were burning a hole through my tongue as I walked back to the kitchen.

Miranda was sitting at the table, a bottle of water instead of wine in front of her. Jason was standing, leaning against the kitchen island.

"I almost told Cole I loved him," I blurted out.

Jason blinked slowly. "Wow. That was random."

"Why didn't you?" Miranda asked, twisting in her seat.

"I don't know. It just seems too . . . it's too soon," I said, walking around the island to the fridge, in bad need of the full sugary power of a Coke. "And really bad timing to drop those three words."

"Is there really any perfect time?" Miranda folded her arms across her chest.

Jason grinned as he moved to the other side of the island and leaned into it. "I'd say anytime other than the mayor of the town admitting to killing women and then shooting himself would be it."

She shot him a look. "Okay. I'll give you that, but that's all."

"Where's Cole heading to again?" Jason asked, crossing his arms and leaning against the counter.

I took a drink of the carbonated goodness and then lowered the bottle to the counter. "He was going over to the mayor's house."

"Why?" he asked.

Fiddling with the lid, I shrugged. "He wanted to see the scene for himself."

Miranda glanced over at Jason. "Is it some inherent cop thing that makes him want to visit a crime screen?"

"I think it's more of seeing everything with his own eyes kind of thing." I took another drink as they stared at me, and the look on Miranda's face said there was more. And there was. These two people were my closest friends. I could share my suspicions with them. "Do you guys . . . think Mayor Hughes really did those things?"

Miranda's dark brows knitted together. "Yeah," she said slowly. "He killed himself and left a letter saying he did those things."

"Tyron said it looked like a suicide, but he hadn't been over there yet. I don't even know if the agents had been there at that point." Stepping back, I leaned against the counter. "It just . . . it doesn't make sense."

"Crazy typically doesn't make sense," Miranda replied. "And serial killers are a special brand of crazy."

"Actually, serial killers are usually the opposite of crazy," Jason said, shrugging one shoulder. "They're usually very smart."

"Killing people for pleasure is the height of insanity," she replied. "That's my opinion and I'm sticking to it."

I looked at Jason. "So you don't think the mayor was a serial killer?"

His gaze slid to mine. "I don't know what to

think, but he admitted to everything, right? The vandalism. Cutting off Angela's finger and sending it to you? We may never know why he did it."

A fine shiver curled down my spine. Angela's finger? My heart dropped. "What did you say?"

His gaze came to mine. "What?"

Ice dripped across the base of my neck. "You said he . . . he cut off Angela's finger and sent it to me. No one has confirmed that it was her finger. I didn't even tell you that was in the suicide note."

"Yeah, you did."

"No," I whispered. I *knew* I didn't tell him that. We just had this conversation. "I . . . I didn't."

Miranda frowned as she looked up at Jason. "She didn't tell me that."

"Well, it doesn't take a huge leap of logic to assume that's what he did," Jason explained. "The finger was missing from Angela and . . ." He trailed off, straightening.

My lips slowly parted. It was safe to assume that if anyone was copying the Groom, they'd cut off the ring finger. "The police had never confirmed that Angela was missing a finger or that it was sent to me."

"Shit," Jason muttered.

A cold, harsh realization slammed into my gut as I pushed away from the counter. Air lodged in my throat. Panic burst through me. "Miranda—"

Jason whipped around so fast, I almost couldn't believe it was possible. His fist connected with her temple, the fleshy thud knocking the air out of my lungs. She didn't even have a chance to cry out or blink.

Miranda slid out of the chair, crumpling onto the floor. Once down, she didn't move. Shouting, I started toward her, but drew up short when Jason stepped in front of her.

"I wanted a little more time." Jason reached up and removed his glasses, carefully folding and slipping them into the front pocket of his shirt. "But this was bound to happen."

CHAPTER 28

OH MY GOD.

My heart beat frantically in my chest as my mind raced to catch up with reality.

It was Jason.

Oh my God, it was *him*.

Jason spared a brief glance at Miranda. "I really didn't want to hurt her. I like her. Did she tell you about us? I was hoping that when this was over, she and I would take it to the next level." His gaze slid to me. "You, on the other hand, I fucking hate."

"If . . . if you like Miranda, then please, let me help—"

He shot forward so quickly I didn't have a chance to move. He grabbed my hair with one hand, and then I doubled over, crying out as his fist caught me in the stomach. Air punched out of my lungs and pain radiated down my spine as he yanked my head back. My arms pinwheeled until I reached back and gripped his arm.

Jason jerked me back up and against him until our faces were inches apart. "Oh, you fucking bitch. You're going to pay attention to me and not her. I've waited too long for this for you to be distracted. Would've preferred some real good alone time but I got to make do."

I stared at him with wide eyes, seeing a face that I trusted but not recognizing the mask of hatred and fury.

"Do you understand me?"

When I didn't answer, pain exploded across my jaw. Starbursts blinded me as Jason let go of my hair, and I fell forward, my knees smacking off the floor. I caught myself with one hand.

"On your knees." He laughed, and that sound sent chills down my spine. "How familiar."

Slowly, I lifted a trembling hand to my cheek as I worked my jaw. A fiery ache shot across the side of my face but it didn't feel broken.

"You don't even get it, do you?" He circled me. "But damn, Sasha, you were getting so close to figuring it out."

I lifted my head as my thoughts swirled to make sense of what was happening.

"I overheard you saying it yourself the other night. What if there . . . was always two of them." He stopped directly in front of me. His smile was cruel and cold. "What if there wasn't just one Groom the whole entire time?"

"Oh God," I whispered, horror locking me into place.

"What if there were two who worked together?

One who was smart enough to make sure there was no evidence of his presence left behind. One who spent the last ten years being smart. You know, not-killing-where-you-eat kind of thing."

Head thumping, I leaned away from him. "You . . ."

Jason cocked his head to the side and widened his eyes. "Yeah. Me." Slowly he knelt down in front of me, and I jerked back against the fridge door, putting space between us. The sadistic smile fixed on his face. "You and I have spent some special time together before. Kind of disappointed that you never realized it."

My stomach soured and my head spun as I scooted to the left.

His gaze followed me. "Just think," he murmured. "You've lived all these years thinking you helped put the Groom in his grave. That you got away." His hand snapped and his open palm caught my mouth. I cried out as I fell to the side. "But this whole time, you only put one of us in the ground. I've been having fun this whole entire time. I just made sure there was no pattern. I strayed far from home and picked women that no one would miss. Remember what I said about serial killers?"

I pulled myself away, my gaze flickering wildly around the room. Panic threatened to dig in deep, but I couldn't let it. I needed to get help. I needed to get a weapon. My phone was on the counter, but that was of no use at this point.

Jason's fist closed around my hair. "Do you remember?"

Blood trickled down the corner of my mouth

as I focused on getting my tongue to work. "Th-They're smart," I forced out, and my words sounded mushy to me.

"That's my good girl."

My stomach turned. "I am not your girl."

"Yeah, you're just a dumb bitch, and there's nothing more I hate in life than a bunch of dumb bitches." He sighed as he rose, pulling me up with him. I staggered to my feet. "You should ask my wife. Then again, she's dead, so that's not going to happen."

"My God," I whispered.

"Cameron was different," he said, dragging me toward the kitchen island. "At first. I think I might've actually loved her. Then one day she decided she wanted kids. I didn't. We fought. Obviously, I didn't take that well. She never really kept in contact with her family. Lucky me. No one even gives a damn she's gone."

I closed my eyes. That wasn't true. Someone gave a damn.

"Then you came back home. Couldn't believe it when Miranda told me you were coming back. Fucking pissed me off. You were here, prancing around, and I just couldn't deal with that. Fuck no. You should've stayed away."

My hands flew out as he slammed my head forward. A crack of blinding pain stunned me as my forehead hit the edge of the counter. My legs gave out, and I crumpled to the floor.

Jason stepped back. "Just think. Let it sink in. Every single time you hugged me. Every single time you called me and asked for a favor. You opened your doors to me. Left me alone in here. I've had free rein of the place." He laughed. "I helped your mother do dishes."

Moaning, I twisted onto my side, pressing against the base of the island. I was going to be sick. God, I was going to be sick.

"This whole entire time I was punishing you, making you regret coming home. Dragging it out so you can feel just the tiniest measure of pain that I've felt."

Head spinning, I looked to the side and blinked rapidly. He was going to kill me if I didn't get up. He was going to kill Miranda. Wet warmth ran down the side of my face. This wasn't going to happen. I wasn't going to be his victim again. I was going to get out of here. Miranda would be okay. I would hug my mom again. I would get to tell Cole that I loved him.

"You don't even know why," he said, as my cell-phone started ringing.

My lips felt weird. "I . . . I don't care."

"Oh," Jason laughed. "You do. You want to know why. Everyone always wants to know why."

I reached up, gripping the edge of the counter. *Get up. Get up.*

He was suddenly in my face. "You got my father killed."

I froze as I stared at him. I didn't want to believe what I heard. His father?

"Vernon was my father," he repeated. "My real father."

It clicked into place slowly, painfully. Jason had come here all those years ago to find his real father.

He'd told us that he'd never found him, and we never had a reason to not believe him. "The . . . the fire that killed your mom and stepfather . . ."

"That was me." He winked, and my phone started ringing once more. "It's amazing how people, even law enforcement, will see what they want to see. I mean, no one wants to believe an all-A student who watches *Star Trek* and marathons of *Firefly* is capable of murdering his parents."

Jason was a monster.

"I found my father pretty quickly and you know what I found?" he said, curling his hand around the back of my neck. "I really take after my dad. Must be a genetic thing." Lifting his gaze to the ceiling, he shrugged a shoulder. "Except he was a lot calmer than me. More patient. You did get that right. My father wanted to spend the rest of his life with his brides," he said, lips twisted into a cruel semblance of a smile. "I just wanted to see what their insides looked like."

"Jesus," I muttered.

"He doesn't have a thing to do with this." Jason rose and dragged me with him. "Oh, and thank you for telling me that I had yet another relative here. Good ole Mayor Mark Hughes."

A new horror filled me.

"He had no idea we were related, that Vernon had a son. I doubt he would've welcomed me into the fold if he did," he said, laughing under his breath. "I paid him a little visit, made sure he took the fall for everything. Come to find out he really did vandalize your car and did that really weird shit with the deer and your mother's truck." Jason chuckled again as he pulled me back from the counter. "What a dumbass. He about pissed himself when he realized who I was, when I made him hold the gun to his own head. Man, putting that kind of fear into someone is a beautiful thing."

I swallowed. "They'll figure . . . it out. That it wasn't a suicide."

He snorted. "No. They won't. Not these dumbasses. But now I'm going to have to get real creative about this mess." He paused. "And you know who is a really great suspect? One Cole Landis."

"You—"

Jason grunted as he shoved me forward. My upper body slid across the island. Pots and pans scattered across the island, clanging off the floor. A container of uncooked rice Mom had left out flew across the room. My cellphone went flying, and then I was falling. I twisted at the last second, hitting the floor. My hip smashed into a pot, and sharp pain flashed down my leg. I reached out behind me, my hands smacking along the floor as my phone starting ringing once more.

In under a heartbeat, he was on me, one hand on the center of my chest as he reached up into a drawer. The knives—holy shit, he was going for the knives. "This is going to be messy. Hard to clean up after. Maybe pinning this shit on Cole isn't going to work. Probably going to have to leave town."

I bucked my hips as I slid my hand along the floor. My fingers brushed the cool handle—the skillet, the iron skillet. So close.

"When I'm done with you, I'm gonna dump your body right where it always belonged," he said, pulling a knife out of the drawer. Light glinted off the blade. "I think that would make Dad happy."

"Your father was a twisted fuck," I spat, swinging the cast-iron skillet with all my strength. "And so are you."

The crack was like a shot of thunder, echoing throughout the kitchen, and shot down my arm. Jason yelped as his grip loosened. I wrenched free, flipping over and scuttling on my knees. Pushing up, I whipped around, facing him.

Wild, wide eyes fixed on mine. Eyes I'd once trusted, was familiar with. Eyes I even loved in a little way. Eyes now full of hatred and fury. Slowly, like water easing between rocks, the emotion faded from them.

Jason shifted to the side, his left leg going out on him first. He went down to his side, arms outstretched toward me, *still* coming at me, *still* wanting to hurt, but I was out of reach.

He was never going to get to me again.

Jason shifted forward, hitting the floor face-first. His body twitched once, twice, and then stilled.

Breathing heavy, I stepped back as I lowered my aching arm. A faint stream of blood seeped across the floor, sinking into the crevices between the tiles.

It was him.

It always had been him.

My stomach churned as bile rose so swiftly I doubled over, vomiting. I'd trusted him. He'd helped me afterward, telling me I was safe, after he'd done horrible, horrible things to me. My entire body burned. I'd trusted him with my mother and my friends. I'd trusted him when he—

Straightening, I clenched the pan. *Pull it together, Sasha, pull it together.* I limped back, my gaze darting to where Miranda lay motionless. I needed to check on her, but I didn't want to take my eyes off Jason.

I opened my mouth to call her name, but only a hoarse croak came out. I swallowed the burn and tried again. "Miranda?"

When I glanced over at her, she hadn't moved. What if she—no. I cut those thoughts off. She wasn't dead. There was no way. I couldn't let myself believe that. I needed to focus on getting help.

Face throbbing, I scanned the disaster that was the kitchen for my cellphone. Pots were everywhere. Shards of ceramic. Spilled rice. Limping toward the counter, I held on to the cast-iron skillet. I eased around the island, getting closer to Miranda as I kept my eyes on Jason.

Kneeling, I placed a hand on her chest. "Miranda?" After a moment, I felt her chest rise. "Miranda, honey, I need you to get up."

A soft moan drew my attention. Jason wasn't moving. I took a risk and looked at Miranda. Her eyelids fluttered.

Hope sparked. "Miranda—"

A roar blasted through the room, and my head jerked up. Jason was on his feet, arm and knife raised in the air. He raced toward me. My heart felt like it stopped in my chest as I lifted the skillet, fully preparing to bash his skull into the rest of the wall. I swung, but Jason sidestepped at the last second, and I hit air.

I cried out as pain shot up my arm and into my shoulder. The skillet slipped from my fingers, clanging off the floor. Before I could react, another burst of pain exploded alongside my head. My legs gave out once more and I hit the floor. For a horrifying moment, I thought he'd stabbed me in the head, but it had been his fist.

Jason grabbed a fistful of hair and yanked me onto my feet. "You think we're done? That I'm going to go down that easy? Oh, fuck no." He circled an arm around my neck and started walking. "I'm not going to die here and neither are you."

Dazed, I stumbled over my own feet as he half dragged, half carried me toward the back door. Instinct screamed at me to fight back, but I was having a hard time getting the message from my brain to my limbs.

Shoving open the back door, he veered to the left, toward the staff staircase. I tried to grab the frame of the door, but he pulled me through. All it took was seconds. *Seconds.* That was it, and we were in front of the cellar door.

The scent of earth and dampness invaded my senses as he forced me into the main cellar. I grabbed at his arm, my nails digging into his shirt as he continued in the darkness and through another door—the wine cellar. The light was on, and I suddenly thought of what James had said about the light being on down here.

I struggled in his hold. "What are you—?"

"I didn't say you could talk." Reaching around me, he shoved aside a rack of wine. The bottles rattled as the entrance to the unused part of the cellar came into view. "Ever been down here?" he said.

I didn't get a chance to respond.

Jason shoved me into the dark room. I fell forward, blindly throwing out my hands. I went down, my palms smacking off the dirt-packed floor. I couldn't see anything in the darkness.

"You haven't." He walked around me, confident in where he was stepping. "No one comes into this part. Probably should've. Too late now."

My breath caught as a light came on suddenly, flooding the space with dull yellow light. I sucked in dusty, dank air and shrank back as my gaze flew over the damp bricks and the floor.

There was a crumpled body lying in the corner, lying on his side. I recognized the old, worn flannel shirt. "James!" I cried out.

Jason blocked me, standing between us. "Don't even think about moving."

"Is he . . . is he dead?" The words tumbled out as I stared around Jason's legs. I didn't see him move.

"I don't know. Took the knock to the head like a champ," Jason replied without an ounce of compassion. "I like the guy, but he came down here this morning, poking around. My fault. Should've turned that damn light off. If he isn't dead, he'll be dead soon enough."

My God . . .

Praying that James was okay and that he would somehow survive this, I looked around the room. Rope hung from the old metal hooks embedded deep into the stone. Some of it was frayed. Pieces had rust-colored splotches. Scratches dug deep into sections of the stone, as if an animal . . . or a person had attempted to claw their way out.

And they had.

Oh God, someone had been down here, and they'd scratched at the stone in desperation. What appeared to be chips of fingernails were broken off in the marks, and the ground had stains, dark and muddy-looking *stains*. Stuck to the wall, above the horrifying marks, were items. A floral scarf. A badge. A woman's blouse—

"Like what I've done with the place?" Jason asked.

I saw it—saw it all—and it reminded me of another time when the light had finally come on, and I saw the horror around me, the horror I'd been held captive in. This wasn't just a cellar. This was a tomb.

"Oh my God," I whispered.

Jason had been holding them here, those poor women, killing them in the cellar under the Scarlet Wench.

I ALMOST COULDN'T process what I was seeing as I rose to my knees and it had nothing to do with the blows to the head.

"You have Miranda to thank for me knowing about this part of the cellar," Jason said, standing in front of me. "And yourself. Do you remember telling me about the tunnels when we were in college?"

Pressing my lips together, I didn't answer.

"You guys were talking about how creepy the cellar was," he continued. "Not sure if you realize this or not, but those bricks came down in the cemetery ages ago. I took them down before we took you."

I jerked.

"I used to come in here when you were sleeping, walk around the inn. You had no idea. Every once in a while, I visited, even after you left town. I guess it made me feel like I was still close to you." He knelt, and I lifted my chin. Blood trickled down the side of his face. "I had complete access to this place. Made copies of the keys just in case someone closed up the entrance. Could've done anything this whole entire time."

My stomach turned. There was a good chance I was going to be sick, knowing that he'd been in this house when my mom was here, alone and completely unaware.

"I kind of stumbled onto this part of the cellar." His hand snapped out, curving around the back of my neck. His grip was painful. "Then I remembered Miranda saying once that no one ever used this part. Seemed fitting. How does it feel?" he asked. "Knowing that they were down here this whole time? That they were alive while you were upstairs in the kitchen, eating and drinking? When you were in your apartment fucking and they were down here dying?"

I sucked in a wheezy breath. "You're a sick bastard."

"Yeah. Yeah." He twisted my head back. James was still motionless in the corner. "I've heard worse. There's something I want you to understand. I killed them because of you, because you had to fucking come back and rub it in my goddamn face—" He stopped suddenly, lifting his gaze to the ceiling.

Footsteps.

There were *footsteps* upstairs.

"Sasha!" Cole's voice rang out from above, his voice tinged with panic and anger.

I opened my mouth to scream, but Jason was on me, clapping his hand over my mouth so all that came out was a muffled grunt. He lifted me to my feet, circling an arm around my chest, clamping my arms to my side.

"Listen," Jason murmured into my ear. "Listen to him upstairs. He has no fucking clue you're down here. None. And he won't. Not until it's too late. But he'll know." He wrenched me back, away from the opening in the cellar. "I'll make sure he finds out that you died while he stood right above you."

My heart slammed against my ribs as I heard Cole speaking. I couldn't make out the words—it was either to Miranda or he was on the phone.

"If I can't pin the blame on him, maybe I'll kill him?" His breath against my ear sent shivers down my spine. "But I like the idea of him living with the knowledge of losing you twice."

I hated him—hated him with every fiber of my being. He was worse than a sociopath. He was a monster.

Digging my fingers into his hand, I tried to pry him away as he laughed quietly in my ear.

"Do you know these tunnels branch out? One goes a little further down the street, into another house?" He pressed his head against mine. "I just want you to know before I kill you, that I'll escape."

There was no way I was letting that happen.

No way.

An explosive curse sounded from upstairs and then I heard Cole shout my name once more. The rage building inside of me diminished everything else—the terror and pain. I was not going out this way. I was not going to give this bastard another second of my life.

Lifting my leg, I slammed my foot down on his.

He grunted, but held on. Without thinking, I kicked my head back, connecting with his skull.

Jason yelped out a curse.

Then I went wild.

Swinging my arms back, I hit every part of him I could reach, which wasn't much, but my fists connected with his sides, and his head. I kicked back, digging my foot into his shins.

I shoved my body backward, knocking him into the wall. The thud was audible, and I wasn't sure it was enough to be heard, but I had to try. I threw myself backward again, and his head cracked off the wall. His hand slipped from my mouth.

I screamed—screamed with everything I had in me. "Cole!" My voice echoed throughout the cellar, and I had no idea if he'd heard me. "Co—"

"You stupid bitch!" Grabbing my hair, he twisted me around and shoved me forward with brutal force. There wasn't enough time to protect myself from the blow. I hit the brick wall and the burst of fiery pain was blinding. A heartbeat passed and he threw me backward. I hit the floor, sending plumes of dirt into the air. He was on me, his knees pinning my hips as he circled his hands around my neck.

I'd taken my final breath before I realized it would be my last.

His fingers dug into the skin of my throat painfully. I beat and clawed at his hands, trying to loosen the grip. It didn't work. Lifting my hips, I couldn't throw him off. He was like a man possessed. He *looked* possessed. Blood streamed down his face, his eyes dark and full of hate, face contorted with anger—anger at me for daring to live, to survive.

But I couldn't breathe.

I didn't want his face to be the last thing I saw, but I refused to close my eyes. I glared back at him even as my lungs burned. Weakness infiltrated my muscles, turning my arms and legs into lead. They became too heavy to lift. My arms slipped to my sides, falling against the floor.

A wide smile crept across Jason's face. A full smile, showcasing bloodstained teeth. The corners of my vision darkened just as I heard a popping sound.

Jason jerked forward, letting go of my throat. Cool, beautiful air rushed into my throat, expanding my lungs. Slowly he lowered his chin. My gaze followed. Bright red splattered across the center of his chest. A second later, his legs folded like a paper sack and he fell. No twitching. Nothing this time.

Heart racing, I lifted my gaze to the opening in the cellar. I opened my mouth and croaked out one word. "Cole."

I JOLTED AWAKE from my nap, gasping air as I sat up in bed and pushed the blanket to my waist. Faint sunlight streamed through my bedroom window. My throat was hoarse, as if I'd been screaming, and—

My bedroom door opened, and Cole strode in, worry pinching his features.

I'd been screaming.

Again.

"Hey," he said, walking to the bed.

Placing my hands over my face, I squeezed my eyes shut. "Sorry."

"Like I said before and I'll say it again, the last thing you need to do is apologize for a nightmare." The bed shifted as he moved closer and I felt his fingers on my arm. He lowered my hand and then the other. "How bad was it?"

I shrugged a shoulder. "Not that bad."

"Sasha."

Lifting my chin, I looked over at him. Like every

time in the last week, since the night in the cellar, his gaze took stock of the injuries. I'd healed a lot, but the corner of my lip was still sore and the side of my jaw was mottled in a lovely shade of blue and fading purple. There were bruises elsewhere, like along my hip, that still ached, and I had at least one headache a day.

But I was alive, so I could deal with the bumps and the aches.

I could also handle the nightmares, and that meant I was also going to do my best to be open with Cole. He wasn't having it any other way.

Lying down in the stack of pillows, I stared up at the ceiling. "I had a nightmare that he . . . he was in here while I was sleeping."

Cole cursed.

"It'll stop." I looked over at him. "It will."

His jaw was hard. "It took ten years for the nightmares to stop the first time."

"But they did, because you . . . you are here." That sounded cheesy, but it was true. "These will stop too."

He nodded stiffly as he positioned himself against the headboard and stretched his long legs out, crossing them at the ankle. "You're right," he murmured.

I stared at him, knowing what he was thinking. It was there, a shadow in his eyes for the last week. He was thinking what if he hadn't gone to the mayor's house. He was thinking what if while there, he hadn't discovered the security camera the mayor had hidden in his office. He was thinking what if they hadn't played back the video and seen Jason in the room with the mayor. Saw him forcing Mayor Hughes to write the suicide letter and everything else. He was thinking what if he hadn't heard me shout his name from the cellar.

It was Cole who'd been calling my phone, trying to warn me as he, along with Tyron and the agents, had raced to the inn.

I tried not to think about what would've happened if Cole hadn't showed when he did. Nothing good came from that. At all.

My gaze shifted to the ceiling and I let out a soft, slow breath. James had been finally woken up yesterday. The blow had cracked his skull and put him in a coma, but he'd survived the attack by some kind of miracle. It really had been touch-and-go, because he'd been in the cellar all day, but that old man was going to outlive a nuclear war.

I'd done a lot of soul searching this week, and I wasn't the only one. Although Miranda had recovered physically, I knew the emotional and mental side of things would take a lot longer to get over. She'd been friends with him all these years, had become more and wanted more. Even though Miranda had never said it, I knew she had loved Jason— loved him as more than just a friend.

And I couldn't imagine what she was going through, but I would be there for her, whenever she wanted to talk about it.

Jason had been smarter—much smarter—than his father. He'd fooled everyone around him. In the days after the confrontation with him, things were revealed about him.

Cole had discovered unsolved suspicious murders in Pennsylvania, Maryland, and Virginia, but since

Jason had changed the method of murder and appeared to pick vulnerable victims at random, it was hard to see a pattern.

Until the agents took a look at the basement here and the one in his home.

His cellar had been worse than the one below the inn, a true carnival of horrors. He'd collected *trophies*, and not just clothing like he'd kept here. Hair. Pieces of skin. Toes. God, the list went on and on. It would take months for the investigators to collect the DNA and ID the victims.

There was a part of me that almost couldn't believe it. That teeny, tiny piece of me that couldn't fathom that he could be two different people. The Jason we trusted. He had access to the inn whenever he wanted. I'd left him here multiple times alone, giving him ample opportunity to snatch a key and to make a copy. And then there was the Jason who was a complete monster.

I exhaled slowly.

"It'll get better." Cole leaned over and dragged the strands of hair back from my face. "I can promise you that."

I smiled as my gaze traveled over his striking face. There was several days' worth of scruff on his jaw. In all honesty, I would've been a complete mess if it hadn't been for Cole. He'd been there through the worst of the pain, when walking from the bed to the bathroom caused my body to ache. He'd sat with me when I told Mom about Jason, and didn't shy away when the inevitable burst of emotion followed. Cole was there the first time Miranda and I met after the night in the kitchen.

That . . . that had been the hardest.

"You still with me?" Cole's hand lingered gently on my cheek, since it was still a bit swollen.

"Yeah," I whispered, reaching up and placing the tips of my fingers on his arm. There had been a hundred different things running through my head when I'd been trapped in the kitchen and cellar with Jason. I'd made good on several things. I wasn't a victim. I got out of there. Miranda would be okay. I hugged my mom again. There was one thing I hadn't done.

I hadn't told Cole that I loved him.

And I was scared out of my mind to do so even though he'd been there for me. There was a part of me, probably a stupid part of me, that still feared he wouldn't want to be in this for the long haul, because things . . . things were going to be rough.

Nerves filled my belly, but I wasn't going to chicken out. Life was too short. "I want to tell you something and I don't want you to feel pressured to answer the same, okay? I just want to get—"

"I love you," he said, eyes a warm blue.

I blinked. "What?"

One side of his lips kicked up. "I love you, Sasha."

My lips parted.

He cocked his head to the side. "You were going to say it first, right? And you were worried that I would feel obligated and say it too, so now you know a hundred percent that it isn't because I feel obligated."

I stared at him a moment and then I sat up, ignoring the twinge of pain along my side. Cole moved with me. "You . . . you love me?"

His eyes searched mine. "I loved you ten years ago, Sasha. I loved you the entire time you were gone. And I loved you since the moment I walked into the dining room and saw you standing there."

Oh my . . .

The half grin appeared. "Or maybe you were going to tell me you wanted Japanese takeout and this is about to get really, really awkward."

"No." A laugh bubbled up in me. "I was going to tell you that I love you."

"Was?"

My lips curved up at the corners. *"Am,"* I corrected, scooting so that our faces were inches apart. "I love you, Cole. I've been in love with you since our first date."

His grin spread as he leaned in and when he spoke, his lips brushed mine. "I'm so glad this didn't get awkward."

"Me too." I paused. "But Japanese takeout does sound amazing."

Cole chuckled. "I do love you, Sasha. That's something you never have to doubt."

Tilting my head just the slightest, I pressed my lips to his. The kiss was soft and perfect. "I won't."

Carefully, he eased me back down onto my back and he shifted so he was on his side beside me. "I'll call your favorite in—steak and shrimp, correct?" When I nodded, he slid the tips of his fingers down my arm, leaving a trail of acute shivers in their wake. "But first I want to make sure you're doing okay."

Cole had been doing that a lot this last week. Checking in, making sure I was processing everything. Truth was, this was a work in progress.

Nightmares were going to linger longer than the aches. It would be some time before I didn't expect an officer to walk through the inn doors, but knowing I still had all this goodness inside me, all the love around me . . .

I had Miranda.

I had my mother.

I had Cole.

"Yeah, I'm okay." I took a deep, cleansing breath. "It's really over now."

EPILOGUE

IN THE STANDING oval mirror that belonged to Grandma Libby, tears showed brightly in my mother's eyes. She stood beside me, one hand clutching the front of her pale blue blouse and the other hovering over her mouth.

"You look so incredibly beautiful, honey." Her voice thickened. "I feared I would never see this day. It's like a dream come true."

"Mom," I whispered. A knot burned the back of my throat, a messy and amazing knot. "Don't make me cry. I'll ruin all of Miranda's hard work."

"And that would make me very unhappy." Miranda appeared at my left. She winked when her gaze met mine in the mirror. "You do look amazing."

Miranda was in a pale blue dress, a color that was absolutely stunning on her, and the Grecian style was beyond flattering. Her braided hair was pulled up in an elegant twist, just like my mother's. I smiled at her, and fought the urge to apologize for the hundredth time, because there were still shadows in her eyes. I was getting better at not doing that, because deep down I knew what happened to her, to all of us, wasn't my fault.

It had been the Groom's.

It had always been Jason and his father's fault. No one else's, and eventually I knew I wouldn't feel the need to apologize. One of these days, I supposed, but today wasn't going to be a day I spent focusing on the past.

"Today's about the present," I announced out loud.

Neither woman was surprised by what I said, because they understood where my thoughts had gone. Mom folded an arm around my bare shoulders. "It's about the present and future."

Exhaling slowly, I stared at my reflection. My dress wasn't white. That was still never going to happen, but the gown I'd found was a beautiful champagne color, and moved like silk and water. It was a simple gown with a pearl-beaded heart-shaped bodice that gathered under the breast and then flowed out. Miranda had curled my hair earlier, parted the mass down the middle, pinned the sides back behind my ears, and let it fall in loose waves down my back. I wasn't wearing any jewelry. No veil. The dress was a huge step. Everything else felt like too much.

"You ready?" Miranda whispered.

Finding it hard to speak, I nodded. She moved over to the table in Mom's kitchen and picked up the bundle of champagne-colored roses. A pale blue ribbon dangled from the stems. Placing the wedding bouquet in my hands, she stretched up and kissed my cheek.

"I am so happy for you," Miranda whispered, her

voice thick with emotion. "So freaking happy for you."

"Thank you," I croaked out, fingers spasming along the cool stems.

Miranda glanced over at my mom. "I'll be downstairs."

When she left the room, Mom faced me. Her eyes glimmered with unshed tears. "There is so much I want to say to you, but I know if I get started I'll start bawling, and I'm saving my tears for the pillow."

I laughed. "You've been watching *Dance Moms*."

"Possibly." Her inhale was shaky as she reached out, smoothing my hair at the temple. "But I want to tell you that I am so incredibly proud of you."

"Mom," I whispered, feeling the wetness gather in my eyes.

She clasped my shoulders. "My beautiful daughter . . ." Cupping my cheek, her smile wobbled. "It's time."

We still had a few moments, but I knew if we lingered, both of us would end up sobbing uncontrollably, and I didn't want to be a mess. We left the room and took the main staircase. The inn was closed for the weekend, so the hum of conversation I heard as we reached the top of the staircase was all from people we knew.

Lit garlands twisted around the railing, twinkling, and the air smelled of crisp balsam and pear. It was the last weekend of November, and the entire inn was decorated for Christmas. From where we stood, I could see one of the four Christmas trees. This one wasn't the largest, but was set to the right of the staircase and could be seen outside, through the glass panes in the doors.

Gathering the skirt of my dress, I headed down the stairs, and stopped while Mom walked ahead. The conversation lulled as I focused on taking deep, even breaths. Nervous energy was bouncing all through my system, but it wasn't fear. Oh no, it was eagerness and anticipation. It was a thousand different emotions but none of them bad or frightening.

James appeared, and I smiled when I saw him. Never in my life had I seen him wearing anything other than an old shirt and jeans that had seen better days.

His salt-and-pepper beard was trimmed, and the black trousers, white dress shirt, and pale blue tie seemed so out of place on him, like he was wearing another man's clothes, but he cleaned up nicely.

"You look so handsome," I told him.

He didn't smile. Didn't grin. That wasn't him, but those dark, soulful eyes softened. "You ready, girl?"

Twisting at the waist, I looked up the staircase, and I could almost see my father standing there, nodding at me, telling me I was ready. He would be proud of who I'd chosen to escort me, and I was ready. I nodded.

"Then let's get this show on the road," James said gruffly.

In a daze, I threaded my arm through his and we walked to our left. Folding white chairs had been brought in to accommodate the small ceremony, and the dining tables had been temporarily cleared out to make room for the garland-covered arbor. Those tables would be back out later, for the reception, but right now, the whole area was a winter wonderland with a touch of love.

My gaze flickered over the people seated. I saw Cole's parents and family. I recognized Tyron sitting near my mother. Miranda was waiting at the arbor, along with the pastor Mom had known for years, and Derek, who stood next to Cole.

Air hitched in my throat when I saw him. Heart thumping like a steel drum, my knees felt weak as our gazes collided and held. I saw his lips part, could practically feel the unsteady inhale he took. Raw emotion crawled over his striking face, and those pale blue eyes that matched the dresses that Miranda and my mom wore, the same color as the ties secured loosely around James' and Derek's necks. The same color threaded through the roses I carried.

Oh my God, he was the most beautiful man I'd ever seen. Felt that way all those years ago when I first saw him in class, and I still believed that, today more than ever, because he was about to become my husband.

I was actually going to get married.

Cole's full, expressive lips curled into a smile, and there was no stopping my response. I felt my grin race across my face, and James had to pick up his pace to keep up with me.

"Damn, girl," James grumbled as we reached the arbor. "He ain't goin' anywhere."

"Truest words ever spoken," Cole replied.

The crowd laughed, and even though my cheeks flushed, I wasn't embarrassed. I only had eyes for

Cole. Miranda took the bouquet from my hands and stepped back while James shuffled over to one of the chairs. I only guessed that was what had happened, because I was 100 percent focused on Cole.

He took my hands in his and said in a low voice, "It's taken us a long time to get here."

A strangled, emotional laugh erupted from me as I squeezed his hands back. My heart beat fast. "Too long."

"But we're here," he said, tone rich and deep.

And we were, after all this time, after everything that had happened. Despite the fact I'd sworn I'd never wear a wedding gown, never allow a ring put on my finger, Cole and I were here.

What did Grandma Libby always say?

Never say never.